Kate Ellis was born and brought up in Liverpool and studied drama in Manchester. She has worked in teaching, marketing and accountancy and first enjoyed literary success as a winner of the North West Playwrights competition. Keenly interested in medieval history and "armchair" archaeology, Kate lives in north Cheshire with her engineer husband, Roger, and their two sons. *A Painted Doom* is her sixth Wesley Peterson novel. *The merchant's House, The Armada Boy, An Unhallowed Grave, The Funeral Boat, The Bone Garden* and *A Painted Doom* are also published by Piatkus.

Also by Kate Ellis

For more information regarding Kate Ellis log on to
Kate's website: www.kateellis.co.uk

The
Skeleton Room

Kate Ellis

PIATKUS

Copyright © 2003 by Kate Ellis

First published in Great Britain in 2003 by
Judy Piatkus (Publishers) Ltd of
5 Windmill Street, London W1T 2JA
email:info@piatkus.co.uk

The moral right of the author has been asserted

A catalogue record for this book is available from the British Library

ISBN 0 7499 3376 3

Printed and bound in Great Britain by
Mackays of Chatham plc, Chatham Kent

With many thanks to Judy Lees for all her help.

20 July

The woman in the red T-shirt lay on the sharp grey rocks far below; distant and tiny, like a small fish caught in the teeth of some gigantic sea creature.

The figure on the cliff top above stared down and swayed slightly to the rhythm of the waves. The sea would soon swallow the woman in the red T-shirt and carry her off. Over the centuries the sea had claimed many lives around this coast. So what was one more?

Seagulls shrieked overhead like souls in torment while fat bees buzzed, busy in the greenery. For a moment the watcher stood listening to the sounds of nature, then took a step forward, careful not to go too near the edge. There was no movement down below on the rocks; the woman in the red T-shirt lay there twisted, her lifeless limbs spread out against the grey stone in a clumsy parody of sunbathing.

The watcher felt in a pocket to check that the letter was safe before glancing at an expensive watch. It was time to go now, to get away before others came along to enjoy the awesome beauty of the cliff top.

It had been easy this time. In fact murder became easier with each passing year.

Chapter One

My sorry tale begins in the year of Our Lord 1771 when I was newly appointed to the parish of Millicombe. At the hour of ten o'clock one Friday in April of that year, I was called to the hamlet of Chadleigh to visit a certain farmhand called George Marbis, who, by all accounts, was close to death. His daughter, Margaret, had run along the coast path to Millicombe at that late hour and my maidservant showed her into the study where I was composing my sermon for the following Sunday. The girl, Margaret, a poor, thin creature, pleaded with me to come with her, saying that her father was most troubled and had asked to see me. As vicar, I felt obliged to give the dying man some words of comfort, so I went with Margaret to Marbis's cottage, which I found to be a dark, foul-smelling place, hardly fit for the animals he tends.

Marbis was indeed close to meeting his Maker, and I prepared to utter the words of comfort I use at such unhappy times.

But Marbis would have none of my prayers. He clawed at my sleeve with his bony hands and said that he wished to speak with me in private. Margaret, who had cared for her father since her mother's untimely death in childbed, busied herself about the cottage, and the dying man bade me stoop so he could whisper in my ear. His breath was

2

noxious but I obliged him. Yet afterwards I wished I had
refused, because what he had to tell me was a secret so
vile that it were best not to hear it.

From An Account of the Dreadful and Wicked Crimes
of the Wreckers of Chadleigh *by the Reverend Octavius*
Mount, Vicar of Millicombe

23 July
Ian Jones watched his colleague wield the sledgehammer,
fearful that one misplaced blow would bring the huge
edifice of Chadleigh Hall crashing to the ground.

'You sure that's not a supporting wall, Marty?'

''Course I'm bloody sure.'

Marty Shawcross raised the hammer while Ian scratched
his shaved head. At least they'd have plenty of time to get
out if the ceiling started to collapse.

A few foundation-shaking thuds later, when the dense
cloud of plaster dust had begun to settle, Marty and Ian looked
at the small jagged hole that they had made in the wall.

'You were right. Looks like a doorway. It's been
blocked off.'

'What did I tell you?' Marty reached out and pushed the
loose plaster from the edge of the hole. 'Do we carry on or
what?'

'Ours not to reason why – ours just to do what's on the
plans. Give it another bash.'

Marty obeyed and dust and debris flew into the air as the
hole expanded. The men coughed and Ian took a grubby
handkerchief from his pocket and held it to his face.

'We're meant to be knocking through to the next room
but this looks like some sort of cupboard or ... I'm having
a look.'

'Go on, then. Rather you than me.'

Marty watched as Ian poked his head through the hole
and quickly pulled it out again.

'Can't see a bloody thing. Got your lighter?'

Marty, a incorrigible smoker, pulled a cheap disposable cigarette lighter from his trouser pocket and handed it to Ian, who lit it and held it just inside the gaping hole.

After a few seconds of silence, Ian turned to face his companion. The blood had drained from his face, leaving it as white as the plaster dust that was settling on the splintery floorboards.

'What is it? What did you see?'

It was a while before Ian felt up to answering.

Neil Watson had dived down to the wreck of the *Celestina* several times. But, being a creature of habit, he preferred to work on dry land, dealing with the artefacts the divers were bringing up from the seabed, viewing their video footage and writing reports in the disused beach café that they were using as their site headquarters.

He was unused to working in such splendid isolation. He missed the hustle and bustle of a land-based dig and the chatter of his colleagues, most of whom were working aboard the boat or diving beneath the sea.

But today he had company. A couple of bored-looking youths – Oliver Kilburn and his friend, Jason Wilde, aged eighteen and both at a loose end since the finish of their final school exams – had volunteered to help with the finds from the wreck. And as Oliver's father was Dominic Kilburn, the businessman who owned the beach, Neil felt he could hardly complain that the pair were unreliable and turned up only when it suited them.

Satisfied that the boys weren't doing too much damage to the delicate objects brought up from the seabed, Neil stepped outside the café onto the sandy concrete steps that led down to the beach. He shaded his eyes against the sun and squinted at the dive boat, which bobbed near the rocks, watching the figures on the deck, divers in shiny black with brightly coloured air tanks on their backs.

Neil knew that their main enemy was the weather. The

ship's timbers had been uncovered by a freak storm three weeks before and discovered by amateur divers, who had reported their find to the relevant authorities. And, if nature decided not to cooperate, another storm could cover the remains of the *Celestina* up again just as quickly. They were working against the clock, and Neil Watson preferred to work at his own pace.

'How's it going, then, Dr Watson?'

Neil swung round. A tall man was standing on top of a rock to his left, outlined against the sun. Neil shielded his eyes, feeling small and subservient as he gazed up at the towering figure. But perhaps this was Dominic Kilburn's intention.

'We're making good progress. They've uncovered more of the timbers and found a lot of interesting stuff. Your son's in there washing the pottery they brought up this morning – high-status stuff, probably from the captain's cabin. Want to take a look?'

Neil pointed at the shabby wooden building near by which had been a beach café and ice-cream shop in the days when the cove had been the property of a neighbouring girls' boarding school which had allowed its use by the public.

But Dominic Kilburn's mind was on more important things than old pottery. 'Is there any sign of . . .?'

'No. Nothing like that.'

'Can you use metal detectors down there? Speed things up a bit?'

'I can assure you that we are carrying out a thorough investigation of the site. We'll use metal detectors if they're considered appropriate,' said Neil with academic dignity, as though Dominic Kilburn had made an obscene suggestion.

Kilburn jumped down off his rock, walked up to Neil and put his face close to his. 'I'm footing the bill for this, so if I say get a move on, you get a move on.'

Neil pretended not to notice the threat in Kilburn's voice.

'You can't just strip the wreck of anything that might be worth a few bob, you know. Everything has to be recorded, photographed and drawn *in situ*, and any finds need to be conserved properly. We don't cut corners. We're archaeologists, not treasure hunters.'

'So what about all these stories? Surely you've found some signs of . . .'

'Don't get your hopes up. There's a chance we won't find anything like that.'

Kilburn was about to reply when his son appeared at the café door. Oliver Kilburn was tall, classically good looking with fine fair hair. Neil noticed a distinct family resemblance and wondered, not for the first time, whether the boss's son was a helper or a spy in their midst. Kilburn greeted Oliver with a scowl, seemingly annoyed by the interruption, but before he could say anything the sound of raised voices drifted over on the breeze, clear above the cry of the seagulls and the thunder of the waves. Something was happening.

Neil shaded his eyes and looked out to sea. A dinghy was approaching, its outboard motor thrusting it through the waves at full speed. Without a word he left the Kilburns, father and son, and ran towards the waterline to meet it. When the dinghy reached the shore Matt jumped out, anxious to relay some news. Neil glanced back and saw that Dominic Kilburn was standing beside his son, watching expectantly, no doubt hoping that Matt was bringing the news he had been waiting for since he had first heard the story of the *Celestina*.

But what Matt had to say didn't concern sunken treasure. After a brief conversation, Neil took his mobile phone from his pocket and looked at it despairingly. There was no signal. He swore under his breath and looked up to find Dominic Kilburn and his son standing beside him.

'What's going on? What have they found?'

Neil didn't answer. 'I need to get to a phone. There's no mobile signal around here.'

'There's a cottage up on the cliff top. You pass it on the way down to the beach,' said Oliver Kilburn in an attempt to be helpful.

'Thanks,' Neil mumbled. At least the boy's suggestion had been a good one.

He looked out to sea again, ignoring Dominic Kilburn's repeated questions. He could see that the diving team were dragging something onto their boat but he didn't hang around. He rushed off up the sand, leaving a neat trail of footprints behind him, and scaled the steep and overgrown path to the lane above.

When he reached the top he paused to catch his breath, but then he ran on. Fifty yards down the lane he found a small, brick-built cottage fronted by a long and overgrown garden. The gate bore the name 'Old Coastguard Cottage' on a rustic wooden plaque, but Neil had no time to take in the architectural niceties: he rushed up the garden path, ignoring the tall, toppled flowers that ambushed his legs, and banged on the front door. The sound was urgent – but then it was meant to be.

A thin, dark-haired man in his early thirties opened the door a fraction and peeped round suspiciously, as though he feared a raid of some kind. When Neil explained the reason for his visit the door opened a little wider, and after a few seconds he was allowed into the hallway.

The man pointed to an old-fashioned telephone, which stood on the hall table, and he watched in silence as Neil dialled the numbers: 999.

'Police,' Neil said calmly, instinctively turning away from the man. 'We've found a body in the sea at Chadleigh Cove.'

When Neil turned round he saw that the colour had drained out of his host's face.

The two policemen climbed out of the car and admired the view. Chadleigh Hall had been built at a time when pleasing proportions were all the rage.

'It'll be nice when it's finished,' commented the elder of

the pair, a big man with unruly hair, an expanding midriff and a prominent Liverpool accent.

'What are they doing to it?'

'Turning it into one of them posh country hotels. Nothing that need concern us on our salaries.'

The younger man smiled. 'I suppose we'd better see what all the fuss is about.'

As if on cue, a uniformed constable appeared, shaded by the magnificent Georgian portico. He raised his hand in greeting. 'Sorry to drag you out, sir,' he said, addressing the older man and ignoring his companion. 'But a couple of workmen have turned up a body. They were knocking a wall through and they found a skeleton. I reckon it looks suspicious,' he added seriously.

'Right, then, George, lead us to it.'

The constable led the way through what was once, and no doubt would be again, a magnificent entrance hall, now filled with scaffolding, large paint pots and the tools of the builder's trade. They ascended a sweeping, dust-covered staircase and passed through a series of rooms, each stripped bare to the plaster and awaiting the attentions of electricians and decorators.

The younger CID officer breathed in, the smell of fresh paint reminding him that he had promised his wife that he would decorate the bedroom some time soon – work permitting.

Stepping through another doorway, they found themselves in a smaller room, as bare as the rest. Two men were sitting on wooden stools: the smaller of the pair was a monkey-like man with the wizened skin of a heavy smoker, the larger sported a fine beer belly and had more hair on his body than on his head. They stared at the newcomers.

'This is Detective Chief Inspector Heffernan and er . . .' The constable hesitated. He knew Gerry Heffernan – everybody knew Gerry Heffernan – but he hadn't come across his colleague before, although he'd heard of his existence:

there weren't that many black detective inspectors in the local force.

'Detective Inspector Peterson,' the younger man said quietly.

'They've come to ask you a few questions,' the constable said with relish.

'Right, then, let's get on with it, shall we,' Heffernan began, looking from one to the other. 'Which of you found this skeleton?'

'We both did, I suppose. But Ian went inside to have a look and I stayed out here. It gave me the creeps just looking at it.' Marty Shawcross shuddered.

'Can you tell us what happened?'

Marty looked at the policeman who spoke. Detective Inspector Peterson possessed a quiet air of authority which Marty assumed was bestowed by his police warrant card.

'We didn't know it was there,' Marty said defensively. There was no way they were going to lay any blame on him. 'The plans said this wall was to be knocked through so me and Ian started and there was this sort of room and ...'

'It must have given you a shock.' Wesley Peterson did his best to look sympathetic.

'Nearly gave me a bleeding heart attack seeing that thing staring at me.'

'Me and all,' Ian chipped in, not wanting to be left out.

Heffernan plunged his hands into his trouser pockets and looked Marty in the eye. 'Well, if you've recovered perhaps you could give a statement to the constable here while me and Inspector Peterson have a look at what you've found.'

Marty nodded. 'We thought we were just knocking through to the room next door. We reckoned it was a cupboard or something. It's nothing to do with us really. We just ...'

Wesley Peterson decided to interrupt the protestations of

9

innocence. 'Do you know anything about this place? Who were the previous owners?'

Marty shrugged his shoulders, still on the defensive. 'It used to be some posh girls' boarding school. Then it was empty for a few years until Kilburn Leisure bought it and decided to turn it into a hotel. There's going to be a health spa and a golf course and . . .'

Wesley looked around at the chaos, the protruding electrical wiring and the debris-strewn floor. 'Very nice,' he said, imagining the finished result.

'It'll be a bit beyond our pockets but the Chief Constable might give it a go,' mumbled Gerry Heffernan with what sounded like envy. He nodded to the constable, who was hovering near the door, preparing to usher Marty and Ian away.

Marty raised a hand, as if about to say something. But the constable shot him a discouraging look and the two men filed out meekly.

Wesley Peterson watched them disappear through the doorway. 'I can't see that their statements are going to tell us much.'

'We've got to go through the motions, Wes. And you never know, one of them might have done it.'

'Hardly likely.' Wesley grinned at his boss. 'I bet this room – if it is a room – has been sealed up for years.'

'We'd better take a look, I suppose. After you.'

Wesley ventured into the room first. Although the entrance had been enlarged since Marty's initial discovery, he had to lower his head as he crossed into the unknown. The space was pitch dark, and Wesley wrinkled his nose at the musty odour of decay. He could hear Gerry Heffernan breathing close behind and he found some comfort in the thought that he wasn't alone. And at least, unlike Ian and Marty, he knew what to expect. He flicked on the torch he had borrowed from the constable and moved its beam about the room.

It was small, this chamber of death: around eight foot by

nine. As the light played around the cobweb-covered walls he could make out a dark shape in the corner.

The torch beam came to rest.

'Ruddy heck,' Heffernan murmured.

Wesley said nothing. He stared at the thing sitting there; a complete skeleton slumped on a large, solid-backed, wooden chair. Its wrists appeared to be tied by wisps of rope to the chair's arms and the skull grinned up at them, as if pleased to have some company. A hank of fairish hair was still attached to the skull and decayed scraps of cloth and tissue clung to the bones. Wesley looked away.

'Poor sod. Looks like he's been tied up in here and left to die.' Gerry Heffernan began to back out of the room. 'Has someone called Colin Bowman?'

'He was in the middle of a post-mortem but he said he'll be here as soon as he can.'

'Come on, Wes, let's get out of here.'

Wesley didn't protest. He would be as glad as his boss to be out of that tomb chamber. Wesley, who had studied archaeology at university, had seen many bones in his time, but somehow these filled him with a particular horror. It was the circumstances – the squalid little room, the chair and the remnants of rope that suggested the victim had been alive when he was left in there; that he had been helpless as he listened to his tomb being sealed before facing a slow death in the darkness.

They stepped outside into the larger room, a room on the first floor which would probably have been used as a bedchamber when the house was built in the eighteenth century but which was now earmarked as an office for the new hotel.

'How long do you think he's been there?' Heffernan asked anxiously. If it was less than seventy years it was their job to launch an investigation.

'Haven't a clue yet but there's bound to be something that'll give us a hint. And by the way, I think it's a she.'

11

Chief Inspector Heffernan looked at his subordinate in wonder. 'How do you work that one out?'

'The look of the skull. I could be wrong but . . .'

Gerry Heffernan said nothing. Man or woman, the skeleton in the sealed room at Chadleigh Hall – soon to be the Chadleigh Hall Country Hotel – was something he'd rather not think about.

The constable announced the arrival of the pathologist.

Gerry Heffernan was relieved to see Colin Bowman. Last time he had encountered a suspicious death he had had to make do with Colin's locum – and Gerry hadn't quite made up his mind whether he approved of lady pathologists like Laura Kruger. To Gerry Heffernan a woman's place was with living patients, preferably in a mother-and-baby clinic.

Colin, his usual relaxed self, indulged in his customary ten minutes of social chitchat before borrowing a torch and venturing into the small chamber where the skeleton sat, now the focus of the police photographer's attention. Wesley and Heffernan waited outside the room for the verdict: there wasn't room in there for all of them.

After a few minutes Colin emerged, his amiable face serious. 'Nasty business.'

'How long do you think it's been there?' Wesley asked. 'It is old or . . .?'

'Well, I can pronounce life extinct but not much else at the moment. If I had to hazard a guess I'd say she – and I'm pretty sure it's a she, incidentally – has been there for some years. But how many years . . .'

'Can't you give us any idea?' Gerry Heffernan sounded impatient. If he wasn't under any obligation to investigate the unknown woman's gruesome death, he wanted to get back to the police station for a nice cup of tea.

'Sorry,' said Colin Bowman. He picked up his bag. 'Well, gentlemen, if you can arrange for the remains to be brought to the mortuary, I can make a more thorough examination.' He looked around. 'This place was a school for years, you know. A girls' boarding school. An aunt of my wife's was an old girl.'

'And did she tell you if they used to wall up their pupils when they misbehaved?' said Wesley with a smile.

'She never mentioned it and I can't really ask her as she's in South Africa.'

Heffernan slapped Wesley on the back. 'Time we were off, Wes. We can't do much here until Colin's given us his verdict and I want to catch up with some paperwork.' He sounded subdued, serious. Not his usual ebullient self.

Heffernan had begun to march towards the staircase and Wesley followed, wondering what had brought about the boss's change of mood and this unaccustomed desire to catch up on paperwork – he usually behaved as though it didn't exist. Perhaps the thought of the woman in the sealed room had affected him more than he would care to admit.

'Are you okay, Gerry?'

''Course I am.'

Neither man said anything as they walked towards the car. Then Wesley decided to break the silence, to distract them both from thoughts of death.

'How are Sam and Rosie settling in?' Gerry Heffernan's children were both home from university for the summer.

'Okay. Rosie's got herself a job playing the piano in some posh restaurant. And Sam's working for a landscape gardening company. Makes a change from last year.'

Wesley grinned. Last summer Gerry's son, Sam, had found a particularly enterprising way of supplementing his student loan. It was something Wesley could hardly forget.

He was about to unlock the car door when his mobile phone rang. Heffernan looked irritated. 'Whoever invented those things should be shot,' he muttered as Wesley answered it.

After a brief conversation Wesley turned to his companion. 'A body's been found in the sea off Chadleigh Cove. They want us there. It's not far away.'

'I know where it is, Wes. We used to take the kids there when they were little. Nice beach. Kathy always used to like places where you didn't get the crowds of day trippers.'

Wesley noticed a faraway look in his boss's eyes, the look that always appeared when his late wife's name was mentioned.

He opened his mouth, about to mention that Neil Watson was working on some eighteenth-century shipwreck at Chadleigh Cove. But he thought better of it. 'I suppose we'd better get over there.'

'Two bodies in one day, eh?' said Heffernan gloomily. 'Don't suppose we've got much choice.'

The beach was inaccessible to vehicles so the police and ambulance personnel had to make their way along the steep path that led down from the cliff top.

Neil Watson had watched as a couple of the divers working on the wreck had carried the body ashore. A woman's body, barely recognisable after the sea creatures had feasted greedily on the eyes and soft flesh, swathed in sodden and shapeless cloth, filthy with mud and seaweed. There were no shoes on the waxy, swollen feet but there was a wedding ring on her finger, cutting into the bloated flesh.

The divers stood around on the golden sands, not quite knowing what to do. When Dominic Kilburn had seen their discovery, he had pleaded a business meeting and left. But Oliver still hung around, watching.

A young constable in shirtsleeves, first on the scene, busied himself trying to convince everybody that there was nothing to see. But nobody seemed to be taking much notice of him.

When Heffernan and Wesley arrived the body was ready to be moved by a couple of well-built ambulance men. The police surgeon – or Forensic Medical Examiner, as he was now known – had pronounced life extinct and had authorised the woman's last journey to Tradmouth Hospital mortuary to lie with the Chadleigh Hall bones in a room of stainless-steel drawers.

There was nothing more to be done until they knew her identity and Colin Bowman had determined exactly how she died. Just as Gerry Heffernan was suggesting that they return to the station for a cup of tea, Wesley spotted a familiar face.

He walked towards Neil Watson, his feet sinking in the fine sand: it was difficult for a man wearing a suit on a sunny beach to look anything but out of place. Neil saw him and grinned.

'That body's not going to hold us up, is it?' Neil had always put his work first, ever since he and Wesley had been students together at Exeter University; not a thought for the unfortunate woman who'd just been pulled out of the sea.

'I shouldn't think so. Tell me about this shipwreck, then. How are you getting on?'

Neil was only too pleased to satisfy his old friend's curiosity. 'The ship was called the *Celestina*. According to the records, she hit the rocks one night in 1772 and sank out there, just where the dive boat is.' He pointed to the divers' small vessel that bobbed at anchor a couple of hundred yards out to sea.

Neil looked round to make sure Oliver Kilburn wasn't in earshot. 'Dominic Kilburn of Kilburn Leisure owns the manor of Chadleigh and he has rights to any wreck in the sea off his land.' He frowned, trying to remember the exact terms. 'Any ship wrecked as far out to sea as a man on horseback can see an umber barrel, that's it. It's one of those archaic manorial things.'

'So why are you here?'

'The County Archaeological Unit's coordinating every-thing and making sure that anything of historic interest is dealt with properly, but Dr James, who's an expert in marine archaeology, is leading the actual dive. Kilburn's making a great show of cooperation, saying how he values our help and all that. But I get the feeling we're just here to keep the authorities happy, and we're as welcome as a plague of cockroaches in his hotel kitchens.'

'So how's it going?'

'Okay so far. Of course, it's Jane who loves all this underwater stuff, and she's having the time of her life working with Dr James: she hangs on his every word.' He grinned, pointing to a tall blonde in a black wet suit who was standing down by the water's edge.

'I read somewhere that there are a lot of wrecks around this coast.'

'Oh, yes. It's famous for them.'

'So why's Kilburn so interested in this one? What's in it for him?'

Neil smiled knowingly. 'I dare say I can let you in on his little secret. According to contemporary records, the *Celestina* was on her way home from Portugal to Tradmouth carrying a cargo of gold coins and jewels. And as far as we know they're still down there waiting to be found. And if Kilburn has this ancient manorial right to the wreck, then legally . . .'

'Any sign of them?'

'Not yet. And we're trying to keep the whole thing quiet. The last thing we want is treasure hunters.'

Large quantities of gold had always eluded Neil on his past forays into archaeology. But there had to be a first time.

'How's Pam?' Neil asked suddenly, shielding his eyes from the light.

'She's okay. But she can't wait for the end of term.'

'I keep forgetting when the baby's due.'

Wesley was rather surprised that Neil even remembered Pam was pregnant: such things usually passed him by. 'Not until November but . . .'

Wesley was interrupted in mid-sentence by a loud voice behind him. 'I thought it was you. What are you digging up this time?' Gerry Heffernan had arrived.

16

'A shipwreck,' Neil answered. 'Was it murder, then?'

Heffernan looked confused.

'The body in the sea – was it murder?'

'I hope not. The weather's nice and the holiday season's coming up so the last thing we want is more work. Has Wes told you about the skeleton we found at Chadleigh Hall?'

'No, he's been keeping that one quiet.' Neil looked at Wesley expectantly.

'Some workmen have just found a skeleton in a sealed room at Chadleigh Hall, about half a mile from here.'

'How long's it been there?' Neil sounded interested.

'We don't know yet.'

'Let me know if you want me to have a look at where it was found,' said Neil. 'Examining the historical context and all that.'

'Skiving off work, you mean,' Gerry Heffernan mumbled under his breath.

Neil grinned. 'Call it helping the police with their enquiries. How about it?'

Gerry Heffernan shrugged. It would do no harm. Neil's expert eye might spot something that would confirm that the skeleton was a couple of centuries old – and that would give them the excuse they needed not to begin an investigation. 'Okay, then. You and Wes put your heads together and say the skeleton was killed by William the Conqueror while he was down here on his holidays in 1066. And if you do find it's less than seventy years old I don't want to know. Right?'

The chief inspector turned and marched off down the beach.

The doors of Tradmouth police station swung open and a woman walked in. She hesitated and then made for the front desk.

'Er, my friend's gone missing,' she began nervously. 'What do I do? I mean, do I just tell you or . . .'

17

The large, bearded desk sergeant drew himself up to his full height. The woman standing on the other side of the reception desk was what Sergeant Bob Naseby would have described as a bit of all right. She wore tight white trousers, a short striped T-shirt and the golden sandals on her dainty feet revealed a set of perfectly painted scarlet toenails. A pair of sunglasses was perched on top of her golden-blonde head like a tiara.

He turned to the filing cabinet behind him and pulled out the appropriate sheet of paper slowly: Bob Naseby was never a man to be rushed.

'Right, madam, if you could give me a few details. Who is it that's missing?'

'It's my friend. She's been staying with me. She went out last Friday and never came back. We'd arranged to go out that evening so she would have let me know. I'm really quite worried about her.'

The police station door swung open and a man entered, clutching his motoring documents nervously. He stood behind the woman, and Bob feared that he'd soon have a queue on his hands.

Fortunately for Bob, a young woman emerged from a door marked 'Private'. Her fair hair was scooped back in a ponytail and she was neatly dressed in a navy linen suit which looked cool in the warmth of the July day.

Bob called to her. 'Sergeant Tracey, can you have a word with this lady?'

Detective Sergeant Rachel Tracey looked in the woman's direction. She had been going out to fetch a sandwich. But if she wanted a figure like the woman she was about to escort to the interview room, perhaps it was for the best that her plans had been foiled. She pulled in her stomach and forced herself to smile reassuringly.

She led the way to the small ground-floor room, and when they were seated the woman gave her name as Lisa Marriott and lit a cigarette. Rachel pushed an unwashed ashtray towards her, trying to hide her disapproval.

'So tell me about your friend,' she began. 'What's her name?'

'Sally . . . Sally Gilbert.'

'Address?'

'She was staying with me.' The woman recited her address and Rachel wrote it down. 'We work together, me and Sally. She left her husband a couple of weeks ago and she needed a bit of space; some time to think things over. I offered her my spare room.'

'How do you know she's not gone back to her husband?'

'That's the first thing I thought of. I rang him and he said he hadn't seen her since she left.'

Rachel watched the woman's eyes. There was unmistakable anxiety beneath the heavy layers of eyeshadow and mascara. 'I'd better have her husband's name and address.'

Again they were recited without hesitation. She had obviously known the missing woman well.

'Where do you work?'

'The Tradfield Manor Hotel. Sally works on reception and I'm a beautician at the health club. She didn't turn up for her shift today and that isn't like her – she's usually very reliable. I think something might have happened to her.'

'So when exactly did she go missing?'

'Friday, just after lunch. She said she was going to meet someone.'

'Who?'

'She didn't say.'

'Where was she going to meet them?'

'I don't know. She said she'd be a couple of hours and I was expecting her back by five. We were going out for dinner at Languini's – a bit of a treat. It was Sally's idea: she said she might have something to celebrate.'

'Any idea what?'

Lisa shook her head.

'Did she take anything with her?'

'Only her handbag, I suppose.'

'Was she driving?'

'Yes. She went off in her car. It's a white Renault Clio – R reg, but I can't tell you the registration number.'

'Don't worry,' said Rachel. 'And you're sure you've no idea who she was meeting?'

'No. I thought it might be . . .' She hesitated and sucked on her diminishing cigarette.

'Who?'

Lisa Marriott studied her long scarlet nails. 'She was seeing this man but it finished a few weeks ago. I just thought she might be seeing him again but . . .'

'Do you know his name?'

'She just called him Mike. I never met him.'

Rachel sat back to avoid a plume of cigarette smoke. 'Do you know where he lives or where he works or . . .'

Lisa Marriott stubbed out her cigarette and shook her head. 'She said he lived in Neston and he worked funny hours . . . shifts. I don't know anything else.'

'So let me get this straight,' Rachel said, preparing to write it all down. 'Your friend Sally Gilbert was having an affair with a man called Mike. Her husband found out and she left him and she's been staying with you for a fortnight. Is that right?'

'No. Her and Mike finished before she left her husband. Mike had nothing to do with them splitting up. Trevor found out about it but he forgave her. She just got bored with Trevor.'

'Did Trevor know she was staying with you?'

'Of course he did. He was as good as gold. Forwarded her mail and everything.'

Rachel found herself feeling sorry for Trevor Gilbert, the man who had been so accommodating of his wife's whims and infidelities. But then perhaps the worm had turned. Worms often do when they've been pushed too far.

Lisa lit another cigarette. Rachel took a deep breath and coughed.

'Did anything unusual happen before she disappeared? Did she receive any phone calls or . . .?'

Lisa shook her head. Then she remembered something. 'She got a letter that morning. It was strange – she seemed sort of . . .' She searched for the right word. 'Excited about it . . . and a bit secretive. Yeah, now that I remember, she read the letter and then said she was going out to meet someone that afternoon. Then she said we'd go to Languini's that night – she said she might be celebrating.'

'And she didn't give you any clue about who she was meeting?'

Lisa shook her head.

'Did she tell you what was in the letter?'

'No. She just put it in her bag. I was a bit curious but you don't like to seem too nosey, do you?'

Rachel, who had always been blessed with a healthy dose of curiosity, said nothing. She looked down at the missing-persons form.

'Right, Ms Marriott, I'd better have a description of Sally. What was she wearing when she went out on Friday?'

'Cream trousers. And a bright red T-shirt. She'd just bought the outfit – spent a fortune on it. But then Sally never stints herself. She likes to buy the best.' She screwed up her face in concentration. 'And I think she was wearing a gold necklace, a locket, but I can't be sure about that.'

'Handbag?'

'Blue leather. Brand new. Cost a bomb.' There was a hint of envy in her voice.

'What about her shoes?'

'She was wearing red mules to match her T-shirt – stilettos. She always wears high heels – says it makes her look thinner.'

Rachel Tracey began to write everything down in her small, neat hand.

The front garden of Old Coastguard Cottage was a riot of anarchic colour. Tall hollyhocks and foxgloves tumbled over the crumbling path that led to the green front door, an undisciplined mob of flowers lying in wait to attack the legs of any passer-by.

The man stood at the cottage window and watched the scene outside. The archaeologist's phone call had caused an invasion of police and ambulance crews. But now things had gone quiet.

Some of the divers working on the shipwreck had passed the cottage on their way to the Wreckers Inn and he had asked them what was happening. They'd told him that a woman's body had been found in the water at Chadleigh Cove. But he'd known that already by eavesdropping when the archaeologist had called the police.

He had stayed indoors as the police cars passed along the track. Not that the local police were anything to worry about – he didn't know them and they didn't know him. Then, when the van bearing the woman's body had passed by, he had watched from the window. Death had always fascinated him; its rituals and its reality.

He looked at his watch. Now that things were quiet he could take a walk in the fresh air. When he left the cottage he made sure the front door was firmly locked – you couldn't be too careful, even in the beautiful Devon countryside. Once he was satisfied that the cottage was secure, he stepped out onto the lane and strolled towards the chapel that was hidden in a hollow behind a cloak of trees.

The lane soon petered out, dwindling into a cliff path. To his left lay the vast, glistening sea, and just ahead of him he could see the little stone chapel built for the Iddacombes of Chadleigh Hall on the edge of their land. Now it was disused and locked, visited only by the occasional walker and by the shades of the dead who slept in its tiny grave-yard.

Nettles brushed against his legs as he walked towards the moss-covered memorial, little more than an over-large gravestone, which stood on the south side of the chapel. He pushed his way through the high grass and bindweed until he reached his goal. Then he squatted down and read the inscription.

'To the memory of those who perished on board the *Celestina*, 24th July 1772.'

He read the names – twenty-eight in all, all buried here in the rich Devon earth. At the top of the list were Captain Isaiah Smithers, Master, and his wife Mary Anne. The man smiled. It was a happy coincidence that he had found Captain Smithers here, so close to where he was staying. A real piece of luck. Providence even.

He walked around the neglected chapel before heading back to the lane, stopping dead when he spotted a car parked between him and the cottage. The gate leading into a field of crops stood open to his left and he darted in behind the tall hedge, where he stood, statue still.

Concealed by foliage, he watched as two men climbed into the car. One of them was young, black and smart, and his companion was older, slightly unkempt and a little over-weight. They were chatting amiably: probably a pair of plain-clothes detectives. The man knew the signs.

When the car had driven away he hurried back to Old Coastguard Cottage and shut the door behind him. If he kept his head nothing could go wrong.

At 10.30 that night a white lorry sporting the bright red Nestec logo swung out of the factory gates and onto the road leading to Exeter and the M5 motorway.

But before reaching Newton Abbot the driver pulled into a lay-by and lit a cigarette. He had promised his wife he was giving them up but he was in urgent need of a dose of nicotine. And as he wouldn't be home that night, she wouldn't smell the tobacco on his breath. It was a little sin she would never know about – along with a few others.

He sat there in the darkness, his engine switched off. The road was quiet but from time to time a car flashed past, a blur of headlights like the eyes of some fast swooping predator, intent on its goal. He inhaled the smoke and closed his eyes.

Then a sudden noise made him jump. The driver's door was flung open and he felt strong hands dragging him out of the vehicle. He flopped helplessly onto the cold, rough ground. Then the blow came and he knew nothing more.

Chapter Two

Marbis grabbed my hand and held on to it tightly. Not wishing to cause offence I allowed it to rest in his as he spoke.

He was most insistent that I should not speak but listen to the tale he had to tell. I agreed, anxious as I was to be out of that dreadful place, and hoped that his talking would be brief.

I set down here what he told to me upon that night. It was not a story that I shall easily forget.

George Marbis's tale began in the year of Our Lord 1732 when he was but ten years of age. His father, old Josiah Marbis, was a man over-fond of strong liquor who frequently absented himself of an evening from the cottage where he lived with George and his mother. George noted his mother's discomfort during his father's absences and yet he suspected nothing amiss, rather that his father was drinking away all the money he earned working on the land. Then, one October night in 1732, George's mother was heavy with child and her pains began when his father was away from the cottage. George was sent to fetch Mother Padley, the midwife, and as he hurried to her cottage through the wind and the rain, he saw lanterns and the shapes of men in the dark. Then he heard screams drifting inshore on the wind. The screams of terrified women and children.

Forgetting his mother's plight for the moment, young George followed the glow of the lanterns in the darkness. They were heading for the shore and George stayed some way behind. He watched from the cliff top as the men scrambled down to the sands, and he saw that a ship had foundered on the rocks, her mast already afloat and her back about to break in the relentless waves. The screams were those of the poor souls trapped upon the ship, and George's first thought was that the men with the lanterns would rescue the people and take them to safety.

But George Marbis witnessed no acts of heroism or Christian charity that night. Rather what he saw would stay in his thoughts until his dying day.

From An Account of the Dreadful and Wicked Crimes of the Wreckers of Chadleigh *by the Reverend Octavius Mount, Vicar of Millicombe*

On his way to Tradmouth police station the next day Wesley took off his jacket and loosened his tie: it was far too hot for formality, even first thing in the morning. Gerry Heffernan, who had discarded his own jacket on the way to work, followed him into the building and glanced back longingly at the busy river, where pleasure boats and private yachts were gliding over the water in the sunshine.

Hungry seagulls circled above the fine array of scented flowers that bloomed in the Memorial Gardens and tumbled from baskets on lamp-posts and window ledges. Even the police station boasted its own colourful display in the small flower beds either side of the main door. Wesley breathed in deeply as he climbed the stairs to the CID office, contemplating another day at work.

Tradmouth's holiday atmosphere had crept through the open windows and invaded the office. A couple of the detective constables were wearing brightly patterned shirts; hardly Wesley's idea of plain clothes. Nobody had ventured in wearing shorts yet, but Wesley suspected that if the weather kept up it would only be a matter of time.

Rachel Tracey had taken off her jacket to reveal a neat, but slightly see-through, white blouse. She was sifting through a pile of reports, but when she saw Wesley she looked up at him and smiled.

'Someone's determined that we shouldn't enjoy the weather. A lorry was hijacked last night between Neston and Newton Abbot. The driver was knocked out and half a million pounds' worth of computers were stolen.'

'How's the driver?'

'He's got a sore head but otherwise he's fine. They kept him in hospital overnight for observation. What happened down at Millicombe yesterday?'

Before he could answer Gerry Heffernan lumbered in and made straight for his office, shouting that he was in urgent need of a cup of tea.

'Well, at least the boss has got his priorities right,' said Rachel in a low voice when she was sure he was out of earshot.

Wesley started to laugh, then he looked up and saw that Steve Carstairs was watching them with speculation in his eyes. He straightened himself up in an attempt to look businesslike. There was nothing Steve would like better than to start a few rumours.

Rachel glanced over in Steve's direction and understood. She'd stick to police matters when he was about. 'So what did you find over at Millicombe?'

'It was at Chadleigh, just outside Millicombe. Some divers working on a shipwreck spotted a body in the water and brought it ashore.'

'Suspicious?'

Wesley shrugged. 'Don't know yet. Probably an accident or suicide. We'll know more when Colin Bowman's done the post-mortem.'

'Man or woman?'

'Woman. And we had another call before that. Some

27

builders found a skeleton while they were working on a place called Chadleigh Hall. Heard of it?'

Rachel nodded. Being a local farmer's daughter she knew the area well. 'It used to be a girls' boarding school – known locally as "Virgins' Retreat".'

'Well, it's possible that one of the virgins had been tied up in a sealed room and left to die.'

A momentary expression of shock passed across Rachel's face. 'I didn't know much about the place, not moving in those sorts of circles, but I never heard of anything odd going on there.'

'And if there was, your mother would know about it?' Wesley grinned. Rachel's mother, Stella, had a talent for uncovering local secrets which the intelligence services would have envied.

'Not necessarily. Millicombe's fifteen miles away. My mother's radar might not reach that far.'

'Anything new to report here?'

'Steve and Trish have been to interview the owner of the hijacked lorry but apart from that it's been pretty quiet. A woman came in yesterday to report that her friend's gone missing but that's about all.'

Wesley looked up. 'Anything to worry about?'

'I doubt it. The woman had an affair, left her husband and then went to stay with a friend from work. I can just imagine the rest: a few tears, a few glasses of cheap plonk and a few "aren't all men bastards" sessions.'

'Has the man she was having an affair with been contacted? Isn't it likely she's gone off with him?'

'According to the friend, Lisa Marriott, the affair finished a few weeks ago, but it's always possible she could have had second thoughts and taken up where she left off. She received a letter just before she disappeared, apparently, then she went out and didn't come back.'

'A grovelling letter from the husband or the other man?'

'Possibly.'

'Have you checked it out?'

'The friend said the boyfriend's name was Mike but she didn't know anything else about him. I've tried to get hold of the husband but there's been no answer. There's one interesting thing, though. The husband's called Trevor Gilbert, and guess what . . .'

Wesley was hot and tired, in no mood for guessing games. 'What?'

'He works for Nestec. The computer firm whose lorry was hijacked last night. He's the warehouse manager. He was the one who saw the consignment of computers off the premises.'

'So you think there could be a link between the hijacking and the woman's disappearance?' Wesley looked at Rachel with admiration. She had deserved her recent promotion to detective sergeant.

'Trevor Gilbert sees half a million pounds' worth of computer equipment onto a lorry which is stopped by masked men on its way to the M5. The driver's knocked out, the lorry's pinched, then it's found abandoned near Exeter with all the valuable stuff nicked.'

'Which points to the hijackers having inside knowledge.'

'And if they want to keep their man on the inside from talking, what better way than to hold his wife . . .'

'His estranged wife.'

'Perhaps they didn't know that. Or maybe he still has a soft spot for her – that's what Lisa Marriott implied, anyway. She might have been kidnapped and held until the job was over.'

Wesley looked sceptical. 'It's possible, I suppose.'

Gerry Heffernan's office door crashed open and he emerged with a mug of steaming tea in his hand, sleeves rolled up ready for business.

'Right, you lot. Some poor woman's been found in the sea near Millicombe and we've got to find out who she is. I want details of any women reported missing on our patch. Aged between twenty-five and forty-five. Come on. Look lively.'

There was a flurry of activity. Trish Walton made for the filing cabinets, beating her colleagues to it.

Wesley reached for the sheet of paper lying on Rachel's desk.

'Right age,' she said.

Wesley didn't reply. He was reading the description of Sally Gilbert. When Rachel had spoken of her, mentioning the probability that she had run off with a lover or was involved somehow in the hijack, he hadn't associated her with the mutilated corpse that had been pulled from the water. But now, as he read her description in Rachel's small, neat handwriting, he knew that they might have a name for the dead woman – the lady from the sea.

'Short dark hair. Last seen wearing a red T-shirt and cream trousers,' he said softly. With a bit of imagination that could describe the sea-sodden garments that had draped themselves around the woman's drowned flesh. 'It could be her.'

'The woman who was found in the sea?'

'I think we should pay this Trevor Gilbert a visit.'

Wesley stood up and made for Gerry Heffernan's office, clutching Rachel's report.

Detective Constable Steve Carstairs sat at his desk behind a pile of paperwork and watched at Wesley Peterson left the office with Rachel.

They were on their way to see Trevor Gilbert, the warehouse manager at Nestec. As soon as Steve had heard about the lorry hijacking, he had thought it smelt like an inside job – or at least a job that needed inside knowledge. Gilbert might be involved, the man on the inside. Or, in view of recent developments, perhaps he'd done away with his missus. But whatever it was, it was a shame that Peterson was going to get the credit . . . as usual.

Steve jabbed his ballpoint pen into the sheet of paper before him on the desk and twisted.

His telephone began to ring, making him jump. He

picked up the receiver and barked his name.

'Steve?'

'Yeah. Who's that?'

The voice sounded familiar yet he couldn't place it. Probably one of his grasses.

'You free tonight?'

'Who is that?'

He wished the speaker would give him a clue ... or a name.

'Meet me in the Tradmouth Arms ... No, you'd better make it the Star. I don't fancy bumping into Scouse Gerry. Eight o'clock.'

A grin spread across Steve Carstairs' face. 'Harry, mate. What are you doing down this way, my old son?' He unconsciously adopted a cockney twang when speaking to Harry Marchbank – he always had. Harry had been a detective sergeant in Tradmouth CID before transferring to the Met, and when Steve had joined the department as a raw young detective constable he had thought the sun shone out of Harry Marchbank's nether regions.

'Scouse Gerry still about, is he?' Marchbank's accent was now so firmly anchored in the Thames that nobody would have guessed at his Newton Abbot roots.

Steve lowered his voice. 'He's DCI now.'

'Bloody hell.'

'And the bloke who replaced you from the Met – he's a bleeding graduate and a member of the ethnic minorities so he gets all the promotion going: he's made it to inspector. And the lovely Rachel hangs on his every word – bet it's not long before he gets into her knickers. She's been promoted to sergeant and all. That leaves me still a humble DC, but I'm white and male so I reckon there's no chance of getting any higher. How's the Met?' he asked longingly.

From the time he'd joined the police force Steve Carstairs had yearned for armed stake-outs, fast cars and drugs busts in some decaying inner city. But the reality of Tradmouth CID and the routine of paperwork meant that he

31

was usually disappointed. But then he had his own flat, new wheels ... and a devoted mum, who took in his washing every weekend and returned it, freshly ironed, on a Monday. His reasons for staying put were piling up with the years.

'The Met's fine,' Marchbank said quickly, anxious to cut the chitchat. 'Look, Steve, I'm down here on business ... trying to trace someone. I'll have to come in and have a word with Stan Jenkins tomorrow.'

'Inspector Jenkins has retired. Scouse Gerry's in charge now.'

Marchbank swore under his breath. 'Okay, it'll have to be him, then, if he's the guvnor. See you in the Star tonight. Eight o'clock.'

'Who is it you're looking for?'

There was no answer. Harry Marchbank had put the receiver down.

Even though Wesley had seen the body of the woman who had been dragged ashore in Chadleigh Cove, he wouldn't have recognised her immediately from the photographs scattered around the living room at 5 Westview Way, Tradmouth. The woman in the photographs was pretty, though inclining towards plumpness. She had dark eyes and sleek dark hair and gazed warmly at the camera, her wide mouth set in a fixed eternal smile.

Wesley picked up one of the framed photographs that sat on the window sill – Sally in her wedding dress. There seemed at first to be no resemblance between the hopeful young bride and the bloated, eaten creature that he had seen lying on the wet sand. But he knew that it was her.

The house was on a brand-new estate on the very edge of Tradmouth on hilly land rejected as unproductive by the farmer who had owned it and sold it to developers for a tidy sum. Number five was detached, expensively furnished, and boasted four bedrooms plus an en suite bathroom. Wesley found himself wondering how much a warehouse manager at Nestec would earn. Surely not enough to finance this little palace. Unless Sally Gilbert's salary as receptionist at the Tradfield Manor Hotel was substantial, which he doubted. Or maybe they just lived in considerable debt: a lot of people seemed to these days.

Trevor Gilbert stood by a large orange sofa which looked as if it hadn't been out of the showroom long. 'I've had the police round here already today,' he said, on the defensive.

'I'm sorry, but we do need to talk to you,' said Rachel Tracey quietly, mindful of the news she would soon have to break.

'What's going on?' Gilbert continued. 'Why don't you get out there and catch the bastards who hijacked the lorry? Why are you wasting time questioning me when you should be after the villains who did it?'

Gilbert was a small man in his late thirties with thinning hair and a belligerent manner. But his aggression couldn't disguise his nervousness as he played with the strap of his wristwatch.

'I think it might be better if we sat down,' Rachel suggested gently. Wesley had asked her to go along with him. She was good with bereaved relatives and Gerry Heffernan's bluntness might not have gone down well with a man who was about to be told that his wife had been found floating dead in the English Channel.

Gilbert looked as though he were about to object. But something in the tone of Rachel's voice made him obey. Wesley caught her eye and nodded. It would probably be best if she did the talking.

'We're not here about the lorry hijack, Mr Gilbert. We're here because your wife's friend has reported her missing.'

Wesley was watching Gilbert's expression, and he thought he saw something that looked almost like relief. Then, after a split second, Gilbert was on his guard again.

'She's got someone else, you know. I said to Lisa when she rang that she'll have gone off with him. Typical of the selfish cow not to let anyone know. She'd never think people'd be worrying about her.'

'This other man . . . do you know who he is?'

'I've no idea,' he said quickly, and Rachel believed him. If Sally hadn't confided in her bosom pal Lisa, she would hardly have confided in her husband.

Rachel summoned all her reserves of tact for the next bit. She took a deep breath. 'There's no easy way of saying this, Mr Gilbert, but I'm afraid that a body's been found which fits your wife's description. Right height, hair, clothes. I'm very sorry . . .'

He stared at Rachel. 'But Lisa only saw her on Friday,' he muttered pathetically. 'What about her car? Has that been found?'

'Not yet. We're looking for it.'

'She'll have gone off somewhere. If you can't find her car it means . . .' He hesitated. 'This body . . . where was it found?'

'In the sea near Millicombe.'

'There you are, then. Sally hated boats and she couldn't swim. There's no way she'd . . .'

'There was evidence of extensive injuries. It's possible that the woman we found may have fallen some distance . . . from the top of a cliff perhaps. There are a lot of cliff paths around that coast. Was your wife in the habit of going walking or . . .?'

'No way. It can't be her,' Trevor Gilbert said with fragile confidence, chewing at a fingernail.

Wesley and Rachel looked at each other. There was one way to find out for certain whether the dead woman was Sally Gilbert.

'Mr Gilbert,' Rachel began, 'would you be willing to have a look at the body for us. It's possible that it's not your wife but . . .'

'It's not her. It can't be.'

'It would still help us if . . .'

Gilbert took a deep, shuddering breath. 'All right, then. But I know it won't be her.'

'We'll take you down to the hospital,' Rachel said quietly, ushering the man out of his living room. It was best to get this over with quickly.

Gilbert walked before them obediently. But when he was about to open the front door he stopped dead.

'Something the matter?' Rachel asked, wondering whether he'd changed his mind.

But Gilbert had picked up a small collection of letters and was staring at them. 'They're for Sally,' he mumbled. 'I promised to post them on.'

Wesley thought it best not to mention that Sally might not be in a position to receive letters. The man had to have hope. 'Has she had many letters since she left?'

'A few,' muttered Gilbert, still staring at the envelopes.

'Anything unusual? Any writing you didn't recognise?'

Gilbert thought for a moment. 'There was one late last week. I forwarded it on to Lisa's address. I, er . . . I think it was from a solicitor. It looked sort of . . . official.'

The word 'divorce' hung in the air unmentioned, but it was clear that this was what Gilbert suspected. Sally had intended to make their separation permanent.

Trevor Gilbert didn't say a word as Rachel drove towards Tradmouth Hospital.

It was five o'clock and the divers had already gone, using the excuse of uncongenial tides. But Neil Watson, who didn't quite understand these things, strongly suspected that they'd headed for the pub. Which was where he intended to go.

Half an hour earlier Jane had come ashore in the dinghy, still wearing her diving suit, her eyes glowing with excitement. Underwater archaeology had always been her passion and she was enjoying every second of the search for the *Celestina*'s secret. But Matt, her boyfriend, didn't share her enthusiasm; he stayed firmly on the dive boat to receive whatever the divers brought to the surface.

Matt and Jane had made their way back to the cottage

they were all sharing, lent to them for the duration by Dominic Kilburn. But Neil lingered on the beach, feeling that the couple might appreciate some privacy. He wondered, in view of the rumours about the treasure on board the *Celestina*, whether someone should be keeping watch on the beach all night to deter any treasure hunters who might take it into their heads to dive down to the wreck. It was a long time since Neil Watson had slept on a beach, but he was up for it if necessary.

He sat on the sandy concrete steps leading to the disused café and breathed in the salty air. Chadleigh Cove had never been one of the popular holiday beaches and had been used mostly by locals. But now it was private – part of the Chadleigh Hall estate recently acquired by Kilburn Leisure Ltd – and its new owners had planted notices saying 'Private property, no admittance' all over the top of the narrow path that snaked up the cliff. Neil wasn't sure that he agreed with notices that threatened trespassers with instant prosecution, and several times he had resisted a strong temptation to tear them down.

However, the signs hadn't deterred a group of adolescents who were running around at the other end of the beach, long limbed and boastful; boys chasing screaming girls in some timeless mating ritual. But then Neil recognised one of them as Oliver Kilburn, whose dad owned the beach, so presumably he could do as he pleased.

The day had been warm and sunny but now he felt a cool breeze on his naked back. He slipped his T-shirt over his head. If the weather kept up it would certainly be warm enough to sleep beneath the stars as he and Wesley had done when they were students helping to excavate a temple on a Greek island. Neil smiled, convincing himself that he felt sorry for Wesley with his responsible suburban lifestyle. Wesley's days of sleeping on beaches were definitely over.

His stomach rumbled as he listened to the sleepy rhythm of the waves. He knew that a meal and a few pints would be waiting for him at the Wreckers, so he grabbed his rucksack and started up the beach towards the cliffs, hoping that Oliver Kilburn and his friends wouldn't decide to interfere with the team's inflatable dinghies which now lay in the shade of the café cum site headquarters. The currents in the cove were treacherous, but that sort of thing doesn't usually worry the young who are out to impress their fellows. The young can do stupid things, as Neil knew from his own experience.

As he neared the path up to the lane, he spotted a figure standing in the entrance to one of the caves in the rock face; a tall figure wearing khaki shorts, his face hidden by a floppy cotton sunhat. Neil decided to investigate on a whim, a feeling he couldn't put into words. He left his rucksack and walked back, the soft sand slowing his steps, and as he drew nearer the stranger turned. It was the man from the cottage on the cliff top who had allowed him to use his phone when the body had been found. He was standing there watching the youngsters, minding his own business, and there was no way Neil was going to tell him the beach was private.

The man spotted Neil and looked mildly embarrassed. 'I saw the signs and I didn't know if I should be down here. Then I saw the kids and . . .'

'As far as I'm concerned you can come down whenever you like.'

The man gave a shy smile, as though reassured. 'What was all the fuss about yesterday?' he asked.

'The divers found a body in the sea.'

'I gathered that much. Was it an accident or . . .?'

'We don't know. It was probably someone who fell off a boat or chucked themselves off a cliff. No doubt we'll read all about it in the local paper in due course.'

The man looked relieved, as if the incident of the body in the sea had been preying on his mind.

Neil held out his hand. 'I didn't have time to introduce myself last time we met. I'm Neil Watson.'

The man shook his hand. 'Robin Carrington,' he muttered.

'Do you live in that cottage or are you here on holiday?'

'It belongs to a friend. I'm down here to do some work.'

'What do you do?'

He hesitated. 'I'm a genealogist. I trace people's ancestors.'

'Really?'

The man sensed Neil's interest and carried on. 'I'm working for a family in the States who think they have local connections.'

'So how did they contact you?'

'Through the Internet. I have my own business.'

'Successful?'

'Oh, yes. They say that after pornography genealogy's the most popular thing on the Internet. It's what people want, a history. I suppose that's what we all want.' He smiled. 'I make a living from it, anyway.'

'This your first time down here?'

'No. I come down every year. I need a break from London.'

'How's your work going?'

Carrington smiled. 'Very well. I've been rooting through local church registers and it turns out that my clients are related by marriage to the family who owned a big house near here: Chadleigh Hall. They were called Iddacombe.'

Neil nodded. He knew about the Iddacombes, local landowners and shipowners. They had owned the *Celestina*.

'My clients are called Smithers and they live in Connecticut. An Isaiah Smithers was master of a ship called the *Celestina* and his wife was an Iddacombe. I read in the local paper that you're working on the wreck of the *Celestina*.'

'That's right. Have you found out much about Captain Smithers?'

'Only that he's buried in the graveyard of that little chapel just along the cliff path; the one that belongs to the hall.'

'I'll have to go along and pay my respects,' said Neil. 'Look, you're very welcome to come down here any time and see what we're bringing up from the wreck. And if you've got any information about Captain Smithers or the Iddacombes . . .'

'Isaiah Smithers' wife was a Mary Anne Iddacombe and she was the daughter of John and Mercy Iddacombe, who owned Chadleigh Hall. She's buried in the graveyard too, and it looks like they died together when the *Celestina* was wrecked. She must have sailed with her husband.'

'Bet she wished she'd stayed at home.' Neil was running out of things to say. And he felt a sudden pang of hunger for the fish and chips waiting for him at the Wreckers. 'I'm off to the pub now for something to eat. Fancy a pint?' He felt obliged to be sociable.

Robin Carrington shook his head.

'I'll leave you to it, then. See you soon maybe.'

He trudged back down the beach and, as he picked up his rucksack, he turned. Carrington was gazing out to sea, oblivious to the antics of the young people near by. Gazing out to the place where Captain Isaiah Smithers had lost his life.

Wesley Peterson made his way back to his modern detached house at the top of the town, strolling through the steep streets, between tubs and window boxes festooned with colour and scenting the early evening air. It had been a beautiful day and it would have been a pity to use the car. He stopped to catch his breath and turned round. As he looked at the rooftops of the town spread out below him, tumbling down to the glistening ribbon of the River Trad, he had no regrets about leaving London and the Met far behind.

As he walked on towards home he thought of Trevor Gilbert. He and Rachel had taken him to the hospital mortuary to identify his wife's body. He had gone into the room with dread, the smell of death and air freshener

39

making his stomach churn, and he had watched as Rachel had taken Trevor's arm gently when the woman's dead face was revealed. The staff at the mortuary had done their best to make Sally presentable, but it was still a distressing experience for a man who had courted her, lived with her and, presumably, loved her.

Trevor hadn't spoken. He had just given an assenting nod as the crisp white sheet was pulled back. He had stayed silent as they had driven him home and had nodded meekly when Rachel had explained that the post-mortem would be carried out in the morning. His sister had been contacted and she had agreed to come over so that he wouldn't be alone.

When Wesley arrived home he saw a space where Pam's car should have been. He felt a pang of anxiety. Even after meetings and lesson preparations, she was usually back from school by half five or six and now it was half past seven. What if she'd had an accident? What if she'd been rushed to hospital – a miscarriage, or something wrong with their son, Michael?

As he put his key in the front-door lock all sorts of terrible scenarios began to unfold in his imagination. He called Pam's name but there was no answer.

He walked through to the living room and called again, but the only sound was the ticking of the clock on the mantelpiece. The emptiness of the house came as a shock when he had expected the usual domestic chaos. The silence disturbed him.

The place was as untidy as he had left it that morning. But one thing had changed: a large sheet of paper lay on the coffee table, a message scrawled across it. Wesley picked it up.

'Della rushed to hospital. Michael next door. Be back soon.'

Wesley sighed. Gerry Heffernan had a huge repertoire of mother-in-law jokes but none of them seemed appropriate for Pam's mother, Della, a woman who could best be described as 'giddy', in stark contrast to Wesley's own mother, who was a sensible family doctor with strict views on child rearing.

He wondered what Della's emergency could have been. Somehow he had never associated the ebullient Della with illness, but then she was in her fifties and she did drink rather more than the government's recommended guidelines. Wesley had always considered her to be a silly woman who made Pam, her only daughter, seem staid in comparison. But then he had a sneaking fondness for his mother-in-law, irritating though she could be, and he would never wish illness or disaster upon her.

Hunger gnawed at his stomach, but he was resigned to the fact that he would have to feed himself. And there was Michael: he would have to relieve the neighbours of the alarming responsibility of a lively toddler who had more energy than sense before they were reduced to quivering wrecks.

When he heard the sound of a car door slamming outside, he rushed to the front door. Pam was on the drive locking the door of her VW Golf. She turned round and gave him a weak smile. She looked tired.

'Have you got Michael yet?' were her first words.

'I was about to. I've only just got in myself. How's Della? What happened?'

Pam didn't answer for a few moments. She was intent on taking the paraphernalia of her work from the boot: files, boxes of books, a bulging briefcase; the working day wasn't over yet. Wesley took a box from her: her pregnancy wasn't showing much yet but it was a fact etched on his mind.

'So how's Della?' he repeated, anxious to know how serious things were.

'Fine. Will you fetch Michael from next door?'

'What happened?'

She turned to him. There were dark rings beneath her eyes and her face was ashen. She looked ill. 'My bloody

41

mother fell down a step outside a pub and broke her ankle. She'd been celebrating the end of term with some of her students and she was somewhat the worse for wear, as far as I can make out.'

Wesley tried hard not to smile. Della lectured in sociology at a further education college and, ever since the restraining influence of her late husband had been removed by his untimely death from a heart attack, she had reverted to the days of her lost youth. Drink, parties and the occasional unsuitable man – it was as though Della was making up for lost time. And it was Pam with her teaching career and young family who had become cast in the role of responsible adult.

After he had called next door to fetch Michael from their neighbours, a retired couple with four grandchildren of their own who could be relied on to help out in an emergency, Wesley placed the tired toddler in his playpen and made for the kitchen. He found a frozen shepherd's pie and put it in the microwave, but when he took the meal to Pam, he found her slumped on the sofa staring into space as Michael whinged with tiredness in his wooden prison.

He handed her the plate and sat down beside her. 'Hard day?' He tried to sound sympathetic.

'You could say that. Thank God it's the end of term. What about you?'

'A lorry hijacking and we've identified the body that was found floating in the sea near Millicombe. And did I mention that someone found a skeleton walled up in a secret room yesterday?'

Pam looked up from her shepherd's pie, interested. 'No. Where was this?'

'At a big old house over at Chadleigh. It's being done up and made into some sort of hotel and leisure complex – some builders found a skeleton tied to a chair in a bricked-up room ... just like in all the best ghost stories, only this one was for real. The hall's near where Neil's working on that shipwreck.'

Pam looked away. She and Neil had gone out together at university but it hadn't lasted long. To Neil Watson relationships came a poor second to archaeology, and she had soon become aware of Neil's flatmate, Wesley's, many attractions.

'Chadleigh Cove, you mean? He's told me all about it. He rang while you were out the other day.'

'You never said.'

'I forgot. I've got a lot on my plate, you know,' she said with more than a hint of reproach. 'If it's not school it's Michael and if it's not Michael it's my bloody mother breaking her ankle when she's rolling out of some pub.'

Pam put her head in her hands and Wesley put a comforting arm around her shoulder. This was real life: kids, work and exhaustion. Not much time for the fun they used to have; not much opportunity for social life, leisure or refined cultural activities. A simple trip to the theatre required the organisational genius of an expert in military strategy, so nowadays they didn't bother and slumped in front of the TV set instead.

Maybe when the kids were off their hands. Maybe when they were Della's age they could spread their wings again. Suddenly Wesley looked upon Della's activities with a whole new understanding.

'So where did you say this skeleton was found?' she asked after a few moments.

'Place called Chadleigh Hall.'

Pam's eyes lit up with sudden interest. 'It used to be a girls' boarding school. My mother was at school there.'

Wesley looked at her, surprised. 'I didn't know.'

'Her family weren't badly off and my grandfather worked abroad for a while so she boarded at Chadleigh Hall. Being locked away with all those poor little rich girls probably accounts for Della's left-wing politics.' She grinned. 'Do you think the skeleton was a pupil who pushed the staff too far? In which case I'm surprised it wasn't my mother.'

Wesley gave her hand an affectionate squeeze. 'We're keeping an open mind at the moment. How long's Della going to be in hospital?'

'They said she'd be out soon but she's going to have to take it easy.' She hesitated, as if she was about to say something else but had thought better of it. She forced herself to smile. 'She'll be fine. What about the body in the sea? Was it a swimming accident or . . .?'

'We don't know yet. The post-mortem's tomorrow.' He didn't feel inclined to talk about Sally Gilbert's death. The thought of it depressed him. 'Apart from Della's little bit of excitement, how was your day?'

'Not too bad. Only one more day to go till the end of term. I should be crossing off the days to my release like they do in prison.' She looked up suddenly and smiled. 'Mind you, things are looking up. The end-of-term presents have started to come in. The score so far is three soaps, two scented candles, an embroidered hanky and a bottle of bubble bath. And one of the kids gave me this.' She reached for her handbag and took out a small oblong box. She opened it and took out a gold chain with a small oval locket set in its centre. 'Isn't it pretty?'

'Lovely,' said Wesley, giving the object a quick glance. 'Is it real gold?' he joked.

Pam laughed. 'Hardly. Probably came out of a Christmas cracker.' She put the necklace down and read from the card that lay inside the box. 'To Mrs Peterson. Thank you for being my teacher and good luck with your new baby. Love from Kayleigh Dilkes. Isn't that lovely?'

'It's an improvement on an apple for the teacher.'

'I know. It's really sweet of her. I mean, Kayleigh's mum can't be well off. I think she works as a cleaner and I don't think there's a dad about.' She looked at the necklace and smiled. 'At least I know Kayleigh didn't pinch it out of her mum's jewellery box – I saw her mum hand it to her as she came into school.'

Wesley smiled and said nothing. Michael was grizzling,

ready for sleep, so Wesley trudged upstairs with the baby in his arms to do a spot of father–son bonding.

When he had left the room Pam poured herself a glass of orange juice before picking up the necklace again to have a closer look. She ran her index finger over the delicately carved pattern, a flower with a tiny blue stone at its centre. She opened the locket and peered inside. And when she spotted what looked like a tiny hallmark near the hinge, her heart began to beat faster. After a few seconds she snapped it shut and threw it down on the coffee table as though the thing were too hot to hold.

She stared at it for a few moments then picked it up again, running its fluid chain through her fingers. The more she looked at it the more she was convinced that it possessed the mellow sheen of real gold rather than the brash glitter of a cheap imitation. There was a small dent on the back, but even if it was damaged surely no hard-up single mother would give away such a treasure – unless it hadn't been hers to give in the first place. Easy come, easy go.

She held it, wishing the hallmark would disappear, wishing that the necklace would transform itself into what she had assumed it was – a worthless piece of costume jewellery. Perhaps she should show it again to Wesley, seek his advice. But then he was a policeman and would feel compelled to ask awkward questions about its origins. And the last thing she wanted to do was to hurt Kayleigh's feelings, to betray the child's trust.

She put the necklace back in its box. There was no need to mention it to Wesley for the moment: she'd deal with it in her own way.

She took a sip of her drink, wishing that the glass contained red wine instead of healthy orange juice. There was nothing she could do about the necklace tonight, even if she wanted to.

Robin Carrington stood at the door of Old Coastguard

Cottage and inhaled deeply. The air was good here, unpolluted. Not like London. The dark was gathering now; not the street-lit electrical glow that passed for darkness in the city, but a dense, velvet darkness, all enveloping. A darkness that hid all imperfections, all wickedness.

He thought about taking a walk to the pub. But Neil Watson might be there and he feared that he had said too much already.

He left the house, glancing back at the telephone on the hall table. When he reached the lane he stopped and listened. He could hear the regular, soporific rhythm of the sea, and he felt a sudden urge to go down to the beach, to stand with the waves lapping at his bare feet, knowing that there was nothing between him and the French coastline but water.

He crossed the lane and started down the steep path, stopping halfway down to stare out to sea. But in the dim moonlight he could make out only the shifting mass of water and the faint outline of the jagged, treacherous rocks.

His work for the Smithers family in distant Connecticut was almost complete, and when he had finished he would leave Devon for good.

He would cross the angry sea and never return.

Dominic Kilburn let himself into Chadleigh Hall and stood in the entrance hall at the foot of the sweeping staircase. It would be splendid when the work was finished; the jewel in Kilburn Leisure's crown.

The builders had all gone home and the place was empty. He listened to the sounds of the sleeping house, the creaks and bumps of ancient ghosts, and when he flicked a switch the bare bulbs shone; tiny glass suns, dispelling the night. At least there was electricity in the place.

Kilburn walked through the rooms slowly, leaving his footprints in the plaster dust on the bare boards. When he reached his destination, he stood for a while, his eyes drawn to the jagged hole in the wall; gaping and impenetrable like the entrance to some fearful cave.

His way was barred by blue-and-white tape – a crime scene, not to be entered. But he ducked under the barrier and, with shaking hands, took a torch from his pocket and shone it into the blackness of the tiny room.

Chapter Three

Tears welled in George Marbis's eyes. Even after the passage of so many years it distressed him to tell of what he had seen. But he continued his story, his voice becoming weaker as he spoke.

Being but ten years of age, George was small and agile, and he reached the shore in the moonlight unseen by the men of the village, who carried with them lanterns and ropes. He recalled the purposeful silence as they marched down the path towards the sand and the screams and cries of distress from the roaring water – the cries of souls in peril.

George crouched behind a rock, hidden from view. He could see clearly in the glow of the full moon and he watched as the men of the village waded into the rolling waves. The village blacksmith, Matthew Kilburn, went first, a rope tied fast about his waist. George saw his face in the moonlight, saw his jaw set in determination. Kilburn strode through the waves towards the broken wreckage of the ship, a hero ready to save the lives of the hapless sailors. George watched as he reached out to a woman who was clinging to a mast, half conscious, expecting that any minute she would be carried to the safety of the shore in his strong arms.

But Matthew Kilburn made no effort to pluck the woman from the angry sea. His large hands tightened around her throat as he throttled the life from her and pushed her beneath the waves.

From An Account of the Dreadful and Wicked Crimes of the Wreckers of Chadleigh *by the Reverend Octavius Mount, Vicar of Millicombe*

The Star stood in the middle of the town, in a back street near the church. Gerry Heffernan had been known to drink in there after choir practice on a Friday night, but on a Tuesday he would most likely be at home or in the Tradmouth Arms next door to his house on the waterfront.

It was eight o'clock and the bar was busy, filled with a cocktail of regulars and summer visitors. But as soon as Steve Carstairs walked in, he spotted Harry sitting in the corner, a pint glass raised to his full lips. He had a little more belly and a little less hair than when Steve had last seen him two years before, but other than that he seemed unchanged. Steve pushed his way through the standing drinkers until he was looking down on his old colleague, a wide grin on his face.

Harry Marchbank looked up. 'Steve, mate. How are you doing? Sit down. What'll you have?'

'I'll get them, Harry. Pint of lager, is it?'

'Well remembered. I'll tell you one advantage this dead place has over London ... the prices are cheaper.' Harry laughed and handed Steve his empty pint glass.

Five minutes later they were settled with their drinks: Harry's pint of lager next to a bottle of some exotic brew which Steve put to his lips at regular intervals.

After a brief exchange of news Harry looked Steve in the eye. It was time to get down to business.

'So what brings you down here?' Steve prompted. 'I thought you said you'd never set foot in Tradmouth again.'

'I never intended to but my guvnor had other ideas. He said that I knew these parts so I'd be the man for the job.'

'What job's this?'

49

'Murder suspect's disappeared. Well, we didn't know he was a murder suspect until after he'd scarpered. A month ago he bumped off his missus, and I'll give him his due, he was very convincing – played the distraught widower to perfection. Everyone reckoned it was accidental death, cut and dried. But then her family demanded a second post-mortem which was done a few days ago – now we're treating her death as suspicious. Our suspect left London a couple of weeks back – said he had to get away to do some work and told his in-laws he was heading this way. He was brought up round here and apparently he comes back regularly.'

'Where does he stay?'

'They don't know.'

'Does he know about the second post-mortem?'

'No. He probably thinks he's got away with it.'

'What about his work? What does he do?'

'He's a . . . oh, what do they call it? He traces people's family trees . . . got his own company on the Internet – the Root Route, he calls it. I ask you . . .'

Steve shrugged. It sounded a funny sort of job to him.

'He said he'd only be away a couple of weeks but now it's almost three so I reckon this story about him working is a load of crap. I reckon he's decided to disappear before anyone started asking questions. Here's as good a place as any to start looking for him.'

'But why have you gone to the trouble of coming down here yourself? Why not just let the local . . .'

'Because I'd recognise the bastard anywhere. And I want him banged up.'

Steve saw bitterness in Harry's eyes as he took a long swig of lager, as though cooling the fires of his anger. Steve wasn't usually a perceptive soul but something told him this wasn't just a routine enquiry. This was personal.

There was something Harry Marchbank wasn't telling him.

*

The next morning Gerry Heffernan sat at the breakfast table and smiled at the two young people sitting opposite him.

'Nice, this.'

'What is, Dad?' It was the girl who spoke. She had a pretty, earnest face, framed by a shock of dark curly hair. She reached for a slice of toast with slender musician's fingers and looked at her father enquiringly, tilting her head slightly just as her mother had done when she was alive.

'Having you two back home.'

Rosemary Heffernan smiled. Her brother Sam said nothing. His mouth was full of toast.

'Ran out of money, didn't we,' said Rosie, helping herself to cornflakes.

Heffernan grinned good-naturedly. The pair were a terrible drain on his pockets but they were all he had.

'At least we've got ourselves jobs,' said Sam as he reached for another slice of toast. 'It's going to be bloody hard work this landscape gardening. Not like Madam here: playing the piano in a restaurant. What kind of job do you call that?'

'At least it's better than what you did last summer,' she teased. 'What was it? Stripogram?'

'Kissogram,' he corrected. 'I never took anything off.'

'At least that's what he told his father.' Heffernan grinned. 'So Eric the Viking has finally hung up his helmet, has he?'

Sam bit into his toast again and ignored his sister's giggles.

'So what exactly did you wear?' Rosie asked innocently.

As Sam kept munching his toast, his face bright red, Rosie realised how much she had missed the innocent pleasure of getting one over on her brother.

The indulgent father leaned back in his chair. It was good to have both of them home. The place had seemed quiet since Kathy's death and it was refreshing to have the house full of argument and music again after the long months of silence.

'Dad,' said Rosie, looking her father in the eye. 'The job at the hotel doesn't pay enough so I'm doing a few hours for this cleaning agency called Ship Shape.' She grinned. 'It's run by an ex-Wren from Plymouth.'

'Surely you don't need to take on more work.'

'I need the money.'

Sam stood up, scattering toast crumbs on to the floor. 'I'd better be off, Dad. See you tonight, eh?'

As his son shot out of the front door, Gerry Heffernan carried the dirty dishes to the sink and turned on the hot tap. Rosie was still sitting at the table and made no effort to help. Then he glanced at the kitchen clock and remembered that Sam wasn't the only one with work to go to.

He left the dirty dishes piled up like the unsolved case files on his desk in the CID office. Something to be dealt with later.

At half past nine Wesley would have considered a sink full of washing-up an attractive option as he stood beside Heffernan watching Colin Bowman slice into Sally Gilbert's discoloured flesh. He hated post-mortems first thing in the morning. Or at any time, come to that.

Both of his parents and his sister were doctors but Wesley had been born squeamish and he wasn't afraid to admit it. When he had witnessed his first post-mortem he had fainted, but things had gradually improved over the years. Now he could at least look at Colin Bowman's handiwork without feeling queasy.

Sally had been an attractive young woman in life. A wife but not yet a mother, as Colin pointed out cheerfully.

When he had weighed the dead woman's internal organs as casually as a greengrocer weighing out potatoes, he gave his tentative verdict. 'From the injuries, I'd say she fell into the water from a great height, possibly off a cliff, hitting the rocks on the way down. She was certainly dead before she hit the water. We'll have to wait for the toxicology report before we know whether she was under the influence of drink or drugs.'

'So it could have been an accident?'

'There's some bruising that could have been caused before her death. In fact there are marks on the top of her arms, just as though somebody's grabbed her. And look at her hands.' He held up the corpse's right hand. 'Badly bruised, and some of the small bones have been broken – almost as if someone's stamped on them.'

Wesley winced at the thought. 'You mean she might have been pushed off a cliff into the sea and then, when she tried to cling on, her killer stamped on her hands?' He wanted to pin the pathologist down to a definite sequence of events.

'It's possible.'

'Oh, come on, Colin, give us a break. Did she fall or was she pushed?' Gerry Heffernan lacked Wesley's diplomacy and patience.

'All I can say is that the injuries are consistent with Wesley's theory. Come over and have a look.'

Wesley declined Colin's invitation to make a close examination of the dead woman's arms and hands, and thought for a few moments before asking his next question. 'Had she eaten before she died?'

Colin nodded. 'She'd partaken of a traditional Devon cream tea shortly before her death. Could do worse for a last meal, I suppose.'

'It's just that her friend Lisa Marriott said Sally Gilbert left the house just after lunch saying she'd be a couple of hours. So she could have met her killer, had a cream tea with him then died soon afterwards. At least that gives us an idea of the possible time of death, but we still don't know where she went into the sea. Do we order a search of the whole coastline?'

'Oh, I don't think there'll be any need for that, Wes,' the chief inspector said with a smug grin. 'I know someone who'll be able to tell us where she went in.'

Wesley looked sceptical. He didn't know how his boss was going to come up with the necessary information without a good deal of routine police work ... short of consulting a very reliable clairvoyant.

'What about the bones from Chadleigh Hall?' Heffernan asked suddenly.

'I've had a good look at them. When I've cleaned myself up we'll go and see, shall we?'

Fifteen minutes later they were looking down at the yellowing bones of the Chadleigh Hall skeleton. It looked smaller than it had done in that room of horror. Smaller and more vulnerable. The bones of a young girl.

'Interesting this one, Gerry, but I must say I can't really tell you much about her.'

'It is a "her", then?' Wesley wanted to be certain.

'Oh yes. A female in her mid to late teens. She was five foot three inches tall and had good teeth with no dental work. She had the good fortune to be well nourished, by the look of the bones, and there are no obvious signs of disease. However, the cause of death isn't obvious either.'

'How old is it, then?'

Colin Bowman smiled. 'That's more Wesley's province than mine. She could have been in there twenty years or a couple of hundred, which I must say seems more likely given the circumstances. But there's no way of confirming that without the appropriate tests.'

'Which can take months,' said Wesley with what sounded like disappointment. 'But a thorough examination of the room she was found in might give us a clue. Neil did volunteer to have a look at it with me.'

'Okay,' said the chief inspector. 'Help yourself. The room's still sealed off as a crime scene just in case, so hopefully nobody will have touched it. And I'd like to get some background on the place. It used to be a girls' school. I want to find out if any of the girls went missing.'

'Actually my mother-in-law is an old girl of Chadleigh Hall.'

Heffernan started to chuckle, a merry sound that seemed inappropriate in a mortuary. 'Red Della ... at a boarding school for young ladies? I don't believe that.'

'I was quite surprised myself. As a matter of fact Della's here in the hospital. She broke her leg.'

'How did she do that?' Heffernan asked.

'Coming out of a pub, would you believe.'

Heffernan nodded, unsurprised.

'We could go and have a word with her if you like.'

Colin Bowman looked disappointed. 'I was hoping you'd stay for coffee.' He looked Heffernan in the eye. 'There's chocolate cake,' he added, as tempting as Eve's serpent.

Gerry Heffernan patted his substantial stomach and moistened his lips. As he had said to Wesley on more than one occasion, they certainly knew how to live down at the mortuary. 'Then how can we refuse, eh?'

They proceeded down the white corridor towards Colin's cosy office. They would make the most of their opportunities while they could.

They found Della easily enough. She was sitting up in bed reading a magazine that featured the word 'sex' several times on the front cover in bold letters.

She looked up and a wide smile spread across her face. 'Well, if it isn't my favourite son-in-law. If you've brought grapes with you I hope that they've been crushed and fermented and poured into a bottle. You can't get a drink in here for love nor money.'

'Hello, Della. I've brought Gerry with me. We'd like to ask you a few questions.'

She held her arms out. 'Put the handcuffs on, then, I'll come quietly. What am I charged with? Loitering on licensed premises or corrupting the young? I plead guilty to both charges.'

Heffernan gave Wesley a look of sympathy.

55

'I hoped you'd give us some information, that's all.'

Della snorted and turned her attention to an article on how to please your man in the bedroom.

'It's about your old school. Chadleigh Hall.'

Della looked up from her magazine. 'What about it?'

'When were you there?'

She thought for a moment. '1960 to '67. Why?'

'It's a bit of a long shot but a skeleton was found in a small sealed chamber off one of the first-floor rooms.'

Della raised her eyebrows, suddenly interested.

'Of course, it could have been there for years, but I wondered if there was any building work done in the time you were there. Or anything strange you remember. Did any of the girls go missing or were there any stories you remember hearing about the house ... or any rumours? Anything, really. We're clutching at straws but we've got to start somewhere.'

Della frowned. 'Whereabouts on the first floor?'

'If you go up the main staircase and turn left you go through one large room and then on into another. It was probably a bedroom when the hall was built. There was a small room, about eight foot square, leading off the second room, and it had been sealed up with the skeleton inside.'

Della sat in silent concentration, dredging the memories of her distant schooldays. After a couple of minutes she spoke. 'That would have been the headmistress's room. I remember it well. I spent a lot of time waiting outside it. There were workmen about when I was ... Oh, let me think ... I must have been in my fourth or fifth year. That would have been 1964 or 1965, I suppose. They did a lot of work on the building. I think they knocked old Frostie's room about a bit, but I can't really remember.'

'Old Frostie?'

'The headmistress. Miss Snowman. Commonly known as Frostie.'

Wesley nodded. He had always felt some sympathy for

teachers with unusual names, knowing the cruelties of the young.

'The workmen must have thought their ship had come in – all those nubile young virgins who hadn't seen anything male in years apart from the ninety-year-old gardener and his neutered tomcat.'

'And do you remember if any of those nubile young virgins went missing around that time? Did any girl leave unexpectedly?'

She closed her eyes, trying to recall the past. 'I seem to remember hearing that one of the older girls had run away around that time but I shouldn't have thought that was uncommon at boarding schools in those days. I think the average modern women's prison would seem like a holiday camp compared with what we had to put up with. Cold baths and lots of jolly hockey. I contemplated running away myself at times. I'll have a think about it and see if I can remember anything more. After all, there's nothing much else to do in this place, is there?'

They took their leave of Della, not knowing whether she had told them anything useful or not . . . and promising that next time they visited they would bring a discreetly hidden bottle.

When Gerry Heffernan walked into the CID office he had a sudden feeling that there was something out of place in his domain.

Then he saw what it was. Harry Marchbank was sitting at Steve Carstairs' desk, scratching his thinning hair. When he spotted Heffernan he stood up and the DCI halted suddenly. Wesley Peterson, following behind, narrowly avoided cannoning into him.

It was Heffernan who spoke first. 'What are you doing back on my patch? I thought I'd got rid of you a couple of years ago.'

The boss's words lacked their usual good humour. He meant what he said. As Wesley had always got on well with

Gerry Heffernan, this was a side of the man he rarely, if ever, saw.

Marchbank had the good grace to look embarrassed. 'I'm, er ... here on official business, sir. I've reason to believe that a murder suspect from our patch has headed this way and my guvnor's sent me to track him down.'

'Without letting us know?' There was menace in Heffernan's voice.

'I said I knew the local lads here so it'd be all right.'

'What makes you think that, then?'

Marchbank didn't answer.

At that moment Steve Carstairs appeared at the office door and hesitated. Then he put his head down, scurried in and sat at his desk.

Heffernan opened the door to his office and indicated by a jerk of the head that Harry Marchbank should step inside. He didn't want the whole office to hear what he had to say.

'You come in and all, Wes. Whatever he has to say for himself he can say in front of you.'

Wesley followed them in reluctantly. He didn't want to get involved in old office enmities but it looked as if he had no option. As Marchbank sat down Heffernan glowered at him from the other side of the desk. The newcomer ignored Wesley, who perched on the office's spare chair, feeling awkward.

'Right. Why are you here? And I want the truth.'

'Like I said, I'm looking for a suspect. He's wanted for murdering his wife.'

'When was this?'

'A few weeks back – end of June.'

'You'd better tell me the whole story.' Heffernan glanced at Wesley, who sat watching the proceedings like an umpire, determined to stay neutral if possible.

'This bloke Robin Carrington hasn't got two pennies to rub together. Then his mum dies and he inherits her house and moves from a seedy bed-sit into a nice four-bedroomed place. But the place costs a fortune to keep up so he gets into a load of debt. Anyway, a year ago he gets married to a young nurse called Harriet Marsden, and once he's married he insures Harriet for a fortune, almost three-quarters of a million. Only it doesn't work the other way – he's not heavily insured, just Harriet. Got it so far?'

Heffernan nodded and looked at Wesley, who, suspecting some kind of reaction was needed, nodded too.

'A few weeks ago the nice house catches fire. His mum had had the place for years and she'd never renewed the wiring and the fire investigators reckon that it was an electrical fire. Anyway, a body was found in the burned-out house. Harriet had been home alone 'cause she was supposed to be on night duty and Carrington had gone out for the day, or so he said. It seemed like an open-and-shut case and everyone reckoned that Harriet had died in the fire: accidental death. But once her mother learned about the insurance she didn't let it rest. She demanded a second post-mortem and last week she got it. And it came up with some interesting findings.' He paused, looking at his audience, who were waiting expectantly for the punch line. 'The second pathologist reckoned that she'd been dead when the fire started so the case has been reopened.'

'And Carrington?' asked Heffernan.

'He scarpered a couple of weeks after Harriet died, saying he was off to do some work in Devon. He doesn't know about the second post-mortem. He thinks he's in the clear.'

'What about Carrington's alibi for the time of Harriet's death?' Wesley asked.

Marchbank turned to him, the trace of a sneer on his lips. Then he turned back and addressed Gerry Heffernan.

'He claimed that he was in some library all day, then spent the evening in a pub. We've checked out the library – it appears he was there. And he says he met his solicitor in the pub – a bloke called Nichols who's not known for his love of the Metropolitan Police Force. He's friendly with more villains than I've had hot dinners.'

'That doesn't mean he was lying on this occasion,' said Wesley, earning himself another sneering glance.

'So do you know where to find this Carrington?' Heffernan asked. He would have hated to admit it but Harry Marchbank's story had got him intrigued.

'Somewhere in Devon – that's all he told Harriet's mum.'

'Devon's a big county.'

'Yeah, but he knows this area. He was brought up in Neston and he comes down this way for a couple of weeks every year. He was due back in London a few days ago but there's no sign of him.'

'Where does he usually stay when he comes down here?'

'Harriet's mum didn't know.'

'So we can presume he's in some hotel or bed and breakfast or renting a cottage?'

Harry Marchbank looked at Wesley. His mouth smiled but his eyes didn't. 'Very clever,' he said patronisingly.

Heffernan leaned forward. 'So what do you want us to do about it?'

'Just a bit of cooperation, that's all. I might need some manpower for an arrest or . . .'

'We're not sitting on our backsides twiddling our thumbs here, you know. We've got a lorry hijack and a couple of suspicious deaths. And that's not counting the usual holiday crime wave; thefts from yachts, burglaries . . .'

'Yeah, right. I get the point. I won't call on the local force unless it's absolutely necessary.'

'But you'll keep me informed of what you're up to. I like to know everything that goes on around here. And if you put a foot wrong I'll be on to your guvnor right away. That clear?' Heffernan looked Marchbank in the eye, challenging.

'Fair enough.'

'Fair enough, sir,' Heffernan barked.

Wesley looked at him, surprised. For an easygoing man, Heffernan was doing a fair impression of the nastier kind of sergeant-major.

60

Marchbank strolled from the DCI's office, his eyes scanning the outer office for familiar faces. They lighted on Rachel Tracey, who had just sat down at her desk, her healthy lunch of sandwich and fruit set before her.

He made his way over and sat on the corner of her desk. 'Long time no see, Rachel. I hear you've made DS. Congratulations.' He picked up the banana that lay on her desk. 'This for the new DI, is it?' He smirked unpleasantly and she snatched the fruit from him.

'Piss off, Harry. I thought I'd seen the last of you.'

'You might be seeing a lot more of me if you play your cards right.'

She turned away. It was best to ignore pests.

'Do you know you can see right through that blouse in a certain light,' was Marchbank's parting shot.

She looked up and saw that Wesley had emerged from Heffernan's office to watch their visitor leave. Her eyes met his and she smiled.

'What's he doing here?' she asked.

'Looking for a suspect. You sound as if you're not pleased to see him.'

'I'll say I'm not. Harry Marchbank is not a nice man.'

Steve Carstairs, at the desk over by the window, kept his head down and said nothing.

Although Sam Heffernan had drunk three cups of strong tea during the course of the morning, he had had nothing else since breakfast and his stomach told him it was high time he had something to eat. He thrust his spade into the dry soil. His hands were sore and blistered with the unaccustomed effort of manual work, but he carried on, uncomplaining. There was no way he wanted his new workmates to think he wasn't up to it. The sweat dripped down his forehead and tickled his nose, forming an annoying dewdrop at the end. When he wiped it away with a filthy hand he smelled the damp, slightly rotten aroma of newly turned soil on his fingers.

The man he knew only as Andy stopped work and leaned on his spade. 'Come on, Sam, get your back into it or we'll be here till next year.'

Sam renewed his efforts and Andy turned to the other man, who Sam knew as Keith. 'He's not doing bad for a beginner, is he?' The remark was followed by hearty laughter, as if the two men were sharing a private joke. Sam thought it best to smile and say nothing. Show willing but don't rock the boat.

'I reckon it's dinner-time,' Andy announced with authority. 'You brought something with you, Sam?'

Sam looked at him, puzzled.

'You brought something to eat? Sandwiches?'

Sam felt himself blushing. 'I'll, er, go down to the shops and ...'

'Bloody long walk to the shops.' Another gale of private laughter.

Sam knew they were right. It was a mile at least into Tradmouth. And it would all be uphill on the way back. He cursed his lapse of memory. He had been in a rush to get to his new job on time and lunch had been the last thing on his mind.

It was best to get it over with. He thrust his spade into the ground with a violence that surprised him and began to walk around the side of the house towards the gate.

'Hello. Don't tell me you've finished already.'

He swung round and saw the lady of the house emerging from the kitchen door. He had seen her when she had brought out mugs of tea to the thirsty workers. She was a tall woman with short hair, fair turning to grey. She looked sympathetic and capable, the sort who might well be a former nursing sister or teacher. But she was also attractive for her age, which Sam estimated to be around the mid-fifties, and she had a figure that would have been more fashionable in the ample days of Marilyn Monroe than the lean times Sam had known since he had first noticed that girls were different from boys.

62

'How's the work coming on?'

'Er, fine. I'm, er, just going out to get something to eat. I forgot to bring any lunch. It's my first day and ...' The sentence trailed off. He could think of nothing more to say. Perhaps he had said too much already, but there was something motherly about the woman, something that invited confidences.

'There's no need for you to go all the way to the shops,' she said with a sympathetic smile. 'I can make you a sandwich.' She suddenly frowned, as if she feared she'd made a terrible faux pas. 'Is that all right? If you'd rather ...'

'No, that's great. Thanks.'

'Come on into the kitchen. No need to let the others know you're getting special treatment.'

Sam followed her into the large kitchen, careful to take off his muddy boots before stepping over the threshold.

'I've got some smoked salmon in the fridge. Is that okay?'

Sam nodded eagerly. He had a weakness for smoked salmon but he wouldn't have liked to have consumed it in front of Andy and Keith, who would probably consider that such refined tastes cast doubt on his masculinity. 'This is very good of you, Mrs ... er ...'

'Carole. Carole Sanders. And you're ...?'

'Sam Heffernan.'

'And it's your first day with Tradmouth Landscapes?'

He nodded, watching her assemble the sandwich. 'I'm a student. I'm just working for them in my vacation.'

'What are you studying?'

'Veterinary Science up in Liverpool.'

She smiled with approval. 'So you're going to be a vet? Very worthwhile job. Would you like to work around here?'

'Yes. I think I'd prefer to work with farm animals rather than just pets.'

She handed him the sandwich, neatly cut in two, on a white china plate, and watched him devour it hungrily. 'Want another?'

Sam nodded. He was a growing lad. And at that moment he preferred Carole Sanders' company to that of Andy and Keith.

He looked around the kitchen: it was large and expensively fitted with all the appliances concealed behind polished-oak cupboard doors.

'Sam, could you fetch me a loaf from the pantry over there?' She pointed to a closed door in the far corner of the room. 'It's on the bottom shelf. You can't miss it.'

Sam hurried over obediently. The pantry was large and in the corner a trapdoor stood propped open – a wine cellar perhaps. He licked his lips as he located the sliced wholemeal loaf: he could have drunk a glass or two of wine with his sandwich, although he doubted that his hostess's hospitality would extend that far. But he couldn't complain.

As soon as Carole Sanders had made the second sandwich, she looked at the kitchen clock and announced that she was going out to work – she worked part time in an office in Tradmouth – but he had no need to rush and give himself indigestion: he could take as long as he liked.

When she had gone, Sam sat for ten minutes alone in the cool calm of the large kitchen, enjoying the break, enjoying not having his every remark smirked at by Andy and Keith. But he'd get used to it. He had to: he needed the money.

He walked over to the pantry and peered down into the space beneath the open trapdoor. In the gloom he could make out a wooden staircase and what looked like racks lining the underground walls. The bases of bottles glinted, reflecting the dim light of the forty-watt bulb in the pantry above. A wine cellar: Mrs Sanders was a woman of taste.

When he heard the sound of a key in the front door, he left the pantry quickly, closing the door behind him. If Carole had forgotten something and returned, he didn't want her to think he was prying ... or planning to help himself to a bottle or two.

But it wasn't Carole Sanders who appeared in the kitchen doorway. It was a woman in her late twenties, pale, with a turned-up nose. Her fair hair was scraped back off her face into a limp ponytail. She wore a light-coloured shapeless cardigan over a Lycra top and a miniskirt that showed off a pair of long, pale legs.

'Who are you?' she asked. Her tone was aggressive and her accent decidedly local.

Sam could have asked her the same question. But he didn't dare.

'I'm, er . . . working on the garden. And you are . . .?'

The woman stepped into the kitchen and edged her way around the cupboards, looking at him with suspicion. He noticed she had taken something off the worktop by the bread bin, something she had quickly shoved into her cardigan pocket. 'I'm Brenda . . . the cleaner. When will Carole be back?'

'She said she wouldn't be back till five. She's gone to work.'

The woman thought for a moment. 'If she comes back before you go can you tell her that I've only been able to do an hour today 'cause I'm doing some overtime at the hotel. And tell her Kayleigh's finished school so I'll have to bring her next time I come.'

'Kayleigh?'

'My daughter. Though I don't know what business that is of yours.' Then, without another word, she scurried away.

When Sam had first entered the kitchen he had noticed a ten-pound note nestling amongst some unpaid bills on the worktop near the door and thought this rather trusting of Mrs Sanders, considering there were strangers in the garden and the back door was open.

He fixed his eyes on the worktop and realised the money wasn't there any more.

The cleaner, Brenda, had looked furtive, guilty. He knew she'd been up to something. And he was as sure as he could be that the money was in her cardigan pocket.

But once the money was found to be missing it would be a matter of his word against hers. And Sam didn't know which one of them Mrs Sanders would believe.

Trevor Gilbert sat in his newly decorated front room, a glass of whisky clutched in his hands. He didn't usually touch the stuff but the sight of Sally's mangled body in the mortuary was still etched on his brain. At least alcohol dulled the pain a little, but Trevor knew the effect would be temporary.

He looked around the room he had decorated for Sally. That had been before he learned of her affair. He would have done anything for her then. His brother-in-law said that he allowed her to walk all over him. But he had loved her, so what else could he do. Until the end he had hoped she would come back. Until he had seen that official-looking letter. The letter in that crisp, expensive envelope marked 'Strictly Private and Confidential', which looked as if it was from a solicitor; the letter he had meekly forwarded to Lisa's address. Perhaps he should have torn it up. But it was too late for regrets now.

He thought of her on top of the cliff, tumbling down, hitting the jagged rocks on the way down to the merciless sea. Then he drained his glass and poured himself another drink from the half-empty bottle. All the trouble at work about the hijacking and now this. Trevor felt tears prick his eyes. At least things couldn't get any worse ... unless the police started asking questions again.

The phone on the window sill had rung a few times before Trevor registered the sound. He put his whisky glass down on the polished coffee table – something Sally would never have allowed him to do – and stumbled towards the window. When he picked up the receiver he grunted a hello, hoping it wasn't the police again.

'A bit of advice,' hissed the voice on the other end of the line. 'Keep your mouth shut or what happened to your wife might just happen to you. Do you understand?'

Trevor opened his mouth to speak but, in his terror, no sound emerged.

'Understand?' the voice repeated.

'I understand,' Trevor whispered into the mouthpiece before the line went dead.

Chapter Four

Young George Marbis watched as Matthew Kilburn lifted the woman's lifeless body from the waves. He was certain then that he had been mistaken in what he saw. Surely the blacksmith had been struggling to rescue her and her clothing had been caught in some wreckage. Surely Matthew Kilburn was no callous murderer who deserved the gallows.

He watched Kilburn carry the woman ashore and place her gently on the sand. She did not move and looked as if she had passed from this life (although George, being a child, had not seen much of our old enemy, death). He saw the glint of a knife and held his breath as Kilburn grabbed the woman's pale hand.

I could tell that the memory of what followed distressed George greatly, and he spoke of it in a whisper so that I had to put my face close to his stinking breath. 'He cut off her fingers,' he whispered to me. 'They had swelled in the water and he cut 'em off for her rings. He threw the fingers away and turned the poor maid over for her purse. He robbed the dead. Such wickedness,' he said.

I uttered words of comfort to calm his troubled mind. Yet he knew the woman had not died in the sea. Matthew Kilburn had strangled the life from her. Such wickedness.

From An Account of the Dreadful and Wicked Crimes

of the Wreckers of Chadleigh by the Reverend Octavius Mount, Vicar of Millicombe

Gerry Heffernan returned to the office looking rather pleased with himself.

Rachel Tracey looked up from her paperwork. 'Good lunch, sir?'

'You could say that, Rach. Wes about?'

Before she could answer Wesley Peterson appeared at the office door, a plastic-wrapped sandwich in his hand.

'Come into the office, Wes. I want a word.'

Wesley smiled at Rachel as he passed her desk, a smile she returned. As he reached Heffernan's office he turned round and saw that she was watching them, no doubt dreaming of the day when she could summon underlings into her own office. She had told him in an unguarded moment that she wanted to get to the top, to concentrate on her career. Work, she had said, was more reliable than men.

Gerry Heffernan interrupted his thoughts.

'I've been to see my old mate George at the coastguard station. I reckon I know where Sally Gilbert went into the water.'

Wesley sat himself down. 'Where?'

Heffernan walked over to the large Ordnance Survey map of the area that hung on his wall, half obscured by a coat stand which he moved to one side.

He pointed at Chadleigh Cove. 'That's where she was found. I told George when she disappeared and he worked out from the tides and the currents where she was likely to have gone in.'

He consulted the scruffy sheet of paper he'd just pulled from his pocket and searched the map, frowning with concentration. After a long silence he spoke. 'Just about here. Monks Island. Popular tourist trap. There are lots of cliffs round there. I reckon we should search the area.'

Wesley didn't know whether to look impressed or sceptical. 'How reliable is this friend of yours?'

Heffernan laughed. 'It's obvious you're not a seafaring man, Wes. If you know what you're doing it's not hard to work out where currents and tides would take a body. She went in around the Monks Island area, a couple of miles from where she was found. No doubt about it.'

Wesley studied the map. 'Have you ordered a search for her car?'

'Already done, Wes. The uniforms are over there now. And I've asked a team to search the cliff path.' He grinned smugly. 'I reckon we should nip over there and see how the land lies.'

Wesley sat himself down. He wanted to get things straight in his mind. 'So what have we got so far? A lorry full of computer equipment that Trevor Gilbert sees off Nestec's premises is hijacked and stolen. Trevor's estranged wife is staying with a friend then she goes missing. According to the friend's statement she received a letter last Friday, then she said she was going out to meet somebody and might have something to celebrate when she got back. But she never came back. She had also been having an affair with a mystery man. All sorts of possibilities there, I suppose.'

'Mm. She could have been abducted to ensure Trevor's silence; lured away by this mysterious letter ... or the letter might have had nothing to do with it. She could have been murdered by her long-suffering husband ... or by her fancy man. Or by somebody else altogether. But it's usually the husband, isn't it?'

'That's what the statistics say.' Wesley didn't sound too sure.

'Trevor Gilbert arranges to meet her for a walk on the cliffs, just to talk things over. Then they have a row and he pushes her into the sea. There are some dangerous cliffs around Monks Island.'

'Where was he last Friday afternoon?'

'He said he was on the late shift. In the afternoon he was on his own in the house. But we'll have another go at him – he could be hiding something.' Heffernan sighed. 'Now what about the body at Chadleigh Hall?'

'Colin can't tell us much about the bones, unfortunately, but I want to have another look at that room. I'd like Neil to give his opinion, see if he picks up on anything we've missed. Do you remember that Della said there was building work done when she was at school there – around the same time as one of the girls went missing?'

Heffernan nodded. 'You reckon it could be the body of one of the schoolgirls? Taking school discipline a bit far, isn't it?'

Wesley shook his head. 'I'm not thinking anything at the moment. I'd just like to find out more about the hall's past, that's all.'

'But if the skeleton is as recent as the school, it means we've got to get the forensic team to go over it and start an investigation.'

'Let's not jump to conclusions. We don't know how old it is yet.'

Heffernan looked at his colleague accusingly. 'What's the use of you having a ruddy archaeology degree if you can't tell how old a skeleton is.'

'It's hard to tell how old bones are just by looking, and radiocarbon dating takes a long time. But the context in which they're found can often give you clues,' Wesley replied patiently. 'That's why I want Neil to have a look.'

'It can't do any harm, I suppose. Anything on the Nestec robbery?'

'I asked Paul Johnson to have a word with any Nestec staff we haven't spoken to yet.'

Heffernan looked at his watch. 'We'd better get over to Monks Island and see how the search is going.'

The telephone on Heffernan's cluttered desk began to ring. He picked it up and barked a greeting into the receiver. A few seconds later he turned to Wesley, a wide grin on his

face. 'They've found her car. It was parked outside a bungalow in the village of Littlebury on the mainland across from
Monks Island and the old couple who live there rang the local
station to complain – they thought the car had been abandoned. What did I tell you?' he added, gloating.

Wesley said nothing.

'Let's get over there, then. What are we waiting for?'

Wesley hesitated. 'We ought to call on Trevor Gilbert
and tell him the post-mortem findings. Don't you agree?'

Heffernan thought for a moment. 'Okay. You go with
Rach – she's good with grieving relatives. Join me at the
carpark at Littlebury as soon as you're finished.'

Wesley opened the door and watched Rachel as she
worked. He wasn't looking forward to telling Trevor
Gilbert that his wife might have been murdered. But
someone had to do it.

Kayleigh Dilkes smiled up at Mrs Peterson, her favourite
teacher. Pam smiled back, feeling slightly awkward.

'Did you like the necklace, miss?' Kayleigh, a nine-year-
old with the small, pinched face of a wise pixie, spoke with
a slight lisp.

Pam hesitated. 'It's lovely, Kayleigh. Thank you. But
. . . well, I was just a bit worried that it cost too much. It's
very kind of your mum, but she really shouldn't have spent
that much money on me.' She studied Kayleigh's face for
any sign of disappointment. The last thing she wanted was
to hurt the child's feelings. Kayleigh was one of the more
likeable children in her class.

But Kayleigh smiled brightly. 'Oh, it's okay, miss.
Someone gave it to my mum and she didn't like it so she
said I could give it to you.' Then the child's face fell. 'But
if you don't like it . . .'

'Oh no, Kayleigh, I like it. I like it very much. Thank
you.'

Kayleigh grinned with relief, displaying a set of crooked
teeth. 'That's okay, then, miss.'

It was time for the children to go: as it was the last day of term, they were finishing early. Pam smiled benignly as Kayleigh skipped out of the classroom to join her friends in the playground. At least she knew now that Kayleigh's mother hadn't spent her own money on the present – but somehow that still didn't solve the problem.

Pam watched Kayleigh out of the classroom window and saw that her mother was waiting for her; a vision in tight Lycra and baggy cardigan. It would be embarrassing but she felt she had to do it and now was her chance. She shot out of the building and hurried across the playground.

'Ms Dilkes,' she called cheerfully. 'Can I just have a quick word?'

Brenda Dilkes froze and looked at Pam suspiciously. To Brenda teachers represented authority, even the young, amiable and pregnant Mrs Peterson.

Pam was pleased to see that Kayleigh had run off with a couple of her classmates. She hadn't wanted the child to overhear what she had to say.

'It was very kind of Kayleigh to give me such a lovely present,' she began. She felt her face redden with embarrassment but it was as well to get straight to the point. 'Only I was a little bit worried. It looked very expensive and I wondered if Kayleigh had taken it without you knowing.' She adopted what she considered to be an expression of innocent concern.

Brenda Dilkes put her hand to her throat. Pam noticed a red mark there: a love bite. 'No, it's okay, Mrs Peterson. I told Kayleigh she could give it to you.'

Pam smiled. 'Are you sure? It looks very valuable. I think it's real gold.'

Brenda smiled as though amused by the thought of a teacher making a fool of herself. 'Oh no. It's not gold. Can't be.' Then she hesitated as though she was having second thoughts.

'If you want it back ... if there's been a mistake ... I'm sure Kayleigh would understand.'

Brenda Dilkes shook her head. 'No. It's okay. I'm sure it's not worth ... Look, someone gave it to me and Kayleigh said you'd like it,' Brenda gabbled nervously. 'She's come on so well in your class and she wanted to give you something nice.'

That was it. Pam felt she had no choice but to accept the gift graciously. She made the appropriate noises of gratitude and walked back to the school building, conscious of Brenda's eyes on her. She was glad that was over.

She longed to nip down to the staffroom for a cup of tea but there was too much clearing up to do on the last day of term. She was sitting at her desk, still feeling uneasy about what she knew Wesley would call 'her moral dilemma', when the door opened and Jackie Brice walked in.

Jackie was Pam's classroom assistant: a mother of five with a large bosom and a heart to match. She had left school with no qualifications, had married young and had become a grandmother at the age of forty. She also lived on the Tradmouth council estate not far from Kayleigh, and she was an expert on other people's business.

'Jackie,' Pam began. 'You live near Kayleigh Dilkes, don't you? What do you know about her family?'

Jackie had been about to remove a child's painting from the class notice-board. But she turned to face Pam, sensing gossip, her favourite pastime.

'Brenda Dilkes ain't wed, I know that much. But that's how it is these days, ain't it. And I don't know who Kayleigh's dad is ... mind you, I don't expect Brenda knows neither,' she added with a ribald laugh. 'She spends a lot of her evenings in the Royal Oak and I've heard she's not too particular about the company she keeps.'

'Where does Brenda work?'

'At that posh hotel – the Tradfield Manor. And I've heard she cleans for a few people around here and all.'

Pam nodded, wondering whether her new necklace belonged to someone she cleaned for or to one of the hotel guests. In which case her mother would tell her to hold on to it. Della was a great believer in the redistribution of wealth – especially if it was redistributed in her direction. But Wesley, of course, held more conventional views.

'Do you know the family well?' Pam continued, encouraging conversation. She realised how little she really knew about the children in her class: teachers tended to see the sanitised side; the side the parents wanted them to see when they turned up in their best clothes to parents' evenings – if they turned up at all.

'Oh yes, they only live in the next street. Brenda's mother was a bit of a girl when she was young – Brenda never knew who her dad was, you know. And her mother before her – Brenda's gran – she had a bit of a reputation: it was said she had more Yanks than Eisenhower in the war.' Jackie laughed. 'Runs in the family, I reckon.'

Pam looked down at the pile of paperwork on her desk. 'Would you say Brenda was honest? I mean . . .' She didn't really know how to continue without implying that Brenda Dilkes was a thief.

'I don't know what you mean.' Jackie sounded wary.

'Do you know if the family's ever been in trouble with the police or . . .'

'Not that I've heard. Why?'

'No reason. I just didn't know much about them, that's all. It, er . . . helps to know the children's backgrounds,' she said, hoping she was sounding professional and convincing.

'You look worried. What is it?' It was typical of Jackie to come straight to the point.

Pam looked up at her and realised that it would be good to confide in someone. 'It's just that Kayleigh gave me a present – a necklace – and I think it's real gold. I asked Kayleigh's mum about it and she said someone had given it to her and she was quite happy for Kayleigh to give it to me. I feel really embarrassed about accepting it but I don't want to hurt Kayleigh's feelings. I don't really know what to do.'

Jackie started to laugh. 'It'll be from one of Brenda's fancy men. I wouldn't worry about it if I were you. Plenty more where that came from, if what I hear about Brenda Dilkes is true.'

Pam smiled. Jackie's words made her feel better. The necklace had probably been a gift from some admirer: the Royal Oak in the centre of the town attracted tourists, sometimes wealthy ones. Or perhaps Brenda's domestic duties at the hotel or in private homes involved more than dusting and polishing.

Pam began to write, uncomfortably aware that Jackie was watching her. The necklace was still in her bag . . . and it seemed that was where it would stay for the time being.

Wesley let Rachel ring the doorbell of 5 Westview Way. He looked around but the close was quiet. No net curtains twitched in the double-glazed windows. There weren't any net curtains full stop. The inhabitants of Westview Way probably considered them old fashioned.

The door opened to reveal Trevor Gilbert, unshaven and red eyed. He stood aside to let them in, and Wesley noticed that his shirt was stained with something that at first glance resembled blood but was probably tomato ketchup. Wesley went ahead of him into the living room. The place was a mess.

Rachel, forgetting her feminist principles for the moment, offered to make a cup of tea. Trevor looked as though he needed it. Wesley saw an empty whisky bottle on the coffee table, a sticky glass beside it. Trevor had been seeking oblivion, but by the look of him he hadn't found it.

'We're sorry to disturb you again, Mr Gilbert. We just thought we ought to tell you the result of your wife's post-mortem.' Wesley studied his feet, feeling he was intruding on the man's grief. But it had to be done. He just hoped that Rachel would hurry up with the tea.

She appeared, carrying a tray. As she handed round the brightly coloured mugs made by an exclusive local pottery

– obviously Sally's choice – Wesley decided he couldn't delay the bad news any longer.

'I'm sorry to have to be the one to tell you this, Mr Gilbert, but it looks as though your wife's death wasn't an accident.'

'You mean she topped herself.' Tears began to well in Trevor Gilbert's eyes. 'She had no need to do that. I would have had her back. I . . .'

Rachel intervened. 'What Inspector Peterson's trying to say is that Sally's death might not have been suicide or an accident. I'm sorry.'

Trevor almost spilt his tea. He stared at Rachel as though she'd uttered an obscenity. 'What?'

'We're treating her death as suspicious,' Wesley said gently.

'What does that mean?'

'We think she might have been murdered.'

'Only think?'

'The pathologist was pretty sure. I'm sorry.'

Trevor put his hot cup on the coffee table and cradled his head in his hands.

'I'm afraid this changes things a bit, Trevor. I'm going to have to ask you a few questions. They're just things we need to know . . . nothing to worry about,' he said reassuringly, knowing that his last statement wasn't necessarily true.

Trevor raised his head. He had aged ten years since Wesley had first met him. 'She wasn't . . . she wasn't interfered with, was she?' He spoke almost in a whisper.

'There was no evidence of sexual assault,' said Rachel, omitting to mention that a couple of days spent in the sea may have obliterated any telltale signs.

Trevor nodded as though, to him, this was a small comfort.

'I'm afraid I'm going to have to ask you to account for your movements on the afternoon Sally disappeared. I'm sorry.' Wesley hoped he sounded sympathetic. He felt genuinely sorry for this man. Even if he had murdered his wife in a fit of rage, who knew what anguish had driven him to it . . . and what agonies of guilt he was experiencing now?

'I wasn't due in work till seven. I was on the late shift, you see,' Trevor began, his voice hoarse. 'I went into Tradmouth for a paper and some milk and . . . I don't think I did much after that. I watched the cricket on the telly in the afternoon. Did some washing. That's it.'

'Did you see anybody who can confirm this? Did anybody call or did you see any neighbours?'

He shook his head. 'Didn't see a soul. The neighbours here hardly say a word to you and I can't remember seeing any of them.'

'Did the postman call with a parcel . . . the milkman come for his money? Anything. Did a neighbour see you hanging the washing out?'

'Used the tumble dryer, didn't I?' He gave Wesley a sad smile, as though he knew he was doing his best.

'Is there anybody we can call?' Rachel sounded concerned. 'A relative or friend? Your sister?'

'No, love. Thanks all the same. I wouldn't be much company. I'm better on my own.'

Rachel nodded. She'd forgive him calling her 'love' this once. She had to make allowances.

As they walked out into the hallway, Wesley glanced back and saw that Trevor Gilbert was opening a new bottle of whisky.

Rachel Tracey drove through the narrow country lanes and at three o'clock they reached the carpark overlooking Monks Island. The small island lay close to the shore, topped by its white wedding cake of a hotel. At low tide you could walk there but now, surrounded as it was by swirling water, it could only be reached by a strange vehicle resembling a tractor on stilts that reminded Wesley of a Victorian bathing machine. He watched, fascinated, as it swallowed its passengers and disgorged them on the island's shore.

Gerry Heffernan was standing, shirtsleeves rolled up, breathing in the salty air and staring longingly out to sea.

They climbed from the car and strolled over to join him.

'You took your time. How did you get on at Trevor Gilbert's?' The chief inspector shuffled from foot to foot impatiently. Something was annoying him.

'He hasn't been able to come up with an alibi for the time she disappeared. Where's Sally Gilbert's car?'

'It's been taken back to the nick. Forensics'll give it a good going over. It was found in a side road up behind those white bungalows.'

The officers who were to carry out the search of the cliff tops stood around in groups, talking quietly. A gaggle of curious tourists loitered some way off, staring. A few families watched, licking ice creams, their holiday entertainment provided courtesy of the local constabulary. Gerry Heffernan turned and looked at them and Wesley feared he was about to make some witty remark that might damage relations between police and public. But he held his tongue for once.

'Let's get on, Wes. I can't do with an audience. If I wanted to be watched while I was working I'd have gone on the stage.'

'What about the search of the cliff tops?'

'We've got all available officers on it. But it's a big job. At least it hasn't rained since Friday ... which makes a change.'

'Her car's been found here so it looks as though your friend George was right. She must have gone into the sea somewhere near by. What about the island?'

'They're searching the cliffs on the seaward side.' Heffernan thought for a moment. 'If someone arranged to meet her, the island would be a good place. It's popular with visitors but most of them stick to the hotel or the café and pub down near the shore. If she met her murderer in the café and he suggested they go for a walk round the island . . .'

'Sounds feasible. We'll just have to see what the search comes up with.'

Heffernan nodded as he looked longingly at a child's chocolate ice cream. They would have to wait and see.

Detective Constable Paul Johnson drove out of Tradmouth with Steve Carstairs sitting silently beside him in the passenger seat.

As they turned onto the Neston road Steve broke the silence. 'Did you know Harry Marchbank's back?'

'Yeah. I saw him coming out of the office yesterday. How is he?'

Paul followed the signs to the Neston industrial estate.

'Same as ever.'

Paul didn't answer. He had been a probationer when Marchbank had left and he couldn't say he was sorry to see the back of him. DS Marchbank had been an arrogant sod: Paul much preferred his successor, Wesley Peterson.

'What's he doing down here?'

'He thinks one of his villains has gone to ground on our patch . . . a bloke who murdered his wife.'

'And?'

'He's looking for him, isn't he?'

There was a note of sarcasm in Steve's voice which Paul ignored. He knew Steve Carstairs too well to rise to his bait. 'Here we are,' he said as he steered the car through an open pair of metal gates that bore the name 'Nestec'. The building ahead of him was long, low and glaringly new. Five years ago the Neston industrial estate had been green fields.

The two policemen parked in the designated area for visitors, and as they walked towards the main entrance they passed a lorry that was being loaded with cardboard boxes. Paul remembered that Trevor Gilbert was warehouse manager here. Trevor Gilbert's wife was dead and, according to Rachel Tracey, Trevor was at home. But this one man's personal tragedy hadn't slowed the wheels of commerce. Nobody was indispensable.

They reported to the receptionist, a plain woman with frizzy hair whose spectacles dangled from a gold chain around her neck. She asked them to wait, but they hardly had time to make themselves comfortable on the grey designer chairs provided for waiting visitors before a tall, fair-haired man appeared, his hand outstretched in greeting. Paul shook the hand firmly and made the introductions.

'Sebastian Wilde,' he said with a wide smile. 'I was expecting your DCI Heffernan or . . .'

'I'm afraid DCI Heffernan's busy, sir. You'll have heard that your warehouse manager's wife has been found dead.'

Sebastian Wilde's broad, freckled face assumed an expression of sincere concern. 'Terrible business. I've told Trevor to take as much time off as he needs, of course. And I said if there's anything we can do . . .'

'We're treating Mrs Gilbert's death as suspicious.'

Wilde's mouth opened in shock. 'That's terrible. We all assumed it was an accident. Do you mean she was murdered?'

'It looks that way, sir. If we could have a word in private . . .' Paul glanced at the receptionist, who was making a great show of not listening.

Wilde ushered them into his office. 'If I can help in any way . . .' he began as he sat down in a large black leather chair.

Paul and Steve sat in smaller chairs on the other side of the desk. Paul sneaked a look around the office; a model of sleek simplicity, designed by someone with a liking for grey and stainless steel.

Paul took out his notebook and Steve gave him a hostile glance. 'How well did you know Mrs Gilbert?'

'I met her on social occasions, of course. I often throw parties for my staff or take them out for dinner. I like to think of Nestec as one big happy family. A happy

81

workforce is a successful workforce, you know. They deserve some reward for all their hard work.'

Paul looked Wilde in the eye. 'Have you considered the possibility that Trevor Gilbert was mixed up in the hijacking of your lorry? The man on the inside, as it were.'

Wilde shook his head. 'Trevor's been with me since I started the company. I'd say he was completely trustworthy.'

Steve sat forward. Paul was doing too much of the talking. 'You see, our DCI reckons that Sally Gilbert's death might be connected with your stuff being nicked. What if her husband gave information to the villains and then they abducted Sally to keep him quiet? What if it all went wrong and they ended up killing her? It happens.'

Paul thought Steve was pushing it a bit. He noticed that the colour had drained from Wilde's face.

'Surely not in this case. I told you, I'd stake my life on Trevor being completely trustworthy. Ask anyone here. Ask the warehouse staff: they'll all say the same.'

'We might just do that,' said Steve with a hint of menace.

Paul tried the gentler approach. 'Do you know of anyone who might have a grudge against Mr Gilbert ... or the company? Any sacked employee or ...'

Wilde spread his large hands on the desk, a gesture of openness. 'Nobody at all. I always choose my staff carefully, Constable. Most of them have been with me since Nestec started up. It's a family firm and there's never been any bad feeling: none at all.'

'We would like to talk to Mr Gilbert's colleagues, if that's convenient,' said Paul as Steve shot him another hostile glance.

'Of course. Anything to help.'

Wilde stood up, smiling helpfully. 'If there's anything you need just let me or my secretary know.'

'Nice bloke that Mr Wilde,' Paul observed as they made their way to Nestec's warehouse.

Steve grunted and said nothing.

When Rachel got back from Monks Island she decided to take Trish Walton with her to the Tradfield Manor Hotel. Some instinct told her that Lisa Marriott would talk more openly to a couple of women.

In days gone by the Tradfield Manor would have been described as a 'gentleman's residence'. But ten years ago, at the time when the average gentleman couldn't support twenty-three bedrooms and extensive stables, it had been acquired by Kilburn Leisure, which had transformed the main house into a country hotel and the stables into a health club.

It was well known that Kilburn Leisure had just acquired Chadleigh Hall near Millicombe too. The company seemed to be spreading its octopus-like tentacles all over the area. But then, with the difficulties faced by farming and fishing, leisure and tourism were becoming the lifeblood of the region. And leisure was Kilburn Leisure's business.

Rachel and Trish watched the well-heeled clientele saunter into the health club with something approaching envy. They too longed to relax in the sauna, to swim in the azure waters of the pool or to be massaged and pampered by the team of well-manicured beauticians. But they had a job to do.

As they entered the building music oozed from discreetly concealed speakers. The usual repertoire of light classics and songs from a more leisured age added to the ambience of easy elegance – just what Kilburn Leisure had ordered.

They found Lisa in the beauty salon sipping a cup of coffee. She wore starched white, a parody of a nurse's uniform. Her hair was scraped up into a ponytail, but wisps of blonde hair escaped at the sides, transforming the look from clinical to glamorous. Rachel found herself wondering how long it took to put on the mask of make-up each morning.

'I can't be long,' Lisa began. 'I've got a bikini-line waxing in twenty minutes.'

Trish winced at the thought of this modern form of torture but Rachel said nothing. There were things she needed to ask Lisa – and any other members of the staff who knew Sally Gilbert. The waxing might have to wait.

'We wanted to ask you a few more questions about Sally. We're now treating her death as suspicious.'

A wave of shock passed beneath the thick mask of foundation. 'You mean she was murdered?'

'It's likely. Yes. Did Sally know Monks Island at all?'

Lisa hesitated, studying her long scarlet nails.

'Did you ever hear her mention Monks Island?' Rachel prompted. Lisa was hiding something and she knew it.

'Yes. She . . .'

'Go on.'

'That Mike she was seeing – he took her there for a meal once. They went to the hotel. She told me all about it . . . full of it, she was. Said it was the best meal she'd ever had. Expensive, mind. But he paid,' she added triumphantly.

Rachel, disappointed that the message of female equality didn't seem to have filtered through to some quarters, took her notebook from her handbag and began to write.

'We'd like to talk to this Mike . . . just so that we can eliminate him from our enquiries. I know you said you didn't know his surname or where he lived, but is there anything you can remember; anything she said about him that you might not have thought was important at the time?'

Lisa put her cup down on a stainless-steel trolley and glanced at the watch pinned to the front of her uniform, as though she were a nurse taking a patient's pulse.

'He worked shifts, I remember that much. And I think he was married – I mean, he must have been or she wouldn't have been so secretive. She wasn't scared of Trevor finding out but she still wouldn't say much about him to me. I mean, if he wasn't married she'd have been showing him off to me, wouldn't she. It must have been him who was holding back.'

'But he still took her to Monks Island for a meal? He can't have been short of a bob or two.' Rachel turned to Trish, who nodded in agreement.

'She never mentioned he was rich or anything. She was really cagey.'

'As if she was ashamed of him?' Trish suggested.

'No. I don't think it was that.'

'Could it be somebody who works here? Or a guest in the hotel? Someone who comes to Tradmouth regularly on business, for instance?'

Lisa shook her blonde head and the ponytail bobbed from side to side. 'I would have known if it was anyone here. And I can't think of a Mike on the staff who'd fit the bill. There's a young lad in the kitchens and the manager's called Mike but I'm sure I would have known if it was him. No. From the way she talked, I'm certain he didn't work here. I'd have known.'

Rachel didn't doubt the truth of her last statement. 'When did the affair start?'

'About six months ago we were having lunch and she said she'd met this man. I was a bit shocked really. I'd always thought she was quite happy with Trevor. I mean, Trevor's dull but they had a nice house and ... well, you know what I mean.'

Rachel nodded. 'Go on.'

'She used to tell Trevor she was going out with me but she'd go out with this Mike instead. After a while she got bolder and she told Trevor I'd split up with a boyfriend or something and that I wanted her to stay the night. Of course, she spent the night with this Mike, didn't she. I didn't like it, though. I didn't mind her using me as an alibi for the odd evening ... but nights ... I told her.'

'And what did she say?'

Lisa began to study her nails again. 'By the time I got round to telling her, the affair was cooling off. Then a couple of weeks later she came into work one morning and said she'd split up with him. But that didn't stop her leaving Trevor. She was fed up with him by then. I said she could stay with me – she didn't have anywhere else to go. Her mum was dead and her dad had married again so he didn't want her.'

'But Trevor did.'

Lisa looked up. 'Yeah. I suppose he did. Why were you asking about Monks Island? Wasn't she found near Millicombe?'

'We think that's where she was killed. The currents carried her body round to ...'

'Yeah, I see.' Lisa didn't want to hear the details.

'You knew Sally well. Can you think of anyone who'd want to harm her? Had she argued with anyone at work? Anything?'

'Everyone liked Sally,' Lisa stated simply.

'And Trevor? Would you say Sally could have driven him to kill her? He must have had a lot to put up with. A lot of men would snap if ...'

'No. Trevor's a pussy cat. He'd never have harmed her.'

Rachel caught Trish's eye. The pussy cats on her parents' farm had no hesitation in committing murder if some innocent mouse happened to cross their path.

She suddenly remembered what she wanted to ask. 'That letter you mentioned – the one she received just before she died. Trevor said he forwarded it to her. He suspected it was from a solicitor. Had she been to see a solicitor about a divorce?'

'No. I don't think she'd got round to it. I mean, it's a big step, isn't it? And I'm sure she would have mentioned it.'

Rachel tried again. 'Do you think the letter was from someone she'd arranged to meet? I mean, did she read the letter and then say that she was going to meet someone?'

Lisa thought for a moment. 'Yeah. That's the impression I got. She read it and seemed sort of ... excited and said that she might have something to celebrate later.

Then she said she was going out.'

'And she took the letter with her?'

'Yes. But I think she might have left the envelope lying around. I'll have a look – see if I can find it.' She looked at the watch again. 'Look, is that all? My lady's due in five minutes for her bikini line and I'm dying for a wee.'

Rachel couldn't think of any more questions so she stood up. 'If you come across that envelope, can you let me know?' She handed Lisa her card.

'Sure,' Lisa answered dismissively.

As Rachel left, she had an uneasy feeling that something Lisa had said was important. It was just a question of working out what it was.

The South Devon Yellow Pages lay open on the double bed in Harry Marchbank's room on the first floor of the Trad View Guest House on Newpen Road. Harry sprawled beside the directory on the rumpled duvet, flicking the pages. He had rung round all the hotels and guest houses and some of the places which dealt with holiday lets but had drawn a blank so far. No single man. Nobody answering Robin Carrington's description.

He reached for the photograph that lay on his bedside table; a holiday snap of a young man in a brightly patterned shirt and sunglasses, taken on his honeymoon: the clearest photo he could find. Carrington. He stared at it, willing it to give up its secret. 'Where are you, you bastard?' he muttered to the image.

He slid from the bed and walked to the dressing table, where he examined himself in the mirror. He looked at the round unshaven face, topped by thinning hair. He was ten years younger than Gerry Heffernan but, looking at the bags beneath his eyes and the deep furrows in his skin, he probably looked the same age. Too much booze, too many cigarettes – although he did try to give up from time to time. Too many women.

He had never felt settled in Tradmouth. He had always

longed for London, for something a small town couldn't offer. When he was in his early twenties he had worked in the capital for two years. They had been good years and there had been a woman there who was special. But then his father had had his stroke and Harry had returned to Devon. He would have gone back to London after his father's death but by then he had married a Tradmouth girl: that had been a big mistake. There were no children. Perhaps if there had been he wouldn't be standing here alone in a cheap guest house; he wouldn't be searching for Robin Carrington.

He went into the tiny en suite bathroom and shaved, rinsing his face several times as though the water would bestow him with new life, new vitality. Half an hour later he was ready to face the world. There were a couple of holiday letting agencies that he wanted to visit personally, armed with Carrington's photograph.

He left the guest house, grateful that the landlady was nowhere to be seen. She was a nosey cow who showed too much interest in other people's business. After closing the front door behind him quietly, he stepped out onto the pavement and began to walk down the sloping road towards the centre of the town.

He made for the High Street, his hands in his trouser pockets. It was pleasantly warm and too early in the year for the worst of the summer crowds. You couldn't move on these pavements in August. Looking up at the overhanging black-and-white buildings, he felt no pang of regret that he had left this place for the bustle of the metropolis. He had done the right thing.

Looking to his right down the narrow side streets, he could see the river, sparkling in the sun. Harry pulled a face. He had always hated boats and the sort of people who sailed on them – Gerry Heffernan in particular.

He turned down one of these streets and walked towards the waterfront. The office he was looking for was on his left, with photographs of properties displayed in its window. He pushed the glass door open and walked in, but ten minutes later he walked out again. No luck.

But there were two more places to try in Tradmouth before he spread his net wider and ventured out to Neston or Dukesbridge. He strolled down towards the quayside, making for a row of vacant benches. When he reached his destination he kicked at a seagull scavenging at his feet before sitting down and fumbling in his pocket for a cigarette.

Harry inhaled the smoke and stared out at the river. He watched the ferry scuttling back and forth and the yachts gliding silently across the water as seagulls screeched overhead. He sat back and studied the faces of the passers-by and the people on the decks of the moored yachts. He was looking for one face in particular but so far he was having no luck.

There was an old-fashioned red telephone box about ten yards to his right, near a large cannon which pointed out to sea, the relic of some long-forgotten war. Red telephone boxes were a rarity in the modern world but this one had been preserved because of its setting on the picturesque waterfront. The powers that be had probably concluded, wisely, that crass modernity would look out of place.

Harry froze and the cigarette fell from his fingers. There was a man walking slowly past the phone box, gazing out at the boats on the river. It was him. It was Carrington. He'd know him anywhere.

Harry's heart beat faster, hammering in his chest, preparing for pursuit. But as he stood up the man near the phone box spotted him and began to hurry away, dodging through the queue of cars waiting for the car ferry. Harry gave chase but his quarry was younger and faster. However, the rush of adrenalin made Harry carry on, running, one foot in front of the other, breathless. He reached the High Street and looked from left to right. People. Men, women and children. But no Robin Carrington. He struggled for breath, bent double, uncomfortably aware of the pain passing through his chest and left arm.

It had been Robin Carrington; he'd know the bastard anywhere, was his last thought before he collapsed on the hard, grey pavement.

Chapter Five

George Marbis grasped my hand, his skinny fingers holding me like the claws of some desperate, dying animal. 'Forgiveness,' he whispered. 'Is there forgiveness?' I assured him that the Lord forgives any man who puts his trust in Him and sincerely repents of his sins.

'But there is worse,' he said. 'Much worse. Will I still be forgiven?'

I repeated my assurance but Marbis appeared to find no comfort in my words.

'I must tell all, Reverend, then you must judge for yourself.' I told him not to speak if it tired him but I could sense his spirit would know no rest until he had confessed all. I allowed him to continue, assuring him every now and then that I was still listening to his sorry tale.

It seemed that at the age of fifteen George Marbis had joined the wreckers at their work and the deeds he had witnessed as an innocent child became his own deeds. May the Lord have mercy on his soul.

From An Account of the Dreadful and Wicked Crimes of the Wreckers of Chadleigh *by the Reverend Octavius Mount, Vicar of Millicombe*

'Rachel's been here already,' Wesley said as he parked the

car on the crunching gravel outside the Tradfield Manor Hotel.

'Well, there's no reason why she should get all the fun. Brought your cossie?'

'My what?'

'Your cossie ... swimming costume. They've got a health club with a pool.'

'I always thought swimming was like drinking – not something to be done when you're on duty.' There were times when Wesley never quite knew whether Heffernan was being serious. He certainly wouldn't have put it past him to conduct interviews in the shallow end of the pool if he thought he could get away with it.

Heffernan grinned, showing an uneven set of teeth. 'Only joking, Wes. I can't swim.'

Gerry Heffernan had served as a first officer in the merchant navy before joining the force, even had his master's certificate, and what leisure time he didn't spend singing in the choir at St Margaret's was spent aboard the *Rosie May*, the vessel he had restored lovingly after his wife's death. Wesley found the idea of a man who had lived his life so close to the sea being unable to swim rather bizarre. And he said as much.

Heffernan shook his head. 'You don't understand, Wes. Sailors never learn to swim ... if the sea knows that you don't trust her she takes her revenge.'

Wesley raised his eyebrows.

'I was born with a caul,' Heffernan continued.

'A what?'

'A caul – a membrane around my head. My mum kept it and I've still got it in a tin at home. It's supposed to save you from drowning.'

Wesley knew sailors were a superstitious lot but he had hardly expected it of the chief inspector. 'You're joking, aren't you?'

Heffernan said nothing as he climbed out of the car and Wesley sensed that he had been deadly serious. Gerry

Heffernan constantly surprised him.

Wesley had to quicken his steps to keep up as Heffernan marched towards the hotel's main entrance. At least the boss was wearing a jacket today and a shirt that had had a passing encounter with an iron, however brief. He looked moderately presentable, and Wesley wondered whether this was his daughter, Rosie's, influence. Since the death of his wife, Gerry Heffernan had been in sore need of a bit of care and attention.

'Why are we here exactly?'

'I want to find out everything I can about Sally Gilbert.'

'But Rachel and Trish have already spoken to Lisa Marriott.'

'But I don't want a friend's point of view, Wes. Friends only give the authorised version out of loyalty. I want to find people who didn't like her ... or didn't have any opinion one way or the other. I want to get at the truth. And she might not have told Lisa Marriott everything. There might be someone else around here who knows Sally Gilbert's little secrets. Some of the men, for instance.'

Wesley couldn't argue with that. He followed as the chief inspector marched to the hotel's reception and asked to see the manager. The production of his warrant card ensured that his request was dealt with swiftly by the business-like young woman behind the desk. Wesley tried to imagine Sally there and failed. There was a pile of leaflets on the desk arranged in an elegant fan. A special offer: two meals for the price of one. Wesley picked a couple up and put them in his pocket. It was time he and Pam had an evening out.

A man emerged from a door marked 'Private' at the side of the reception area. He was, Wesley guessed, in his late thirties. He wore a dark suit with a perfectly knotted blue silk tie, a uniform which marked him out as surely as if he had a placard with the word 'Manager' hanging around his neck. Wesley held out his hand and introduced himself.

'Mike Cumberland. Manager,' the man announced,

businesslike. He ran his fingers through his dark, receding hair and turned. They followed him into his office.

'We're making enquiries about one of your employees; a Mrs Sally Gilbert. You'll have heard she was found dead a couple of days ago?'

Mike Cumberland nodded. Wesley watched his eyes but they were giving nothing away.

'The thing is, Mr Cumberland,' Heffernan went on, 'we're now treating her death as suspicious so we want to interview all her colleagues: not the whole staff, just the people who worked with her directly. Can you arrange somewhere private where we can ...'

'Of course. No problem. You think she was murdered?' He arranged his features into an expression of shocked concern. 'We all assumed she'd met with some sort of accident.'

'As my colleague said, sir, we're treating her death as suspicious.' There was something about Mike Cumberland that made Wesley feel that he had to be on his best and most formal behaviour. 'How well did you know her?'

'We were colleagues,' was the non-committal reply.

'Oh aye?' Heffernan looked sceptical.

Mike Cumberland blushed. 'I can assure you that my relationship with Sally was purely that of manager and receptionist.'

Heffernan leaned forward and looked the manager in the eye. 'I've heard of kids playing doctors and nurses ... is manager and receptionist the same, then?'

Wesley sat, expressionless. Sometimes Heffernan didn't realise that not everyone shared his sense of humour. He watched Cumberland's face, but he was relieved to see that the man hadn't taken offence. In face he was smiling.

'I'm afraid not, Chief Inspector. As I said, my relationship with Sally was purely business.'

'Did you find her attractive?'

Cumberland hesitated, blushing. 'If you want an honest answer, no. She wasn't my type.'

'Do you know if she had any particular friends on the staff here?'

'There was Lisa Marriott, of course – she's one of our beauticians. Apart from that, she seemed to be friendly with everyone. And before you ask, I didn't know much about her private life. I don't consider it my job to pry into my employees' affairs unless it's affecting their work.'

'She left her husband a couple of weeks ago. Did you know about that?'

'I hear gossip. But as it didn't affect her work at all, I took no notice. That was her business.'

The office door opened and a man walked in. He was tall, well over six feet, with a shock of grey hair and piercing blue eyes. Mike Cumberland stood up and looked guilty, like a schoolboy who had been caught doing something unsavoury behind the bike sheds. The newcomer was no mere colleague. He was a man with authority.

'I assume these gentlemen are from the police.' The man looked Wesley and Heffernan up and down.

'Yes.' The manager was showing telltale signs of being flustered. 'This is, er . . .'

'Detective Inspector Peterson and Detective Chief Inspector Heffernan.' Wesley felt he ought to cover up the manager's lapse of memory. 'And you are?' He knew quite well who the man was but he wasn't feeling particularly deferential.

'I'm Dominic Kilburn. I own this hotel.' He looked at the two detectives as though he expected them to be impressed. Then he thought for a moment before pointing an accusing finger at them. 'Heffernan and Peterson. You're the pair who are holding up the work on Chadleigh Hall. You've sealed off a couple of my rooms. When can I get my men back to work?'

Heffernan opened his mouth but Wesley spoke first. 'We found human remains at Chadleigh Hall and it appears to be a case of murder. We're obliged to investigate . . .'

'Yes, but surely you can let my men get on with the

95

work. Presumably you've taken these remains off the premises and . . .'

'I'm afraid the rooms have to remain sealed off for the time being. I can assure you, we won't take any longer than we have to,' Wesley lied. He'd taken a dislike to Dominic Kilburn and he felt that a little inconvenience might do the man good.

'Yes, but when . . .'

'When we've finished,' said Heffernan bluntly. 'Okay?'

Wesley expected fireworks; threats of tale-telling to the Chief Constable. But Kilburn nodded brusquely and looked at Heffernan with something approaching curiosity. Wesley suspected that not many people stood up to Dominic Kilburn.

Mike Cumberland was watching nervously. 'If that's all, gentlemen, I'll arrange that room for you.'

'What's this?' Kilburn asked, suspicious.

'One of your staff has died in suspicious circumstances. I presume you have no objection if we interview her colleagues. We won't take longer than necessary.'

Kilburn opened his mouth to protest then decided resistance was useless. He nodded. 'Of course my staff will do their best to cooperate with the police. That goes without saying.'

'Did you know Sally Gilbert, sir?'

'Sally . . .' Kilburn looked puzzled and turned to Mike Cumberland, as if for help.

'One of our receptionists, Mr Kilburn. Dark hair, about five foot five . . .'

'Can't say I know her.'

Wesley had a nagging feeling that Kilburn wasn't telling the truth, but he acknowledged that he could be mistaken. He knew that if Kilburn swore that grass was green he wouldn't be inclined to believe him. Prejudice, he thought philosophically as he left the office, takes many forms.

But work called, and the two policemen were shown to the meeting room where they would conduct their interviews with the staff who knew Sally Gilbert.

It was going to be a long day.

Harry Marchbank tore the oxygen mask off his face. Why did this have to happen now, just when he had Carrington in his sights?

He tried to sit up but the effort made him breathless and he slumped back onto his pillow again. He couldn't stay here, helpless in hospital. He couldn't let Carrington go free, not now he knew he was in the area. A small, plump nurse bustled past and Harry raised his hand, trying to attract her attention. But she was on her way to another patient and it was a few minutes before she returned.

'Now you know you shouldn't have pulled your mask off, you naughty boy,' she said with bossy disapproval. 'Come along. Put it back.'

Harry, who hadn't been called a naughty boy since he was twelve, felt he had no option than to obey. There was something strangely comforting about being looked after by a motherly figure who had your welfare at heart. Harry felt suddenly meek and safe, as if he'd regressed to the cosy, cocooned days of childhood.

'I want the phone,' he said, gazing into the nurse's blue eyes.

'You should rest.'

'I've got to make a call.'

The nurse knew the telltale signs. Sometimes it was better to give in than to allow the patient to become agitated. 'I'll see what I can do,' she said in a soothing voice.

'You do that, love. And make it quick, eh.'

'Put your mask back on,' the nurse ordered brusquely. The man was beginning to annoy her, but she wheeled the telephone trolley to his bed to prevent a rise in his blood pressure.

Two minutes later Harry Marchbank was speaking to a puzzled Steve Carstairs.

*

Keith and Andy had gone off in the van, leaving instructions that Sam Heffernan was to mow the lawn. It was part of the regular contract, they had explained, smirking. When Tradmouth Landscapes weren't providing Mrs Sanders with a new pond, pathways, fencing and patio, they tidied her garden every week. Keith and Andy had taken the lawnmower out of a brick outhouse before going off for 'supplies'. Sam was about to say that he didn't realise that pubs sold garden equipment, but he thought better of it. It was probably best not to make waves. He was the new boy; the student. It'd be wise to keep his head down.

The sweat dripped off his face as he pushed the heavy petrol mower up and down the lawn, leaving satisfying stripes behind him. He was used to hard work – assisting at the birth of a calf can be quite taxing – but not at such a sustained level. At least, he told himself, he would be fit by the time he returned to Liverpool at the end of the summer.

As he was pushing the mower back towards the house, he spotted a sun lounger near the back door which hadn't been there a minute before. On it sat a young man, around Sam's own age or possibly younger. He wore checked shorts and dark glasses and swigged lager from a can. Although Sam couldn't see his eyes, he sensed that he was watching him.

Self-consciously, he carried on mowing, walking slowly up and down, avoiding looking at the newcomer. But the time came when he had to switch the engine off and return the machine to the outhouse.

He was dragging the great oily beast back to its home when he heard a languid voice saying, 'You're new.'

Sam stopped. 'Yeah.' He was about to walk on when the young man spoke again.

'You the student?'

'That's right.'

'I thought so. Auntie Carole's mentioned you. I'm Jason Wilde, by the way – the prodigal nephew. My mum's rarely at home so I come to Auntie Carole's for a few home comforts. But then you've met my Auntie Carole, so you'll know what I mean. She's my dad's sister but I can't see any resemblance myself.' He smirked unpleasantly, and Sam concluded that all was not well between father and son.

Jason Wilde reached down and produced a can covered with beads of moisture: well chilled. 'Have a beer.' He held the can out temptingly and Sam stepped forward and took it.

'Thanks. Cheers,' Sam said as the ring-pull gave a satisfying hiss. He poured the icy liquid down his throat. It felt good.

Jason took a swig from his can. 'You met Brenda yet?'

'The cleaner? Yes.'

'What did you think?'

Sam didn't know what he was expected to say.

'She's not bad for her age, is she, and she's always grateful for a bit of attention, if you see what I mean.' Jason winked suggestively. 'She nicks things, you know. I've told Auntie Carole about her, but will she listen? She feels sorry for her and she says it's hard to get cleaners these days so she doesn't mind the odd thing going walkabout.'

'Perhaps she should tell the police?'

Jason looked at Sam as though he was being particularly naive and snorted. 'And have the pigs crawling all over the house and poor old Brenda hauled off to Holloway or wherever it is they send them? No way.' He took another swig from his can and put it on the ground. 'I think Auntie Carole feels obliged to keep her in work. All that Lady Bountiful stuff. Middle-class guilt – doing her bit.'

'Does Brenda just work for your aunt or . . .?'

'Oh, no. She cleans for some old couple who live in a lighthouse and she works at one of the hotels my mate's dad owns as well. She does okay for herself.' He grinned unpleasantly and scratched his bare torso.

'Good,' was all Sam could think of to say. He felt awkward, as though he were being assessed for some unspecific purpose. 'Are you at uni, then?' he asked, trying to make conversation.

Another snort. 'No way. I've just finished school and I'm buggered if I'm going back. My dad'll give me a job. He owns Nestec, the computer firm. Have you heard of them? I'd be no good on the technical side – Dad employs nerds to deal with that sort of thing. I reckon marketing and PR would be right up my street.'

Sam smiled. Jason's last statement was probably true.

'I'm taking a break at the moment,' Jason continued. 'I told Dad I wanted to think things over. Me and Olly have been over at the new place his dad's bought . . .'

'Olly?'

'Oliver Kilburn. We know each other from school. His dad owns Kilburn Leisure. You've heard of them, I presume?'

Sam had but he wasn't going to admit it.

'They've just bought a place called Chadleigh Hall near Millicombe which has its own private beach. There's a shipwreck there and a load of archaeologists are down there making nuisances of themselves . . . or so Olly's dad says. Olly and I have been helping them out.'

'That sounds interesting.'

Jason raised his eyes to heaven. 'It's bloody boring, actually. They record everything, measure it, film it, photograph it and clean it. I wouldn't mind but they're only finding rusty old iron and soggy wood so it hardly seems worth all the effort. Olly's dad reckons there's loads of gold down there but I think someone's been having him on.'

'My dad told me they'd found a skeleton at Chadleigh Hall.'

'Works for Kilburn, does he?'

Sam detected the hint of a sneer in his voice. 'No. He's a policeman.'

This was a conversation stopper. Jason took a long drink from his can.

'I'd better get back to work. Thanks for the beer.' Sam began to push the mower towards the crumbling brick outhouse, but Jason leaped up from the sun lounger. 'I'll put that back for you. Might as well make myself useful.'

Sam let him take the mower and watched as he opened the flaking green door, suspecting that Jason hadn't suddenly decided to help out of the goodness of his heart.

It was more as if there was something in the outhouse he didn't want him to see.

Steve Carstairs had received a phone call from Harry Marchbank but there wasn't much he could do about it now. On the chief inspector's orders he was stuck in the carpark gazing out on Monks Island. The dead woman's car had been taken away long since and the remaining police officers were questioning arriving visitors, hoping that somebody had been there the previous Friday and remembered seeing Sally Gilbert.

Steve sat in the driving seat of the unmarked police car with DC Trish Walton beside him, watching the proceedings. A steady stream of cars was arriving. Word had got around. Trish put her hand on the door handle. 'Come on. Let's go and give the uniforms a hand.'

Steve didn't move. 'Bloody ghouls,' he muttered. 'They've only come 'cause they heard on the radio that there was a police search here.'

'So they want to bring a bit of excitement into their dull lives. It doesn't mean they weren't here last Friday. Someone might have seen something.'

Reluctantly Steve left the comfort of the car, clutching a clipboard with a picture of Sally Gilbert on the front. 'Did you see this woman here on Friday afternoon?' He was expecting the answer to be 'no' every time.

He touched Trish's arm, wondering whether this was his opportunity to try his luck with her at last. But he knew he had to watch his step. One false move would make him the laughing stock of the station canteen. He knew what Rachel Tracey and her feminist cronies were like.

He straightened his collar and gave Trish what he

considered to be an irresistible smile. 'We'd better go and talk to some ghouls, then.'

They began to stroll across the carpark, their clipboards clutched to their chests, when Steve's mobile began to ring.

He looked down at the instrument, hoping it wasn't Harry Marchbank again. He really didn't have time for Harry right now. He had other irons in the fire.

'So Sally Gilbert was either a candidate for sainthood, a devious little schemer or a tragic romantic heroine, depending on who you talk to.' Wesley Peterson flicked through the statements taken from the dead woman's colleagues at the hotel, feeling rather overwhelmed by the wealth of conflicting information.

'Is any of this stuff any use, do you think?' Gerry Heffernan sounded disappointed.

In the two hours they had spent questioning the staff of the Tradfield Manor Hotel, they didn't seem to have learned much more about Sally than they knew already. She worked on reception. She spent money as if it were going out of fashion. She went home to her nice house and her boring husband. She had left the same boring husband after an affair with an unknown man. She didn't gossip much about her private life, more's the pity. Lisa Marriott knew her best, but even she had only received the edited version of Sally's triumphs and woes. People knew only what Sally Gilbert wanted them to know.

There was still no clue to 'Mike's' identity. Wesley rather favoured the manager Mike Cumberland in the role of the phantom lover, but Heffernan had his misgivings.

Wesley pushed the pile of statements to one side. 'I was always taught that one of the first rules of detection is find out all you can about the victim. And from what we know so far, it seems likely that her death's just a crime of passion; either the jealous husband or the mysterious Mike.'

'Don't forget the Nestec connection, Wes. If Trevor

102

Gilbert was involved in the hijacking then Sally might have been abducted to keep him quiet.'

'But to kill her . . .'

'Something went wrong. They panicked.'

Wesley shrugged. It was possible. He thought for a moment. 'Whoever killed her couldn't have known her that well.'

Heffernan looked at him, puzzled. 'How do you mean?'

'If that mysterious letter she received was summoning her to some sort of meeting with her killer, we have to remember that it was posted to the house she shared with Trevor first. He forwarded it on. The murderer didn't know she'd left her husband.'

'If the letter's relevant. It might have nothing to do with it. Trevor thought it was from a solicitor. Get someone to have a word with all the local firms, eh; see if anyone had been writing to Sally. If we find out that she'd been to see about a divorce and it was a letter connected with that, I think we can forget the letter theory. She said she'd have something to celebrate: perhaps that something was her freedom from Trevor.'

'But the address . . .'

'She might not have known how long she'd be staying with Lisa. And she knew that her tame, well-trained husband would meekly forward it on to her wherever she was.'

Wesley nodded. He couldn't fault his boss's logic.

Heffernan scratched his head. 'We've got to find this Mike character.'

'I still think Mike Cumberland's the best bet. They worked closely and . . .'

Heffernan looked him in the eye. 'Wesley. Have you led a sheltered life?'

Wesley looked puzzled.

'Mike Cumberland wouldn't be interested in Sally Gilbert if she lay on the hotel reception desk stark naked.'

Wesley opened his mouth to answer but the phone began to ring before he could speak. Heffernan answered it and, after a brief conversation, looked up at Wesley with a satisfied smile on his lips.

'They think they've found where Sally went into the sea: on the cliff top at the far side of Monks Island – signs of a struggle. I want to get back there now. Coming?'

Wesley stood up. 'Yeah. Any objections to stopping off on the way? We'll be passing Chadleigh Cove and I want a word with Neil.'

Gerry Heffernan took his jacket from the coat stand and said nothing.

Neil Watson was only too glad to leave his waterlogged artefacts and drive the short distance to Chadleigh Hall. At least Oliver Kilburn and Jason Wilde hadn't turned up on the beach that day, which meant he didn't have to worry about leaving them unsupervised with the finds and equipment. He didn't trust them, and as far as he was concerned they could stay away for good, but he hardly liked to say that to Dominic Kilburn.

'Here we are,' Wesley announced as they pulled up outside a grand Georgian mansion, half hidden by a network of scaffolding.

Neil opened the car door, climbed out and stretched.

'I didn't tell you, Wes. I've found out that the captain of the *Celestina* was related to the family who lived here.'

'So there's a link between your wreck and the hall?'

'Looks like it.'

Gerry Heffernan, who had been uncharacteristically quiet, slammed the passenger door. 'Here we are, Wes. Your mother-in-law's alma mater. I would have thought St Trinian's was more her style.'

Wesley ignored him and made for the grand portico; the main entrance designed to impress.

'So what is it we're supposed to be looking at?' Neil asked. He walked beside Wesley, his hands stuck firmly in the pockets of the combat jacket he was still wearing in spite of the warmth of the July sun.

'I wanted to show you where the skeleton was found. I'm looking for anything that'll give us a date.'

'What you mean is that we need to identify the newest thing in the room. If we find, say, a coin from 1900 the room could have been sealed up later than that but not earlier.'

'Exactly. The room's pretty bare but it's worth a look.'

Gerry Heffernan looked a little confused but nodded sagely.

They reached the room that once served as Miss Snowman's study in the distant days of Della's youth. Wesley ducked under the blue-and-white tape that decorated the crime scene and Neil followed. But Gerry Heffernan hung back; he had no wish to enter that chamber of death again. It stank of death: slow, agonising death. He walked away and looked out of the window onto the pleasant parkland scene outside. He could make out the glistening sea through the trees: it was nearer than he had thought. He mentioned something to Wesley about going outside for some fresh air and ambled out of the room.

Wesley handed Neil the torch he had brought with him from the car and allowed him to enter the skeleton room first. He said nothing to guide him. It was best that he came to his own conclusions.

The two men moved silently about the tiny chamber. Wesley spent some time examining the chair, looking for any telltale signs that might date it. It was a roughly made, solid wooden chair with a tall back and no decoration, the sort that was sometimes found polished up by the fire in country pubs. He touched the seat that the corpse had sat on and withdrew his hand quickly, not having the benefit of a forensic team's plastic gloves.

Neil had turned his attention to the area near the door. He knelt down in the dust and began to run a filthy finger along the gap between floor and wall.

'Gotcha,' he said with a smile of triumph, pulling a tiny object from its hiding place.

He handed it to Wesley. 'There's your answer. Someone was in here between 1960 and whenever the coins went decimal and they left the evidence.'

Wesley stared at the small, dusty, strangely shaped coin in his hand. 'What is it?'

'My mum used to have a box of old coins ... the ones before everything went decimal. If I'm not mistaken this one was known as a threepenny bit. Funny little thing, isn't it.'

There was a shuffling outside in the main room. Thinking Gerry had returned from his wanderings, Wesley stepped through the doorway and saw Marty Shawcross, one of the workmen who had made the initial grim discovery, standing awkwardly in the middle of the floor, shifting from foot to foot as if waiting in a queue. When he saw Wesley he straightened himself up and cleared his throat.

'Can I help you?'

Marty hesitated as though trying to find the right words. 'Er, I was ... er, it's just that ...'

Wesley assumed what he supposed to be an encouraging expression. 'Go on.'

'I asked Ian and he said I should tell you. It's just that ... Well, the hole we made in the wall ...'

'What about it?' Wesley knew that he had to be patient. It would all come out eventually.

'It's just that it wasn't old plasterwork ... not as old as the house. That hole; it was already a doorway and Ian and me, we reckoned it hadn't been blocked off that long ago.'

'Are you telling me the plasterwork you knocked down to get into that room was fairly modern ... not eighteenth-century?'

There was relief on Marty's face. 'Yeah. That's it. It wasn't horsehair plaster like the old stuff. It ...'

Wesley nodded. Marty had just confirmed Neil's findings. 'Thanks for telling me.'

'Is that all right, then?' Marty asked nervously.

'Well, you've just doubled my workload, but apart from that ...' said Wesley, with a weary smile.

Steve Carstairs was back on duty at eight. Overtime. He just had time to get something to eat and see what Harry Marchbank wanted. Visiting the sick wasn't something Steve enjoyed – he usually avoided it if he could. But Harry had said it was urgent. A matter of life and death.

As Steve walked into the ward, he realised he should have brought something; flowers or grapes were traditional. But somehow he had never thought of Harry Marchbank as a flowers-and-grapes type. And he doubted that a bottle of vodka – Harry's favourite tipple – would be allowed.

Harry spotted him and began to raise himself up on his pillows. Steve saw that he was wired up to some sort of machine that emitted muted electronic bleeps. The dark shadows beneath his eyes stood out against grey-tinged flesh. He didn't look well. In fact he looked bad.

Steve approached the bed slowly and forced his mouth into a smile. 'Harry, my old mate, how are you doing?' he said with false bonhomie. 'What have you been doing to yourself? You look like you're wired up to the national grid.' Make light of it, he told himself. Don't treat Harry like a sick man.

Harry was sitting up, trying to act as though he were in the best of health. He looked round, clearly not wanting to be overheard. 'Bloody quacks. They reckon I've had some sort of heart attack. A warning, they said.' He pulled at the wires, making Steve afraid that he was about to dislodge something vital. 'Look at all this lot. Load of bloody fuss about nothing. I just had a bit of indigestion and came over all dizzy. It was when I started running in that heat, that's what did it. There's nothing the bleeding matter with my heart.'

'Don't tell me, tell them,' Steve said quickly. But Harry wasn't listening.

He leaned forward. 'I saw him,' he said in a loud

107

whisper. 'I saw Carrington. He was here in Tradmouth. When he spotted me he made a run for it. I followed him and that's when this happened.' He paused, as though trying to catch his breath. 'Look, mate, you've got to track him down for me. I can't do anything while I'm stuck in here, but as soon as the quacks let me out I'll take over.'

'Sorry, Harry, but I've got a lot on at the moment. We've got a murder and . . .'

'I'm not expecting you to do my job for me. Just a few discreet enquiries. You know the sort of thing. According to his mother-in-law, he comes down this way on his own for a couple of weeks every year but she doesn't know where he stays. I've checked out all the letting agencies in Tradmouth but I've not tried Neston yet . . . or Dukesbridge. All I'm asking you to do is make a few phone calls. It's just that I'm afraid he'll get the wind up and scarper now he knows I'm here.'

'I don't know.'

'Come on, Steve, it's not much. Just a couple of phone calls to help out an old mate.' Harry lay back on his pillows and assumed a martyred look. He hadn't expected so much resistance to his suggestion, but he calculated that if he looked ill enough Steve would feel obliged to cooperate.

'Okay. I'll see what I can do.'

'Good lad,' said the invalid with renewed vigour. 'There's a picture of Carrington in my locker. Not a good one, more's the pity, but we can't have everything, can we.'

Steve took the photograph from the locker and stared at it. 'Not much to go on,' he said, disappointed. 'Couldn't you get a better one?'

'That's all I've got. He drives a silver Nissan – I've written the registration number on the back of the photo. And don't let Scouse Gerry get wind of what you're up to . . . or our dark friend. Wouldn't trust him as far as I could throw him, smug bastard.'

Steve nodded solemnly as he placed the photograph in his

wallet. 'I can't promise anything but I'll do my best.'

'That's all any of us can do, isn't it, son.'

Harry closed his eyes. Sooner or later he'd catch up with Robin Carrington.

Wesley Peterson arrived home at six, hoping that Pam was feeling up to doing the cooking. He was tired. But then there was every likelihood Pam would be too.

He found her lying on the sofa watching Michael, who was posting brightly coloured shapes into a box and emitting a low grizzling whine. He was tired too after his day at the childminder's. The television droned in the corner; some advert full of gleeful actors offering loans at amazingly low rates of interest.

Wesley stood in the doorway for a few moments, taking in the scene and asking himself why they put themselves through this, why they rushed to and fro exhausting themselves. But he knew the answer: they couldn't live as they did without money and, as neither of them had large private incomes or lottery wins, that meant either getting into debt or working for it. Wesley's parents had raised him to prefer the latter option.

'How are you?' He asked the question out of habit but one look at Pam's drawn, pale face told him the answer.

'Okay,' she said bravely. 'Michael's had his supper. I'll put him to bed and then I'll make us something.' She thought for a moment. 'I suppose we should really get one of the neighbours in to baby-sit and go and see my mother.'

Wesley flopped down in the armchair, fearing that it was going to be hard to get back up again once he was settled. 'No need. I saw her this morning. She was demanding strong liquor and reminiscing about her schooldays. Not much wrong with her.'

Pam looked at him, surprised. 'That was nice of you. I'm sure she appreciated . . .'

'I might be popping in tomorrow as well.'

'What's brought this on?' Pam hadn't expected her

109

husband to take such an interest in the health of his mother-in-law.

'She's helping us with our enquiries. We've evidence that the body we found at Chadleigh Hall might date from the time the place was a school – about the time your mother was there.'

Pam pressed her lips together. She might have known this elaborate display of family devotion had something to do with work.

'We had to start somewhere and your mother just happened to be handy.'

'Handy isn't a word I'd use to describe my mother,' Pam muttered under her breath as she stood up. She bent to lift Michael from his playpen and winced with sudden pain.

'What is it?' Wesley asked anxiously.

'I'm okay. Just a twinge. It's nothing. Don't fuss.'

Wesley stood up and took Michael from her. The baby chuckled, glad to be released from the confines of his prison, and pulled at his father's hair, a new game.

'You sit down,' Wesley ordered. 'I'll put Michael to bed and make the supper. Okay?'

Pam sank into the soft cushions of the sofa and smiled weakly. 'Thanks,' she said softly, stroking her stomach.

He stood with a contented Michael in his arms, watching her. She caught his eye and shifted in her seat.

'You're not wearing it,' he said.

'What?'

'The necklace . . . your gift from a grateful pupil.'

Pam blushed. 'Er . . . no. Not today.' She opened her mouth to say something else but thought better of it.

'You should wear it. It's pretty. It looked expensive, you know.'

'Well, I'm sure it wasn't,' she snapped. She lay back against the cushions, her legs spread out inelegantly. 'Can't you stop playing Mr Plod for one minute, Wesley? Can't you see a piece of jewellery without wondering whether it's been nicked? Lighten up, will you. You're off duty.'

Wesley looked at her, hurt. 'I only said that it's a nice necklace. I didn't mean . . . I'll give Michael his bath.'

He left the room with Michael wriggling in his arms, nearly pulling him off balance as he climbed the stairs. Perhaps there was something in what Pam said. Maybe his work was taking over every waking moment of his life . . . and his dreams too sometimes. He had seen it happen so many times – the tunnel vision, the abandonment of family life. He wouldn't end up like that.

Half an hour later he returned to the living room to find Pam stretched out on the sofa with her arms around a cushion, cuddling it as a child cuddles a teddy bear for comfort and security.

He knelt down on the floor beside her and took her hand.

'Sorry for snapping at you,' she whispered, giving him a weak smile. She opened her mouth to speak then hesitated, as if something was worrying her.

'What is it?'

She took a deep breath. 'Nothing,' she said quietly. 'Nothing at all.'

Robin Carrington walked from Old Coastguard Cottage to the Wreckers. He needed a drink. He had meant to pick up some cans of beer in Tradmouth but events had disrupted his plans and his well-considered shopping list still lay dormant in his pocket. He would get something to eat at the pub and do some shopping tomorrow. Tradmouth was risky now, so he would try Neston and hope for the best.

He had been confident that it was all over, that he was in the clear, so the sight of Harry Marchbank had shaken him. Something must have happened back in London: perhaps they had found new evidence; perhaps he had made a mistake. From the look on Marchbank's face when he had seen him in Tradmouth, he knew the truth. But it was doubtful that he would find out where he was staying. There were still people Robin could trust.

He put his hand up to his head, knowing that his developing headache was caused by tension. Things weren't going as smoothly as he would have liked, but surely his luck would change soon. It would take only one stroke of good fortune to turn everything around. In the meantime, he would concentrate on his work. At least that was going well: he had already traced the Smithers family to Tradmouth where, according to parish records, they had worked as carpenters for several generations.

But there were times when he needed a break from history, and for the second time that day he found himself thinking about Brenda Dilkes and the good times they had shared together in the past. She would probably be in the Royal Oak that evening, and it was a pity that a visit to Tradmouth was out of the question now that Marchbank was about. But even though that particular avenue of pleasure was closed to him, there couldn't be any harm in having a quick drink at the Wreckers, well outside the small fishing port of Millicombe where tourists and yachtsmen gathered. The Wreckers would be safe.

He met nobody on the lane. There was usually someone; the archaeologists or divers. Or those two loud and arrogant young lads who hung around the beach, helping or hindering. But this evening it was quiet.

Nine o'clock, still light in July. He could see the pub's roof through the trees. Chadleigh was a tiny hamlet in the shadow of its thriving neighbour, Millicombe. It was too small to possess its own church and its only pub, the Wreckers, wasn't Devon's prettiest drinking establishment, although a yellowing notice in the bar announced that the place was over three hundred years old.

As he walked he tried to remember what the notice said. It was something like 'in the eighteenth century this pub was the haunt of Chadleigh's notorious wreckers, who would lure ships onto the treacherous rocks in order to plunder the cargo and rob the passengers and crew of any valuables'. That was all. No more information for the curious. But he supposed those few words said it all. Robbery. Mugging on a grand scale. More ambitious than the bastards who had once stolen his mobile phone in London.

When he reached the pub he stooped to enter the low door to the lounge bar. Once inside, he bought himself a pint of bitter and placed it on a lonely table.

Then he noticed Neil Watson sitting in the corner, saying goodbye to his two companions, a man with a straggly ponytail and an attractive blonde woman who were leaving hand in hand. When they had gone, Neil spotted him, picked up his glass and walked over to his table.

'Mind if I join you?'

'Not at all.' Robin did his best to sound casual, welcoming. He knew he had to take care but history was a safe subject. 'Have you found out anything more about the *Celestina*?'

'Not really. Only that it belonged to a lady called Mercy Iddacombe. She was a big shipowner and she had a town house in Tradmouth: Chadleigh Hall was her country estate.'

'That's interesting. Do you remember me saying I was tracing the ancestors of an American family called Smithers and I'd found a connection with the Iddacombes?'

Neil nodded.

'Well, I looked up the name Iddacombe in the phone book and I found a George Iddacombe whose family lived in Chadleigh Hall before the war. I rang him and told him about your shipwreck. He said he wouldn't mind if you contacted him – he might be able to tell you something about his family's history.'

'Why not? It's a good idea.'

Robin Carrington wrote down the number and address. Even if he had to keep a low profile from now on, there was nothing to stop Neil doing some detective work for him. A mutually beneficial arrangement.

As Carrington walked back to Old Coastguard Cottage he felt rather pleased with himself. But he was still impatient for action. He had expected the call to come days ago. And he was beginning to wonder whether it ever would.

Brenda Dilkes could hear Kayleigh's television up in her bedroom, blaring out the signature tune of *EastEnders*. The television had been Kayleigh's Christmas present the previous year. She liked Kayleigh to have what all the other kids had. She didn't like her going without.

The door bell rang, making Brenda jump. She wasn't expecting anyone. She walked into the hall slowly, her eyes on the shape behind the frosted glass in the front door. A tall shape: a man.

She opened the door cautiously. There was no chain: she had never got round to having one put on, even though burglaries on the Tradmouth council estate were increasing. Security had never been one of her top priorities.

As soon as the door was opened, a large and expensive white trainer appeared on the cheap nylon carpet. Its owner barged his way in and shut the door behind him.

'Hello, Brenda.' Jason Wilde stood in the hallway, an arrogant grin spreading across his face.

There had been lots of men: men she'd picked up in the Royal Oak; men at the hotel; men whose houses she'd cleaned who were grateful for extra services when their wives weren't about. The encounters were mutually beneficial: they got what they wanted and she got a bit of extra spending money.

But she never knew quite what to make of Jason Wilde. She didn't know whether he was just a harmless spoiled brat whose dad owned a computer firm – or something more dangerous.

She looked at him suspiciously. 'What do you want?'

He came closer and she backed away. 'I think you and me can do each other a favour.'

'What do you mean?' She glanced upstairs. She could hear angry voices from Kayleigh's television. Why did she always have to have it on so loud?

'There's a storeroom at the hotel. Olly Kilburn says it's never used – nobody ever goes near it. Now he can't get his hands on the key ...'

'His dad bloody owns the place.'

'I know, but he can't go asking for the key without arousing suspicion.'

'And what makes you think I can?' Brenda's voice became harder. This was business.

'Because you're in a position to nick it. And you're a lady of many talents.' He put his hand up to her hair and stroked it.

Their eyes met, a new understanding between them. 'My daughter's upstairs.'

'She's watching telly.'

'What if she comes down?'

Jason didn't answer. When Brenda turned and walked slowly into the lounge, he followed, taking off his shirt.

Chapter Six

As the man charged by God with the care of their immortal souls, I am ashamed to say that I discovered that the villagers of Chadleigh appeared to look upon the wrecking of a ship on their shore as a blessing, almost as a gift from the Almighty Himself. For the plunder taken from the unfortunate vessel brought them more prosperity than they could gain by the toil of their hands. And thus I return to George Marbis's sorry tale. As I have said, he joined the wreckers himself at the age of fifteen and after many years one Jud Kilburn, the son of Matthew Kilburn, who had by now passed from this life, became their leader. Jud Kilburn was even more vicious than this father, and it worried him not whether the poor souls on the broken ships lived or died, and if they lived he would send them to their Maker happily if their possessions tempted him or if they had witnessed too much.

It fell to George Marbis to lead a horse along the cliff top with a lamp fixed upon its head to lure unhappy ships onto the rocks below. As one of the wreckers' number, George's ears were stopped to the cries of the dying by his share of the pickings. How easy it is for men to ignore evil when it is to their advantage.

From An Account of the Dreadful and Wicked Crimes

of the Wreckers of Chadleigh *by the Reverend Octavius Mount, Vicar of Millicombe*

Trevor Gilbert woke at dawn. The pills the doctor had given him had sent him off to sleep all right but he still woke early, a thousand horrors flitting through his head. He lay in his sweat-soaked bed, keeping to his side. As though Sally were still there sleeping beside him. He put out a trembling hand, feeling the cool smoothness of her unoccupied pillow. Then the truth hit him like a punch to the stomach. She was dead. She would never come back.

Trevor rose from the shambolic bedclothes and staggered to the window. He lifted the curtain aside; an expensive fabric, the best. Sally always had to have the best. It was daylight outside but there was no movement in the street below. Only the birds called defiantly from unseen trees; the countryside scolding its encroaching concrete neighbours. Westview Way's human dawn chorus of clattering crockery and spluttering car engines was yet to come.

The new car squatted in the drive below the bedroom window. Sally had insisted on having something new – something she would be proud to be seen in. But now the only vehicle she would be seen in would be a shiny black hearse. Trevor felt tears sting his eyes, and soon they were rolling down his cheeks and onto the clean white paintwork of the new window sill as he thought how Sally the laughing bride had become Sally the bloated corpse, lying on a cold mortuary slab. He knew what had caused the grim transfiguration. He knew everything; the truth that was too painful even to contemplate. But the police must never find out. He must be strong. Strong and silent as the grave.

He let the curtain fall and looked around the bedroom. The floor was strewn with dirty underwear; unwashed cups stood on the table beside the grubby bed. When Sally was there it had been pristine, immaculate. Now the place was falling into decay, like her lifeless body.

He wondered whether he should try to go to work.

Sebastian Wilde had told him to return whenever he felt up to it, even if it was only for a couple of hours. Nestec needed him, he had said with what had sounded like sincerity.

But could he face his colleagues again? Could he even talk to them after what had happened?

At seven o'clock exactly Trevor Gilbert went downstairs and poured himself a drink.

Wesley hadn't slept well. Neither had Pam. She had risen several times in the night to walk around and fetch herself drinks from the kitchen.

Wesley clambered out of bed with a headache and staggered downstairs. Pam was still asleep, curled up in foetal comfort. He knew it would be up to him to make the breakfast.

They left the house at the same time, Pam driving off with Michael in the child seat beside her. He would be dropped off at the childminder's before she drove on to school. She had to go in today even though the children had finished for the holidays: an in-service training day, she said. When she had thought he wasn't looking he had detected a worried look on her face. But there was no time to talk. And he wasn't sure what he would have said to her if there had been. They left for work, going their separate ways.

When he reached the office he found Gerry Heffernan pacing up and down like an anxious expectant father. He spotted Wesley and stopped in his tracks.

'I've been waiting for you. Where have you been?'

Wesley didn't answer. He followed the chief inspector into his lair and slumped down on the chair, yawning.

'Keeping you awake, are we?'

'Sorry, I didn't sleep too well.'

'Me and all. Rosie went out early this morning. She's cleaning offices for this agency called Ship Shape. Woke me up at half five having a shower.'

118

'But it's good to have her and Sam home?'

Heffernan gave a secretive smile. 'I suppose it is. Sam's fallen on his feet. He's working for a gardening firm, and when he forgot his sandwiches the lady of the house provided him with a slap-up lunch. All right for some.'

But Wesley's mind wasn't on matters domestic. He sat for a few seconds studying his hands, gathering his thoughts. 'So where do we start?'

Heffernan looked at his cluttered desk and made a gesture of despair. 'What have we got? Sally Gilbert murdered by person or persons unknown and shoved into the sea. We've found nothing in her car to give us any clues. I had a word with Steve – another man who's looking the worse for wear – and nobody's admitted seeing anything suspicious on Monks Island last Friday – but it's early days yet.' He leaned forward confidentially. 'Have you noticed that Steve seems to be sniffing around our Trish?'

Wesley twisted in his chair and looked out through the office window. Trish Walton was sitting at her desk and Steve was standing next to her, bent over. The boss was right. There was certainly something, some eye contact, some electricity between them, that hadn't been there yesterday. He had suspected that Steve had been interested in Trish for some time. She was a sensible young woman – perhaps she would be good for him.

'Have you heard anything more from that DS Marchbank yet, the one from the Met? He thought we had one of his murder suspects on our patch?'

'Can't say I have ... and I don't particularly want to either. His suspect's details have been circulated and that's all he's getting for the moment.'

Wesley sensed the subject of Harry Marchbank was closed. 'Lisa Marriott says that Sally had a handbag with her, a posh new leather one that cost a fortune. It's always possible that it went into the sea but it's not turned up so far. No sign of her shoes either – probably at the bottom of the English Channel.'

'Maybe the murderer nicked the handbag. Perhaps it was a mugging that went wrong.' Heffernan sighed. 'We're not getting anywhere, Wes. Do you think we should arrest the husband? Put some pressure on him and see if he talks?'

'It might be worth a try.'

Heffernan looked up and grinned. 'I think we should have a nice little day trip to Monks Island – have a cream tea in the café there and ask some questions. Someone must have seen Sally that day.'

'I'm glad I didn't have much breakfast,' said Wesley, contemplating the rich Devon scones with jam and clotted cream – packed with hazardous cholesterol ... but he'd take the risk this once.

'What about our other little puzzle?'

'What puzzle?'

'The Chadleigh Hall skeleton. We'll have to open the case now that your mate says it probably dates from the sixties.'

Wesley almost wished that they could have stayed in ignorance until the Sally Gilbert case was cleared up. But the skeleton intrigued him. He wanted to know who she was and what had driven somebody to leave her in that chamber, alone and terrified, to face a slow and agonising death. Somehow he couldn't come to terms with it happening as recently as the 1960s: surely something like that couldn't have happened in the era of the Beatles, miniskirts and free love.

'I'll get Forensic over to have a look and I'll try to track down some of the staff of the girls' school. I expect Della will have some inside information. She has her uses at times.'

'But first things first, eh. Let's get across to Monks Island and see what's happening.'

As they left the CID office, Wesley glanced back at the officers, buzzing with purposeful activity like bees in a hive. Only Steve Carstairs appeared to be staring into space with other things on his mind.

Mercifully, the roads were clear as they drove out to Monks Island. The sun was shining. That was eight days in a row; probably some sort of record. Puffs of snowy cloud, insubstantial as foam on waves, raced across the pale blue sky. Perfect. Surely it couldn't last.

There were still signs of police activity on the island. A large police caravan dominated the carpark on the mainland, a sure indication that something was happening. The tide was out and a wide umbilical pathway of damp sand joined the island to the coast. Wesley and Heffernan strolled along it, Wesley a little nervous about incoming tides. But Heffernan, who was reputed to know about that sort of thing, seemed unconcerned.

As soon as they reached the security of the island, Wesley took in his surroundings. A series of wide steps led up from the beach to a steep track. A tiny pub no bigger than a cottage with ancient white-painted stone walls stood to the right, overlooking the mainland. A few yards farther on, past a utilitarian white café, was a path leading to a large white building half hidden behind trees: a hotel, classic art deco, layered like a wedding cake with rows of gleaming windows and topped by a central tower. The pale green paintwork against the white of the walls gave the building an appearance of modernity, of freshness. Wesley looked at it, picturing the interior which, he imagined, would be light and airy.

Heffernan watched his colleague. 'That place used to attract everyone who was anyone in the old days, you know. Royalty, film stars – you name 'em, they came here.'

'I can believe it. Have you ever been inside?'

Heffernan snorted. Wesley took it for granted that this meant no.

'Where shall we start?'

Heffernan looked around. 'How about the café? Then we'll ask at the pub.'

'And if we have no luck there, we'll try the hotel?'

The chief inspector didn't answer. He was already walking towards the café which was dwarfed by its more impressive neighbour.

Once inside the café, Heffernan ordered a cream tea, purely in the line of duty, and Wesley did likewise. But it didn't take them long to discover that none of the staff there remembered serving a woman dressed in red T-shirt and cream trousers the previous Friday. They all stared at Sally Gilbert's photograph blankly. They'd never seen her before.

Wesley couldn't help feeling a little smug. He had remembered something about Sally Gilbert: she was a lady who had expensive tastes, who never took the cheapest option. He had noted as much when he had visited 5 Westview Way. Sally Gilbert, he suspected, lived way beyond her means. She would choose the hotel with its glitzy connections any day.

After a brief enquiry at the pub which produced a blank look from the young barman, they made for the hotel. Heffernan hovered at the entrance. But when Wesley strolled into the building confidently, the chief inspector had no choice but to follow.

They followed painted signs with bold 1930s lettering until they reached the tearoom. The place was filled with light and greenery beneath a huge glass dome. White wicker furniture completed the picture. If the stars and royalty of the pre-war years were to return here, they would still feel at home. Which was more than Gerry Heffernan did.

He nudged Wesley. 'Come on, Wes, let's get this over with.'

Wesley smiled. It was the first time he'd seen his boss at a social disadvantage. Normally he bluffed it out.

Wesley took a seat near a white grand piano, which would no doubt be put to use later in the day. 'Tea? Coffee? Toasted teacake? Another cream tea?' he asked his companion casually.

'I didn't think we were going to . . .'

'Come on, Gerry. This is all in the line of duty.'

'Wesley,' Heffernan whispered under his breath. 'I don't like it here.'

'Why? What's wrong with it?'

'I don't feel right. I'm not dressed for this sort of thing.'

Wesley was quite surprised at his boss's new-found sensitivity. That sort of thing had never worried him in the past. His jacket was wrinkled and his shirt slightly frayed at the collar. He was a widower in need of a good woman – but good women weren't that easy to find.

A young waitress, dressed classically in black dress and white apron, hurried over to take their order. Wesley ordered a coffee and a tea. He didn't intend to gorge himself at the hotel's prices. He noticed that Heffernan had chosen the corner seat, almost hidden by a large potted palm, as though he wished to be inconspicuous.

When the waitress returned, he explained why he was there and produced Sally Gilbert's photograph.

The waitress took it from him and stared at it. She hadn't been working the previous Friday, she explained. She'd been at her cousin's wedding. But she'd show it to some of the other staff.

The girl was well spoken and helpful. Wesley guessed she was a student. He looked across at Heffernan, who was still lurking in the undergrowth, amazed that he should feel intimidated by such a pleasant and inoffensive young woman.

'What's the matter, Gerry? You look like a villain on the run who's found himself next door to the local nick. What's wrong?'

But before Heffernan could answer, the girl had returned with a man. Her companion was tall with silver hair and wore an immaculate black suit and discreet grey tie. He had an air of subservient authority and Wesley guessed he was the head waiter.

He looked at Wesley with well-controlled disdain. 'You

were enquiring about one of our guests . . . sir?' The accent was cut glass, the tone sneering. Policemen, and black policemen at that, should know their place.

But Wesley wasn't going to rise to the bait. 'Not a guest exactly. The lady might have been here in the tearoom last Friday afternoon.' He noticed that the man was holding the picture of Sally by the corner, as if it were something dirty. 'Do you recognise her from the photograph? She was wearing a red T-shirt and cream trousers.'

'I believe I did see her last Friday.'

'Only believe?' Heffernan growled from the undergrowth. 'Did she come in here or didn't she?'

Wesley detected a sudden flash of alarm in the head waiter's eyes. Hitherto the boss had kept in the background but now he was sitting forward in full view. He pulled out his warrant card and flashed it at the man, who was trying hard to maintain his icy demeanour. Wesley suspected that there was some history between these two.

'We think a woman was murdered near this hotel, sunshine. If I liked I could order this place to be torn apart. Now was she here or wasn't she?'

The head waiter knew when he was beaten. 'Yes. She was here. She sat at that table over there.' He pointed to a table by the window, a table that had a panoramic view of the sea.

'Was she with anyone?'

'No. She was on her own. But she kept looking at her watch as though she was afraid of being late for something.'

'But if she was expecting to meet someone they didn't turn up?'

'No. Unless she'd arranged to meet them somewhere else.' The man looked at Wesley, a little uncertain of how to treat him.

'Did you serve her?'

'No. I was at the desk. I always keep an eye on things from there when I'm sorting out the evening bookings and

124

menus. Lilly actually served her.'

'Then can we talk to Lilly?' Wesley asked, trying to hide his impatience.

'Of course.' The head waiter nodded to the girl, who scurried off through a door marked 'Private'.

'Are you sure that she was alone?'

'Yes. I remember that quite clearly.'

'Did you watch her the whole time she was here?'

The waiter looked quite offended. 'Of course not. It was a very busy time. I had things to do. The manager was in an important meeting so I had to arrange the refreshments for that too.'

'And you didn't see or hear anything suspicious that day, anything out of the ordinary?'

The man shook his head and Wesley told him he could go.

'Do you know him?' Wesley asked as soon as the head waiter was out of earshot.

'Know him? I'll never forget him. I brought Kathy here on our wedding anniversary one year and he humiliated me. He said I couldn't come in his poxy restaurant because I hadn't got a jacket and tie on. Sent us away like a couple of naughty kids and we ended up eating fish and chips on the harbour at Millicombe.' A grin spread across his face. 'It didn't half give him a turn when I showed my warrant card, though. It was almost worth it to see the look on his face. If Kathy was still . . .' His voice trailed off.

Before Wesley could think of anything to say, a tall woman appeared. He guessed she was considerably older than the head waiter, probably the longest-serving member of staff. She stooped slightly and, in the same black-and-white outfit as her young colleague, reminded Wesley of a vulture he'd once seen at the zoo.

'I'm Lilly. Mr Broadbent said you wanted to see me.'

'That's right. Please sit down.' Wesley smiled to put her at her ease before asking her the same questions as he had asked her colleagues.

But this time they were in luck. Lilly remembered the lady all right. She'd ordered a cream tea and Lilly had the impression that she was early for some sort of appointment – killing time. Lilly had wondered whether she was meeting a man as she had been wearing what Lilly considered to be rather a lot of make-up. And perfume – the expensive stuff. But in spite of the designer clothes, in Lilly's opinion she'd been a bit common really – more money than class. But then a lot of them that came to the hotel these days were like that: not like the old days.

Wesley allowed her to talk, speaking only when the flow dried up. 'Did you see her with anybody else at any point? Please think hard.' He gave Lilly what he considered to be his most appealing smile.

Lilly wrinkled her beak-like nose. 'Now you come to mention it, when she left I watched her go. She'd left me a rather generous tip. Now as I remember she reached the hotel entrance and stopped. I could see her from where I was. She was standing next to someone and I'm sure she was speaking to them.'

'How long for? Where did they go?'

Lilly looked apologetic. 'I'm sorry. A couple came into the tearoom and I had to take their order. I didn't see. I'm sorry.'

'You've been very helpful.' There was never any harm in a bit of encouragement. 'Can you describe the person she was talking to?'

The nose wrinkled again. 'I didn't actually see the person. It was more of . . . more of an impression. They were wearing a hat and I thought . . .'

Gerry Heffernan leaned forward, awaiting the verdict.

'I might be wrong but I thought . . . I thought it could be a man.'

'Well, that narrows it down a bit,' muttered Gerry Heffernan, raising his eyes to heaven.

The call came through at midday. They had received

confirmation from Forensic that the blood and hair found on the rocks beneath the disturbed cliff top on Monks Island definitely belonged to Sally Gilbert, and one of her red shoes had been found tangled in seaweed in the water below. After organising all available officers to interview everyone working or staying on the island and ordering a thorough search, Gerry Heffernan decided it was time to return to Tradmouth.

Wesley drove back through the narrow, hedge-lined lanes with Gerry Heffernan slumped in the passenger seat, deep in thought. It wasn't until they had reached the outskirts of Tradmouth that he broke the silence.

'I reckon it must be the fancy man, whoever he is. Sally Gilbert puts on a load of make-up . . .'

'She always wore a lot of make-up,' said Wesley, stating the simple fact.

But Gerry Heffernan wasn't to be put off. 'She tarts herself up and goes to meet someone . . . a man . . . in one of the poshest places around. What if this Mike asked her to meet him, to renew their relationship, or whatever they call it? She might not let on to her mate Lisa until she'd decided it was all back on again.'

'And she's early for their date. Lilly said she thought she was just killing time.'

'Or he keeps her waiting. What is it they say? Treat 'em mean, keep 'em keen. I can't see Trevor keeping her waiting, can you? And I can't see her dolling herself up for him either. My money's on the fancy man. What do you think?'

Wesley didn't answer. He was concentrating on parking the car in the police station carpark.

'So who's Mike?' Wesley asked suddenly as he pushed open the station's swing-doors. 'Mike Cumberland, the manager? There's always a chance you're not right about his sexual inclinations, you know.'

Heffernan gave a dismissive grunt. 'Mike's a common name,' he mumbled. 'Even your little lad's called Michael.'

127

'Yes, but how many Mikes did Sally Gilbert know?'

There was no answer. Wesley had made a good point and Heffernan knew it. Perhaps it would be worth having another word with the manager of the Tradfield Manor Hotel.

They found the CID office half empty. Most of the officers were out and about asking questions, and the few who were still there, manning the phones and sifting through paperwork for information, hardly looked up when their two senior officers appeared in the doorway. Only Steve Carstairs glanced up guiltily from his computer.

'Steve. A word.' Heffernan had noticed the furtive look on Steve's face.

Steve obeyed the boss's beckoning finger. His face was sulky as he slunk into Heffernan's office.

Heffernan came straight to the point. 'Have you heard from Harry Marchbank?'

Steve hesitated. 'Er, he's in hospital. But he thinks he'll be out in a couple of days.'

Heffernan glanced at Wesley, who was sitting in the only available chair apart from the chief inspector's own.

'What's the matter with him? Nothing trivial, I hope.'

'Suspected heart attack.'

Heffernan was silent for a moment. Wesley watched his face and saw nothing: no gloating, no sympathy.

'How is he?' Wesley asked. He thought he should say something.

'He says he's fine. Says they're fussing over nothing.'

Heffernan stood up. 'And what made you keep this little gem of information to yourself?'

'Don't know, sir. Didn't get the chance to tell you, we've been that busy.'

'Been to see him, have you? Been visiting the sick?'

Steve blushed. 'I popped in last night, sir.'

'And what did Marchbank have to say for himself when you "popped in"? Did he ask you to do his legwork for him?'

Steve looked at the boss. By some form of telepathy, he seemed to have guessed the truth. But Steve's only instinct was to cover up for Harry ... as he always had in the past. 'No. Nothing like that.'

'You sure?' Heffernan looked him in the eye.

'Yes, sir. Got enough on my plate with this murder and the Nestec robbery, haven't I?'

'Never a truer word spoken. I want you to telephone every computer retailer in the area; see if anyone's tried to flog them Nestec's stuff. You've got all the serial numbers, haven't you?'

Steve nodded sulkily.

'Then after that you can get over to Littlebury where Sally Gilbert's car was found – knock on any doors that haven't already been knocked on. Someone must have seen her – she wasn't the invisible woman. Take Trish with you when she gets back. You can do your courting-couple act. I'm sure you're good at it. Off you go.'

Steve scuttled back to his desk, picking up a couple of heavy telephone directories from the shelves on the way.

'You were a bit hard on him, Gerry.'

'Nonsense. If I wasn't he'd be disappearing off doing Harry Marchbank's legwork every time my back was turned. You didn't know Marchbank when he was here. He had Steve at his beck and call. Where do you think Steve acquired his more endearing qualities? Harry Marchbank, that's where. Can't say I'm sorry he's in hospital and out of our hair. Steve's been improving a bit lately. Pity if Harry Marchbank went and spoiled all that, eh.'

When Wesley had first arrived in Tradmouth, Steve Carstairs had given him a hard time. Wesley had come across racists many times in his life and Steve, unfortunately, had appeared to be one of them. But recently his attitude seemed to have softened. As Heffernan had said, it would be a pity if Harry Marchbank went and turned the clock back.

The chief inspector stood up. 'I think we should take a

stroll to the hospital and have a little chat with Harry – set him right on a few things. Then we'll drop in on your dear mother-in-law.'

'Why?'

'I thought you were interested in that skeleton at Chadleigh Hall. Now that your mate Neil's gone and added to our workload, I suppose we'd better follow it up. I want to see if she has any interesting reminiscences about her schooldays. You know the sort of thing – jolly hockey sticks, feasts in the dorm, tying up the new girl and leaving her to die in a sealed room ...'

Wesley smiled. 'I'm not sure that Della played hockey.'

'More a fag-behind-the-bike-sheds type, I should think. Come on.'

The walk to Tradmouth Hospital took five minutes. The two men strolled together in amicable silence through narrow streets filled with shoppers and early tourists; people going about their business unconcerned by death. Wesley almost envied them.

They found Harry Marchbank sitting up in bed, minus his oxygen mask. If Heffernan hadn't been told otherwise, he would have thought he was malingering. The visitors approached under the patient's hostile gaze.

It was Heffernan who spoke first. 'Hello, Harry. Steve tells me you've not been well. I thought I'd come and find out for myself. I thought you might have been telling him tales.' He picked up the chart clipped to the end of the bed and examined it closely, although Wesley doubted that he could understand the thing.

'Why are you here?' Harry said, glancing at Wesley.

'Call it visiting the sick and needy. We're off to see an old lady in the next ward soon. We like to do our bit.' The chief inspector beamed down at Marchbank like a malevolent cherub.

Wesley, glad that Della couldn't hear herself being described as an old lady, wondered where this conversation was leading.

'So what's wrong with you?'

'They think I had a heart attack but they can't find anything wrong with me now. I told them it was indigestion, but would they listen? Bloody doctors ...'

Heffernan looked at Wesley. 'Don't say that in front of our inspector here. Most of his family are doctors. Isn't that right, Wesley? Raised the whole tone of the office has our Inspector Peterson. We're even getting Steve Carstairs house-trained at last.'

Heffernan paused, glaring at the patient in the bed. 'I'll come straight to the point, Marchbank. I never liked you and I was glad to get shut of you. And the last thing I want is you coming back and taking my officers' minds off their work. I don't want you asking Steve to do your legwork for you while you're stuck in here. Right? He's got enough on his plate as it is. And I don't want you stirring things just as they were beginning to settle down either. Understand?'

Marchbank smirked. 'Crystal clear ... sir.'

'So have you tracked down your man yet?'

Marchbank shifted against his pillows, giving Wesley a hostile glance. 'You could say that. I saw him in Tradmouth on the waterfront. He ran for it and I was after him when all this happened. The bastard's somewhere around here and when I get out of here I'll get him.'

Wesley had been watching the man in the bed: there was something in his attitude – the almost fanatical determination in his eyes – which didn't quite add up. There was something he wasn't sharing with them. 'You seem very keen to get this man,' he said quietly. 'Almost as if it's personal.'

Harry Marchbank looked at Wesley, his eyes full of venom, leaning forward as though he were about to spit in his face. 'You don't know nothing about it. Think you're so bloody clever, don't you. Why don't you go back where you came from ... we'd all be a bloody sight better off.'

'You mean they're missing me at the Met?' Wesley couldn't resist goading the man.

'You know what I mean. I hear you're married to a white woman. I think that's awful. I think . . .'

Wesley looked him in the eye. 'Nobody cares what you think, Marchbank. I can see now why everyone in Tradmouth was so glad to see the back of you,' he said calmly, before walking out of the ward without looking back.

Gerry Heffernan had followed him, and as soon as they were outside the swing-doors he put a hand on his shoulder. 'Don't let him get to you, Wes. That's what he wants.'

'I know. I've met his type before, unfortunately.' He walked to a corridor window overlooking the river and stared out, watching the craft flitting purposefully along the water. As his initial wave of anger began to fade he turned to Heffernan, who was standing by his side. 'I reckon Harry's probably a sad man behind all that racist, bullying front; a bit pathetic really.'

'You think so? I reckon he's just a nasty bastard.'

'Sometimes the job attracts that type . . . inadequate men who think it'll give them their little bit of power . . . make them someone.'

Heffernan looked at him, surprised. 'Didn't know you went in for psychology in your spare time, Wes.' He had never thought of Harry Marchbank like that before, but maybe Wesley was right. Maybe there was unhappiness; a deep inadequacy, behind the man's unpleasantness. 'At least we haven't got to put up with him in Tradmouth any more, thank God.' He touched Wesley's arm. 'Come on, let's go and see what Della has to say for herself.'

Wesley made for the next ward and for once he was pleased to see his mother-in-law. Della was guaranteed to get the bitter taste of Harry Marchbank out of his mouth. She was sitting in the chair by her bed, looking bored. Her eyes lit up when she saw the two men enter the ward. Entertainment was about to be provided.

'Well, if it's not my favourite son-in-law. How's Pamela? Poor girl, she looked so tired last time I saw her.'

She looked into Wesley's eyes anxiously. 'She is all right, isn't she? I feel so helpless being stuck in here when I could be helping her.'

Della had never been one for taking any domestic responsibility off her daughter's shoulders – she was more likely to turn up at unsocial hours expecting to be wined and dined than to roll up her sleeves and help with the cooking and childcare. But Wesley thought it best not to draw her attention to this fact, so he just smiled and gave the answer she expected to hear: Pam was fine – positively blooming.

She beamed at Heffernan. 'Nice to see you, Gerry. Is this a social call?' she asked, obviously glad to be the centre of attention of two members of the male sex.

'Not exactly. We'd like to ask you some more questions about your schooldays.'

'Can't think why. The most exciting thing that ever happened to me was when we found the French mistress's knickers on the washing line and I hoisted them up the flagpole. You're not arresting me for that, are you?'

Wesley ignored her last remark and focused on the matter in hand. 'We've evidence that the skeleton we found in Chadleigh Hall might date from the 1960s, around the time you were there.'

Della hadn't expected this. She sat quite still for a few moments, shocked.

'I know it's a long time ago, but do you remember anything that might help us identify the skeleton? Last time we spoke you mentioned some workmen. And a girl who ran away. Have you remembered any more? Anything at all?'

Della shook her head. 'Sorry. It's all a bit vague.'

'What about old school friends? Are any of them still around?'

'The only ones I've kept in touch with are miles away.'

'What about teachers?' There was a chance that staff would remember more than the unobservant young, busy with their own teenage preoccupations.

Della thought for a moment. 'Frostie's still alive apparently. Which is surprising – she seemed ancient when I was at school. She was in the local paper a few weeks ago; something to do with painting.'

She saw that the men were looking puzzled. 'Not painting walls – painting pictures, watercolours. She had some paintings in an exhibition – somewhere in Neston, I think it was. Miss Amelia Snowman, retired headmistress. As I said, I was just amazed she was still alive.'

'You don't happen to know where she lives, do you?'

Della shook her head. 'I have no desire to meet that woman again – even if she has turned into a harmless old lady who's taken to painting watercolours in her retirement. I just remember her as an evil, sadistic old bat.'

Wesley, who could imagine that Della would have provoked this quality in her teachers, said nothing. He looked at his watch. It was time they were going.

An artistic spinster called Miss Snowman whose face was splashed all over the local paper couldn't be that difficult to track down.

Steve Carstairs sat on the edge of Trish Walton's desk. She looked up at him and smiled. Then she saw that Rachel Tracey was looking at her, so she returned her attention to the pile of statement forms on her desk.

'How's it going?' Steve asked, lowering his voice.

'I've drawn a blank with the people in Sally Gilbert's address book. Most of them hadn't seen her for ages – just exchanged Christmas cards, that sort of thing. I'm just going through all these statements from people on Monks Island, but they were all struck blind and deaf last Friday afternoon. I mean, a woman's shoved off a cliff and nobody sees a thing. Funny, isn't it?'

'Hilarious. You up for a bit of house-to-house later?'

Trish felt her cheeks burning. 'Why not.'

Steve picked up a paper clip from her desk and began to

straighten it out absent-mindedly. 'If you wanted a cottage down here and you didn't want to go through the usual agencies or holiday letting places, where would you go?'

Trish thought for a moment. 'There are adverts in the papers . . . private lettings.'

'Mmm. Suppose so,' he said unenthusiastically, imagining himself trawling through endless back copies of the local and national papers.

'Or there's always that place in Neston.'

'What place?' He leaned forward, suddenly interested.

'There was all that trouble about it a few months ago, remember? It's a sort of information centre for squatters in the middle of Neston called Home from Home and it's run by some vicar who says he's providing a service for the homeless. It gives out information about empty second homes and holiday properties – usually in isolated places where nobody would know what was going on. It's all very organised, like a sort of New Age estate agents – only they don't hand over the keys. And they're careful to keep on the right side of the law so there's not much we can do about it.' She looked him in the eye and grinned. 'Why? Thinking of moving out of your flat, are you?'

But before he could answer, Trish's phone rang. Steve mouthed, 'See you later,' and scurried back to his desk. Even though Trish's suggestion about Home from Home was a long shot it might be worth looking into. But after the boss's warning about getting involved with Harry's work, he'd have to tread carefully.

Harry was a mate – he'd been good to him in the old days. He owed him a favour.

There were times when Robin Carrington felt that he needed a break from poring over old documents in dusty archives. He would have liked to have gone into Tradmouth again; have a drink in the Royal Oak, perhaps meet up with Brenda. But after the shock of seeing Harry Marchbank, he wasn't prepared to take any risks.

He hoped that Neil Watson had contacted the Iddacombes – George and Marjorie – in the converted lighthouse they called home. When he had spoken to them on the phone they had seemed interested in the discovery of the *Celestina* and their links to the American Smithers family. But when they had invited him to visit them he had made his excuses and declined. Why should he put himself in a vulnerable situation when he had found Neil Watson to do the job for him?

But there was one gamble Carrington was willing to take. If Marchbank had spotted him in Tradmouth, that was where he'd keep looking, so Neston, eight miles upstream, would probably be safe.

With this in mind he drove to Neston and parked in the carpark of the biggest, most anonymous supermarket in the town. After shopping for a few essentials, he left the car there and took a walk around the winding back streets, fascinated by the New Age shops; the crystal and health food shops staffed by earnest-faced women who looked as if they rarely smiled, let alone laughed.

He passed Neston's grand parish church without going in. He had had enough of things ecclesiastical over the past couple of weeks, as he had spent much of his time trawling through church records kept in Exeter. He had found Captain Isaiah Smithers' baptism in the register of St Margaret's, Tradmouth, and the entry for his burial – and that of his wife, Mary Anne – at Chadleigh Hall's chapel, the cause of their deaths given as drowning with a note in a spidery hand saying that Isaiah was Master of the *Celestina*, wrecked in the cove.

When he had cast his net wider, searching through the registers of other churches in the area, he had come upon an entry in Millicombe parish church's marriage register: Isaiah Smithers, ship's master, had married Mary Anne Iddacombe, younger daughter of the late John Iddacombe Esquire and Mistress Mercy Iddacombe of Chadleigh Hall, in 1771. Robin had noted the date with surprise. Captain

Smithers and Mary Anne hadn't been married long when they died, side by side, in the swirling, hungry waters of the English Channel. When he had discovered their grave in Chadleigh Hall's little graveyard, he had pictured them as middle aged and many years married when they took their last fatal journey. But Isaiah had been twenty-six and Mary Anne ten years his junior – sweet sixteen. Too young for life to end.

He knew the Chadleigh Hall connection would please his clients: a long time ago he had discovered that there was nothing people liked better than to find they were related to gentry. And the rest of his job would be relatively simple. It wouldn't be long before he had a full family tree for Mr and Mrs Smithers of Connecticut, dating back to the early seventeenth century. When he had gathered all the information he would print it out and post it to them, arranging for their payment to be sent to his solicitor in London to be forwarded on to him when things were more settled. Not that the money would be an issue now ... not like it used to be.

With these thoughts whirling in his head, Carrington wandered into a gloomy second-hand bookshop. He remembered the place from previous trips. One year he had spent hours searching through its shelves and had come away with a slim volume of local tales, published in the reign of Queen Victoria. Once again he made for the local history section at the back of the shop, his footsteps echoing on the dusty floorboards.

Standing in front of the tall bookshelf, he breathed in deeply. A unique smell – the smell of slightly damp paper, musty and strangely comforting. He scanned the books with their faded brown, green and blue bindings, the titles hard to make out against the muted colours. There were no bright paperbacks here, only the venerable, forgotten volumes of yesteryear; the kind of books that had always fascinated Robin Carrington.

He was searching for some reference to Chadleigh or

137

Millicombe – something that would tell him more about the places and their people – and after half an hour he found what he was looking for. A slim brown volume entitled *An Account of the Dreadful and Wicked Crimes of the Wreckers of Chadleigh* by a Reverend Octavius Mount. He pulled the book from the shelf and flicked through it.

After a few minutes Robin Carrington found what he was looking for: the name Captain Isaiah Smithers. And five minutes later he left the shop, clutching the small, dusty book close to his chest.

As Carrington was emerging from the bookshop, Wesley Peterson was driving through Neston's narrow and crowded streets.

'What's this woman's address again?'

'Laburnum Cottage, Berry Ducis – just outside Neston. Rachel said it's near Berry Ducis castle. According to Rach she's looking forward to our visit – she'll be getting the kettle on so put your foot down.'

Wesley's foot stayed exactly where it was on the accelerator. Speed wasn't an option on the congested roads of summertime Neston. And the likelihood of the Miss Snowman Della had described fussing over a pair of policemen with hot cups of tea was remote. But he didn't say so: he wouldn't rob Heffernan of his hopes.

Miss Snowman's thatched cottage was picture-postcard pretty. A pair of large laburnum trees stood in the front garden, giving the place its name. All Wesley knew about laburnum trees was that they were pretty when in flower but highly poisonous and hazardous to children. Perhaps Miss Snowman, who had been charged with the care of the young for so many years, preferred it that way.

Heffernan nudged Wesley's arm when he had rung the door bell. 'You do the talking, Wes. You sound posher than me.'

Della's former headmistress answered the door. Wesley had calculated that she would be in her eighties or nineties.

But if the woman who stood before them, with a ramrod-straight back and sharp blue eyes, was that old she certainly didn't look it. Time had been kind to Miss Snowman, which is more than her former pupil, Della, had been.

'I presume you're the policemen. Identity please,' she said, in the same voice that must have forbidden running in the corridor all those years ago.

Wesley and Heffernan meekly handed their warrant cards over for examination. Miss Snowman stared at the cards and then at the men. Once satisfied, she handed them back and stood aside to let them into the cottage.

'You'll have tea.' It was an order rather than a question.

When they were settled in a pair of chintz armchairs, sipping Earl Grey tea under the former headmistress's stern gaze, Wesley decided to break the ice.

'My wife's mother is an old girl of Chadleigh Hall.'

'Really?' She looked at him with something approaching disapproval. 'What's her name?'

'Della Stannard . . . her maiden name was Kelly.'

Miss Snowman glowered. Her eyebrows were still black, unlike her hair, which now matched her name. She was good at glowering. 'Della Kelly.' She thought for a moment. 'A naughty girl if I remember right. Always in trouble.'

She looked away. Wesley had expected her to ask what Della was doing now – whether she had made the transition from naughty girl to useful member of society. It seemed to be a natural thing for a former teacher to ask. But it appeared she had no interest in the fate of her old girls. The subject was closed. Perhaps it hadn't been a good idea to mention Della after all.

Heffernan gave an almost imperceptible nod. It was time to get down to business.

Wesley began. 'Chadleigh Hall's being converted into a hotel, Miss Snowman. When one of the walls was knocked down a room was discovered – a room that had been sealed up for years.' He paused, watching her face, but her

139

expression gave nothing away. 'It was a wall in what used to be your study, Miss Snowman.' Again no reaction. He delivered the punch line. 'The body of a teenage girl was found in the sealed room and we suspect she was put in there some time in the 1960s.'

At last Wesley detected a worried look in the old woman's eyes. 'That's impossible, Inspector. Absolutely impossible. Don't you think I would have noticed dead bodies being carried around my school? It's an outrageous suggestion.'

'So you know nothing about this body?'

'Of course not. Who could she have been? I mean, has she been identified?'

'Not yet. We wanted to ask if any of your pupils went missing around that time. Della ... er, my mother-in-law mentioned that one of the older girls disappeared while she was there. What can you tell me about it?'

There was no mistake. Miss Snowman's face had clouded. She knew something. 'There was a girl. She went off one day after a tennis match ... ran away.'

'You contacted her parents, of course.'

'Naturally.' She glanced at Wesley, worried. 'But she didn't return home. The police were called, of course, but then her parents received a letter from her saying she was safe and well. She'd gone to London with some unsuitable young man. The search was called off. I believe her parents tried to find her but ...'

'But what?' Heffernan spoke for the first time.

'I don't think they had any success. Presumably she'd thought that it was enough just to let them know she was safe. She'd also said in the letter that she didn't want to see them again. Of course, I never heard anything more about it. She'd made her choice and that was that.'

'Tell us about the girl.'

'Her name was Alexandra Stanes. A quiet girl ... but sometimes they're the worst. She was average height, I suppose, light brown hair, quite pretty. Not too bright.

140

Easily led.' She paused as though she was about to say something more but had thought better of it. 'That's about all I can tell you. She wasn't a very memorable girl. In fact the most memorable thing she ever did at Chadleigh Hall was to disappear into thin air.'

'Were her friends interviewed at the time?'

Wesley was sure he wasn't mistaken: Miss Snowman looked uneasy.

'I believe so. Yes.'

'And did any of them throw any light on her disappearance?'

Miss Snowman shook her head, her lips pursed.

Wesley carried on. 'I believe you had builders in around the time she left.'

Miss Snowman looked up at Wesley sharply. 'Who told you that? Della Kelly, I suppose.'

Wesley nodded.

'Yes, I had some alterations done to my study and my secretary's room. I wanted a wall knocked through to the passage but the builders began the work then said it couldn't be done. Supporting wall or something. They said the whole place would collapse around my ears if I insisted. So they concentrated on improvements to the kitchens and did some work in the attics.'

'We'll need the names of the builders. Do you remember?'

She looked at Wesley and sniffed disapprovingly. 'Young man, I'm not senile, you know. Of course I remember the builder. It was Mr Kilburn. His son runs the business now. In fact he's done rather well for himself. He's branched out and he owns several hotels: Kilburn Leisure. Have you heard of them?'

'Oh yes. We've heard of them,' said Gerry Heffernan, catching Wesley's eye.

Sally Gilbert had worked for Kilburn Leisure. And Sally Gilbert was dead.

*

The call came through to the CID office at 3.30. Six of Nestec's stolen computers had turned up at a second-hand computer shop in Morbay.

Steve Carstairs sat beside Rachel as she drove through Morbay's crowded streets. It was coming up to holiday time: the season of crowded pavements, traffic jams and petty crime on the promenade. As they drove slowly past shops crammed with bright plastic buckets and spades, inflatable dinghies and Lilos suspended from shopfronts shifted gently in the breeze.

Rachel's foot hit the brake as a couple in baseball caps dragging a pair of young children with dirty faces and dripping ice creams stepped in front of the car. Steve swore but Rachel kept her eyes ahead, knowing that if her companion had been driving he might have just added to Devon's accident statistics.

Morbay Computer Services occupied a small shop in a run-down side street well away from the seafront. The place hardly reeked of high technology, resembling more the old-fashioned electrical shops that Rachel remembered vaguely from her childhood.

A jangling bell announced their arrival as they stepped into the small shop. Rows of grey computer screens, blank as sightless eyes, were piled up on shelves.

Steve gave Rachel a nudge as a small, balding man appeared from the back of the shop. If the weather hadn't been so warm he would have been wearing an anorak.

'You called us about the computers from Nestec?' Rachel gave him her most charming smile. The man responded with a blush.

'They're in the back,' he said, before leading the way to what seemed like a cave formed out of cardboard boxes. He pointed to a pile of boxes in the corner. 'There. If I'd known they were nicked I'd never have bought them, but I was told they were second hand, that a firm had folded after getting some new equipment. They just wanted to get what they could for it.'

'Is that usual?'

The man looked embarrassed. 'It happens sometimes.'

'So when did you find out they'd been nicked?' Steve asked, as though he suspected the man of robbing Nestec's lorry personally.

'When a copper came round with a list of stolen items to look out for. I noticed the batch numbers and ...' He looked at Steve. 'I'm the victim here, you know. It's me who's losing money. Two grand I paid for those computers. Thought it was a bargain. Some bargain.'

'Yes, sir. We know. It's very public spirited of you to call us.' Rachel smiled again, making up for her colleague's shortcomings. 'Now can you describe the person who sold you the equipment?'

The man frowned. 'Just a lad, he was. He said he was in charge of IT in a firm that had gone bust so I assumed he was in his twenties, but he looked younger.'

'Tall or short?'

'Average.'

'Hair?'

'Brown. Shortish.'

'Accent?'

'Didn't really have one.'

'Anything else you can tell us about him? Anything he said? Anything at all?'

'No. He wasn't here for long. He just said he worked for a small firm that had gone bust and he was trying to get the best price for some nearly new computer equipment. He had a van outside and he brought in the boxes. He went away for a couple of hours while I checked the equipment then he came back and I paid up. Two grand for six new computers. I thought I had a good deal.'

'Did he sign anything? Give you any sort of paperwork?'

'Hang on a minute.'

The man scuttled off into another room and returned a few minutes later with a sheet of paper. 'Here we are. He gave me this receipt for the money. "Received the

143

sum of two thousand pounds for six second-hand Nestec computers."'

'Is there a name?' Rachel asked, ever patient.

'Yes. It's signed . . . it looks like D. Duck.'

Rachel and Steve looked at each other.

'Is that D for Donald?' Steve muttered.

'And is there a name for the company?' Rachel enquired.

'Yes. Celestina Products. Never heard of them. Have you?'

'Any news on the Sally Gilbert case?' Gerry Heffernan asked loudly when he returned to the CID office.

Trish Walton spoke first. 'Nothing new, sir. We're interviewing all the people on Monks Island who were definitely there on the day Sally Gilbert died. I've made a list.' She handed the boss a sheet of paper. 'Steve and Rachel are following up a report that some of Nestec's stolen computers have turned up in Morbay.'

Wesley smiled at Trish encouragingly. She'd only joined CID recently after a period of secondment and she was shaping up well.

'Let's hope Steve is behaving himself,' Heffernan muttered as he made for his office, with Wesley following.

'Trish is a sensible girl.'

'I didn't mean that, Wes. I meant with Harry Marchbank leading him astray.' He paused for a moment, frowning. 'Do you reckon we should go and have a word with this builder Kilburn?'

'If he's still alive.'

'Shouldn't be hard to find out. Dominic Kilburn of Kilburn Leisure's his son: we'll pay a call to his offices.'

'I don't think we made a very good impression when we saw him at the hotel.'

'We don't have to make a good impression, Wes.'

'No, but I don't think there's any point in getting on the wrong side of the Dominic Kilburns of this world. They can make things awkward for us.'

144

Heffernan grunted. Wesley was probably right. But he hated to admit it. 'I reckon Kilburn senior must be prime suspect for the Chadleigh Hall killing.'

'Or one of his workmen.'

'The voice of reason speaks again.' He grinned at Wesley. 'Let's pay Kilburn Junior a call, shall we. His offices are in Neston – I looked up the address. He'll be able to tell us where to find his dad.'

Wesley looked longingly at the cup of steaming tea on one of the detective constable's desks. But he comforted himself with the thought that, with any luck, they'd be offered refreshments at the well-appointed offices of Kilburn Leisure Ltd.

They drove out to Neston again and found Kilburn Leisure's offices housed in a grand Georgian villa on the outskirts of town. A brass plate, polished to mirror brightness, confirmed that they had come to the right place. The villa's paintwork was gleaming white and the door – the original – was painted a rich glossy red. A pair of bay trees with abundant, dust-free leaves stood either side of the entrance. Not a thing out of place. Dominic Kilburn's father may have been a jobbing builder but this place bore no resemblance to a builder's yard.

A young receptionist, cool and efficient beyond her years, greeted them and asked them to wait. The only reading matter provided for their entertainment was a collection of Kilburn Leisure's brochures, including one describing the as yet unformed delights of Chadleigh Hall. Luxury bedrooms with en suite Jacuzzis; swimming pool; health club; conference facilities; nine-hole golf course. No mention of skeletons.

It was ten minutes before Dominic Kilburn put in an appearance. Wesley formed the impression that their wait had been deliberately engineered to emphasise the fact that he was a busy man who was not at the beck and call of anybody, least of all the local constabulary.

He shook hands, but when they announced that they

wanted to talk to him about Chadleigh Hall his impatience was obvious. 'I suppose you've come about that skeleton. Look, there's nothing I can tell you about it. I only bought the place a year ago and the building work didn't start till May. I wanted to have the place opened by September but . . .'

'I'm sorry, Mr Kilburn,' said Wesley. 'We believe it's possible that the skeleton was put into that room in the 1960s so we're obliged to investigate. I'm sure you'll understand.'

Kilburn didn't reply.

Wesley continued. 'We've been talking to the former headmistress of the girls' school that used to occupy the hall. She says your father's building firm did some renovation work in the mid-1960s.'

Kilburn looked wary. 'So?'

'We'd like a word with your father. If you give us his address we can leave you to it.' Wesley smiled expectantly, as though he was anticipating instant cooperation. The tactic sometimes worked.

Kilburn hesitated. 'He's an old man. He's eighty-four. I don't want him bothered.'

Wesley did his best to look sympathetic. 'I can assure you, sir, that all we want is an informal chat. His address?'

Another hesitation. Gerry Heffernan, watching from the wings, had a feeling that Kilburn's reluctance had little to do with filial concern.

'He's in a retirement home,' Kilburn said after a long silence. 'Prawlton Towers in Tradmouth. On the road to the castle. Look, I don't want him upset.'

Wesley looked straight at him. 'You have my word that we'll do nothing to upset him.'

He caught Heffernan's eye. It was time to move. There was no point in staying any longer. They had what they wanted.

As they left the building, Wesley turned and saw Dominic Kilburn watching them from the window. Staring, expressionless.

Wesley climbed into the car and drove away.

Sebastian Wilde of Nestec had seemed delighted to hear that some of his stolen computer equipment had been found. It was the best news he'd had all day, he had told DC Paul Johnson, who had telephoned him with the glad tidings, and he was happy to hear that someone from CID would be round in due course to give him some more details.

Paul reported back to the office that Trevor Gilbert still hadn't returned to work in Nestec's warehouse. But then a man whose wife had just been found murdered was entitled to grieve in private.

Wesley sipped his tea from a flimsy plastic cup. He and Heffernan had called at the station to catch up with any developments before they made their way to Prawlton Towers. But there was nothing new to discover. The questions piled up and the answers came slowly . . . when they came at all.

There was no point in hanging around when they could be following up at least one of their cases, albeit one that dated back a few decades. Gerry Heffernan suggested that they walk the half-mile or so to Prawlton Towers and Wesley didn't argue. He knew the virtues of exercise and thought that the boss looked as though he could do with some.

They walked purposefully through Tradmouth's narrow streets until they reached the road leading to the castle, which had a calf-aching gradient. Wesley walked on past tall, pastel-painted houses to his right – homes fit for retired sea captains to live in – and a spectacular view over the river to his left. He walked ahead. Gerry Heffernan was lagging behind a little, breathing heavily.

'Hang on, Wes.'

'You shouldn't eat so many chips in the canteen,' answered the doctor's son, slowing his pace a little.

They continued to climb. Wesley, whose walk home each

day provided the necessary training for such a trek, was still slightly ahead when they reached the great oak door of Prawlton Towers. He waited for Heffernan, taking the opportunity to examine the building.

His first thought was that Prawlton Towers was a monstrosity; a great stone edifice that had been designed by an architect with a taste for Gothic horror. He could count three pepper-pot towers protruding from the roof, and there was always the possibility that there might be more round the back. It was the sort of place that any vampire would snap up for a seaside retreat. And as for its present function, Wesley thought it wasn't the kind of place where he'd like to end his days.

The front door was opened by a woman with short dark hair. As with many overweight people, it was difficult to estimate her age. Her plump face, above a cascading set of chins, was unlined, and her blue nylon uniform barely contained her expanding hips, straining over her middle until the seams looked likely to give way at any time. She looked at them suspiciously with small eyes that reminded Wesley of a pig's. But he tried to banish the thought from his mind. He was judging her before he knew anything about her – the true definition of prejudice. The woman probably couldn't help how she looked.

She didn't smile as they announced themselves but told them to wait while she went off to find the matron. She disappeared, walking slowly with a rolling gait, leaving the two men alone in the hallway, taking in their surroundings.

The hallway must have been impressive at some time in the past but now the paint was flaking on the sweeping staircase and the red patterned carpet had worn away in places to reveal the grubby woven canvas beneath its matted pile. The place was cluttered with the detritus of the sick elderly: a brace of commodes; a stair lift; a trio of sagging wheelchairs upholstered in split black plastic. The faint aroma of urine drifted in from somewhere.

'Please God I'll never end up in a place like this,' Gerry

Heffernan mumbled under his breath.

Wesley gave a brief, bitter smile. He was about to say something when a woman appeared, as thin as her colleague had been fat. She had a slit of a mouth, painted scarlet and tightly shut. Her eyes were watchful, suspicious. She looked like the sort of woman who'd give nothing away, and Wesley had an uneasy feeling that she wouldn't make things easy for them, especially if Dominic Kilburn had already been in touch to ask her to make sure his father wasn't upset.

Wesley gave her what he considered to be his most charming smile, but her expression didn't change. He introduced himself and Heffernan and assured her that they only wanted a quiet word with Mr Kilburn. Nothing to worry about. Just a chat about a job he'd once done.

The matron pressed her lips tighter together and looked as though she was about to refuse. Then, unexpectedly, the lips twitched upwards.

'I don't suppose it'll do any harm. But remember, Mr Kilburn's in his eighties and . . .' She hesitated. 'Well, he can be a little confused.'

Wesley assured her that they would do their best not to upset the old man and the matron gave a brisk nod, satisfied for the moment. She was giving them the benefit of the doubt. Innocent until proved guilty. But they would have to tread carefully with old Mr Kilburn: if they upset him, his guardian dragon might not give them a second chance.

They were led along a dimly lit corridor. The plain doors of the residents' rooms bore the names of their occupants on thin pieces of paper tacked onto the wood with drawing pins, as though their occupation of the rooms was a temporary arrangement and the names might have to be changed quickly. This intimation that the Grim Reaper was loitering in the shadows was hardly encouraging for the residents, Wesley thought.

Mr Kilburn's room was at the end of the corridor. Matron knocked in a businesslike manner and didn't wait for an answer before she opened the door: there was no lock – safety reasons. Wesley had the passing thought that he'd rather keep his privacy and his dignity than have his safety policed like that of a child.

And it was as a child that the matron addressed Mr Kilburn. He was sitting in a tall, plastic-upholstered armchair, staring at the newcomers with vacant, rheumy eyes. He had once been a big man but his body had shrunk, leaving his clothes hanging, scarecrow-like, off his bony frame.

'Now then, Jack,' Matron began with forced jollity. 'You've got visitors. The police.' Wesley expected her to complete her sentence with the words 'isn't that nice?' but she stopped herself just in time.

'Right, love,' said Gerry Heffernan, who wasn't easily intimidated. 'If we can just have a chat with Mr Kilburn ... We'll call you if we need anything, eh?' He looked at her expectantly and she took the hint and disappeared.

'Bet this place is worse than the army,' Heffernan began. It was a fair bet that Kilburn had served in the forces.

'Navy man myself,' Kilburn answered, looking up with interest, his eyes now more alert.

'Me too.' Gerry Heffernan settled himself down on the edge of the bed.

Wesley thought it wise to let him do the talking. He could tell he was already striking up a rapport with the old man.

'Served on the *Ark Royal*, I did, in the last lot.'

'Really?' Heffernan sounded impressed. 'Bet you could tell some tales. I was in the merchant navy ... first officer but I got my master's ticket.'

'Aye-aye, Captain,' the old man chortled, raising a bony hand in a feeble salute.

'You had your own building business and all, didn't you? We've met your son, Dominic. Done very well for himself. You must be proud.'

The old man's face cracked into a smile. 'He's a good

150

lad. Visits every Sunday, he does. He's got his own hotels, you know.'

Jack Kilburn was looking quite happy. Either he'd forgotten they were the police or he was enjoying the company of a fellow seafarer so much that he chose to ignore the fact for the moment.

'I know. He's bought Chadleigh Hall, hasn't he? Going to turn it into a posh place with a golf course and ...'

'Oh, aye. Chadleigh Hall.' The old man's face suddenly clouded.

'You did some work there once, didn't you? Knocked down some walls when it was a girls' school. Do you remember?'

There was a sudden wariness in Jack Kilburn's eyes. 'It were a long time ago.'

'Did you ever meet a girl there called Alexandra Stanes? She was a pupil at the school.'

'There were a lot of girls about giggling and flirting with our Dominic and that other lad who used to work for me then ... what was his name? Pete Bracewell, that's it.'

Wesley wrote the name carefully in his notebook. 'Where can we find Pete Bracewell now?'

'How should I know? Worked for me for about five years then he buggered off somewhere – Dorset, I think. Last I heard he'd got a job with the council – bin man. I said did he want to do an apprenticeship but he never did: quite happy labouring, he was. Wasn't very bright, was Pete.'

'What about the girls? Do you remember any of them?'

'They were just girls. Posh girls. Used to take one look at me and turn up their snotty little noses. Didn't stop 'em giggling when they saw the young lads, though.'

'So your son Dominic was working there too?' asked Wesley, doing some quick mental calculations. It was strange, he thought, that Dominic Kilburn hadn't mentioned the fact when they had asked about Chadleigh Hall during their visit to his office. He guessed that Dominic would

151

have been in his late teens around that time – certainly old enough to be taking an interest in schoolgirls. Or to strike up a relationship with Alexandra Stanes.

''Course he was working for me,' the proud father said. 'Took over the business when I retired, didn't he?'

Gerry Heffernan leaned forward. 'Bet your Dominic had a good time with all those girls,' he said with a conspiratorial wink. 'Young lad like that – bet they couldn't leave him alone. I know when I was that age ...'

But Jack Kilburn turned away. 'I don't remember. We had work to do and that headmistress was an old harridan. If we'd got up to anything like that we'd have been out on our ears, I can tell you.'

Heffernan leaned back again. His ploy hadn't worked.

Wesley decided on the direct approach. 'Mr Kilburn, do you remember knocking a wall through in the headmistress's study? You see, a skeleton was found in a sealed-up room adjoining that study during the present building work and there's evidence that the room had been entered during the 1960s. What can you tell us about it?'

Jack Kilburn's eyes flickered in panic. 'Where's that nurse? I want the toilet. Nurse!' he shouted in a querulous voice, thin and broken. 'Nurse!'

The old man's breathing was getting faster and shallower. 'Nurse!'

'I'll get her,' said Wesley, making for the door.

As Jack Kilburn was led off to answer the call of nature, Wesley had the uneasy feeling that he had used his frailty as a weapon against them, to stop them getting at the truth. Kilburn hadn't seemed confused during their conversation. On the contrary. He had watched the old man's eyes and seen understanding there. Understanding and fear.

Jack Kilburn knew more about Chadleigh Hall than he had admitted. In fact Wesley wouldn't have been surprised if he knew the whole story. But it was a matter of proving it.

*

They returned to the office at ten to five. The walk from Prawlton Towers into the town was downhill. Easy. But it still made both men long for a decent cup of tea.

They walked into the office, only to find that most of the officers were out and about making themselves useful and asking questions. Those that remained at the station had telephone receivers fixed to their ears or busy fingers running fast over computer keyboards like those of expert pianists. At the end of the room stood a large notice-board with Sally Gilbert's smiling photograph pinned at its centre.

Wesley stood staring at the image for a few seconds, but his thoughts were interrupted by Trish Walton, who bustled over with a sheet of paper in her hand. He gave her a welcoming smile. He considered Trish, like Rachel Tracey, to be a sensible, hard-working policewoman. He just hoped that Steve Carstairs' interest wouldn't lead her from the path of righteousness. He was sure she could do better for herself.

'There's been a message from Monks Island. Apparently Sebastian Wilde of Nestec was at the hotel there on the day Sally Gilbert died. He went for a meeting with the hotel owner, who's thinking of putting in one of Nestec's computer systems. He was there from eleven thirty to around three. The probable time of Sally's death. Her husband worked for Wilde. It's a link.'

Wesley nodded. 'You're right, Trish. It is a link. I'll let the boss know.'

He walked slowly to Heffernan's office, deep in thought. It seemed that all roads led to Nestec.

Rosie Heffernan sat at the piano and played a gentle Chopin nocturne, an antidote to her day: she had risen at five o'clock and had spent the first part of the morning cleaning two sets of offices in the High Street; then she had come home to catch up on her sleep before rushing off to the Tradfield Manor Hotel to entertain the ladies and business-men who lunched by playing a selection of light classics on the restaurant's grand piano. She had arrived home at 4.30

feeling tired and sweaty. But a shower and a change of clothes had improved her mood.

Her fingers rippled over the piano keys. It was a familiar piece, one she had played for an examination. The music came to a dreamy end and she sat perfectly still, savouring the moment, the satisfaction of a piece well played, until the sound of her father's key in the front door brought her thoughts back to matters domestic. Such as what they would eat for dinner. Sam hadn't yet returned so he wouldn't have a say in the decision. But then Sam had never been fussy about what he ate.

'Rosie. You in?' Her father's voice drifted through. 'What's for tea, love?'

Rosie smiled. Dad never changed. And Sam wasn't much better. As with most men, their stomachs came first. When her mum had been alive ... She pushed the thought from her mind. Her mother was dead: killed in a hit-and-run accident. And they had been left to get on with their lives.

Gerry Heffernan appeared in the doorway, a grin on his chubby face. 'Hiya, love. Not got the tea on?'

Rosie gave her father an innocent smile. 'Why don't you make the tea, Dad? You're a better cook than I am.'

Gerry Heffernan turned in the direction of the kitchen. Somehow he'd never got the hang of sexual equality – but he guessed this was it. And he knew Rosie was right: since Kathy's death his cooking skills had improved. It had been a matter of necessity: man shall not live on ready meals for one alone.

'I don't know whether Sam'll have room for anything when he gets in,' Heffernan said. 'He's still working at that woman's. Mrs Sanders ... the one who gave him lunch. If I know Sam he'll have been gorging himself again.'

'Some people have all the luck.'

'She sounds a nice woman, that Mrs Sanders,' he said casually.

Rosie didn't answer. The previous night Sam had commented, almost as a joke, that he'd like to introduce his new employer to their dad: she was a widow who worked part time in a Tradmouth office, around his age, comfortably off and nice with it.

Rosie had left the room, stunned at her brother's disloyalty to their mother's memory. If Mrs Sanders, or any other woman come to that, set foot in the house, Rosie Heffernan felt that she wouldn't be able to handle it.

Logic told her that as she and Sam were away for most of the year, it would be good for their father to have company. And yet the thought of somebody usurping her mother's place almost made her feel physically sick, and she was surprised that Sam didn't feel the same. Perhaps men saw things differently.

She resumed her playing: something relaxing by Debussy that drifted through to the kitchen, where her father was wrestling with some obstinate chicken pieces. But after a minute or so her musical flow was interrupted by a shouted request to switch on the television. There was something on the local news he wanted to see.

Gerry came through from the kitchen and sat himself down on the settee, spreading himself out, making himself comfortable.

'Everything okay in the kitchen?' Rosie asked, her stomach rumbling.

'Everything's under control. Shhh ...' He put his finger to his lips. The item he had been waiting for had come on at last.

A young man was standing in a carpark with Monks Island clearly visible in the background. He held a microphone to his mouth like a steel ice cream. 'Police today appealed for anyone who saw this woman on or near Monks Island to come forward.'

A photograph of a smiling Sally Gilbert flashed up on the screen. 'She was wearing a red top and cream-coloured trousers similar to these.' Another photograph flashed up of a top and trousers, the nearest copies the WPC given the job could find.

'And she was last seen at the island's famous hotel on Friday afternoon. It is thought she was killed shortly after leaving the hotel around three o'clock, and the police are anxious to know if anybody saw her with anyone at or around that time.'

Another photograph appeared, this time a handbag, carefully chosen to match Lisa Marriott's description of Sally's. 'The police are anxious to trace the dead woman's missing handbag. If anyone knows its whereabouts or can help in any way, please contact the incident room on . . .'

Gerry Heffernan rose from his seat and scratched his backside.

Rosie looked at him. 'Okay, Dad?'

Heffernan grunted. 'That should get all the local cranks and weirdos reaching for their phones.'

He sat down again to watch the rest of the news while Rosie hurried into the kitchen, having detected a suspicious smell of burning. If she wanted her food to be edible she'd have to do it herself. Her father's mind was on other things.

Peter Bracewell kept to the same routine every night when he reached his three-bedroomed house on the outer edge of the Tradmouth council estate. He got home, greeted his wife with no physical contact, stripped off his clothes in the bathroom and stood in the shower for ten minutes, swilling away the dirt, other people's dirt. The council provided him with thick overalls but he still felt the filth from the bins he emptied – the congealed, week-old food; the discarded disposable nappies; the contents of cats' litter trays; and worse – permeated his hair and his clothes until he reeked of the unpleasant substances he handled every day.

But he liked the job. He liked his mates at work. He preferred it to the first job he'd had when he was sixteen – working as a labourer for Jack Kilburn, the builder. Jack had been a hard man to work for; vindictive and harsh. And word had it that his son Dominic – hotel developer and local entrepreneur – wasn't much better.

There was a plastic runner laid over the hall carpet, ready each night for Peter's homecoming. He went straight upstairs to perform his nightly ritual and emerged from the bathroom half an hour later like a butterfly from a cocoon; cleansed and purified. It was only then he could begin to relax.

That night – after an evening meal of egg and chips cooked by his devoted wife, Sandra, who had returned a couple of hours before from the Tradfield Manor Hotel, where she worked part time in the wages office – he settled down to watch the local news. The first item was about the Sally Gilbert murder – an appeal by the police for witnesses. Then a photograph flashed on the screen and he sat forward, hoping Sandra hadn't noticed his sudden interest. But she was too busy clearing the table. He strained his ears to listen to the rest of the news item, then slumped back in his armchair. He had to think.

When Sandra was safely in the kitchen washing the dishes, Peter Bracewell crept outside and made his way down the narrow back garden towards the shed that was his refuge from the world. He kept his treasures there. Things he had found. Things of interest. Things of value. All cleaned up and neatly filed away. And he had amassed quite a collection over the years; everything from antique clocks to silver spoons and old porcelain. It never ceased to amaze him what people threw away.

But he hadn't intended to keep his latest acquisition for himself. It wasn't to be stashed away and gloated over. Sandra had been going on about wanting a new handbag for her birthday and the one from Monks Island was real leather and virtually new. It had probably cost a hundred quid or more – none of your plastic rubbish.

He had wiped it and polished it before wrapping it in tissue paper, ready to present it to Sandra on her birthday in two weeks' time. Its contents lay discarded in one of the shed drawers, and now Pete hardly dared to open it and take a look at them.

He knew what the name on the credit cards would be: Sally Gilbert.

Chapter Seven

George Marbis passed from this world with my assurance of forgiveness as comfort. Now that I was aware of the evil he had revealed, I preached often against the crime of wrecking and the importance of Christian charity to any in need of help. I informed the constable, who assured me that he would be vigilant and would call soldiers from Plymouth if he learned of a ship being lured to the shore and plundered. Although I am sorry to say that he failed in his duty and it was put about later that he had joined the wreckers himself on many occasions.

But now I would relate the tragic story of the Celestina, *wrecked on our shore some fifteen months after George Marbis's death. It is a sorry tale but one that must be told. I first met the* Celestina's *master, Captain Isaiah Smithers, about a year after old John Iddacombe died, leaving Mistress Mercy Iddacombe a wealthy widow with a fine town house, an estate at Chadleigh and seven fine ships sailing out of Tradmouth. It so happened that she was in need of a new master to take command of the* Jane Marie, *one of her ships sailing for Newfoundland, and young Isaiah Smithers – a mate aboard a Tradmouth schooner, who was seeking his first command – came to her attention.*

He was a handsome, well-set young man, and Mistress

Iddacombe took a great liking to him. There was much talk, in fact, that the pair were lovers, for Mistress Iddacombe, although many years older than the young captain, was a comely woman. Of course, I dismissed such tales as the idle gossip of evil minds. But then there is rarely smoke in the chimney without a healthy blaze in the hearth.

From An Account of the Dreadful and Wicked Crimes of the Wreckers of Chadleigh *by the Reverend Octavius Mount, Vicar of Millicombe*

Wesley Peterson climbed from his bed, intending to creep out to the bathroom. Pam appeared to be asleep and he didn't wish to disturb her. But his efforts were in vain. The bright sunlight streaming through the bedroom curtains had woken her already, and as soon as she heard her husband's soft footsteps on the carpet she opened her eyes.

'What time is it?'

'Five to eight. Go back to sleep. Have a rest. School's out so you're a free woman. Make the most of it.'

'Fat chance. I've got to see to Michael.'

He couldn't argue with that. A toddler has no thought for a pregnant and exhausted mother. It's an age of total self-ishness, of looking after number one. Some people, Wesley thought, never grow out of that phase – notably most of the criminals he had met during the course of his career. Michael, however, would eventually mature and blossom into a kind, considerate human being – if they were lucky.

But it was too early in the morning for philosophy. And he was running late. He cleaned his teeth with one hand and held his electric razor with the other.

He left Pam in bed and crept downstairs to make himself some breakfast. Nothing fancy; cornflakes and orange juice from a carton which proclaimed itself to be pure. There was just time to make a pot of tea. He took some up to Pam on a tray. He would probably be home late that evening so

160

he felt he had to do his bit.

Pam sat up and attempted a weak smile. She still looked washed out but Wesley imagined that things would start to improve now that she no longer had to work every day.

He kissed the top of her head. 'Have you found a baby-sitter for tomorrow night?'

She looked puzzled for a moment. 'Tomorrow night?'

'The meal at the Tradfield Manor.'

'Oh, yes. I've asked Gaynor down the road. It's a while since we've been out for a meal. I'm looking forward to it.' She leaned back on her pillow. 'Did I tell you that I'm meeting Neil today?'

'No.' Wesley felt slightly put out that his wife had made an assignation and not told him about it.

'He rang yesterday and asked me over to Chadleigh for lunch. He wants to show me what he's found in his ship-wreck.'

'What about Michael?'

'I'm leaving him with Mrs Miller.'

Wesley nodded. One more day with the childminder couldn't make much difference to his son's development. He looked at his watch. It was time to go. He experienced a split second of reluctance to leave. But there was work to do: two murders and a hijacking.

After instructing Pam to drive carefully, Wesley Peterson walked to the police station, enjoying the early morning sun and the scent from the tubs and window boxes he passed on his downward journey into the ancient centre of the town.

He could see the wide river glinting ahead of him. Ships had sailed out from Tradmouth bound for the Crusades and in the Middle Ages the river had bristled with the masts of wooden merchantmen bringing wine from Bordeaux. In the time of Good Queen Bess captured Spanish galleons had been towed triumphantly into port; and in later years ships had sailed out with cargoes for the settlers in the New World and had returned with catches from the rich fishing grounds of Newfoundland. Now, however, the River Trad teemed with yachts, pleasure craft and ferries. Times had changed.

When he arrived at the office Rachel was already sitting at her desk, cool and unharassed. She looked up and smiled, but before she could say anything the telephone on Wesley's desk began to ring.

He picked up the receiver and announced his name.

'I'm ringing about the woman who was killed. Sally something.' The voice was certainly a man's but it was high and squeaky, taut with nerves.

'Sally Gilbert. Do you have something to tell us?'

At that moment Steve Carstairs came in, talking loudly to a giggling Trish Walton, showing off. Wesley put a finger to his lips. Steve fell silent and gave Wesley a resentful look.

'Is there something you want to tell us?' he repeated patiently. This one probably needed time.

'It's just that I think I found her bag. I saw it on the telly last night and I thought I'd better ring.'

Wesley reached for his pen. This sounded important. 'Where did you find it?'

'In a bin. I work for the council. I . . .'

'Where was this bin?'

'Monks Island. The hotel bins. It was a brand-new handbag just stuck on the top of all the rubbish so I thought . . .'

'You thought nobody wanted it so you'd take it. Present for your wife?' It was a guess.

'That's right. I thought someone with more money than sense had decided they didn't like it and thrown it out. It's surprising what people get rid of.' The man sounded almost pleased that Wesley understood. 'I thought it'd be empty but then I looked inside and there was all this stuff. I was going to give it in to a police station but . . .'

'But you never got round to it?' How many times had Wesley heard this line before?

162

'That's right. I won't be in any trouble, will I? I mean, there was only a purse with twenty quid in it and some make-up and keys and a photograph. The money's still in the purse.' He hesitated, as though deciding whether to admit to something. 'There's some credit cards and all. I didn't look at the name till last night when I saw it on the telly. But it says Mrs S. Gilbert. That's her, isn't it?'

'Yes,' Wesley answered quietly, awaiting more revelations.

'I haven't taken anything. It's all still there. I was going to bring it in at the weekend.' The word 'honest' was hanging in the air.

'I'm sure you were, Mr, er . . .'

'Bracewell. Peter Bracewell.'

'Right, Mr Bracewell, if you give me your address, someone'll be round to pick up the bag and take a statement.'

As Wesley wrote down the details, he wondered where he had heard the name Peter Bracewell before.

Then he remembered.

Neil Watson sat on the edge of a worn chintz sofa in the drawing room of Bear Head Lighthouse, sipping tea from a bone-china cup with an uncomfortably small handle. He put the cup back in the saucer, fearful of spilling the hot tea on his jeans. He was aware that his fingernails were dirty, an occupational hazard.

He looked out of the window onto the calm sea, thinking how different the tranquil scene would be in rough weather. The *Celestina* had sailed these waters – and she had been swallowed by them.

'I believe that the ship we're investigating used to belong to one of your ancestors,' he began.

Mr and Mrs Iddacombe glanced at each other. 'That's right,' Mr Iddacombe answered wistfully. He was a tall man whose pale bald head reminded Neil of an egg. He had a youthful look but he must have been seventy if he was a day. 'Mr Carrington told me about it when he phoned. He said he's been doing a family tree for someone in America who's related to the captain of the *Celestina* and that's how he came across our family. I'm surprised he's not come to see us himself. We did ask him.'

Neil was surprised too but he thought it best to say nothing.

'Your family used to own Chadleigh Hall, I believe?'

'That's right. My father moved out just before the Second World War, then it was used by the Americans as a base. After that it became a girls' school and now it's going to be some sort of hotel, isn't it, dear?' He looked at his wife for confirmation but she didn't answer.

'Did you ever live there?'

'When I was very young but I don't remember much about it.'

'And have you heard about this skeleton that's been found?'

There was a crash as George Iddacombe's teacup fell onto the parquet floor.

'I'm sure it's nothing to do with us,' the woman said quickly before shouting, 'Brenda ... Brenda. Can you come in here with a cloth?'

Shortly after Mrs Iddacombe gave her imperious order a young woman scurried in. The Iddacombes ignored her as she cleaned up the mess. But Neil's eyes were drawn to her. She was skinny with mousey hair tied back in a pony-tail and a wide mouth. She wore a top that seemed too small for her, stretched tight across her swelling breasts, and a skirt that had ridden up to reveal an expanse of pale thigh. Neil imagined her naked for a second then turned his mind to other things. He'd been too long without female company.

When Brenda, whoever she was – presumably some kind of maid or cleaner – had gone, the Iddacombes poured more tea as though nothing had happened.

'Had you heard any stories that could relate to the

skeleton? Sometimes these old houses have their legends and ...'

George Iddacombe looked as though he was about to speak but his wife got in first. 'Of course not. There was nothing like that.' Marjorie Iddacombe stood up stiffly. 'If you'll excuse me, Dr Watson ...'

Neil knew when he was being dismissed and wondered why.

He made a hasty exit, looking back at the lighthouse and its squat white tower which had once kept ships from going aground but which had been replaced years ago by something more modern.

The Iddacombes knew something about Chadleigh Hall, he was certain of it.

Sam Heffernan was left alone again in the half-finished garden. His colleagues had the habit of disappearing at regular intervals and returning some time later reeking of smoke and beer. Today they had absented themselves early, telling Sam that they had to pick up essential supplies. He suspected those supplies would be liquid and come in a pint glass.

He felt it was time he had a break. Last night his body had ached from the unaccustomed effort of digging. He had lain in a hot bath to ease his stiff muscles until his flesh had wrinkled and his sister had battered on the door demanding that he let her use the bathroom. It was good to be home but it still wasn't the same as it had been when his mother was alive. There was a gaping hole in his life where she had been, always fussing, always caring, laughing at each teenage rebellion. Kathy Heffernan had been special. But now she wasn't mentioned in the house. Nobody spoke her name for fear of causing pain.

He noticed that the sun lounger was back in place near the kitchen door and he wondered if Mrs Sanders' nephew, Jason Wilde, was spending another day skiving at his aunt's place. But there was no sign of him.

The other day Sam had had the impression that there was something in the outhouse that Jason hadn't wanted him to see. And now that he was alone, he had a chance to satisfy his curiosity. Sam was his father's son: he disliked unsolved mysteries, and Jason had been up to something. Presumably Keith and Andy had seen nothing suspicious when they had fetched the mower: but then they probably hadn't been looking.

He strolled towards the outhouse, looking around to check that Jason hadn't emerged from the back door or that Mrs Sanders wasn't watching from the kitchen window.

But there was no sign of life, so he opened the splintery door and stepped inside. The only light seeped in through a small, filthy window, curtained with cobwebs, and it took Sam's eyes a few seconds to adjust. He could make out the shape of the mower standing beside an ancient rusty wheelbarrow and other relics of the house's gardening past. Beyond them he could see that a pathway had been cleared through the disused flower pots, leading to another door. Sam tried the door and it opened.

This new chamber had no window and was as dark as a tomb. But in the pale light that trickled in from the doorway he could just make out some shapes. Where he had expected to find assorted outdoor junk, he could see the dim outlines of large cubes. Boxes. He opened the door wider to let more light in but it was still too dark to make out the printed words on the sides.

Without a torch it was useless. He closed the door behind him and crept out into the fresh air.

Just as he retreated from the outhouse, Mrs Sanders appeared around the corner of the house, laden with bulging supermarket carrier bags, staggering under their weight. Sam rushed forward to help her, and she allowed him to take the bags.

'Thank you, Sam. That's very kind of you. How's the pond coming on?'

'Fine,' he lied. Without Keith and Andy he hadn't made much progress.

'Where are the other two?'

'Out getting supplies.' He thought it best to give the authorised version.

'Would you like a coffee? You look as if you need one.'

'Thanks. I was just checking the mower.'

He watched her reaction but detected nothing out of the ordinary.

'That outhouse must come in useful.'

'It was a bit of a mess but my nephew Jason cleaned it out for me. I said he could use it to store some things ...'

'What things?' he said before realising he was sounding too inquisitive.

'I've no idea. Why don't you ask him?' She smiled at him. 'Put the bags over there, will you. It's the same every time I go to that supermarket. I always end up buying far too much.'

Mrs Sanders poured fresh coffee from a tall glass cafetière and told Sam to sit down. She was sure that he deserved a break.

Sam felt awkward at first, but there was something about Mrs Sanders; a cosy, motherly quality, that made him relax. They were sitting on a pair of stools sipping their coffee when Sam spoke. 'It's a nice house.'

'Thank you,' she said, a faraway look in her eyes. 'I love it. I nearly lost it once but ... well, it worked out all right in the end.' She gave him a sad smile. 'Have you any brothers and sisters, Sam?'

'A sister, Rosie. She's a music student. She finishes next year.'

'What does she play?'

'The piano and the violin.'

'Your parents must be very proud of you both,' she said quietly.

'My mother died a few years ago. My dad's on his own now.'

Before she could make the appropriate sympathetic noises the door to the kitchen burst open. Brenda, the cleaner, was standing there, duster in hand. She looked at Sam and scowled, as though she had wanted Mrs Sanders to herself.

'I'm sorry I'm late, Carole. I've just come from the Iddacombes and I had to pick Kayleigh up from her friend's. I hope you don't mind. She won't be no trouble.'

Sam noted the use of Mrs Sanders' Christian name and wondered whether this was an example of the middle-class guilt Jason Wilde had mentioned: an attempt at matiness.

But if Carole Sanders was put out, she did a wonderful job of concealing it. 'Of course that's all right, Brenda. You know I'll look after Kayleigh any time. No problem.'

'Has Brenda worked here long?' Sam asked when she was out of earshot.

'Oh yes .. must be about five or six years now: Kayleigh was just a toddler when she first started. She comes to me three times a week and she cleans for an elderly couple who live in a lighthouse.' She smiled at the thought that an elderly couple could choose such an eccentric home. 'And she works at the Tradfield Manor Hotel as well. I look after Kayleigh for her sometimes. I like to help her out when I can.'

Sam remembered the missing ten-pound note but thought it best to say nothing. It probably wasn't his place to interfere.

He decided to change the subject. 'Tell me, Mrs Sanders . . .'

'Carole, please.'

'Tell me, Carole, I was wondering why this place is called Gallows House.'

Carole looked at him for a moment before answering. 'This used to be a farm and the old entrance stood next to a crossroads. There was a gallows there where they used to hang local criminals ... just over there where you're putting up that fence.' She pointed out of the kitchen window.

Sam shivered as though a sudden blast of icy air had disrupted the warm day.

Peter Bracewell's house was well kept. The council had recently painted the outside a tasteful cream and the Bracewells had done their bit by keeping the garden regimentally neat. Marigolds formed a guard of honour for Wesley and Rachel as they marched up the front path, and no weed had dared to squeeze under the fence to infiltrate the well-manicured lawn. A brand-new Vauxhall Vectra with gleaming green paintwork was parked in the drive: a rusty heap like the one sitting outside the house next door would have looked out of place.

'Wish my garden looked like this,' Wesley mumbled.

'It'll be because he has to clear away people's rubbish all day. I don't blame him for wanting to come home to order instead of chaos.'

'Didn't know you went in for psychology.'

Rachel smiled at him, a hint of a challenge in her eyes. 'There's a lot you don't know about me.'

The door was answered by a thin, dark-haired woman with sharply chiselled features who stared at them, expressionless, for a few moments before stepping aside to let them in. Then, without a word, she poked her head out of the door as if to check that no neighbour had witnessed their arrival. But judging by the state of the neighbouring houses, Wesley imagined that their occupants would hardly be bothered by a visit from the police: in fact they probably regarded such visits as a hazard of everyday life.

'My husband's through here,' the woman said calmly in an accentless voice. Then she walked ahead of them, leading the way into the living room.

A man sat on the settee, a dapper, long-faced man of medium height dressed in clothes that wouldn't look out of place in a golf club bar: a pair of beige slacks and a short-sleeved, open-necked shirt in a neat blue check. His grey hair was tidily cut and he had an aura of cleanliness about him, as though he'd just emerged from the shower. If Peter Bracewell dealt with dirt and rubbish all day, he certainly didn't bring his work home.

Or perhaps he did. Sitting on a low wooden coffee table was a blue leather handbag, polished up for the occasion and looking shop-display fresh.

Bracewell saw that Wesley was looking at it. 'I thought someone had chucked it out so I brought it home for my Sandra.' He glanced up at Sandra, who, hovering in the doorway, smiled shyly. 'That's new, I thought. Someone with more money than they know what to do with has got sick of it and chucked it away.' The man's voice was nervous, uncertain. 'I didn't look inside it till I got home and I've been meaning to take it into the police station but I haven't had time.'

Sandra Bracewell offered tea. Wesley gave Rachel an almost imperceptible nod and she followed the woman out into the kitchen. Peter Bracewell would probably feel more comfortable on his own.

Wesley sank down on the settee that was too low and soft for true comfort. 'So when did you find it?'

'Friday, it was. We do Monks Island on a Friday around four o'clock.'

'And none of your colleagues saw the handbag?'

'Yeah. Wayne, one of the lads, he saw it first and said it was too good to chuck out. I said Sandra was on about getting a new handbag and I'd take it for her and clean it up ... bit of a surprise for her birthday, like. Wayne didn't want it – he's just split up with his missus. That's it, really. I brought it home and shoved it in the shed. We went away to stay at my sister's in Weymouth for the weekend and I didn't look at it again till yesterday.'

'You didn't open it when you found it?'

'Why should I? It had been thrown out. I thought it'd be empty,' Bracewell said convincingly, avoiding Wesley's eyes.

Wesley knew he was only getting the authorised version

170

which would, no doubt, be backed up by Wayne if he were questioned. But it wasn't the theft of a handbag he was interested in. It was Sally Gilbert's murder. He would get someone to speak to Wayne, but something told him one portion of the story was true. They had come across Sally's handbag in the hotel bins, probably discarded by the murderer in the hope that it would be crushed and destroyed with the rest of the hotel rubbish.

'Did you find the bag on top of the rubbish or . . .'

'Oh yes. It was on top or we wouldn't have spotted it, would we. There's a lot of rich people stay in that hotel. It's amazing what they can afford to throw out.'

Wesley smiled. Any spoils from the bins at the Monks Island hotel were probably regarded as a perk of Bracewell's job.

'Can any member of the public get to the bins or are they kept in a locked area?'

'Anyone can get to them if they wanted.'

A pity, Wesley thought. If access had been through the hotel the list of suspects would be somewhat shorter.

As Sandra Bracewell and Rachel returned with a tray of bone-china teacups, Wesley pulled on a pair of plastic gloves. No doubt Peter Bracewell and others had deposited fingerprints all over the bag's contents by now, but he felt he should play by the book just in case. He leaned forward and opened the bag carefully, as though it were a bomb primed to go off. There wasn't much inside: a purse containing about twenty pounds; a small wallet bristling with bright plastic credit cards – Sally Gilbert's friends and husband had hinted that she was a woman who liked to spend money; a pair of unused, neatly folded tissues; a small photograph of a man Wesley didn't recognise who would no doubt be identified in due course; a small make-up bag whose expensive contents looked newish; and a comb. Compared to most women, Pam included, she had travelled light. He closed the bag again. There would be plenty of time to examine its contents back at the station.

Rachel produced a plastic evidence bag and he put Sally Gilbert's handbag inside it, out of harm's way.

Wesley turned to Peter Bracewell. 'The dead woman's friend said she'd seen her put a letter in her handbag. Did you find it?'

Bracewell shook his head.

'You used to work for Jack Kilburn, the builder.' He watched Bracewell's face for signs of unease.

'That was a long time ago. Must be over thirty years – first job I ever had. Why?'

'Do you remember doing some building work up at Chadleigh Hall near Millicombe? It was a girls' school then.'

Bracewell hesitated, playing with the wedding ring he wore. 'I remember working there but that's about all. It was just another job.'

There was something in Peter Bracewell's body language, in the way he looked Wesley unblinkingly in the eye, which made it obvious that he was lying . . . or at least not telling the whole truth.

'Have you heard that a skeleton was found there in a sealed-up room on the first floor?'

Bracewell swallowed hard. 'Yes. It was in the local paper.'

'We have evidence that the room was opened up in the 1960s as part of the building work.'

There was no mistaking it. Peter Bracewell was squirming in his seat.

'And the skeleton was that of a teenage girl. Did you have anything to do with the girls at Chadleigh Hall? I must say I wouldn't blame you if you did. All those pretty girls who hadn't seen a male in months.'

Wesley noticed Peter Bracewell glance at his wife. Sandra Bracewell gave an almost imperceptible shake of the head.

'I just got on with the job. I don't know anything. I can't even remember much about it after all these years.'

172

'You worked with Jack Kilburn and his son, Dominic?'

Bracewell nodded.

'Didn't you get on with them?'

'They were all right.'

'Was it just the three of you?'

'Yeah. At that time there was just the three of us.'

'So why did you leave?'

'I was offered a job along the coast with my brother-in-law. I moved on.'

'Did you ever meet a girl at Chadleigh Hall called Alexandra Stanes?'

Peter Bracewell's body stiffened. 'Can't say I did.'

As Wesley gathered up Sally Gilbert's handbag, he knew that Peter Bracewell was hiding something.

When Neil Watson returned from the Iddacombes' lighthouse, he experienced a sudden urge to see their ancestor's ship for himself. After enduring the long ritual of donning a diving suit, he plunged beneath the waves and floated weightless in the silent, murky world, watching as his companions swam gracefully, kicking their flippers as they glided like sleek seals, down to where the bones of the *Celestina* lay.

He breathed deep, even, audible breaths. He felt more relaxed than he had on his first dive and realised that he was almost beginning to enjoy the underwater experience, even though he still found it frustratingly slow.

When he had first been down to the wreck, he hadn't been able to see much because clouds of sand had been billowing from the seabed like a thick fog. But today conditions were better: he could see the blackened skeleton of the *Celestina* resting on the bottom and, although the wreckage was well scattered, he could just about make out the shape of the great broken vessel.

The more experienced divers were blowing away the sand around the protruding timbers with a machine that resembled the hose from some monstrous vacuum cleaner, causing more of the ship to emerge slowly from the muddy seabed. He watched Jane as she measured, photographed and labelled an object the size of a house brick before marking its position on a chart. Then she worked carefully in the heavy silence, coaxing the thing, misshapen with the concretion of centuries, free from its resting place.

After twenty minutes Neil signalled to Matt and they swam back to the surface together.

'We seem to be finding a lot of those iron ingots in what we think was the hold,' said Matt as they climbed aboard the dive boat.

'No gold, then?'

Matt grinned and shrugged his shoulders.

Neil shielded his eyes and looked towards the shore, where he spotted a familiar figure by the café.

After discarding his diving gear, he climbed into one of the inflatables and steered it towards the beach.

When Wesley returned to the station, he found Gerry Heffernan pacing up and down the office impatiently looking at his watch. As the day was hot he wore no jacket and his sleeves were rolled up as though he were about to begin some heavy manual task: digging in the literal rather than the abstract sense.

Wesley walked in carrying Sally Gilbert's handbag in its plastic evidence bag. He had already been the butt of a few good-natured jokes from his colleagues. Bob Naseby on the front desk had concluded that as the bag didn't match his shoes he should go home and change. Wesley had laughed – he felt that it was expected. Perhaps he should have let Rachel carry it.

As soon as Heffernan spotted him, his face lit up with a grin of anticipation. 'You've got the bag, then. Anything interesting inside?'

Wesley placed Sally's handbag on his desk and opened it with plastic-gloved hands. 'When it's been checked for fingerprints we can have a good look, but as far as I can see the most interesting thing is this photograph.' He drew the picture out carefully and held it up for the boss to see. 'It's not Trevor Gilbert. Could it be the elusive Mike?'

'It could be her brother for all we know.'

'She was an only child.'

'Or her dad when he was young?'

'Too recent.'

Heffernan shrugged his shoulders. 'Okay. We'll take copies and we'll start asking around ... see if anyone knows him. We'll try Lisa Marriott and Trevor first. It could be one of Trevor's colleagues at Nestec. Sebastian Wilde said that Nestec was one big happy family ... did a lot of socialising. If he wasn't someone from the hotel where Sally worked, she could have met him through Nestec.'

It was a possibility but Wesley was keeping an open mind. She could have met Mike picking up frozen peas in her local supermarket for all he knew – in fact he had heard that the frozen-food section was rife with that sort of thing ... not that he'd ever attempted to find out.

When the bag had been dispatched to undergo the ritual of examination, Wesley picked up a list from his desk. He liked lists; liked crossing off tasks when they were done. It was one way he prevented his workload from defeating him. There was Sally Gilbert's murder; the skeleton found at Chadleigh Hall; the hijacking of Nestec's lorry and the theft of half a million pounds' worth of computer hardware. And something else that wasn't on his list, something that nagged at the back of his mind.

Then he remembered what it was: Harry Marchbank's search for the London man who had murdered his wife for the insurance money. But Marchbank, as far as he knew, was still stuck in hospital. And Wesley found it difficult to drum up much enthusiasm for his manhunt anyway. He had enough on his plate.

'What next?' Gerry Heffernan's voice behind him made him jump.

'We told Sebastian Wilde we'd have a word about those computers turning up in Morbay.' He looked down at the photocopy he'd made of the picture in Sally's bag. 'We can ask him if he recognises this man too.'

They left the police station, and as they walked round to the carpark Heffernan put on his jacket, which provided him with a thin veneer of sartorial respectability.

'Do you still think Sally Gilbert's death is connected with the lorry hijack?' Wesley asked as Heffernan struggled with his seat belt.

'Your guess is as good as mine. But I think there's something odd about the computers turning up at that shop. Almost looks like the work of amateurs.'

'I was thinking the same thing,' said Wesley. He pondered for a moment. 'And I think Peter Bracewell, our friendly neighbourhood bin man and discoverer of lost handbags, knows something about our Chadleigh Hall skeleton. He seemed uneasy when I mentioned it. Almost guilty.'

'Can you see him tying up a young girl and walling her up in that room?'

'In a word, Gerry, no. But I could be wrong, of course.' He thought for a few moments. 'If she was put in there alive she must have taken a while to die – wouldn't Miss Snowman have heard noises when she took over her office again?'

'Unless the girl was gagged. Or, of course, she might have been dead before she went in there.'

'Then why tie her up? Forensics say there were definitely traces of rope around her wrists and ankles – the old-fashioned stuff, not your modern synthetic type. Not that they've come up with anything else useful,' he added, disappointed. 'I want to see Jack Kilburn again. He definitely knew something.'

'It's just a matter of getting past those old gorgons who are supposed to be looking after him. And there's his slimy son, remember.'

'And this Alexandra Stanes, who went missing from the school. What do we know about her?'

'Someone's digging out the file as we speak, Wes.'

'What about her dental records?'

'They would only have been requested if an unidentified body had turned up and they thought it might be her. After all this time they might not even exist.'

'Not like you to be so pessimistic, Gerry. Have you heard anything more from Harry Marchbank?'

'Why do you ask?'

'No particular reason.'

'Harry Marchbank's someone I'd rather not think about. As far as I know he's still in hospital, but Steve'll be the one to ask. One of the great double acts of history, those two – Laurel and Hardy, Abbott and Costello ... Marchbank and Carstairs. I just hope they're not thinking of making a comeback.' He scratched the small piece of midriff that protruded from his straining shirt. 'How's your Pam?'

'Fine. She's going for lunch with Neil today.'

'He's not getting her diving, is he?'

'I hope not.'

'My Sam tried scuba diving once.'

'How is he?'

'He's working at a posh house on the road into Tradmouth. And you'll never guess who it belongs to.'

Wesley didn't even try.

'Only Sebastian Wilde's sister.'

'It's a small world,' said Wesley, his mind on his driving.

'Sam tells me that Wilde's son, Jason, has been hanging around there making the place look untidy. He reckons he comes to sponge off his auntie.'

Wesley glanced at the proud father who was sitting, beaming, in the passenger seat. He was a man unsuited to living alone, and Sam's and Rosie's homecoming had done wonders for his mood. He had been conducting a decorous semi-courtship with a widowed American lady called Mrs Green – but the relationship had become stuck at the level of friendship, and Wesley was unsure whether Sam and Rosie had even learned of her existence. She had recently moved away to live near her daughter in Scotland, and Wesley felt that it was about time the boss found some fresh female company – but he was no matchmaker.

They followed the road signs to Neston, and Wesley drove down the narrow A road, passing through villages and fields dotted with sheep and cows, grazing placidly in the rolling green landscape.

Soon they were sitting in Sebastian Wilde's office, sipping filter coffee from chunky green cups.

'Good news about the stuff turning up,' said Wilde with a fixed smile. 'Let's hope the rest is found soon.'

'Yes, sir. I'm sure it's only a matter of time.' Wesley gave the man a reassuring smile. 'I'm afraid the owner of the shop wasn't able to give us a very good description of the man who sold the computers to him. He was young but that's about all. Signed himself D. Duck on the receipt. But we're going over the stuff for fingerprints. If the thieves have a criminal record we'll catch them. The van driver's made a good recovery, I hear.'

'Yes, thank God. If he'd been badly injured . . .' Wilde shook his head. 'Well, it doesn't bear thinking about, does it?'

'Have you put in an insurance claim for the stolen goods?'

'Of course. But now some have turned up, I suppose . . .'

'Yes, sir. It might be as well to inform your insurers.'

Wilde didn't look too pleased about this and Wesley didn't blame him. It meant that whatever claim he had made would be delayed . . . and for all they knew, the rest of the stolen computers might not be recovered. It would hit Nestec's cash flow badly.

But Gerry Heffernan's mind wasn't on high technology. He leaned forward and looked Sebastian Wilde in the eye.

178

'You never said you were on Monks Island last Friday.'

Wilde looked somewhat alarmed. 'Should I have done? I didn't think it was important.' Beads of sweat had begun to moisten his brow.

'Sally Gilbert, the wife of your warehouse manager, was meeting someone on Monks Island. We've found evidence that she was murdered there. Was it you she'd arranged to meet?'

'No. Certainly not.' Wilde sounded quite offended. 'I was there for a meeting with the owners of the hotel. They're putting a new computer system in and Nestec are bidding for the contract. I went there myself because I thought it would be good business to give them the impression that they were dealing with the top man, if you see what I mean. It seemed to work. The meeting went very well. And before you ask, I didn't see Sally Gilbert. I arrived about eleven thirty; we had a working lunch – a very good one, incidentally – in the manger's office and I left as soon as our business had finished at around three o'clock.'

'A long meeting – eleven thirty till three,' Wesley commented.

'We had a lot to cover; all their hardware requirements and the software to go with it.'

'And you stayed in the manager's office the whole time?'

'I was given a guided tour of the hotel, but apart from that we were in his office, yes. I'm sure the hotel manager will confirm what I've told you. And the IT manager and the . . .'

'Thank you, sir. I'm sure that won't be necessary. Sally Gilbert had a cream tea at the hotel and then she was seen to go outside and meet somebody – this would be just after three o'clock. That somebody wasn't you, was it, sir? If you'd just finished your meeting and . . .'

'No, Inspector. It wasn't me. I didn't see Sally that afternoon.'

Wesley produced the photograph found in Sally's bag

and handed it to Wilde. 'Do you recognise this man?'

Wilde shook his head and handed the picture back. 'I'm sorry. I've never seen him before. Now if you'll excuse me . . .'

'Is Trevor Gilbert back at work?'

Wilde looked a little perplexed at the sudden change of subject. 'Yes. He's in the warehouse. Do you want to see him?'

Wesley and Heffernan looked at each other. 'We might have a very quick word . . . just see if he recognises the picture. We won't take up much of his time,' said Wesley.

'Not unless he has something to tell us,' Heffernan added with the hint of a threat.

As they left Wilde's office Wesley noticed that Gerry Heffernan was looking uncommonly pleased with himself.

'We've got him rattled, Wes,' he said softly as they climbed into the car. 'Sebastian Wilde is not a happy man.'

Pamela Peterson sat on a rock at the top of the beach, and stretched out her limbs in the warm rays of the sun. Peace at last. Shrieking gulls and crashing waves. No children clammering for her attention at school. No lesson plans and paperwork. No baby. No Della to visit in hospital. No Wesley getting in tired and late. Just sun on her face and sand between her toes. It couldn't last.

'Enjoying yourself?'

She opened her eyes and saw Neil looking down at her. 'You could say that.'

'We'll go for lunch in about half an hour, if that's okay. Want to come into the hut and see what we've found?'

This was the nearest Neil ever got to a proposition. She smiled and held out her hand. He took it and helped her up.

'You all right?' he asked, suddenly concerned.

''Course I am. Why?'

'It's just with you being . . .'

'I'm pregnant, Neil, not ill. I'm fine.' She touched his cheek playfully. 'Come on, let's see this hut of yours. Have you just been down to the wreck?'

He nodded.

'Exciting?'

'I suppose it is, in a funny sort of way.'

He led the way to the site hut. It was empty. Oliver Kilburn and Jason Wilde hadn't turned up as they had promised. Underwater archaeology was a laborious process and he presumed they had been lured away by more instant thrills.

The finds were laid out in a large water tank at the end of the room.

'There's no sign of all the gold coins and jewels that are supposed to be down there. Looks like the *Celestina* was carrying iron bars – pretty boring.'

'People always like a good story,' Pam said with a smile.

'Too right. But there were contemporary reports that the *Celestina* was carrying treasure.'

'Are you sure she wasn't?'

'We haven't found anything to indicate she was, let's just put it like that. Unless the wreckers got it all. Chadleigh's wreckers were notorious. They used to lure ships onto the rocks then nick anything they could lay their hands on.'

Pam thought for a moment. 'The wreckers would have been ordinary villagers, right? Wouldn't someone have noticed if they all started flashing round gold like a load of lottery winners?'

'Probably.' Neil scratched his head. 'Right, then, what have we found so far.' He consulted a clip board. 'There are some wooden artefacts, including a bucket, and quite a well-preserved shoe. Then there's an anchor, about fifty iron bars, covered in concretion, but you can make out the shape; a small selection of eighteenth-century coins; two small cannon – probably carried in case they were attacked by privateers; what looks like the remains of a sextant; a cooking pot; some fine blue-and-white pottery – probably from the captain's table; an eighteenth-century pistol plate; the ship's lantern; and last but not least, the ship's bell with what appears to be the name – which we'll be able to see once it's cleaned up. A marine conservation expert's coming over from Plymouth tomorrow to give us a hand.'

Pam nodded politely and peered at the dark, misshapen objects in the tank. When she looked up she saw that Neil was staring at her throat and her hand instinctively went up to the necklace she was wearing; the necklace Kayleigh Dilkes had given her.

'Nice necklace,' said Neil. 'Present from Wes or have you been treating yourself?'

Pam looked at him, surprised. Neil seldom noticed such things. 'Neither,' she answered. 'It's a gift from a grateful pupil.'

'Very nice. Looks like real gold.'

She hesitated. 'I think it is. That's the trouble.'

'How do you mean?'

'It's hallmarked but I've not told Wesley yet. I offered, very tactfully, to give it back to the kid's mother – I mean, the family aren't well off and I felt really embarrassed – but she wouldn't take it. I didn't press the matter because I didn't want to hurt the poor kid's feelings.'

'So what's the problem? Why are you keeping it a secret from Wes?'

She looked at Neil as though he was being particularly naive. 'Well, the mother's a cleaner so I thought there was a chance that she'd nicked it from somewhere. Mind you, she's reputed to have a lot of men friends and she did say it was an unwanted present.'

'Maybe it was.'

Pam shrugged. 'Probably. But you know what Wesley's like. Any possibility that it might be stolen goods and he'll turn into Mr Plod and say it puts him in an embarrassing position.'

Neil laughed. 'I've always thought that honesty was one of Wes's greatest faults.'

They were interrupted by a shy tapping on the café door. Neil gave Pam a questioning look before opening the door wide to find Robin Carrington standing on the threshold, shifting from foot to foot self-consciously, as though he didn't know whether he had a right to be there. Neil invited him in, and as he entered he glanced awkwardly at Pam. He had expected Neil to be alone.

'Me and Pam are going up to the Wreckers for lunch. Do you want to come?'

Carrington hesitated, weighing up the situation. After a few seconds he decided that Pam was no threat – probably a colleague or girlfriend of Neil's – and he felt he could do with a bit of company. 'Why not?' he answered, trying to sound enthusiastic.

The three made their way up the steep cliff path towards the lane at the top. Pam was wearing a long cotton dress, loose to camouflage her expanding waist. She held the hem over her arm as she climbed, and when she looked back she saw that Neil was hovering behind her solicitously, ready to steady her if she stumbled. Carrington walked some way behind him. She regretted that Neil had asked him. She could relax with Neil, whom she'd known for so long: but with Robin Carrington, the quiet stranger, she would have to be on her best behaviour.

She was tired when they reached the Wreckers; the climb and the walk had exhausted her, and the ancient wooden settles in the pub lounge weren't the most comfortable of seats for a pregnant woman with an aching back. But Carrington's presence forced her to be polite and hide her discomfort.

When Neil went to the bar to order their food and drinks, Carrington looked at Pam and smiled. 'You're a friend of Dr Watson's, then?'

'We met at university. He was sharing a flat with my husband. They were studying archaeology together. Are you here on holiday?'

'No. I'm down here working.'

'What do you do?' Pam asked.

'I trace people's ancestors. I'm working for an American

183

family called Smithers at the moment – researching their family tree. In fact it's lucky that I met Neil because the *Celestina*'s captain was an ancestor of my client. Apparently he married the daughter of the Iddacombes, the owners of a big house near here – Chadleigh Hall.'

'That sounds interesting,' said Pam politely. The man was talking quickly, as though something was making him nervous. Perhaps he was just awkward with strangers.

'So your husband's an archaeologist too?'

'Not exactly. He's a policeman. A detective.'

Maybe she was imagining it, but a momentary flash of shock crossed Robin Carrington's face before the mask of politeness returned. 'Really? I've seen a lot of police around here recently. A body was found in the cove, but I haven't heard much about it since, whether it was an accident or suicide or . . .'

'I really don't know. He doesn't tell me everything.' She didn't feel like discussing Wesley's work at that moment. She wanted a break.

When Neil returned with the drinks he sat himself down and looked at Robin. 'I went to see the Iddacombes this morning.'

'They're still about?' Pam said, surprised.

'Descendants of the hall's owners. Come down in the world like most of us. They didn't tell me anything that I didn't know already.' He looked at Pam. 'But they became very cagey when I mentioned that skeleton in Chadleigh Hall, so I reckon they knew something about it. Maybe Wes should have a word with them.'

Pam noticed that Robin Carrington was looking decidedly uncomfortable.

Then he gave an awkward smile. 'I found a book in Neston about the wreckers of Chadleigh and there's a reference to the *Celestina*. I thought you might like to borrow it, Neil.' He spoke with forced enthusiasm, and Pam had the feeling that he was trying to change the subject.

She picked up her mineral water, longing for a glass of

184

wine, and sat back, wriggling her bottom until she was more comfortable. She'd make the most of her leisurely lunch, even though she wasn't keen on Robin Carrington's company. A change was definitely as good as a rest.

Steve Carstairs planned to take a late lunch. He had something to report to Harry Marchbank – a spot of investigation he'd been carrying out in his rare idle moments. The others had thought he was working on the Sally Gilbert case or the Nestec robbery. But his last visit to Neston had been about something else altogether.

He had found Home from Home – motto 'We match the homeless with a home' – in a tiny back street in Neston. A pair of young men in torn black garments, beads and dreadlocks, who were hanging around outside passing a joint to each other, confirmed that he was in the right place. They had been too stoned, he thought, to realise that he looked more conventional than an average Home from Home client: in their state they probably wouldn't have noticed if he'd had two heads.

But the young woman on reception had all her wits about her and looked him up and down suspiciously. Steve knew her sort – a bolshie, police-hating, feminist with a ring through her nose, probably a lesbian. Having labelled her so efficiently, he was quite shocked when she smiled coquettishly at him, fluttered her eyelashes and proceeded to be helpful when he produced his warrant card. They never liked to get on the wrong side of the police, she explained. They ran a service for those in need, not criminals. The shock rendered Steve less aggressive than usual, and he managed to talk to the woman pleasantly and even ended up asking her out for a drink, which she declined on the grounds that she was washing her hair. But you couldn't win them all.

But he did elicit some interesting information before his untimely rejection. Home from Home had come to learn of a cottage just outside Millicombe that was empty – a

185

holiday home left unoccupied for most of the year. Nobody resembling Robin Carrington's photograph had sought Home from Home's services – the woman was quite sure of that – but a couple of weeks ago she had told some 'clients' about Old Coastguard Cottage. It belonged to some London lawyer and was used only for a couple of weeks a year: a criminal waste. The homeless couple and their dog who had gone to view the property had returned, rather annoyed, saying that it appeared to be occupied by a young dark-haired man with a silver-coloured car: Steve supposed this roughly answered Carrington's description.

Armed with this interesting snippet of information, Steve returned to Tradmouth and nursed it until he could visit Harry in hospital.

Feeling lucky for once, he hurried down the polished corridors of Tradmouth Hospital, like a dog anticipating a reward from his master.

Marchbank was waiting for him, sitting propped up against the stiff white pillows, frowning impatiently. His flesh had lost its pallor and he looked better; better and anxious to be out of there.

'Steve, my old mate. Good to see you. They're letting me out of here tomorrow – given me a clean bill of health. Well, not clean exactly. I've had to put up with all these bossy females harping on, telling me I shouldn't eat this and I shouldn't drink that.'

'I'd tell 'em to piss off and mind their own business,' Steve said cockily as he sat himself down.

'Don't tempt me. What have you found out for me, then? Any sign of Carrington?'

Steve gave him a smug grin. 'It might be nothing but I've been given an address – a cottage near Millicombe: little place called Chadleigh.'

'And you think he's there?'

Steve shrugged. 'A man answering his description was seen there.'

'Who by?'

186

'Pair of drop-outs looking for a squat.'

Marchbank grunted in disgust.

'The place is called Old Coastguard Cottage. It's pretty isolated by all accounts – on top of a cliff near Chadleigh Cove.'

'How did you find this out?'

'It's an empty holiday home. Some hairy squatters went along all ready to move in and found this young dark-haired bloke in residence. Carrington's young and dark-haired, isn't he? And they said he had a silver-coloured car and all.'

'It wasn't the owner of the house, then?'

'Apparently the owner only uses the place for a couple of weeks a year. He got fed up with the British weather and now he spends his holiday in Tuscany – or so they told me at the squat agency . . .'

'They've got an agency?'

'You'd be surprised what they've got in Neston – end of the bloody hippy trail it is.'

'So who does the cottage belong to?'

'Now that I have checked out. Some bloke from London called Jeremy Nichols.'

Harry Marchbank sat back, a smug smile on his lips.

'Carrington's alibi was provided by Jeremy Nichols – he's a solicitor but not the kind who's the cop's best friend, if you see what I mean. I bet he's lent him his holiday cottage. Now why didn't I check it out? If I'd known Nichols had property down here . . .'

'And Nichols knows Carrington's wanted for questioning?'

'He'll deny it, of course.'

'So what are we going to do?'

'When I get out of here I'll pay a visit to Old Coastguard Cottage. Maybe make an arrest.'

'I don't know whether Scouse Gerry'll let me . . .'

'There's no need for you to come. This one's mine. Just tell me exactly where this place is.'

Steve obliged. But then he looked at Harry Marchbank's face and saw an expression of vicious anticipation. Perhaps he'd better go along with him. Just in case he went too far.

'How's your day been, then, Steve? Got the knickers off that Trish yet?'

Steve grinned. 'Not had a chance. We've been that busy. There was a murder last Friday – some woman got herself pushed off a cliff and . . .'

'It's a popular pastime around here, getting pushed off cliffs.'

'What do you mean?'

'I remember a few years ago there was a woman got shoved off a cliff around this time of year,' Marchbank laughed.

'You joking?'

Harry shook his head. 'Nah. You look it up in the records.'

Steve looked at his watch. He was late. It was time to get back to the station before he was missed.

Trevor Gilbert sat in his tiny office overlooking the loading bay. He could see everything from there. And everyone in the warehouse could see him through the glass wall. Sometimes he felt like a Roman god looking down on the ant-like mortals below . . . but today his visibility made him feel vulnerable. He felt as though they were all watching and wondering. Wondering about Sally . . . and whether he'd killed her.

He hadn't let on to the police how he'd really felt. He hadn't told them about those moments of stark hatred when he'd known she was with another man . . . or talking over his faults and sexual inadequacies with that smug, empty-headed Lisa Marriott. He had longed to put his hands around Sally's throat and squeeze the life from her. He had longed to see her face contort into a mask of horror when she realised he wasn't the meek, accommodating creature she thought she had married. When she saw that the loyal dog had reared up to savage its mistress.

For years she had got the better of him: spending huge sums to get the house exactly as she wanted it; buying designer clothes they couldn't afford; demanding a new car to impress the neighbours; arranging loans; getting them into debt. And as soon as she had surrounded herself with all these possessions, she had left to seek pastures new, bored with her old life. Trevor had gone along with it all because he had loved her.

But now he had got used to the idea that she was gone it almost felt as though a burden had been lifted from his shoulders. She wouldn't distress him any more.

Trevor jumped when the telephone rang. He had almost forgotten he was back at Nestec; back in the real world and not the cocooned world of tea and sympathy ... or whisky and oblivion. He stared at the instrument for a while before answering it.

He put the receiver to his ear and muttered a hello.

'I'm trusting you, Trevor,' hissed a muffled voice at the other end of the line. 'Remember what I told you before. Keep your mouth shut. Okay?'

'Okay,' Trevor whispered before replacing the receiver with a trembling hand.

Trish Walton looked around the office for Steve. But he wasn't there. He had gone out on some mysterious lunch-time mission.

She bit into the cheese sandwich she'd bought in the canteen and opened the brown cardboard file on her desk. The chief inspector had asked her to find it and it had taken several phone calls to various stations before she had managed to track it down. It smelt rather musty, as though it had been stored in some dank cellar for many years. But then it was dated 1964 – a long time before she was born – so what else could she expect?

The name 'Alexandra Stanes' was scrawled in bold letters on the front. She put her sandwich to one side and leafed through the loose sheets of paper. The missing-person report. The description of the sixteen-year-old girl who had disappeared after a school tennis match on the ninth day of June 1964. The statements of her classmates and teachers. It seemed that she had been rather pre-occupied during the match and had lost two sets to love, even though she was one of the school's best players. Then, when the match was over, Alex, as she was known, had got changed and disappeared, taking a few clothes with her, never to be seen again.

A week later her parents, who lived in the Midlands, had received a letter with a London postmark, saying that Alex was safe and well. But they never heard from her again.

That was that. When the letter had arrived the police had lost interest, although they had gone through the motions of sending Alex's details to the Met.

She heard Rachel Tracey laugh and she looked up. Wesley Peterson had just come into the room and was standing by Rachel's desk, sharing some private joke. Trish gathered up Alexandra Stanes's file and walked over to him. DI Peterson was always approachable ... not like some.

'I've got the file on the girl who went missing from Chadleigh Hall, sir.'

Wesley took it from her and made for his desk. She followed him.

'Anything interesting?'

'She disappeared on the ninth of June. When were the workmen there?'

Wesley looked at Trish, impressed. If she had disappeared after the workmen had gone then it was unlikely that they were linked with her disappearance. Unless she had struck up a relationship with one of them. But then how could he have walled her up in the room once the work had finished?

'I don't know the exact dates. The headmistress just said the work was done in the summer term. Anything else?'

190

'I doubt that she's our skeleton, sir. It looks like she ran away all right. She took clothes with her and she even sent her parents a letter from London a week later. Here.'

She handed him a copy of the letter. It was typewritten and short. Strange, he thought, that she should have gone to the trouble of gaining access to a typewriter.

'Dear Mummy and Daddy,' it read. 'Please don't bother trying to find me. I'm very well and very happy. I won't cost you anything now. Alex.'

'Short and sweet. Not "Don't try to find me", "Don't *bother* trying to find me" – sounds as if she felt she was a burden to them. What do you think "I won't cost you anything" means?'

Trish shook her head. 'I don't know. Perhaps they were always moaning about how much the school fees were or something like that.'

'So she decided to teach them a lesson. She said she was *very* happy. A boy, do you think?'

'Well, it sounds like there was a boy or a man around somewhere. But that's just a guess. There's a statement in the file from Alexandra's best friend, a Carole Wilde. According to this Carole, Alex hadn't said anything definite about a boyfriend but she'd seen her talking to one of the young workmen on a few occasions. She said Alex wasn't the gossipy type, she was secretive, kept things close to her chest.'

Before Trish could say any more Gerry Heffernan emerged from his office. 'Wes!' he shouted, causing every-one in the room to look up from their work. 'What about them photos of Sally Gilbert's bloke? Are you getting someone to show them around to the people she knew or what?'

Heffernan sounded as though something was annoying him. And Wesley knew it couldn't be anything that had happened that day. He took the Alexandra Stanes file from Trish and followed the boss into his office.

'Anything wrong?'

'Wrong? What makes you think that? We've got two unsolved murders, an unsolved robbery and a room full of officers running around like headless chickens. What could be wrong?'

Wesley didn't answer. He knew Heffernan was letting off steam.

'And bloody Harry Marchbank's being let out of hospital tomorrow, so I've heard. Well, he's not having any of my team to help him with his little manhunt.'

Wesley nodded, suspecting that Marchbank's recovery had triggered the boss's bad mood.

'Trish has found the file on the missing schoolgirl.'

'Good. Bright girl, Trish,' Heffernan muttered absent-mindedly.

Wesley gave Heffernan a quick résumé of the file's contents before the chief inspector took it from him and placed it on his desk, where it had many similar files for company.

Heffernan took a copy of the photograph found in Sally Gilbert's handbag and waved it at Wesley. 'Stick it on the board, will you. And make sure everyone's got a copy.'

Wesley stepped into the outer office and walked over to the notice-board where the photographs and details relating to Sally's death were displayed. On a blackboard next to it was chalked a list of suspects, Heffernan's comments – some witty – beside each one. Wesley found a spare drawing pin and attached the photograph of the mystery man to the board before clearing his throat.

'Can I have a quick word, please, everyone.'

Faces looked up from desks. He had his audience's full attention.

'This photograph was found in Sally Gilbert's handbag. Now it's important that we find out who this man is. He could be the man Sally was seeing and we all know how important it is that we question him . . .'

'Sir. I know him.'

It was PC Carl McInnery who spoke. Everyone turned

towards him, curious. 'He works at Neston nick. He's in Traffic. His name's Mike Battersley.' McInnery flushed behind his freckles, as though uncertain whether he'd done the right thing.

'Anyone else know him?'

A couple more hands went up; people who'd seen him around but didn't know him well.

Wesley thanked McInnery and stood staring at the photograph for a few seconds. Mike Battersley – the Mike who'd eluded them since the investigation began – must be a prime suspect. But arresting a fellow police officer was not something Wesley was looking forward to.

Chapter Eight

I thought little of Mercy Iddacombe and Captain Smithers. I had the care of nigh on five hundred souls in the village of Millicombe itself and I spent a deal of time hunting in those days before the infirmities caused by a fall from my horse prevented it.

Mistress Iddacombe owned a fine house near the hamlet of Chadleigh. She seemed to me to be a most charming woman, and on those occasions she honoured me with an invitation to dine she talked of the ships she had inherited from her late husband, the cleverness of her son, James, the accomplishments of her daughters, Caroline and Mary Anne, and the virtues of the handsome captain of the Jane Marie, *Isaiah Smithers.*

James said little but the two young ladies were, I admit, pleasing, Caroline being the elder and prettier. Mary Anne, I thought, was a quiet creature, lacking her sister's conversation.

So it was that I was surprised one wet May evening when Mary Anne Iddacombe called upon me to request that I marry her in secret to Captain Isaiah Smithers.

From An Account of the Dreadful and Wicked Crimes of the Wreckers of Chadleigh *by the Reverend Octavius Mount, Vicar of Millicombe*

Mike Battersley had been on night duty and the two uniformed officers from Tradmouth who called on him to say that Chief Inspector Heffernan wanted a word about the death of Sally Gilbert found him asleep.

Battersley was a good-looking man in his early thirties whose dark hair and olive skin gave him a Mediterranean appearance and the need to shave twice a day. He dressed quickly, asking no questions, and emerged from the front door of his small terraced house bleary eyed and sporting an embryonic beard.

He said nothing in the police car. He had driven many people in trouble to Neston police station in the course of his work, but he had never before been on the receiving end. He stayed silent during the long wait he had to endure at Tradmouth, not speaking until he was facing Gerry Heffernan and Wesley Peterson in the interview room, tape rolling.

It was Gerry Heffernan who asked the first question. Mike Battersley knew Heffernan only by reputation – he appeared stupid but he wasn't. And he'd heard about the black inspector too. He was supposed to be clever – a cut above. The sight of the two sitting there, ready to analyse his every word, made Battersley's hands shake as he lit a cigarette.

'We found your photo in Sally Gilbert's handbag. Is there anything you'd like to tell us?' Heffernan beamed at him across the desk, inviting confidence.

'I was seeing Sally but it was all over. I've not seen her for about three weeks. Honestly.'

'But she still carried your photograph around in her bag. It can't have been all over as far as she was concerned,' Wesley Peterson stated reasonably.

'Who was it who finished the affair, Mike?' Heffernan leaned forward.

'Me,' Battersley whispered.

'Say that louder for the tape, please, Mike.'

'Me. I'd got fed up with her. All she was interested in was spending money. She kept wanting to go to all these expensive places and . . .'

'Including Monks Island?'

'Yeah. We had dinner there one night. In the end I reckoned it wasn't worth it. I couldn't afford her on my salary. She needed a millionaire.'

'She never paid her way?' Wesley asked.

'You must be joking. Spent all her money on clothes and make-up and she had a nice house too – all the latest stuff. Don't know how she managed it. I felt sorry for her poor husband, if you want the truth. If you're looking for Sally's killer I reckon you should be looking at that poor sod. Don't know how he stood it, myself. Her spending like there was no tomorrow, then messing around with me. And even after he had her back she walked out on him. I bet she pushed him that little bit too far and he snapped.'

'Where were you on Friday twentieth July?' Wesley kept his tone formal. He had a sneaking suspicion that Mike Battersley might be right about Trevor Gilbert, but he wasn't going to let him know that.

'I'd been up all night scraping some young tearaway off the Exeter road. He'd nicked a car and turned it over – didn't live to tell the tale. I did some shopping when I came off duty then I went to bed around noon. Got up again around six and had something to eat.'

'Any witnesses?'

'I live on my own.'

'So there's nobody who can confirm your story?'

'No.'

'Why did Sally keep your affair so secret? She never made much effort to keep it from Trevor and yet you never met her friends. Why was that?'

'Because I was still with my wife at the time. She threw me out three weeks ago when she found out I'd been seeing Sally. Okay?'

Wesley looked him in the eye. 'You must have been angry with Sally for breaking up your marriage.'

Battersley stubbed out his cigarette violently.

'Did you send her any letters?'

'Why should I do that?'

'Did you send her a letter a few days before she died asking to meet her?'

'No. Of course I didn't.'

'When did you last see her?'

'I told you. About three weeks ago.'

'Did you and Sally quarrel?'

Battersley looked awkward. 'Doesn't everybody?'

'Were the quarrels ever violent?'

Battersley shook his head. He looked tired and unshaven. He looked as though he'd had enough.

Gerry Heffernan pointed an accusing finger. 'I think you arranged to meet Sally Gilbert at Monks Island. I think you had a row. I think you shoved her off the cliff top and stamped on her hands when she tried to hold on. I had a little look at your record before you were brought in. Nasty temper you've got. You were disciplined for punching a fellow officer a while back when you were working at a nick in Plymouth. Did Sally say something that made you lose your temper, Mike?'

'No.'

'Come on, Mike, we've all been there. Women can be very unreasonable, can't they. Is that why you did it, Mike? Wouldn't she let go? She still carried your picture about ...'

'I didn't see her that day. Why won't you believe me?'

Mike Battersley's clenched fist came down on the table with a bang, making three discarded plastic cups jump up and land on their sides. Cold coffee spilled out and oozed across the table. Wesley took a clean white handkerchief from his pocket and cleaned up the mess.

'Temper, temper,' said Heffernan, a slight smirk playing on his lips. 'I think we'll take a break now. Let's hope that by the time we come back, you'll have decided to tell us the truth.'

Gerry Heffernan stood up and swept from the room like a galleon in full sail. Wesley nodded to the constable sitting by the door, who returned the suspect to an unwelcoming cell.

Wesley caught up with his boss in the corridor. 'What do you think, Gerry? Is he our man?'

'If it's not the husband, it's usually the boyfriend.'

'I suppose so ... statistically speaking. But we're not dealing with statistics, are we?'

'My money's on Battersley – he's got a temper. And if it's not him, I'd say it's Trevor. Neither of them have got alibis and they've both got thumping great motives. It's just a matter of finding out which one and locking him up.' He looked at Wesley and saw doubt in his eyes. 'You're not convinced by my brilliant argument?'

'Why arrange to meet at Monks Island? That shows some degree of planning. Has Trevor Gilbert's place been searched?'

'Yes. There's nothing incriminating and Forensics haven't come up with anything to link him to Monks Island.'

Wesley nodded. He had some sympathy with Trevor Gilbert.

'Mike Battersley's car's being examined now and his house searched.'

'Let's hope they find something.'

Heffernan scratched his head. He'd hoped to be back in time for a civilised meal with his son and daughter, but it looked as if he'd be working late.

On their return to the CID office, Trish Walton bustled forward, a piece of paper in her hand. 'There's been a phone call from Lisa Marriott. She says to let you know that she's found the envelope. Does that make sense?'

Heffernan looked blank. Wesley thought for a few moments. Then he remembered.

He turned to Heffernan. 'The envelope Sally Gilbert received just before her death. The letter she seemed so excited about. Lisa said she took the letter with her and left the envelope. She thought it looked official – as if it was from a solicitor or someone like that. We didn't find a letter in her bag,' he added significantly.

'Right, Trish, ring Lisa Marriott back and tell her to hold on to it.' Heffernan looked at his watch. 'We'll be round soon – probably tomorrow at this rate. Okay?'

Trish hurried off. Heffernan watched her brush against Steve Carstairs' desk. Steve looked up at her and winked and she gave him a coquettish smile in return.

'Well, Wes, I think that while Mike Battersley's down in the cells contemplating the error of his ways, we should pop over to Nestec and have another word with Trevor Gilbert. Give him a nice surprise.'

Wesley sighed. He'd told Pam he'd try to be home early so that she could visit her mother, who was now out of hospital and struggling on crutches. But it couldn't be helped – Della would just have to cope on her own. And Pam should be taking it easy anyway, not running around after her mother. Perhaps his working late would give Pam an excuse to put her feet up.

They left the station and headed for Neston to see Sally Gilbert's husband. Or was he more than a husband? Was he her murderer?

'So the *Celestina* belonged to the owner of Chadleigh Hall?' Jane asked as she struggled out of her diving suit.

Neil was sitting on the concrete steps outside the café, drinking from a can of Coke. 'Yes. She was owned by a widow called Mercy Iddacombe. She inherited seven ships from her husband when he died. He was mayor of Tradmouth at one time – a solid citizen. They had a posh town house in Tradmouth – Ship Street, not far from the church. And when the money started rolling in her husband bought an estate out at Chadleigh.'

'Go on,' said Jane. 'What else have you found out?'

Neil took another swig from his can and made himself comfortable on his makeshift seat. 'I found a book about Tradmouth shipping in the library: it said that Mercy was known as a bit of a dragon – knew everything that was going on aboard her ships. Her operation was certainly profitable. She started off with seven ships and ended up with fifteen. Doubled her money.'

'Good for her,' said Jane.

'Found anything interesting down there today?'

'More of those iron bars, by the look of it. Not a sign of any treasure.'

'Perhaps the Chadleigh wreckers found it – but if they did, we'll never know.'

'Or maybe Mercy Iddacombe was working an insurance scam – saying crates were full of treasure when they were really full of old iron. It's been known.'

'Maybe. It'd be an interesting story if we can prove it.'

'Have you noticed how Dominic Kilburn seems to have lost interest now it looks as though his treasure doesn't exist?'

'Mmm. And his son and his mate haven't turned up to "help" for a few days. With the rights to the wreck Kilburn might have been a rich man. Somehow it makes you glad we haven't found that gold, doesn't it?'

Jane smiled. 'There'll be no more diving today so Matt and I are going back to the cottage.'

Neil watched her go, climbing up the steep pathway to the top of the cliff. He'd work for a while then go back to the cottage to play gooseberry. He wished Pam had stayed longer. He had enjoyed her company.

'What is it?' said Trevor Gilbert when Gerry Heffernan appeared at the door of his tiny office. The words came out in a nervous squeak. Gilbert looked terrified. Dark patches underscored his eyes and he hadn't shaved or ironed his shirt, as though the effort of turning up to work looking reasonably smart had been too much for him.

'We just thought you'd like to know that we're questioning a man in connection with your wife's death. Ever heard of a Michael Battersley?'

'Is that who ... is that who she was seeing? Did the bastard kill her?'

Trevor spat out the question with controlled venom, but Wesley had the impression that the emotion was feigned, that the words were half hearted; almost as though he had lost interest.

'We're still questioning him,' Wesley said, non-committally. He wasn't sure but he thought he could detect a momentary wave of relief pass across Trevor Gilbert's face. 'We'll keep you up to date with any developments.'

Heffernan gave a discreet nod. It was time to go. They had relayed the news to Gilbert and now wasn't the time to begin any in-depth questioning. Wesley turned, and he could see curious faces staring at the office; Trevor Gilbert's colleagues wondering what the police had to say. Or perhaps wondering whether Trevor was being arrested for his wife's murder. There was nothing like a visit from the police to relieve the boredom of the working day.

The two policemen walked across the concrete forecourt, narrowly avoiding being hit by a white van with the Nestec logo on the side which swept up to the loading bay too fast for safety. Gerry Heffernan mumbled something under his breath that Wesley thought it best to ignore.

A familiar figure emerged from the office entrance. Sebastian Wilde was with a boy who bore a striking resemblance to him: his son, no doubt. A chip off the old block. Wilde spotted them and strolled over, taking his time. He was smiling with his mouth but his eyes weren't joining in.

'Chief Inspector, what can I do for you? Is there any more news about my computers?'

The boy with him stared at the ground, as though he would have preferred to have been elsewhere.

'Not yet. We'll let you know. We just called in to tell Mr Gilbert that a man's being questioned in connection with the murder of his wife.'

'I'd appreciate it if you'd let me know you were on the premises in future, Chief Inspector.' There was a more than

201

a hint of reproach in the man's voice.

'We didn't want to bother you. This your lad, is it?' Heffernan grinned at the youth, who was standing slightly behind his father, looking awkward.

'Yes. This is my son, Jason. I'm giving him a lift to my sister's place, so if you'll excuse us . . .'

Wesley stood aside to let them through and the two men watched as father and son made their way to a sleek red Jaguar standing in a parking space marked 'Managing Director'.

'Do you get the feeling that we we're not exactly welcome, Wes?' Heffernan said as he watched the Jaguar drive away.

'Some people just don't appreciate us,' Wesley replied with a smile.

After they had been driving for a few minutes, Gerry Heffernan began to feel in his jacket pockets. Then he swore under his breath.

'What's the matter?'

'I've left my keys at home and Rosie's out this afternoon. I'll have to get Sam's. The place he's working is just along this road. Gallows House. Keep a look out for it, eh.'

Carole Sanders had just returned home from work when she heard the door bell. A visitor. She wasn't expecting anyone.

She smoothed her hair before rushing to answer the door. When she reached the hall she saw that a little girl of about nine was sitting on the stairs playing with an electronic hand-held game. Kayleigh. Carole knew that Brenda brought her here for free food and any other unconsidered trifles that could be snapped up. But she didn't mind: good cleaners were hard to find and Brenda was useful in many ways. She smiled at Kayleigh as she passed and Kayleigh smiled back.

She opened the front door and found a man standing in the porch. He wasn't particularly tall but he was well built with an untidy shock of hair and, in spite of his jacket, shirt and tie, a generally uncared-for appearance. Behind him stood a smartly dressed, good-looking young black man with watchful, intelligent eyes.

'Sorry to bother you, love,' began the older man. 'But is a Sam Heffernan working here?'

'Er, yes, he's in the garden, but ...' Carole sounded wary.

'I'm his dad. I've forgotten me keys so I came to borrow his.'

Carole's expression softened. 'Please come in. Sorry I'm a bit disorganised but I've only just come in from work.' She stood aside. 'Go through to the kitchen. Would you like a cup of tea?'

'Normally I wouldn't say no, love. But I've got to get back home.'

Gerry Heffernan was beaming broadly as he entered the huge kitchen and Wesley noticed that he was watching the woman appreciatively as she disappeared out of the back door.

'Very nice, this, Wes,' Heffernan announced appreciatively, looking around. Wesley felt vaguely embarrassed. Gerry Heffernan looked as if, given half a chance, he'd get his feet well and truly under the table.

The woman reappeared. 'I've told Sam you're here, Mr Heffernan. I'm Carole Sanders, by the way.'

Heffernan beamed. 'Call me Gerry, please. And this is Wesley Peterson.'

'Pleased to meet you. I believe you're a policeman, Gerry?'

'Our Sam's told you, has he?'

'And you, Mr Peterson?' Wesley couldn't decide whether there was approval in Carole's voice.

'Yes.'

'It makes me feel very safe having two policemen in the house,' said Carole lightly.

There was a moment of awkwardness, of hesitation,

when nobody knew quite what to say.

Carole broke the silence. 'Are you sure you won't have that cup of tea?'

'No thanks,' said Wesley quickly, thinking of Pam. 'We'd better not be long.'

'Sam tells me your daughter's studying music, Gerry,' said Carole, making conversation.

Wesley noticed a thin little girl peep round the kitchen door and disappear. He wondered who she was. Carole Sanders looked too old to have a child that age. Perhaps it was a grandchild.

'Yeah. She's marvellous. She's got herself a job playing the piano at the posh hotel down the road.' Heffernan beamed with paternal pride.

'Are you musical? Does it run in the family?'

He blushed. 'Well, I sing in the choir at St Margaret's.'

Before Carole Sanders could comment the door was flung open and a young man burst into the room. 'Auntie Carole, is it okay if . . .?' Jason Wilde stopped when he saw Gerry Heffernan and stood rooted to the spot, his mouth opening and closing like that of goldfish.

Wesley made the connection. Carole Sanders was Sebastian Wilde's sister. Jason was her nephew.

'This is my nephew, Jason,' she said with what sounded like affection.

'We met earlier.' Now that he looked at Carole, he could see a resemblance between her and her brother, Sebastian Wilde.

'Not professionally, I hope.' It was hard to tell whether she was joking.

'Not really. We went to Nestec to see one of the staff and your nephew was there with his father.'

'About that terrible robbery . . . the lorry being hijacked?'

'Something like that,' Heffernan said non-committally. 'Well, I'd better get the keys off Sam and let Wesley here get back to his missus and kiddie.' He felt a sudden desire o keep the conversation going. 'He's got another on the way, you know.'

Carole smiled shyly and turned to Wesley. 'Congratulations. When's the baby due?'

'Not for a while yet. November.'

'Is your wife keeping well?'

'She's a bit tired. She teaches at Tradmouth primary school so she'll be able to put her feet up now term's finished. Do you have any children, Mrs Sanders?'

Carole smiled sadly. 'No, I haven't,' she answered. Wesley wished he'd never asked.

Jason Wilde had been hovering on the threshold. He muttered something to his aunt about going to find Brenda, then he disappeared in a cloud of embarrassment.

Once Jason had left the room, Gerry Heffernan hesitated, reluctant to leave.

But Wesley thought he'd better make a move. 'We'll go out the back way and pick up Sam's keys. It's been very nice to meet you, Mrs Sanders.'

'Yeah,' Heffernan agreed, his eyes glowing. 'I hope we meet again.'

'Maybe you can stay for a cup of tea next time.' Carole Sanders smiled at Heffernan, a hint of something in her eye that Wesley thought might have been a come-on. Perhaps Gerry's luck was in at last.

Sam was cleaning himself up at the garden tap when they found him. He announced that he had finished for the day and begged a lift. There was no sign of his colleagues, Keith and Andy: they had sneaked off half an hour ago.

'Nice woman, that Carole,' Heffernan said to Wesley in a low voice as he climbed into the passenger seat of the car. Sam sat in the back, happy to be chauffeured.

'Mmm.' Wesley was concentrating on getting out of the gateway of Gallows House, awkwardly situated near cross-roads on a blind bend.

'Carole Sanders. Carole Wilde as was,' Heffernan

mused. 'I've heard that name today but I can't remember where.'

Wesley Peterson was relaxing in the bosom of his loving family when Steve Carstairs parked his new car, his gleaming black pride and joy, outside the Royal Oak and strolled inside, hands in the pockets of the expensive leather jacket he wore come rain or shine.

He looked around the pub and spotted Harry Marchbank in the corner. Harry hadn't wanted to meet at the Star as it was likely that Heffernan would be in there on a Friday evening. Harry had a pint of bitter and a whisky chaser lined up in front of him as though he was in for a heavy night. He hardly looked like a man who had just been discharged from hospital. And at the rate he was going, Steve thought, he'd soon be back in there if he didn't watch out.

Steve went to the bar and ordered himself a pint and another for Harry. A thin, fair-haired woman standing at the bar in an outfit that left little to the imagination, looked him up and down and smiled. But he wasn't in a position to take advantage of anything she had to offer. Harry was waiting.

Harry growled a greeting and accepted his fresh pint. 'I bloody need this after being stuck in that place,' he said before downing his whisky in one.

'Should you be, er . . .'

'Oh, don't you bloody start. Any developments?'

'Not since I saw you last.'

'I want to check out that cottage tomorrow. Coming with me if Scouse Gerry lets you off the lead?'

'I would but we've got a lot on at the moment and I don't know if . . .'

'I'll come in first thing and use my powers of persuasion – cooperation between forces and all that.'

'Best of luck.' Steve stared into his half-empty pint glass. The pub was beginning to fill up; mainly with well-heeled locals and yacht owners.

After a few seconds of silence Steve spoke. 'Harry.'

'What?'

'You know what you said about that woman getting pushed off a cliff?'

'Yeah.'

'Was anyone charged?'

'Why do you ask?'

'I just wondered.'

Harry thought for a few moments. 'Stan Jenkins was in charge of the case. It was a girl from Neston – worked in a building society. Marion somebody. She lived with her parents and she just went out one day without telling anyone where she was going and her body was found at the foot of the cliffs at Little Tradmouth – signs of a struggle at the top. The boyfriend was brought in but there wasn't enough evidence to stick so he was never charged. And now there's the one you told me about – the woman on Monks Island. It sounds similar.'

'You're sure?'

'Why?'

Harry saw that Steve was looking serious, deep in thought. Not like Steve at all.

'Ah, forget it, Steve. Think how many cliffs there are around this coast – people are bound to get pushed off them from time to time, especially in summer when quarrelling couples go for walks and that.' He shook his head and smiled. 'You're not getting conscientious in your old age, are you? Is it our coloured friend's influence, eh? Or are you trying to impress that Trish with your brilliant deductive powers so that you can get her into bed? Come on, you've got better things to do at your age than to start imagining that some loony's going round pushing people off cliffs.'

'What happened to this Marion's boyfriend?'

'If I remember right, he emigrated to Australia shortly after.' Harry stood up and thrust his hand into his pocket. 'Have another drink.'

As Steve sat alone, staring into what remained of his

beer, he concluded that Harry was probably right. There was nothing in it.

Gerry Heffernan spent Friday night at choir practice at St Margaret's and had a quick drink with a couple of tenors in the Star afterwards. But when he went to bed at 11.30 he couldn't sleep. He found himself thinking of Carole Sanders: imagining himself taking her for dinner, taking her flowers that would be received with gushing delight. Dinner at Monks Island – minus the censorious head waiter – followed by a moonlit walk.

He told himself he was being silly, like a schoolboy smitten with a girl he'd seen on the school bus. And he was being disloyal to Kathy's memory. He rolled over in an attempt to make himself more comfortable.

Perhaps it was meant. Perhaps Sam going to work at Gallows House and him forgetting his key was all part of the Great Scheme of Things.

Maybe he'd have a word with Wesley – ask his opinion. He'd mention Carole and see what he thought.

Carole Sanders – née Wilde. He'd heard the name Carole Wilde but he couldn't remember where. He closed his eyes and tried to stop thinking. It was time to get some sleep.

But just as he was nodding off it came to him suddenly, leaping up from the depths of his memory. The name had been in the file on Alexandra Stanes's disappearance. Carole Wilde had been Alexandra's best friend.

With this thought circulating in his head and the night too clammy for comfort, Gerry Heffernan didn't get to sleep for another couple of hours.

'Sir, can I have a word?' Steve Carstairs hovered on the threshold of Heffernan's office. It was half past eight on Saturday morning and, the chief inspector thought, too early for one of Steve's 'words' which usually presaged a report of some cock-up or other.

'Can't it wait?' Heffernan felt as lousy as if he'd had a

night on the town – but he didn't even have the satisfaction of a good time remembered. 'Is Inspector Peterson about yet?'

'No, sir.' Steve felt smug at the thought that Wesley was late.

'Tell him I want a word as soon as he comes in.'

'Sir, I was talking to Harry Marchbank last night.'

Heffernan looked up. Steve saw that he looked tired. 'So? Hope he's not been leading you off the path of righteousness . . . not that you ever needed much leading.'

Steve's face reddened. 'It's about this suspect he's looking for. He thinks he's tracked him down and he'd like some back-up when he makes the arrest. I'm willing to go with him.'

'I'm sure you are. But I've got other little treats in store for you. I want you to contact every computer shop within a forty-mile radius and see if any more of Nestec's stolen goods have turned up – that'll include Plymouth, Morbay and Exeter, so it'll keep you out of mischief for a while.' Heffernan grinned wickedly as Steve bit back his resentment.

'Perhaps I'll allow Marchbank to take a couple of uniforms with him if I'm feeling generous. Is he going to let me know when he wants this back-up or am I supposed to read his mind?'

'He says he'll let you know later.'

'That's good of him. I suppose he'll show his face as soon as he's read the paper and his butler's run his bath for him. What does he think we're doing? Sitting on our backsides twiddling our thumbs all day, waiting in case he has a villain he wants catching?' He muttered something under his breath that Steve couldn't quite make out.

Steve was rescued from further embarrassment by Wesley's arrival. He scurried out of the office, barely acknowledging Wesley as he strolled in.

Heffernan stood up, his initial tiredness fading. 'Wes. I remembered last night where I'd heard the name Carole

Wilde. She was Alexandra Stanes's best mate and she was interviewed when she disappeared. Mrs Sanders is Sebastian Wilde's sister – she was Carole Wilde before she married. I think we should have a word with her.'

'But is she the right Carole Wilde?'

'No harm in asking.' Heffernan grinned.

'Is Sam over there today?'

'No. Unlike some of us, he's got the weekend off. If we time it right we'll get to Mrs Sanders' in time for morning coffee, eh?' Heffernan smoothed his hair and looked down at his newly ironed shirt. Wesley sniffed the air. There was an unusual and not unpleasant smell. Aftershave. Gerry Heffernan was wearing aftershave.

Wesley thought that it would be best to say nothing. But he'd have something to report to Pam after work.

'Don't forget we said we'd visit Lisa Marriott about that envelope she found – the one Sally Gilbert's mysterious letter came in. She said she'd be at the hotel today but she'd take the envelope with her if we wanted to call in and get it.'

'Good. Rosie's playing the piano in the hotel restaurant this lunch-time. We'll go over and listen.' He hit his head with his hand as though he'd just remembered something. 'Oh no, I can't go. I've got a meeting with the Chief Super at twelve. You'll have to take Rachel. Anyway, I don't suppose Rosie'd want her old dad embarrassing her. Poor lass, all this cleaning's given her hands like a washerwoman. Still, these students need the money these days. Pity they haven't got a rich dad like that Jason Wilde.'

Wesley didn't comment. But from the little he'd seen of Jason Wilde, he hardly seemed a good advert for the merits of having money in the family.

An hour later they were driving out of Tradmouth, up the steep hill at the side of the Naval College and past the council estate. Just before they reached the open country, they turned into the drive of Gallows House.

The little girl they had seen the day before was amusing herself outside, throwing a tennis ball against the wall near the kitchen. She could hardly play in the garden because it looked like a bombsite: the pond was dug but not yet lined and wooden fencing lay around in neatly wrapped piles.

When Carole Saunders answered the door she invited them in, smiling but looking slightly puzzled. Wesley began by asking who the little girl was and Carole told him it was Kayleigh, her cleaner's daughter. Brenda was working at the Tradfield Manor that day so Carole was looking after her. Not that Kayleigh needed much looking after. She was a sweet little thing.

Wesley tried to think where he'd heard the names before. Then he remembered. It was a Kayleigh who had given Pam that necklace she had taken to wearing: and Pam had mentioned that Kayleigh's mother was called Brenda and worked as a cleaner. It was too much of a coincidence. It must be the same one.

Once they had mugs of freshly brewed coffee in their hands, Heffernan sat like a dumbstruck schoolboy and allowed Wesley to do the talking. He came straight to the point.

'Were you at Chadleigh Hall school in the sixties?'

Carole looked surprised. 'Yes, I was. Why?'

'It's just that we came across your name – your maiden name – in one of our files. You were friendly with a girl who disappeared from the school – Alexandra Stanes?'

'Yes. She went off to London.'

'Did she confide in you at all?'

Carole hesitated. 'Alex was always quite secretive. I thought she was planning something but she never told anyone what it was – not even me.'

'Who did you think she'd gone off with?'

'I don't know. Someone said she'd had a boyfriend up where her parents lived . . . in the Midlands somewhere. As I said, she was a very private sort of girl. She never told secrets. If she'd had any, we wouldn't have known.'

'But it said in the file you were her best friend,' Wesley said, looking the woman in the eye. He had a sister and he

211

knew that teenage girls normally confided their innermost feelings to a 'best friend'. But perhaps in the repressive atmosphere of Miss Snowman's school for young ladies, such things were discouraged and the old British virtue of 'keeping yourself to yourself' had reigned supreme. Times change.

'That doesn't mean she told me everything. We all have things that we would rather remained secret, Inspector Peterson. Perhaps she was afraid that if someone else knew she was planning to run away it would get back to one of the staff and she would be stopped. Alex never seemed happy at Chadleigh Hall. But then the educational ethos of the time didn't exactly encourage personal happiness.'

'We know,' said Wesley. 'We've met Miss Snowman.'

'Then you'll know what I mean.'

'Yes, I do. My mother-in-law went to Chadleigh Hall. She was in one of the years below you, I believe. Della Kelly.'

Carole thought for a moment. 'The name's familiar but we didn't have much to do with any of the younger girls, I'm afraid. Miss Snowman had strict views on desirable friendships,' she added with a sad smile.

'Miss Snowman said Alexandra was easily led. What do you think she meant by that?'

'I've really no idea. I wouldn't have described Alex that way, far from it. Perhaps she got her mixed up with someone else. She must be quite elderly by now so perhaps her memory's not what it was.'

Wesley opened his mouth to speak but Gerry Heffernan, still sitting on the edge of the settee with his mug in his hand and on his best behaviour, cleared his throat. 'Do you remember some builders who were working there around the time Alexandra disappeared?'

'Yes. It was Jack Kilburn and his son Dominic. My nephew, Jason, is very friendly with Dominic's son Oliver. Dominic Kilburn never noticed me all those years ago, of course. But we noticed him all right. He was very good looking in those days.'

'What about the other lad who was working there – Peter Bracewell?'

'I'm sorry, I don't remember. Why are you asking all these questions about Alex? Her parents received letters saying she was safe. Surely . . .'

Wesley interrupted. 'I don't know whether you read in the local paper that the skeleton of a young woman was found at Chadleigh Hall. There was evidence that she might have been killed around the date Alexandra disappeared. So you see . . .'

Carole Sanders' hand went to her mouth. 'Oh dear. I don't know what to say.'

Wesley had an idea. 'Do you know if Alexandra had had any dental work done? You see, the skeleton has no fillings or . . .'

'No, I'm sorry; I can't remember.'

'And there's nothing more you can tell us?'

Carole shook her head.

'I'm sorry we've given you such a shock, love,' Heffernan said gently, edging a little closer to her on the settee.

She gave him a weak smile. 'I'll be fine. But I'm sure you're wrong. I'm certain Alex went off to London.'

Wesley watched as his boss put a comforting hand momentarily upon Carole's. He withdrew it almost immediately and blushed. Wesley stood up.

'If you remember anything, anything at all, please let us know,' he said with formal politeness.

'I will.' She looked at Gerry Heffernan and smiled shyly.

Definitely something to report to Pam. Given how tired she had looked that morning when he had left for work, she needed something to cheer her up. Perhaps he'd take her some flowers tonight along with the news that Cupid seemed to be taking aim at Gerry's heart.

Carole saw them out, standing smiling at the door to wave them off. But as soon as their car was out of the drive, she rushed back to the hall table, looked up a number in the address book that was lying there, and picked up the telephone.

'Do you think it's time we tracked down Alexandra Stanes's parents?' Wesley asked when they returned to the station.

'Mmm. But it's not something I'm looking forward to. How do you tell someone their daughter might have died like that, eh?'

Wesley shuddered. He had no answer to the question. He was almost glad that he had his forthcoming call on Lisa Marriott at the Tradfield Manor Hotel to take his mind off it.

When he and Rachel arrived at the hotel they made for the health spa, where they found Lisa in her crisp white uniform sipping coffee, sitting, feet dangling, on a high hospital couch. She had kicked her high-heeled shoes off for comfort and looked faintly embarrassed as they walked in.

'I was just having my break – my next client's not due till eleven thirty.' She sounded as if she was trying to convince them she wasn't shirking. Not that they cared either way – but Wesley supposed Dominic Kilburn, the hotel's owner, might.

Rachel smiled to put Lisa at her ease. 'Have you got the envelope for us, the one from the letter Sally seemed so excited about?'

Lisa slid down from the couch. 'Yes. I put it in a plastic bag for you like I've seen them do on the telly. I thought that was the right thing to do if it might be evidence.' She said the last word with relish.

She delved into her capacious handbag and brought out a plastic bag containing a seemingly undamaged envelope. TV police dramas had their uses.

Wesley took it from her and examined it. It was a thick cream-coloured envelope with a discreet pale blue stripe running along its gummed edge; it was good quality, expensive. The address was typed – the address Sally had shared with Trevor Gilbert – but it had been tidily crossed out and Lisa's address written above in small neat letters after the words 'Please forward, thank you'. Trevor was a man who remembered his manners. The words 'Strictly private and confidential' were typed in the top left-hand corner and the envelope was postmarked Tradmouth and dated the Saturday before Sally's death.

There was no hint of what it had contained. No firm's name printed on the envelope; no sender's address written on the back. It certainly looked to Wesley like the type of solid, reliable envelope used by professionals; accountants, solicitors or architects. But without a name they had no way of knowing. He had a feeling that the envelope wasn't going to be much help, but they took it away with them, just in case.

They left Lisa enjoying what was left of her coffee. It struck Wesley that he had never actually encountered Lisa when she was doing any work, her 'clients' being always imminent but never actually there.

Rachel looked into his eyes and gave a shy smile. 'Anything else you want to do while we're here, Wesley? Massage, swim in the pool, slap-up lunch?' She sounded as if she'd be keen to take on all three. But Wesley assumed she was joking.

'Another time, perhaps. The boss's daughter's playing piano in the restaurant this lunch-time but I don't suppose we can go in and say hello without eating something.'

'Pity,' said Rachel as they began to walk towards the reception area.

Wesley spotted a woman dressed in neat navy blue disappearing into a lift ahead of them carrying an armful of files. She looked familiar, and after a few seconds he remembered where he'd seen her before. 'Isn't that Peter Bracewell's wife?' he whispered. 'What was her name? Sandra?'

Rachel nodded. 'She must work here.' She looked

around. 'I must say I'm impressed with the Tradfield Manor. It's a nice place.'

'Pam and I are coming here for dinner tonight. There's a special offer on – two meals for the price of one.'

Rachel said nothing.

'I believe the food here's very good,' Wesley continued. 'You should try it while the offer's still on.'

'Not much fun eating on your own,' she said sharply, regretting the words as soon as they left her mouth. Self-pity wasn't an attractive emotion.

But before Wesley could reply, he spotted two young men walking past the reception desk. There was something furtive about them, as if they were up to something. Wesley stopped dead.

'What is it?' Rachel asked in a whisper.

'That's Jason Wilde – Sebastian Wilde's son: I saw him yesterday. And that lad with him's Oliver Kilburn: he was at Chadleigh Cove when Sally Gilbert's body was found. His dad owns this hotel.'

'What do you think they're up to?'

Wesley grabbed a leaflet advertising local visitor attractions from a wooden rack and pretended to study it. 'They might recognise me,' he whispered to Rachel. 'You stand in front of me and keep an eye on what they're doing.'

'A woman's come out to meet them.' Rachel spoke in a low undertone. 'She's wearing an overall – looks like a cleaner or a chambermaid. She's giving them something. Looks like a key.'

Wesley couldn't resist turning to see what was going on. The boys and their female companion seemed engrossed in their own affairs, unaware that they were being watched.

Suddenly Mike Cumberland, the hotel manager, emerged from his office and the woman hurried away as though she knew she wasn't supposed to be there.

Wesley saw Oliver Kilburn give Cumberland an arrogant stare and stroll off towards a door marked 'Staff only' with

Jason Wilde following behind. The boss's son, apparently, could get away with anything.

As soon as they were out of sight, Wesley and Rachel marched up to the reception desk.

Steve Carstairs was triumphant. He had finished his phone calls in good time, confirming that no Nestec computers had been offered to any other outlet in the area. Then Gerry Heffernan, who seemed to be in an uncommonly good mood, had relented and told him he could go and help Harry Marchbank with his search for Robin Carrington.

Steve drove, navigating his nearly new Ford Probe along the narrow lanes, fearing for his glossy paintwork as the hedgerows tickled the sides of the car. He finally pulled up in the carpark of the Wreckers Inn. They would walk the rest of the way. It wasn't far. Just down the lane.

As he and Harry emerged from the car, he noticed a group of people milling around the pub entrance. Steve recognised one of them as Wesley Peterson's scruffy, long-haired friend – the archaeologist, Neil Watson – and he turned away, hoping he hadn't been seen. Some of the others were stowing what looked like diving equipment in the boots of parked four-wheel-drive vehicles. Steve knew that they were working on a shipwreck down in the cove. Not that he was interested in that sort of thing.

He and Harry marched down the lane. From the look of fierce determination on Harry's face, he didn't reckon much to Carrington's chances if Harry got his hands on him. But he was also curious about why this case meant so much to his former colleague, why Harry was pursuing him like Inspector Dew after Crippen ... another wife-murderer.

Old Coastguard Cottage came into sight. Steve hoped they'd got the right place. He wanted to get this over with. It was lunch-time and he was hungry.

A rickety wooden garage stood about ten yards away

from the cottage to the side of the colourful garden. Steve walked up to it and peeped through the filthy window. There was a car. A silver Nissan.

'Harry. This his motor?'

Harry looked in the window and nodded. 'Looks like it. Come on.'

Steve left it to Harry to knock on the door. It was his collar – the reason why he'd come all the way down to Devon. It was only right that he should be in at the kill. Harry knocked softly. No aggressive 'Police, open up'. The door opened slowly but Steve couldn't see who was behind it.

Harry pushed the front door open and barged into the hallway. A young man stood pressed up against the wall and Steve watched as Harry grabbed him, twisting his arm up his back before whispering viciously in his ear. Suddenly Steve felt uneasy, afraid that Harry would go too far. And he regretted coming on his own; Harry might have behaved himself better with someone else present.

'Robin Carrington, I'm arresting you for the murder of Harriet Carrington ...'

But he was interrupted by the sharp ring of the telephone on the hall table – an old Bakelite model. It was a long time since Steve had heard a phone make such a noise. Harry pushed Carrington against the wall and picked up the receiver. 'Watch him, Steve,' he ordered before saying hello to the caller.

'Robin,' said an anxious female voice on the other end of the line. 'Robin, is that you?'

Harry Marchbank answered in the affirmative. With any luck he might net a female accomplice at the same time.

'Look, I won't stay on long, 'cause I'm ringing from a call-box. I've moved down the coast to a new place. Has Jeremy sent the insurance cheque yet? How soon do you think you can get over here?'

Harry's voice was hesitant. 'Sorry, love, this isn't Robin. I'm a friend of his ... met him down the pub. Who shall I say's calling?'

The woman sounded annoyed. 'Tell him it's Harriet. His wife.'

Harry hesitated a moment, as though he'd had a shock. 'He can't come to the phone at the moment but I know he wanted to know where you were.' Steve thought Harry sounded innocent, convincing.

'Who is that?'

'Just a sec, love.' Harry covered the mouthpiece and turned to Robin Carrington, who was now crouching against the wall, his head in his hands. 'There's a lady here says she's your dead wife. A voice from the grave. I think we should have a word down the nick, Robin, don't you?' He put the receiver to his ear again. 'Hello, love, you still there?' But the caller had rung off.

Steve was watching Harry Marchbank's face and he was surprised to see a smile of relief. Almost of joy.

Rachel and Wesley walked down a corridor. Its walls had been painted magnolia a few years ago and were in need of a fresh coat, and its floor was covered with green linoleum; a backstage area strictly for staff rather than guests. They forged ahead until they reached a door marked 'No Entry'. Then they stood, wondering what their next move should be.

Suddenly they heard voices: a male – no, two males – and a female, raised in disagreement. The female was saying something about wanting her cut. But the rest was muffled, like voices heard under water. After a minute or so they made a decision. They were going in. Rachel pushed the door open.

They stepped into a large gloomy storeroom, half under ground. It was filled with the detritus of the hotel – bulky grey shapes were outlined in the weak light that crept in through a tiny barred window: mattresses; bed bases; furniture, mostly old and dust covered. To one side stood a pile of large cardboard boxes, stacked neatly one on top of the other.

A door closed somewhere in the distance – another entrance to the room perhaps. Suddenly Wesley felt himself being shoved to one side by strong hands and two figures, young and male, dashed past. He grabbed at them but they dodged him neatly like experienced rugby players. As they passed Rachel they knocked her off balance and she staggered, clutching at a cardboard box, before falling on the dusty floor, bringing a tower of heavy boxes tumbling down around her.

The two young men didn't stop. They dashed out of the door and all Wesley could do was watch their receding backs. But he wasn't too worried. He knew who they were.

Chapter Nine

Mary Anne Iddacombe was but sixteen and possessed a delicate beauty and a sweet nature. When she called upon me with her request, I spoke to her at length and I sensed an iron resolve behind her words. She loved Isaiah Smithers and she would have him.

At the back of my mind were the rumours of her own mother's indiscretions with Captain Smithers, and I felt I had to learn the truth before I consented to the girl's request. I decided to speak plainly, but my words were greeted with astonishment. Her mother's dealings with Captain Smithers had always been most proper. Her mother's affections, she assured me, were placed elsewhere, and Lord Mereham had been paying her much attention of late.

Thus reassured, I requested that she and the captain call upon me the next day.

If I had known what the future held for that unfortunate couple, I should have spoken with more caution.

From An Account of the Dreadful and Wicked Crimes of the Wreckers of Chadleigh *by the Reverend Octavius Mount, Vicar of Millicombe*

Wesley walked slightly behind Mike Cumberland, who strutted towards the staff entrance, bestowing a hospitable smile on any guest who happened to come into view. Cumberland used the hotel foyer as an actor uses the stage – to give a performance. Once he was behind the scenes, the obsequious smile disappeared.

'Who was that woman Oliver Kilburn was talking to?'

'That was Brenda Dilkes – one of our cleaners.'

Wesley raised his eyebrows. Brenda Dilkes again. Kayleigh Dilkes's mother: the appreciative parent who had provided Pam with the pretty gift.

'And the boys – did they get out through reception?'

Cumberland looked annoyed. 'Yes. They came dashing through and nearly knocked an elderly guest flying. I'm going to have a word with Mr Kilburn. I mean, I know Oliver's his son but it puts me in a very difficult position if he's going to come to the hotel and behave like . . .'

Wesley stopped him in full flow. 'Had you any idea that they were using your hotel to store stolen computers?'

'Of course not. If I'd known, I would have told the police . . . naturally.'

'Naturally,' echoed Wesley.

'And if Brenda Dilkes was aiding and abetting them, I can assure you that her days at this hotel are numbered too. That storeroom is usually kept locked.'

'Who has access to the key?'

'It's kept in the housekeeper's office.'

'Would Brenda be able to get it?'

'Officially not but . . .' He didn't finish the sentence. They had reached the storeroom door.

Rachel was inside sitting on an old mattress, holding her head. She smiled weakly as Wesley asked whether she was all right.

'I can call the hotel doctor if the young lady's hurt,' Cumberland offered anxiously.

'I'm fine,' Rachel replied. She looked at Wesley and shook her head. She didn't want any fuss.

Wesley began to examine the cardboard boxes. The name Nestec was clearly visible, printed on the sides in large black letters. They'd taken a risk hiding them here.

'We'd better find that woman who was with them,' said Rachel. 'She's obviously involved.'

'Mr Cumberland says she's a cleaner – name of Brenda Dilkes.'

Rachel touched her head and winced.

'Are you okay? I think you should go to hospital and get that checked out.'

Rachel glared at him, her mouth arranged in a determined line. 'I'm fine. There's no need . . .'

'You're going. I'll pull rank if necessary. You've had a blow on the head and passed out. You can't be too careful with concussion.'

'It's a bit sore but I'm fine. Don't fuss.'

'The inspector's right,' Cumberland chipped in. 'I'll call the hotel doctor and ask him to have a look at you.'

'Okay, but we'd better find those boys and Brenda Dilkes,' Rachel said as Wesley took his mobile phone from his pocket.

Ten minutes later, as Rachel was being examined by the hotel doctor, news came through that Brenda Dilkes couldn't be found in the building.

While Wesley waited in reception, he noticed that Mike Cumberland was watching him, a smile playing on his lips.

'Fancy a drink while we're waiting?' he said with a hint of something else behind the question.

'Not while I'm on duty, sir,' Wesley answered formally, staying firmly on his own side of the reception desk.

'We're waiting, Robin.' Gerry Heffernan sat next to Harry Marchbank in the interview room. Just like old times. He wanted to get the full story before Carrington was hauled back to London – not that it was any of his concern really, but his curiosity had got the better of him.

'Okay.' Robin Carrington hesitated for a few moments, collecting his thoughts. 'We were short of cash. In debt up to our necks. Harriet had this idea. If we insured her life

223

and made it look as though she'd died, then she'd nip off to France and I'd join her as soon as I'd finished this job for the Smithers family in the USA and the insurance money came through.'

'And when you left for Devon you didn't know about the second post-mortem?'

'Her mother was talking about demanding one but I never thought she'd go through with it.'

'She needed a bit of persuading but I managed it.' Marchbank grinned unpleasantly and Carrington stared at him in disbelief. 'So if you didn't know we were on to you why did you run when you saw me in Tradmouth?'

He shrugged. 'I suppose I panicked. I had the feeling you'd been suspicious about the fire and you seemed to have it in for me so when I saw you I decided it was best to lie low.'

'And this Harriet, your wife, was quite prepared to let her own mother think she was dead?' Heffernan asked.

'They'd never got on, not since ... well, not since she found out her father wasn't her father. But that's another story. And her mother never liked me. The old bitch had to put her oar in, didn't she?'

Marchbank leaned forward. 'The second post-mortem found that the victim had been dead before the fire started. If it wasn't Harriet, who was it?'

Carrington shifted in his seat nervously. 'Harriet saw this homeless woman hanging around near our local shops. She used to beg ... probably on drugs. Harriet planned it all. She gave this woman money every time she saw her and got chatting to her. The woman was having trouble with her teeth and Harriet paid for a visit to the dentist – using Harriet's name. The woman was around the same age and height as Harriet: she even looked a bit like her and ... Harriet planned it all. It wasn't my idea.'

'Crap.' Marchbank banged his fist on the table, earning himself a dirty look from Heffernan. 'Do you expect us to believe that?'

'Go on,' said Heffernan quietly. Marchbank was behaving as if he was emotionally involved and Heffernan wondered why.

'She invited the woman for a meal. It was awful. She smelt and . . .'

Heffernan was tempted to observe that perhaps the poor woman hadn't had his advantages in life but didn't, not wanting to interrupt Carrington's flow. 'What happened?' he prompted quietly.

'Harriet had some stuff from the hospital . . . insulin, I think it was. She injected her and . . . and I arranged it so that the old wiring would catch fire. We dressed her in Harriet's clothes, put her watch and jewellery on and put her up in the bedroom as though she'd collapsed with the smoke. I identified her and because of Harriet's little act of charity the woman's dental records were in Harriet's name. Harriet was very thorough – she'd thought of everything. The whole thing was her idea.'

Heffernan smiled. How many times had he heard this before? Funny how every crime was somebody else's idea. 'Go on,' he said.

'Then it was just a matter of Harriet going straight to France; she set off as soon as she'd done her bit with the insulin – she didn't want to risk anybody seeing her when she was supposed to be dead. She got the train to Plymouth and then the ferry and when she reached France she started looking for a cottage. She promised to let me know as soon as she'd found somewhere suitable – that's why she was ringing. While she was seeing to things in France, I was to tie up the loose ends here and finish the job the Smithers had hired me to do while I waited for the money to come through. Jeremy was dealing with the financial side. He was going to send me the cheque for the insurance – the house and Harriet's life. All our debts, all our money problems, solved in one go. We thought we were in the clear. We thought it couldn't go wrong.'

'So you were here in blissful ignorance while all hell was breaking loose in London?'

Carrington nodded.

'And thanks to your mother-in-law you became a wanted man – for the murder of a woman who was still alive, although you could hardly use that as a defence, could you? And your mother-in-law could hardly have known that by getting her revenge on you, she was making sure that her own daughter went to jail for murder.'

'How could we have known that the old bitch would stir things up?' Carrington put his head in his hands, defeated. He knew it was over.

Heffernan looked at Harry Marchbank, who was sitting quite still with what looked like tears brimming in his eyes. 'So Harriet's still alive? She's okay?' he said softly.

'Yes.'

Marchbank stood up and his chair fell backwards, toppling onto the shiny linoleum floor with a loud clatter. He marched out of the interview room. Heffernan nodded to the constable by the door and followed him out, watching him as he hurried to the Gents. Heffernan hesitated before pushing the door to the Gents open and stepping inside.

He found Marchbank rinsing his face. It was clear he had been crying and his body was still shaking with sobs. He wiped his face with a paper towel and looked at Heffernan, shiny mucus still oozing from his nostrils.

Heffernan hesitated. 'Want to tell me about it?'

Marchbank swung round to face him. 'Just piss off, Gerry.'

'You got it wrong.'

'I thought he'd killed her. How was I to know?'

'What difference does it make? You've still got your collar.'

Marchbank shook his head and reached for another paper towel to wipe his nose. 'I should have left well alone.'

'Why?'

Marchbank looked Heffernan in the eye. 'Harriet's mum and I had a fling when I was in London years ago. If you must know Harriet's my bloody daughter.'

Heffernan stood staring at him, and felt sorry for Harry Marchbank for the first time in his life. Harry had thought his daughter was dead and had gone after her killer. And now he had unmasked his own flesh and blood as a murderer.

He watched as Harry Marchbank broke down in tears.

Steve Carstairs wandered into the CID office looking rather lost. He spotted Wesley and hesitated before speaking.

'I've heard Rachel's gone to hospital. Is it serious?' For once Carstairs sounded quite concerned.

'Just mild concussion; she'll be fine. They're giving her an X-ray but they're just being cautious.'

Trish Walton had overheard. 'Will she be wanting a lift home? She shouldn't be driving if ...'

'Thanks, Trish,' said Wesley. 'But I said I'd pick her up. She's giving me a ring when they've finished with her.'

Steve gave Trish a knowing wink which she studiously ignored.

'Anyone seen Harry Marchbank? I brought his villain in for him and I've not seen him since.'

'Lucky you,' said Trish under her breath.

'So what's been going on? I heard something about the Tradfield Manor Hotel and ...'

Wesley enlightened him. 'More stolen Nestec computers have turned up there. We want a word with Sebastian Wilde's son, Jason, and a lad called Oliver Kilburn, the son of the hotel's owner. We reckon they hid them there. And there's a woman we want to talk to: she's called Brenda Dilkes and she works at the hotel.'

Wesley's speech was interrupted by the arrival of Paul Johnson, who parked his tall, gangling form on a chair next to him.

'We've interviewed the hotel staff, sir, and nobody admits to knowing anything. Oliver Kilburn was seen hanging around near that storeroom a couple of days ago with Jason Wilde. One of the waiters recognised Wilde;

seems he knew him from way back.'

'So the son of Nestec's boss has been found lurking near a pile of computers stolen from his dad's lorry?' Wesley grinned at Johnson. 'Well done, Paul. I want a word with Mr Wilde Junior as soon as possible.'

'Yes, sir.' Johnson looked pleased with himself and scurried off to his desk. Jason Wilde and Oliver Kilburn were pampered schoolboys used to home comforts. They wouldn't be too hard to find, and Wesley was inclined to let them stew for a while.

He looked at Steve, who was surrounded by a tall pile of files. Every so often he took a new one and read it with deep concentration.

'You busy, Steve?'

Steve jumped and immediately looked guilty. 'Yeah. It's this Sally Gilbert case. You still holding Mike Battersley?'

'For the moment.'

'Harry Marchbank reckoned that Sally Gilbert wasn't the first person to fall off a cliff around here at this time of year.'

Wesley looked at him enquiringly, not quite getting the point. 'What do you mean?'

Steve shrugged. He felt foolish and wished he hadn't mentioned it.

'What did Marchbank say exactly?'

'Just that there was another woman who got herself pushed off a cliff at Little Tradmouth a few years back. I don't remember much about it 'cause Inspector Jenkins was in charge of the case. The boyfriend did it apparently, but they couldn't get enough evidence to charge him. There won't be any connection.'

Wesley stood for a few seconds, thinking. 'Possibly not, but I think it's worth checking.'

Steve stared at him glumly, fearing he had just talked himself into more work.

'Tell you what, you check it out. And while you're about it see if there have been any other similar deaths around

228

here in recent years. It shouldn't take long to look up on the computer. Okay?'

Steve said nothing. Next time he'd keep his big mouth shut.

At Gerry Heffernan's suggestion Wesley drove Harry Marchbank to Old Coastguard Cottage. Marchbank had expressed a desire to search the property for evidence and the chief inspector had reckoned that somebody responsible should go along with him to see everything was done properly. He had assured Wesley that it wouldn't take long.

The only thing that had stopped Wesley from making his excuses and seeing to his paperwork was the cottage's proximity to Neil's shipwreck. He hadn't seen Neil for a few days and a quick visit to the beach after the business at the cottage was over wouldn't take up much time.

Marchbank hardly said a word as they drove out to Millicombe. Wesley had thought him a big man when they had first met; a man over-fond of fatty food and alcohol. But now he seemed to have shrunk almost visibly, his cocky swagger replaced by a shuffling stoop. There were no racist jibes; no sneering wisecracks – he didn't look as though he had the energy.

Wesley took the opportunity to ask about the case Marchbank had mentioned to Steve, the death that appeared to be similar to Sally Gilbert's, but Marchbank just shook his head, unwilling to talk. Perhaps Steve had been letting his imagination run away with him.

They reached the front door of the cottage and Wesley opened it with Carrington's key.

'I'll do upstairs if you like.'

Marchbank shrugged as though he didn't care what they did.

Wesley hesitated, wondering whether to say something about Carrington's revelations, but he could think of no words that seemed appropriate. He left Marchbank alone and climbed the stairs leading to the two small bedrooms, both rendered smaller by the owner's choice of over-busy floral wallpaper. The curtains of both bedrooms were closed, but this made little difference as the sun had no problem penetrating the thin flowered cotton.

Fortunately Robin Carrington had been a tidy man. He had treated his temporary home like a hotel, leaving most of his clothes still packed in a large suitcase on the floor beneath the window. But then Wesley remembered that he had been prepared for flight, ready to join Harriet in France as soon as his business here was finished.

He found nothing of interest. A photograph of a young woman, dark and attractive with a determined mouth: Harriet probably. Wesley stared at the picture for a while and thought he could detect a likeness to Harry Marchbank around the eyes. Marchbank's daughter – the woman who had no qualms about murdering for financial gain. If Carrington had been telling the truth – it was still possible that he had instigated the whole project and he was laying the blame on the person who wasn't there to defend herself. Although the French police had now been alerted and it was only a matter of time before Harriet was picked up.

He went downstairs, feeling uneasy, wondering what he'd find. He didn't know Harry – and he wasn't sure that he wanted to know him – and he had no idea how the man would react in the present rather strange situation.

He found Harry sitting on the sofa, his head in his hands, and for a moment he hesitated in the doorway. He cleared his throat and Harry stood up and faced him. 'You finished up there?' He spoke roughly, still the hard man.

'Yes. Are you all right?'

''Course I'm bloody all right. Why shouldn't I be?'

Wesley stepped into the room, looking around. 'Have you found anything?'

Marchbank grunted. 'Nothing much. There's his laptop and a load of history stuff on the sideboard – Carrington was into all that. Ran a business through the Internet. Bloody daft, if you ask me.'

Wesley strolled to the sideboard and leafed through the pile of papers. There were several handwritten family trees; sheets of paper with notes on and photocopies of entries in registers of births, marriages and deaths. On top of them all lay an old book. Wesley picked it up. It smelled musty and its pages were foxed and browned with age. He looked at the date it had been printed: 1789 – the year of the French Revolution, when poor mad George III was on the throne of England and America was enjoying her recent independence from the British crown. He glanced at the book's title – *An Account of the Dreadful and Wicked Crimes of the Wreckers of Chadleigh* by the Reverend Octavius Mount.

Wesley felt an urge to open the book and find out more. But whatever the 'dreadful and wicked crimes' were, they wouldn't figure in his division's crime statistics so there was no time for such indulgences.

'We might as well leave all this stuff here for now until we know what's to be done with it.'

Marchbank said nothing and made for the door.

'What about Carrington's car?' Wesley asked. 'It's in the garage. We ought to take a look.'

Marchbank didn't answer. He stood by the passenger door of Wesley's car, perfectly still, staring out at the heaving grey-blue mass of the sea, past caring.

The rotting wooden garage wasn't locked. The great double doors were almost falling off their hinges, and Wesley had to lift them gently to get them open. Carrington's car – a five-year-old silver Nissan – was sitting inside: some instinct must have told him to keep it out of sight, safe from prying eyes and passing policemen. Wesley felt he had to be thorough and take a look inside. He would feel stupid if there was a pistol in the glove compartment and he'd not found it.

But the contents of the car proved disappointing from a detective's point of view. A box of tissues; a road map; a few cassettes – mostly popular classical; nothing that caught Wesley's interest.

It wasn't until he was about to close the door that he noticed a small white card lying on the dashboard. A parking ticket; the type issued by the council's pay-and-display machines in public carparks. He leaned over and picked it up.

'Littlebury. Fourteen thirty. The twentieth of the seventh.'

Wesley stared at it for a few seconds before its significance registered.

Robin Carrington had been near Monks Island at the time Sally Gilbert died. And Robin Carrington was no stranger to murder.

When Harry Marchbank spotted the Wreckers he said he needed a drink. Wesley left him to it. Marchbank wouldn't want his company and the feeling was mutual.

He made his way down the steep path to the cove, hoping Neil would be there and not away at some meeting or diving beneath the sea.

The fine golden sand seeped over the tops of his shoes as he walked towards the disused café. It was a pity, he thought, that this beach would soon be for the exclusive use of those who could afford the no doubt exorbitant charges of the Chadleigh Hall Hotel. In Wesley's opinion there was something almost immoral about keeping such unspoiled beauty only for those who could pay. But that was the way the world worked. And Dominic Kilburn, once a humble builder who had worked on the hall years before, was going to do very nicely out of it, thank you.

Neil was in the café, his head buried in a pile of drawings and reports. Paperwork – the scourge of the modern age. He looked up as Wesley opened the door and a grin spread across his earnest face.

'Hi, Wes. Like our cannon?' He pointed to a shapeless blackened lump laid carefully on top of a bench. 'It's the third one we've found and there's bound to be more: they had to carry them to protect themselves from privateers.

232

It's going for X-ray and conservation later. Good, isn't it?'

'Very nice. How's it going? Found any of that sunken treasure yet?'

'Lots of iron bars but no treasure. I reckon it's just a story that got embellished over the years. People love that sort of thing – you show me a sunken ship that wasn't supposed to be carrying treasure.' He laughed. 'Kilburn's bloody furious, of course. What use is it being the lord of the manor and owning the rights to the wreck when all you get out of it's a load of rusty old iron?' Neil pushed the papers to one side. 'Pam's looking better,' he said unexpectedly.

'Yes. I heard you had a good lunch.'

'So is this just a social call or . . .?'

'No. I've been giving a suspect's house the once-over.'

Neil looked at him enquiringly.

'That cottage at the top of the cliff. A man called Robin Carrington was staying there. He's wanted for murder in London.'

Neil's jaw dropped. 'I know him. And Pam met him when we had lunch the other day. Bloody hell. Murder?'

''Fraid so.'

Neil shook his head, trying to take it in. 'He's been making a family tree for some people in the States who are related to the *Celestina*'s captain . . . or at least that's what he told me.' Neil shook his head, shocked. 'Murder? He didn't seem the type.'

'They never do. It'd make my job a lot easier if they had horns and a tail and the word "murderer" tattooed across their foreheads. But unfortunately they just look like you and me.'

'Who's he supposed to have murdered?'

'A woman.'

'Crime of passion?'

'Not exactly.' Wesley didn't feel inclined to discuss the details of Robin Carrington's wrongdoings. Then he remembered something. 'I saw this book among

Carrington's possessions. It's called *An Account of the Dreadful and Wicked Crimes of the Wreckers of Chadleigh*. If I get the chance I'll ask him if you can have a look at it.'

'He did mention a book about the Chadleigh wreckers. He said he'd lend it to me.'

'Could the *Celestina* have been wrecked deliberately?'

Neil shrugged. 'There's no way of knowing: she might just have come too far inshore and hit the rocks or she could have been wrecked deliberately for the insurance – that was quite common. Or perhaps she was lured inshore. That's what wreckers used to do. Whole villages would plunder a ship that ran aground. The thing would be stripped before the authorities arrived to stop it.'

'And people like the village constable and the vicar – or the lord of the manor – couldn't they do something?'

Neil laughed. 'Don't be so naive, Wes. The whole village would have been in on it. The village constable probably joined in and the gentry turned a blind eye and took their share of the pickings.'

'And what about the survivors?'

'If they were lucky they were rescued before all the cargo was pinched. But if they were unlucky . . .'

'What?'

'Well, in maritime law a vessel which is driven ashore isn't considered to be a wreck if any person or animal is still alive aboard – and if she's not a wreck then her cargo is supposed to be restored to her owners. So the way some wreckers interpreted it, they could pinch whatever they could lay their hands on as long as it was a genuine wreck. So sometimes they'd kill any survivors and . . .'

'Thanks, Neil. I came down here for a break from work.'

'Don't suppose you're free for a drink tonight?'

'No way. I'm taking Pam for a meal at the Tradfield Manor Hotel – there's a special offer on.' He looked at his watch. 'I'd better get back.'

Wesley made his way back up the path to the top of the

cliff. When he reached the road he turned and shielded his eyes against the sun. The water was a clear blue and a shoal of fish swam in a shifting dark cloud a few metres offshore. He was certain he could make out the vague shape of the wreck near the jagged grey rocks.

As he walked back to the pub to tell Harry Marchbank it was time to go, he had the feeling that something Neil had said was relevant to the Sally Gilbert case. But he couldn't for the life of him think what it was.

When Wesley returned to the CID office Steve Carstairs was waiting for him with a piece of paper clutched in his hand. He had abandoned his habitual expression of bored resentment and had acquired an air of repressed enthusiasm.

'Found anything interesting?' Wesley asked, expecting a negative answer followed by excuses.

But Steve was looking pleased with himself. He placed the paper on the desk in front of him. 'Yeah. I dug out the details of the Marion Bowler case: 1998 it was. Then I did some more digging around and I found that every year for the past few years someone's died falling off a cliff: always in different places but always in July. Most of the deaths were dealt with by uniform or other stations . . . just treated as accidents. And there's no apparent link between them.'

'Go on,' Wesley said encouragingly.

Steve looked at the list. 'In 1997 a woman fell off the cliffs just outside Stoke Beeching but there was no reason to suppose it wasn't an accident. In 1998 we've got Marion Bowler – suspected murder. Then in 1999 a bloke fell off a cliff near Bloxham when he'd told his wife he was going to the supermarket. Suicide was suspected at first but his wife said he'd been quite cheerful when he went out and no note was found so it went down as an accident.'

'So what have you found out about the Marion Bowler case?'

Steve frowned. 'It does seem a bit like Sally Gilbert's

murder. She went out saying she was going to meet someone but she didn't say who. She fell off a cliff at Little Tradmouth and there were signs of a struggle on the cliff top above where her body was found. Her boyfriend was the chief suspect but he always denied it and there wasn't enough evidence to prosecute. He buggered off to Australia not long after he'd got off the hook but Inspector Jenkins seemed pretty sure that he'd done it.'

Wesley nodded. Stan Jenkins was now enjoying – if that was the word – retirement under the strict eye of Mrs Jenkins. 'Are there any others?'

'Last July a man fell off the cliff path overlooking Coreton Cove – in the grounds of that National Trust place near Queenswear: that was treated as an accidental death. The cliff path's dangerous when it's been raining.'

Wesley scratched his head. 'Is there anything to suggest that these deaths had anything in common?'

'Not on the face of it.' Steve grinned as he anticipated showing off his brilliance. 'But I've been reading through the reports and there is something peculiar – some of the relatives said the victims seemed excited about something when they went out. And none of them would say where they were going. It might be nothing but ... What do you think?'

Wesley stared at Steve for a few moments, taking it all in.

'Do you think we might be on to something?' Steve asked, hoping Wesley wasn't going to receive all the credit if something came of it.

'I don't know. See what else you can find out. And well done,' he added. It looked as if Steve had a chance of becoming a good CID officer after all – or maybe it was just a flash in the pan.

Sebastian Wilde was due at Tradmouth police station at four o'clock to identify his stolen computers, which had been brought in and stored in an empty office, carefully catalogued as evidence.

It was all over for Robin Carrington. Tomorrow he was due to return to London, under arrest for conspiracy to murder. Tonight the Tradmouth police were just baby-sitting, if that was the appropriate word: Gerry Heffernan couldn't think of anything better.

Heffernan looked up from his cluttered desk when Wesley burst into his office, a look of cautious excitement on his face.

'Can I have a word?'

''Course you can, Wes. Sit yourself down. Any sign of that Brenda Dilkes yet?'

'No. I rang Carole Sanders' place to see if she was there but she seems to have disappeared. Carole's looking after her little girl but Brenda's not been to pick her up.'

'What about Masters Kilburn and Wilde?'

Wesley shook his head. 'They're not at home. But I've a feeling they won't have gone far.' He leaned forward in his seat. 'Steve Carstairs had a word with me earlier. Harry Marchbank told him that there was a death in 1998 that was very similar to Sally Gilbert's.'

Heffernan looked puzzled. 'Remind me.'

'A girl called Marion Bowler fell off a cliff at Little Tradmouth in July 1998 – evidence of a struggle on the cliff top ... just like Sally Gilbert. It was one of Stan Jenkins' cases.'

'Oh yes, now that you mention it I remember that one. Wasn't it the boyfriend only there wasn't enough evidence to prosecute?'

'That's right. Now I asked Steve to see if he could find any other similar deaths and he managed to unearth a few more. None of them was treated as suspicious at the time and they were dealt with by uniform or other stations.' He paused. 'But now I've had a chance to look at the reports, I think there might be some sort of pattern emerging.'

'What do you mean?'

'None of the victims told anyone where they were going and some of the relatives' statements mention that the victims seemed excited about something. Marion Bowler said she was going to meet someone but wouldn't say who. Remind you of anything?'

'Sally Gilbert. Go on.'

'At first glance the deaths look completely unrelated but . . .'

Heffernan looked him in the eye. 'Do you think it's worth following up?'

Wesley thought for a moment. 'There's no harm in doing a bit of digging. And there's something else. I found a carpark ticket in Robin Carrington's car – he was at Monks Island at the time of Sally Gilbert's death.' He watched Gerry Heffernan's face for a reaction. 'And that's not all. I've not checked the dates yet but Carrington comes to this area on his own every year at around the same time. He says he comes to get away from London and do some work: this solicitor mate of his lends him his cottage. This year he claims to be tracing someone's family tree: that's what he does for a living – he's a genealogist who runs a business through the Internet, or so he says.'

Heffernan caught on quick. 'And you think he might have been down here adding a few names to the deaths register?'

'It's worth checking out.'

'Then get on with it. We'll tell Marchbank he can get off back to London till we've finished with Carrington.' Heffernan slouched back and put his feet on his desk, sending a couple of sheets of paper fluttering to the floor.

Wesley looked at his watch. 'I mustn't be too late. I said I'd pick Rachel up from the hospital and I'm taking Pam out for dinner tonight.'

'Where are you going?'

'The Tradfield Manor. They're doing a special offer.'

'Nice. Have to try it myself.'

But before Wesley could comment, Trish Walton opened the office door. 'Sir, I just thought you should know. Mr Wilde's waiting to see you about his stolen computers.'

'Thanks, Trish. Come on, Wes, let's go and tell Wilde the good news. And let's see what he says about his lad, eh.'

Sebastian Wilde was not a happy man. He had examined his recovered property solemnly, showing no hint of relief that at least some of his lost goods had been found.

Jason, he said, was out with friends: he didn't know where. He promised to let the police know when he turned up but assured them he could have had nothing to do with the theft of his computers. Jason was his son. He knew him. Anything he wanted he only had to ask for. He had no reason to steal, he said with genuine conviction. But his face remained a mask of polite inscrutability: he was giving nothing away.

'Still think Wilde's a possible for Sally Gilbert's murder?' Wesley asked Heffernan as soon as Wilde had left the police station.

'He was on Monks Island for that meeting. What about the son, Jason?'

'That hardly fits in with this new theory about people getting shoved off cliffs every year. Jason would have been a kid when the first few happened.'

'But do you see Sebastian Wilde as a serial killer?'

Wesley smiled. 'When you put it like that, it does sound far fetched.'

'Found any link between the victims?'

'Nothing obvious yet. At the time they were all treated as straightforward, unrelated cases.' He shrugged. 'And perhaps they were. The cliffs around this part of the coast are dangerous and people do fall off them from time to time.'

They were interrupted by Paul Johnson, who gave a perfunctory knock before poking his head around the door. 'There's a lady down at the front desk who says she wants a word with DI Peterson about the Chadleigh Hall case.'

239

Heffernan gave Wesley a nudge. 'Go on, Wes. Don't keep the lady waiting.'

'Did she give a name?' Wesley asked.

'Yes,' Paul replied. 'She said her name was Stanes. Alexandra Stanes.'

Chapter Ten

I married Mary Anne Iddacombe to Captain Isaiah Smithers on the thirtieth day of May. It was a fine day and my two servants, who acted as witnesses to the union, saw the couple exchange their vows as the bright rays of the spring sun streamed through the stained-glass windows. I sensed the couple's delight in each other, although they seemed nervous as they left the sanctuary of the church, as though they were uncertain of the reception that would await them when the truth of their marriage was known. But they need not have feared for I heard later that Mistress Mercy Iddacombe had indeed accepted their union and had begged the pair to regard Chadleigh Hall as their home. I was pleased to see that my instincts about that lady had proved correct. For surely she lived up to her name of Mercy, a kind and forgiving soul.

From An Account of the Dreadful and Wicked Crimes of the Wreckers of Chadleigh *by the Reverend Octavius Mount, Vicar of Millicombe*

Wesley stood for a few moments, staring at her. She was looking down at her feet, avoiding his eyes as though she was ashamed of the lies she had told. Lying to the police didn't appear to have come easily to Sandra Bracewell – born Alexandra Stanes.

Her husband, Peter, stood behind her protectively. When Wesley invited them to follow him to the interview room, Peter put his arm around his wife's shoulders and shepherded her gently. Wesley ordered tea. The Bracewells looked as if they needed it.

'Sorry it's not more comfortable,' said Wesley as they sat down to face him.

He smiled to put them at their ease. He could tell they were both nervous. Peter, looking scrubbed and pink in his spotless light slacks and powder-blue polo shirt, fidgeted with his wristwatch. Sandra sat, stiff and straight-backed, on the edge of her seat – as she'd no doubt been taught to do by Miss Snowman all those years ago.

'I think we should start from the beginning, don't you?'

The couple glanced at each other, and Wesley saw Sandra give her husband a small nod.

'There's not that much to tell really,' Peter began. 'I met Sandra when I was working at Chadleigh Hall. Love at first sight, you might say.' He gave his wife a shy smile. 'She was very unhappy there. She never got on with her parents and they were only too glad to get rid of her at the first opportunity. She hated it at that school, didn't you, pet?'

Sandra nodded but let her husband do the talking.

'Anyway, we arranged to meet in secret and one thing led to another. Sandra never said anything to the other girls – if she had she knew that word would have got round.'

Wesley found himself wanting to hear the woman's version of events, but there was plenty of time for that. 'So you ran away together?'

'Yes. We went to my sister's in Weymouth and eventually we got married. It was my idea to send the letters from London to keep her parents off our backs. My brother-in-law went up there regularly and posted them for us.'

'My parents never tried to find me,' Sandra said in a quiet, husky tone. 'I didn't think they would but . . .'

Her voice trailed off. Wesley looked at her and saw the pain in her eyes. The girl who'd had everything except the most important thing. And it had taken Peter Bracewell to give her that.

'You never contacted your parents later, just to tell them where you were?'

'No. I broke off all contact; it was better that way.'

'What about Carole?'

Sandra gave a weak smile. 'I met her by chance in the street about seven years ago and she recognised me at once. She'd moved back to the area when her husband died and she was working in Tradmouth. We started meeting up sometimes on our days off and . . .'

'Do you work at the Tradfield Manor?'

She looked at him, surprised. 'Yes. Just part time. How did you . . .?'

'I thought I saw you there the other day. Did you know Sally Gilbert . . . one of the receptionists?'

'I only knew her by sight. I work in the wages office.' She pressed her lips together tightly and studied her hands.

Wesley sensed that this line of questioning would get him nowhere. After a few seconds of silence he spoke again. 'You knew we were looking for you. What made you come forward now?'

'I've been wondering what to do since you came round that day. Then Carole rang me and said you'd been round at her house asking more questions but she hadn't liked to say anything to you without asking me first.' She looked down at her hands. 'I thought I'd better come and get things straight.'

Wesley sat back in his chair and gave them a reassuring smile. 'At least we know now that the skeleton at Chadleigh Hall doesn't belong to you, Mrs Bracewell. Thank you for coming.'

'Is that all?' Peter Bracewell sounded surprised.

'Well, I can't see that you've committed any crime, but I'd still like to ask you about the building work at the hall.'

Bracewell looked worried. 'We didn't think we were doing anything wrong. Jack had a few other jobs lined up and he didn't want any hold-ups. He knew there'd be a lot of fuss if it was found and . . .'

'You're talking about the skeleton, I take it?'

'Yes. I don't suppose there's any harm in telling you now. The headmistress wanted her study extended into the next room but we started knocking through and . . . well, you know what we found. It was me and Jack who found it – gave us the shock of our lives. We found a torch and shone it in and saw this bloody skeleton sitting there grinning at us like something from a horror film. We broke down the wall until the hole was big enough to climb through. Jack went in but there was no way I was going in there.' He shuddered.

'So what happened then?'

'Well, Jack Kilburn said we should just seal the room up again and tell the headmistress it couldn't be knocked through. We plastered it all up and that was that. Jack said not to mention it to anyone. He didn't want it getting around.'

When the tea finally arrived, Wesley sat back, considering the implications of what Bracewell had told him. Jack Kilburn had entered the sealed room back in the sixties and the coin Neil had found could well have come from his pocket. It looked more and more likely that the bones were old – possibly from the eighteenth or nineteenth centuries. And if that was the case it wasn't his problem any more.

But Wesley felt this wasn't the end. He still wanted to find out who had left the unknown girl there to die. And why.

'So that's that.' Gerry Heffernan sat back in his chair. 'The Chadleigh Hall skeleton's not our problem.'

'Probably not our problem,' Wesley corrected. 'There's still a chance that she died less than seventy years ago. Neil's met someone who lived at Chadleigh Hall before the war – a man called George Iddacombe who lives in a lighthouse near Bereton. I'd like to have a word with him, just in case he knows anything.'

'But there's only a slight chance of them being recent. I mean, they're more likely to be a couple of hundred years old. That chair's pretty ancient.'

'A sample from the bones has been sent away for dating so we'll know for certain in a couple of months.' Wesley hesitated. 'You know those deaths I mentioned ... people falling off cliffs?'

Heffernan scratched his head and nodded.

'I've been looking through the files to see if I could find any connection between the victims, but as far as I can tell they had nothing in common except that they were ... well, just ordinary, I suppose.' He shrugged. The people who had died either by accident or violence in late July each year for the past five years had been remarkable only in their unremarkability.

Heffernan looked up. 'But you still think it's worth following up?'

Wesley thought for a moment. 'There might be nothing in it but I'd like to dig a bit deeper. I think we should have a word with the victims' relatives and see if we can find some common denominator. I'd like to keep it low key at this stage.'

'I'll leave that in your capable hands, then.' Gerry Heffernan fiddled with some papers on his desk, a faraway look in his eye. 'Did you say it was Carole Sanders who tipped Sandra Bracewell off that we'd been asking questions about her?'

'Yes. She lied to us about not knowing what had happened to Sandra.' He watched Heffernan's face for a reaction.

'I don't suppose she saw it that way. She was just protecting her friend, that's all ... being loyal.'

Wesley noted the swiftness with which the boss had leapt to the lady's defence. Something else to report to Pam that evening. He looked at his watch. Almost five o'clock.

'Let's have a word with Robin Carrington about that carpark ticket before we hit the road, eh.'

They made their way down to the interview room, where Robin Carrington awaited them. He had been brought from the cells and he had lost the worried expression he had worn when Wesley had first seen him. Now he just looked resigned, defeated.

Heffernan spoke first. 'I believe the French police are still looking for your wife.'

'You mean they've not found her?'

'Not yet.'

Wesley placed a plastic bag containing the carpark ticket on the table in front of him. 'We found this in your car. You parked your car at Littlebury, the nearest carpark to Monks Island, on the afternoon of Friday the twentieth of July.'

'So?'

'Can you tell us what you did there?' Wesley asked pleasantly. It was best that the man should be at ease.

'I'd read about Monks Island and I wanted to take a look.'

Heffernan leaned forward. 'And what brought on this sudden urge to go sightseeing?'

Carrington's body stiffened. 'I'd been meaning to go for some time – it's somewhere I'd never been before.'

Heffernan snorted. He didn't believe a word of it. 'How did you come to know Sally Gilbert?'

Carrington looked from one policeman to the other. Wesley watched him and detected early signs of panic.

'Who?'

'Sally Gilbert.'

Heffernan produced the dead woman's photograph from his jacket pocket and threw it across the table. Carrington stared at it for a few moments and shook his head.

'I've never seen her before. Who is she?'

Wesley spoke next. 'Now let's go through exactly what you did from the moment you arrived at the carpark to the moment you left.' He glanced at his watch. This was going to take time.

Robin Carrington told his story, Wesley making notes as

he spoke. This was how it worked: the suspect told the story and then repeated it over and over again while the questioners noted discrepancies; ambiguities to be pinned down and examined.

But even after he had recited his account of the afternoon of the twentieth of July three times, Wesley and Heffernan could detect no hint that he wasn't telling the truth. Perhaps he *was* telling the truth; or perhaps he was just an accomplished liar. Gerry Heffernan's money was on the last option.

'I believe you visit this part of Devon every year?' Wesley asked casually as though he were just making conversation.

'Yes.' Carrington had fallen into the trap.

'At the same time?'

'Usually, yes. Middle to end of July. Jeremy, who owns the cottage, says it's convenient. It's quiet and gives me a chance to catch up on work. There's no Internet connection, of course, but that can sometimes be an advantage. Why do you ask?'

'No particular reason,' said Wesley.

Carrington looked tired and the duty solicitor examined his watch ostentatiously. Wesley caught Gerry Heffernan's eye and stood up. 'We'll want to speak to you again tomorrow. We've contacted the Met to say that you're helping us with our enquiries,' he said to Carrington, who merely nodded, resigned to his fate.

Heffernan followed Wesley out, uncharacteristically silent.

'What do you think?' Wesley asked when they had returned to the office.

'I reckon he did it. But why he did it, I can't tell you.'

Wesley nodded. Robin Carrington, already guilty of the murder of an unknown woman in London, was certainly up there on the best suspects list. And if the earlier deaths turned out to be linked to Sally Gilbert's, then it looked as though he had been in the area every year at the appropriate time.

Heffernan slapped Wesley firmly on the back. 'Come on, let's call it a day.' He thought for a moment. 'Do you think I should mention Sandra Bracewell to Carole next time I see her?'

'That's up to you. There's no harm done.'

Wesley glanced at the clock on the office wall. He'd just have time to pick Rachel up from the hospital before his dinner date with Pam. If he hurried.

Sebastian Wilde opened the front door of the plush barn conversion he called home. He stood for a few moments, listening. The muffled thump of distant heavy metal music drifted down from upstairs; from Jason's room. He was home.

Wilde didn't take his jacket off and loosen his tie as he normally did on arriving home. He placed his briefcase and his laptop gently on the polished wooden floor and climbed the great central staircase that had been hewn for him out of ancient timbers by local craftsmen. The music was louder as he reached the top of the stairs. He walked to Jason's bedroom door and stood for a second, gathering his thoughts before kicking it open.

Jason, who had been lying on the bed with a magazine in his hands, jumped up and let the catalogue of glossy, naked women fall to the floor. 'Dad. You're early,' was all he could think of to say.

Wilde said nothing. He stared at the boy.

'What is it, Dad?' Jason tried to sound casual but his voice trembled slightly.

Wilde's response was to raise his arm and strike his son a glancing blow across the face.

Jason's hand shot up to his stinging cheek.

'I've just been to the police station. They want a word with you about my bloody computers.'

Jason Wilde looked at his father. He had always got round him when he was young – his mother had been the disciplinarian. 'Please, Dad . . . it was only . . .'

'I didn't know you could be so bloody stupid. How could you do it?' Wilde was shouting now. He raised his hand again.

Jason backed away.

Wesley drove to the hospital wondering how long it would be before Gerry Heffernan made some sort of move, before he plucked up the courage to ask Carole Sanders out for a drink or a meal. Every time her name was mentioned he merely blushed and said nothing. No doubt he'd do things in his own time . . . if at all.

When he reached the hospital, keeping an eye on the time, he felt an impulse to take some small offering to Rachel, so he bought a bunch of chrysanthemums from the flower stall at the entrance. He remembered that he had intended to take some flowers to Pam that evening, a peace offering for all his absences from the marital home. He would buy some more on the way out.

He found Rachel sitting in the hospital foyer, looking around impatiently.

'I don't know why I had to come here,' were her first words to him as he held out his floral offering. 'I'm fine.'

'You were unconscious. It's best to get yourself checked out.'

'Lot of fuss about nothing.' She gave him a weak smile. 'But thanks for offering to run me home. They said I've still got mild concussion and I shouldn't really be driving.' She looked him in the eye. 'Were you worried about me?'

''Course I was. Everyone was,' he added hastily.

'So what's the latest? Have they found Brenda Dilkes yet?'

'No. She's not at her address. Her daughter's being looked after by a lady she cleans for but she's not appeared there to pick her up. She was expected three hours ago.'

Rachel's lips formed the word 'oh' but no sound emerged. Her mouth was stuck for a few seconds in a sexy pout. Wesley looked down and played with his wedding ring.

'What about the two boys?'

'All in good time. We'll pick them up soon.'

'Do you think Jason Wilde and Oliver Kilburn actually pinched the stuff from Jason's dad's van?'

'It seems likely. And it looks like Brenda Dilkes was in on it too, or perhaps she just suggested the hiding place. Mind you, there were only twelve computers found in that hotel storeroom and six turned up in that shop in Morbay, so that means that there are an awful lot still unaccounted for. They must be keeping them somewhere and they'd need somewhere big.'

'It'd have to be somewhere well away from Jason's dad.' Rachel smiled at him. 'I hear rumours that the boss has found himself a lady friend. About time, if you ask me.'

'Sam's been landscaping a garden for a certain lady and Gerry's become rather keen on picking him up from work instead of leaving him to get the bus.' He grinned. 'I think he's plucking up the courage to ask her out.'

'What's she like?'

'She seems nice.'

'Is that all you can say? Nice?'

'There's not much else to say. She's the sister of Sebastian Wilde – the owner of Nestec ... and Jason Wilde's auntie.'

'So there's money in the family. Perhaps the boss has struck lucky at last.'

Wesley looked at his watch. 'We'd better be off. I'm taking Pam out for that meal at the Tradfield Manor tonight.'

'Very nice,' Rachel said without enthusiasm.

They walked out together to the carpark, but when they reached the entrance Wesley saw that the flower seller had packed up for the night. Pam would have to do without.

Brenda Dilkes looked at the empty bottle and knew that she had had too much to drink. She lay on the balding candlewick bedspread and stared at the ceiling. She had lain there quite still while the police hammered on the door. She had lain there while the phone rang, once, twice, twenty times. But she hadn't answered it.

She should never have let Jason Wilde involve her in his schemes. But then Jason could be very persuasive when he wanted to be.

She sat up slowly. Her head swam and a feeling of nausea rose in her chest. After a few deep breaths she felt a little better, and the sight of the grubby cream telephone on the chest of drawers reminded her that she should make a phone call. She was supposed to have picked Kayleigh up from Carole's hours ago. But, since she had neglected to pay the bill, she couldn't ring out: she could only receive incoming calls.

She lay back and the dizziness started again, as though she were on a fairground ride or a storm-tossed ship. She opened her eyes. It was better when she opened her eyes.

The front door bell rang, a sharp metallic sound. Brenda pushed herself up slowly, swung herself off the bed and staggered over to the window. She stood quite still behind the curtain, holding her breath. But then she smiled to herself, relieved to see that it wasn't the police at the door.

She slid her feet into a pair of dirty pink mules edged with cereal-caked fake fur and made her way slowly and unsteadily downstairs.

'You look nice. And the necklace goes well with that dress,' Wesley said dutifully. He wasn't lying: Pam did look good in the simple black velvet dress. And the compliment helped to hide the fact that his mind was on other things.

Pam fingered the gold chain around her neck. 'Have you got the voucher?'

This was the awkward part, presenting the special-offer voucher for the meal. He fumbled in his inside pocket and produced it. Fifty per cent off the bill was worth a smidgen of social embarrassment.

But as he took Pam's arm, ready to make their grand entrance into the restaurant, he heard a voice behind him.

'Hello, Inspector. I thought it was you.' Lisa Marriott looked Pam up and down. 'You here for dinner, then?'

'That's right.' Pam noted the thick make-up teamed with the short white uniform. 'Do you work here?'

'In the beauty salon.'

Pam noticed that Lisa Marriott was staring at her throat. Her hand went up instinctively and touched the necklace. 'Is something the matter?' she asked, slightly worried. Perhaps the woman had seen a mark on her skin or some horrible swelling.

'I'm sorry, it's just your necklace. It's just like ... May I have a look?'

'Of course,' said Pam, slightly nervous. She could hardly refuse. She put her hand under the locket and held it out for Lisa to see. Wesley looked on patiently: this was women's stuff.

But after a brief examination, Lisa turned to Wesley. 'Do you know, this is just like a necklace that Sally used to wear. I can't really remember very well but she might have been wearing it when I last saw her ... I think I mentioned it when I reported her missing but then I forgot all about it.' She squinted at the locket again, examining it closely.

'Are you sure?' asked Wesley.

'There can't be two like it. Sally said it was an antique – real gold. There's a little dent in the back here, see.'

Pam undid the clasp with trembling hands and held the locket, examining it closely. She knew Lisa was right. She looked at Wesley, uncertain what to say now that her small deception had been uncovered.

Lisa stood there looking rather embarrassed. 'I'm sorry,' she said. 'Perhaps it's just very like it.' She gave Pam an apologetic half-smile.

Pam felt a rising surge of anger, looking for someone to blame. She glared at Wesley, infuriated that he seemed to be taking the thing so calmly. Tears began to well in her eyes. She thrust the necklace into his hand and marched out of the building.

Lisa caught Wesley's eye and blushed. 'I'm sorry,' she said, lost for other words.

'Are you absolutely positive?'

'Oh yes. I recognised it as soon as I saw it. Sorry if I've got you into trouble with ... er ...'

'That's okay,' he said quickly, before following Pam outside, clutching the necklace in his fist.

He found her near the entrance, sitting on a low wall, sobbing into a crumpled tissue. He sat down beside her and put his arm around her shoulder. 'Did you know it was valuable?'

Pam said nothing. Even though Wesley's question was gentle she still felt like a criminal undergoing interrogation and experienced another wave of anger. He repeated the question. 'I saw there was a hallmark,' she muttered.

'You should have told me.'

'Why?' she snapped.

'It puts me in an embarrassing position, you must see that.'

She turned to him, her eyes narrowed. 'How was I to know it belonged to some woman who'd been murdered? I asked Kayleigh's mum about it and she said it had been an unwanted present. She had a lot of men friends so I thought one of them must have given it to her.' He could hear the frustration in her voice. 'You just don't understand. What was I supposed to do ... interrogate the woman? I had to take her word for it. I could hardly call her a liar, could I? And there was Kayleigh – I couldn't hurt her feelings.'

'So why the secrecy?'

'Because I knew how you'd react. Even now when we're supposed to be having a night out, you're always on duty. You can't bloody stop yourself.'

'I'm sorry,' he whispered, taking her hand. 'But it's not my fault that Lisa recognised it, is it?' He gave her hand a squeeze. 'Come on. We can talk about this later. I don't know about you but I'm hungry.'

She hesitated. Then she looked into his eyes. She knew deep down that it was her own awkwardness, the unease she had felt since she had first seen the hallmark on the gold locket, which was making her so touchy. She was behaving like a bitch, but sometimes behaving like a bitch felt liberating ... as long as you didn't keep it up for too long. Her stomach rumbled and she realised that she was hungry too. Perhaps it was time to call a truce. 'Okay,' she said.

Wesley helped her up. As they walked back into the hotel, Pam slightly ahead, he put his hand in his jacket pocket and felt the necklace there. The question of how it got from Sally Gilbert's neck to Pam's would have to wait until another day.

Chapter Eleven

It grieves me to say that the wrecking of ships off our coast, particularly around Chadleigh, continued and the authorities could do little to stop it. I preached against it many times, earning myself the praise of Lord Mereham, the patron of my living, and Mistress Iddacombe, who was particularly distressed to hear of the evil being done so near to her estate. I was pleased to be invited to dine at Chadleigh Hall on several occasions after the marriage of Mary Anne with Captain Smithers. The Captain was most attentive towards his new mother-in-law and I hoped that there had been no truth in the rumours of an attraction between them. I was concerned for Mary Anne, who looked most ill and hardly uttered a word the whole evening, but then it occurred to me that women sometimes behave thus when they are first with child and that maybe her pale looks foretold a joyous event.

I spent much time in conversation that evening with Mistress Iddacombe's elder daughter, Caroline, who, it seemed, was to be betrothed to Lord Mereham's nephew. As for young James Iddacombe, I feared that he had not inherited his sister's pleasing nature. He spoke to me only to complain that his sister, Mary Anne, had married beneath her, and I sensed that he resented Captain Smithers' position in the household. And when the storm began to rage outside, he absented himself from the company without explanation.

The next morning, as I walked through Millicombe towards the church, I heard the news that another ship had been wrecked not far from Chadleigh. I prayed then that the villagers had heeded the words of my last sermon and aided the poor wrecked souls instead of doing them harm. But I was fearful that the devil had entered the hearts of the people of Chadleigh.

From An Account of the Dreadful and Wicked Crimes of the Wreckers of Chadleigh *by the Reverend Octavius Mount, Vicar of Millicombe*

The meal at the hotel had been eaten in awkward silence and Pam had been up for much of the night with heartburn. Medallions of pork swimming in a thick sherry sauce followed by tarte tatin which lashings of cream had proved too rich for an irate pregnant woman whose necklace was sitting in her husband's pocket in a plastic evidence bag. By the end of the evening at least they had been talking in a civilised manner – although Wesley found the large helping of humble pie he was forced to eat in order to keep the peace less appetising than the meal.

Mental activity rather than indigestion had kept Wesley awake. He turned the case over in his tired mind until nothing made sense. He wondered about the theory that Steve Carstairs, of all people, had dangled before him. A number of deaths, possibly one a year, which might or might not be related.

He thought of Sally Gilbert, pushed off a deserted cliff top in a struggle; about her mysterious appointment and the official-looking letter she had hidden from those around her. Sally, who had a husband who may have been involved in the Nestec hijacking and a lover with a history of violence. Then there was the necklace: Pam had been given it by Kayleigh Dilkes, who, in turn, had been given it by her mother, Brenda, who was somehow involved with the missing computers. But how did Brenda get hold of Sally Gilbert's necklace? Did she steal it? Or had Pam's colleague, Jackie Brice, been right when she had said it had probably been a gift from one of Brenda's gentleman friends? From Trevor Gilbert? The missing computers provided a link between them. And if Brenda was well known for picking up men, perhaps she had encountered Mike Battersley or Robin Carrington.

Wesley lay awake, impatient. He longed to get back to the station; he longed to start asking questions.

At seven he threw aside the duvet and got out of bed. Pam stirred beside him and opened her eyes.

'How's the heartburn?'

'Better.'

He leaned over and kissed her forehead. 'I'm sorry about last night. I'll buy you a new necklace, better than ...'

She managed a weak smile. 'I don't think I want it anyway if it belonged to that woman who was murdered.' She sat up. 'Sorry for being such a bitch. Blame my hormones. I don't even want to see that thing again.'

Wesley sat down on the bed and took her in his arms. They stayed there, cuddled close for a while, until Wesley kissed her and gave her a last affectionate squeeze. 'I've really got to go. I promise I'll take some time off when we've got this case cleared up. I said I'd decorate the bedroom, didn't I?'

'When will that be?'

He forced himself to smile optimistically. 'Who knows, perhaps the necklace is the breakthrough we need.'

She kissed him absent-mindedly but didn't answer.

Sunday passed uneventfully: a day of semi-rest and routine; a day to catch up and collect thoughts. Officers were sent to pick up Jason Wilde and Oliver Kilburn but again neither was at home ... or so the police were told by Sebastian Wilde and Dominic Kilburn. Of Brenda Dilkes there was still no sign.

On Monday morning, after a swift breakfast of corn-flakes and orange juice, Wesley made his way down the hill towards the town. He felt that the walk did him good and cleared his head. And he needed a clear head to deal with the Sally Gilbert case.

Mike Battersley had been released on bail and suspended from his duties in the Traffic Division after being told in no uncertain terms by Gerry Heffernan that he wasn't to leave the area.

Trevor had returned to Nestec full-time, which was probably better than moping at home. Robin Carrington had been charged with conspiracy to murder, arson and defrauding the insurance company just for starters, and was being held in the cells. That trio seemed to be the favourite suspects at the moment, although Wesley had no idea what motive Robin Carrington could have had for disposing of Sally Gilbert. Then there was Sebastian Wilde, who might have been more to Sally than just her husband's boss: he had been on Monks Island at the approximate time of Sally's death. He might have taken the necklace and his son, Jason, might have given it to Brenda.

Or perhaps Sally had been killed by someone else entirely. They had no proof, no evidence. They needed a breakthrough, a bit of luck.

Wesley arrived at the CID office to be told by Trish Walton that Oliver Kilburn and Jason Wilde had been brought in at last and were waiting in separate interview rooms for someone to have a word. She looked at Wesley as though she assumed he'd volunteer and he felt he had no choice.

As Heffernan and Rachel were on their way to speak to Jason Wilde, Wesley was left with young Kilburn. He took DC Paul Johnson with him. He could trust Paul not to say anything that might aggravate the expensive solicitor who would no doubt be supplied by the boy's father.

Wesley entered the room first to find the solicitor – a large grey-haired, grey-suited man – sitting by his youthful client like a mother cow protecting her calf.

Wesley gave Oliver a businesslike smile. 'Now then, Mr Kilburn, you and your friend were seen at the Tradfield Manor Hotel with a number of computers stolen from Nestec. Have you anything you'd like to tell us?'

Oliver Kilburn leaned forward eagerly. 'It wasn't my idea. Jason found all these boxes stashed away in the stables at his place. Loads of them. He thought they were old machines his dad was going to sell off cheap so we reckoned we could flog 'em and make ourselves a bit of cash. I got hold of one of my dad's vans and we put some of them in an outhouse at Jason's Auntie Carole's house. Then Jason reckoned it was damp and his auntie had gardeners in and one of them was getting nosey, so we moved them to an old storeroom at my dad's hotel which no one ever uses. Jason got the key from one of the cleaners he knows.'

'Did you sell some of the computers to a shop in Morbay?'

The solicitor shot Oliver a warning look but the young man ignored him, having decided that honesty was the best policy. 'That's right. We told him something about a firm closing and getting rid of their gear. It was easy. Then . . .'

'Then what?'

'Then the local paper gave the serial numbers of the computers that were nicked from that van. As I said, we thought they were just out-of-date ones; surplus stock.'

'But when you checked the serial numbers you discovered that they were the computers that were supposed to have been stolen? Are you sure that Jason got them from his father's place?'

Oliver nodded. 'Yeah. I helped him shift them. What'll happen to me? I've not done anything wrong.'

He didn't look so sure of himself now. What had sounded like a good idea – turning his friend's father's unwanted computers into cash – had backfired.

'What do you know about Brenda Dilkes?'

Oliver hesitated. 'She cleans at the Tradfield Manor.'

'And how does Jason know her?'

Oliver blushed. 'He said he met her at his aunt's house. He ... er ...'

'What?'

'You know. He pays her for ...'

Wesley raised his eyebrows and said nothing. It seemed that cleaning wasn't Brenda's only source of income.

He sensed that there was nothing more Oliver could tell him. He told him he was free to go after he'd made a statement. They knew where to find him if necessary.

It seemed that the Nestec robbery was solved – and, as they had suspected, it had been an inside job. They just hadn't suspected that it was Sebastian Wilde himself who had robbed his own company.

Heffernan, sitting with his feet up on the cluttered desk, looked up and grinned as Wesley entered his office.

'How did you get on with Jason Wilde?' Wesley asked as he sat down.

'He knows something but he's not saying. The cocky little so-and-so just kept saying 'no comment'. He's got a nasty black eye – looks like someone's been having a go at him. What about young Kilburn?'

Wesley launched into an account of Oliver Kilburn's revelations.

'Believe him?' Heffernan looked sceptical. Then Wesley remembered that Oliver's accusations were against Sebastian Wilde and Carole Sanders was Wilde's sister. A potentially awkward situation.

'Yes, I think I do. Why? Do you think he and Jason hijacked they lorry and he's trying to lay the blame on someone else?'

'He wouldn't be the first poor little rich boy to get his kicks from a crime spree. But I'm keeping an open mind. I suppose we'll have to get a search warrant for Wilde's place.'

'I've already arranged it.'

Heffernan sighed. 'Then we'll have to see what turns up

and what Sebastian Wilde has to say for himself. Anything else to report?'

'We sent someone to pick Brenda Dilkes up but she still doesn't appear to be at home. Steve's still going through those old files to see if any other deaths can be linked to Sally Gilbert's. I'd like to start having a word with the relatives to see if the victims had anything in common.'

'Or knew anyone in common.'

Wesley took the plastic bag that contained the necklace from his pocket and placed it on the desk in front of the chief inspector.

Heffernan looked up and grinned. 'Oh, Wesley, you shouldn't have . . .'

'It's Pam's. Or rather it was given to Pam by one of her pupils – Brenda Dilkes's daughter.'

'So?'

'Pam was wearing it when we went out for dinner on Saturday night to the Tradfield Manor. We met Lisa Marriott.' He paused for the punch line. 'Lisa identified it as Sally Gilbert's.'

Heffernan raised his eyebrows. 'Embarrassing.'

'Pam wasn't amused.'

'Was Lisa Marriott certain?'

'She seemed certain. I want to show it to Trevor Gilbert; see if he can confirm it.'

Heffernan looked at his watch. 'Right. When we visit Nestec to speak to Sebastian Wilde about his amazing vanishing computers, we'll have a word with Trevor Gilbert – kill two birds with one stone.'

They waited until Trish had supplied them with coffee to clear their heads before they drove out to Neston. Gerry Heffernan sat in the passenger seat beside Wesley, firing questions about the Tradfield Manor: the quality of the food; the atmosphere; and most importantly the dent it would make in a policeman's half-empty wallet. He was thinking of asking Carole Sanders out for a meal, he explained, and he wanted to make a good impression.

Wesley assured him that the hotel was satisfactory on all counts and that the 'two meals for the price of one' special offer lasted another week. He thought it best not to mention the fact that if Sebastian Wilde was nicked for stealing his own computers, then his sister might not be over-eager to have a cosy tête-à-tête over the starched white tablecloths with the arresting officer. He didn't want to spoil the boss's good mood.

A team of uniformed officers armed with a search warrant had already been dispatched to Sebastian Wilde's place and they had promised to call Heffernan on his mobile as soon as they found what they were looking for. The chief inspector sat with the instrument in his palm, staring at the thing and willing it to ring. As they reached the outskirts of Neston the telephone emitted a tinny electronic version of 'The Ride of the Valkyries'. Heffernan pressed a key and answered with a gruff 'Yeah?'

After a brief conversation, he turned to Wesley. 'They've found the missing computers piled neatly in Sebastian Wilde's stable block. Oliver Kilburn was telling the truth. Put your foot down, Wes.'

But Wesley drove sensibly. Sebastian Wilde wasn't going anywhere.

The car swept into Nestec's carpark and Wesley parked in a space marked 'Reserved'. A small, rotund security guard wearing a peaked cap watched suspiciously and marched over as the two policemen got out of their car.

'You can't park there.'

Gerry Heffernan got out his warrant card and held it up to the little man's nose. 'I think you'll find that we can park anywhere we like. I take it Mr Wilde's in his office?'

The man's eyes darted round anxiously. Wesley felt sorry for him. 'I'd better let him know you're here.'

Heffernan began to walk towards the offices. 'I'd rather you didn't. I want to give him a nice surprise. Come on, Wes.'

They marched off, leaving the security man fidgeting

with his walkie-talkie, wondering what to do. Then he decided that it was best to do nothing and returned to the glass booth at the carpark entrance to do a convincing imitation of the three wise monkeys.

Sebastian Wilde's secretary was harder to deal with. Like a dragon at the entrance to a treasure cave – or the more obstructive kind of doctor's receptionist – she did her best to convince Gerry Heffernan that her boss was busy and couldn't possibly be disturbed. But Heffernan had decided on bulldozer tactics. He flung Wilde's office door open and walked straight in. Wesley shot the secretary an apologetic smile and followed.

Wilde, sitting behind his desk with a telephone receiver pressed against his ear, looked up at the newcomers and mumbled something to the caller about ringing back later. He stood up, his expression caught between anger and worry.

It was Gerry Heffernan who spoke first. 'I've just witnessed a miracle.'

'What do you mean?' Wilde's voice was wary.

'I've just had my faith in human nature restored. And believe me, after a few years in this job it's taken some battering.' He smiled benevolently. 'Can I sit down and tell you about it?'

Wilde said nothing. Heffernan made himself comfortable in a chair on the other side of the large desk. Wesley stood, watching Wilde's face.

'I've just seen a load of vicious thieves so overcome with remorse that they've returned the goods they stole to their rightful owner. Isn't that nice?'

Wilde fidgeted with a pencil, turning it over and over in his fingers. 'What do you mean? What's this got to do with me?'

'The thieves who nicked your computers, they've returned them. They've left them in your stables for you to find. Now isn't that a stroke of luck? Unless . . .'

Wesley could tell that Wilde was really starting to panic.

The pencil was gripped tighter and turned faster. Until it snapped.

'Unless it was you who staged the robbery in the first place. Hard time for computer businesses, isn't it? I bet you put in an insurance claim pretty smartish, eh? How much was it for?'

Wilde's voice was quiet as he told them. He stared down at his desk, avoiding their eyes.

'And the driver?'

Wilde took a deep breath. He knew when he was beaten. 'I met up with him on the road out of Neston. It was all arranged. I had to knock him about a bit to make it look convincing. He knew what to expect. It was all agreed.'

'So then you drove the van to the rendezvous and took out all the computers?'

Wilde shook his head. 'The computers had never been in the van. Another van had taken them to the stables. The van that I well, I suppose you could call it 'stole' ... was empty. It saved time.'

'So your warehouse manager was in on it?' Wesley asked.

Wilde nodded. 'Trevor didn't want to do it but I persuaded him. I said it'd save the firm. If I got the insurance money and then changed the serial numbers and sold the computers, there'd be a chance there wouldn't have to be redundancies.'

'But Trevor was reluctant to go along with it?'

'As I said, he took some persuading. I knew he was the weak link so I had to keep on at him to keep his mouth shut.'

'And kidnap his wife to keep him quiet?' Heffernan leaned forward. 'You were on Monks Island at the time of Sally Gilbert's death. How do we know you didn't threaten her? How do we know that you didn't take her to the edge of the cliff to scare her and it all went wrong?'

Wilde looked from one man to the other. For a potential murder suspect, he didn't seem too worried. 'I never saw her that day. I was with the hotel's IT manager all the time I was there. He even walked me back to the carpark on the mainland.' He hesitated. 'I suppose it was Trevor who told you about the computers?'

'No. As a matter of act it was a friend of your son's. I don't suppose you were aware of their little scam?'

Wilde didn't answer.

'It seems that your son found the computers you hid and hit upon a scheme to convert them into cash. He was offering them for sale to computer shops. He'd even taken a few and was storing them at another location for easy access.'

Wilde picked up another pencil and snapped it.

Wesley wandered over to the wide office widow that overlooked the entrance. A police car had just drawn up outside – the vehicle that would transport Sebastian Wilde to Tradmouth police station while Wesley and Heffernan made further enquiries.

Wilde was surprisingly quiet as he left. His secretary watched, astonished, as he was led away by two uniformed constables. Then she sat down at her desk, put on the glasses that hung around her neck and resumed her typing. Wesley suspected that she never allowed anything to get in the way of the smooth running of the office. Perhaps Gerry Heffernan needed someone just like her to help him conquer his paperwork.

They found Trevor Gilbert in the glass-fronted office perched high above the warehouse. He eyed them warily as they came in but remained seated at his desk.

'Is there any news?' were his first words. 'Have you charged him?'

'Charged who?' Wesley asked.

'The boyfriend. You were questioning him. Have you charged him yet?'

Trevor had always appeared to treat Sally's extramarital affair with patience and tolerance. But perhaps that had been an act put on for her benefit ... and the police's. Wesley certainly detected a new vindictiveness in his voice.

'We're still making enquiries,' he answered, giving nothing away. 'In fact we're here about another matter. The stolen computers have turned up.'

Trevor's mouth fell open.

'Only they weren't stolen, were they?' Heffernan stepped forward, intimidating the man with his bulk. 'You hid them for Sebastian Wilde. You were in on it.'

Trevor nodded and hung his head like a naughty boy in front of a cane-happy headmaster. 'He said it'd save our jobs. I told him I wouldn't do it but he said that if I didn't . . .'

'What?'

'He said that if I didn't help and keep my mouth shut, something would happen. He didn't say what. I thought he meant I'd lose my job and he'd put the word round that I was no good so I'd never get another. I couldn't afford to lose this job, you see. We'd lived beyond our means for ages. Sally's spending got us in a right mess so I had to go along with Wilde's scheme. I had no choice.' He looked at Wesley . He suspected that of the two he would be the more sympathetic.

'You could have come to us. What is it they call it? . . . blown the whistle,' said Heffernan. 'Sebastian Wilde involved you in a criminal act. He made you an accomplice.'

Gilbert didn't answer. His body drooped as though life had just defeated him and he was waving the white flag of surrender. He wasn't one of nature's whistle-blowers: he probably wouldn't have the courage. It was easier for the Trevor Gilberts of this world to go with the flow. Wesley felt sorry for the man as he searched in his pocket for the plastic bag containing the necklace. He produced it as Gerry Heffernan watched in silence. 'Have you seen this necklace before?'

Trevor looked at it for a while before nodding his head. 'It looks like one of Sally's. She got it from a posh antique shop in Tradmouth. A hundred quid it cost, even though there's a dent in the back.'

'You're sure it's Sally's?'

'Oh yes. I told her it wasn't worth half what she paid for it – I told her they'd seen her coming. But she said she didn't care. She liked it so she bought it. Same with everything – if Sally liked it, Sally bought it,' he said with a hint of bitterness.

'I suppose Sally's death has solved your financial problems?' said Wesley unexpectedly.

Trevor thought for a few moments, wondering how he could answer without incriminating herself. But when the answer came, Wesley knew it was truthful. 'You're right, it has. The mortgage will be paid off now so at least I won't lose the house.'

Wesley nodded. Things must have been bad for the Gilberts if the house was going to have to go. He returned to the subject of the necklace. 'Did Sally ever mention anyone called Brenda Dilkes? She works at the Tradfield Manor as a cleaner?'

Trevor shrugged. 'Sally knew a lot of people from the hotel that I didn't.'

'When did you last see this necklace?'

'I can't remember. I think she took it with her when she left. I suppose she must have done if you've got it otherwise it'd still be with her things at my place, wouldn't it.' Trevor smiled weakly.

Somehow Wesley couldn't bring himself to ask Gilbert any more questions. He felt the man had had enough. It was time they talked to Brenda Dilkes. And there was no time like the present.

Brenda Dilkes was still nowhere to be found. When Wesley and Heffernan called at the hotel they were told that she hadn't reported for work that day. Then they called at her address on the council estate on the outskirts of Tradmouth, but there was no answer, although an inquisitive neighbour pointed out that her small battered Citroën 2CV was still parked outside. Heffernan then suggested that they try

Carole's house, in a coy tone that made Wesley smile. He just hoped Carole's brother Sebastian's arrest wouldn't nip the potential romance in the bud. It was about time Gerry Heffernan had the attentions of a good woman – or any woman, come to that. And Sam seemed to approve, although Gerry had hinted that Rosie didn't seem to share her brother's enthusiasm.

But Carole wasn't at home. To their surprise it was Jason Wilde who answered the door. He stared at them arrogantly, in spite of his bruised right eye, and told them that Kayleigh had stayed the night and Carole had taken her out shopping. He had no idea where Brenda was and he didn't think Carole knew either. His aunt had been annoyed when Brenda hadn't picked Kayleigh up when she was supposed to but had pretended an overnight stay had been arranged: she had kept things as normal as possible for Kayleigh's sake.

Jason was about to shut the door on them when Heffernan stepped forward into the hallway. 'I've got some news for you,' he said with a smirk. He was going to enjoy this. He watched the colour drain from Jason's face as he told him about his father's arrest and the fact that Oliver Kilburn had revealed everything about the Nestec computers. If you couldn't trust your friends, who could you trust?

Jason knew the game was up. To Wesley's surprise, he even promised to present himself at the police station later on to make a full statement. They decided to leave it at that. If he didn't turn up they knew where to find him.

After a few words with Sam, who was busy watering turf in the garden, they climbed into the car. 'What now?' Wesley asked as he drove away from Gallows House.

'Food,' the chief inspector answered. 'I can't think on an empty stomach. How about the Fisherman's Arms? I could murder a hotpot.'

Heffernan took Wesley's silence as consent and slumped back in the passenger seat.

'So it looks like we've cleared up the Nestec hijacking.'

'One down, two to go.'

'You what?'

'One down, two to go. There's still Sally Gilbert . . . and the Chadleigh Hall skeleton.'

'I thought that skeleton wasn't our problem. Peter Bracewell's made a statement and Alexandra Stanes has turned up safe and sound.'

'And who's to say that Alexandra was the only girl to go missing at Chadleigh Hall over the course of its history?'

Heffernan grunted. Wesley had a point, but why make work for yourself? 'It'd have to be in the last seventy years for us to be involved. Before that then it's up to your mate Neil and his cronies. How is he, by the way? Not seen much of him.'

'He says underwater archaeology's too slow and he wishes he was back on dry land. I reckon he'll jump at the chance to go up to Chadleigh Hall.'

'You want to go back there? Why?'

'Well, we've got to give the builders the go-ahead to start work again, haven't we?' Wesley grinned. 'And we've got to be absolutely certain that skeleton isn't less than seventy years old.'

'Seventy years ago: that'd be back in the 1930s.'

'The hall belonged to a family called Iddacombe: they'd been there since the eighteenth century. They moved out during the war and American troops took over the hall as a base. Then after the war the Iddacombes sold it and it became Chadleigh Hall School for Girls.'

'You've been doing your homework.'

'Not me. It was Neil. It's a fair bet that the skeleton's connected with the Iddacombes.'

'Didn't you say there were still some Iddacombes knocking about?'

'Yes. They live near Bereton.'

'And you think one of their family went around murdering young girls?'

'If it was the Iddacombes, it probably won't be our problem. Unless . . .'

269

'Unless what?'

'Unless the girl died in the 1930s or early 1940s when they were still in residence. It might be worth having a word with them to see if they've got anything they'd like to share with us.' He grinned. 'And I think I'll call in at the mortuary after we've had our lunch.'

'Why?' The mortuary wasn't a place Wesley normally chose to visit.

'I just want to see if Colin can tell me anything more about the skeleton. There might be some clue to her identity.'

Heffernan shrugged. He didn't share Wesley's optimism – or his appetite for work. And if it wasn't their job to investigate, his philosophy was to leave well alone. They had enough on their plates with modern-day crime. 'Any more thoughts on the Sally Gilbert case? I reckon Trevor dug himself into a great big hole when you started asking him if he was better off financially now she's dead. Let's face it, he's got the biggest motive and no alibi.'

'But what about those other deaths?'

'What about them? The victims had got nothing in common except that they jumped, fell or were pushed off cliffs ... and people do fall off cliffs from time to time. You're getting over-imaginative in your old age, Wes.' He took his mobile phone out of his pocket. 'I'm going to try Carole's number – see if she's back. I want to see if Brenda's put in an appearance yet to pick up her daughter.'

'Funny Brenda should disappear and leave her daughter like that.'

'Not if she knows the kid's happy with Carole.'

Carole answered her telephone. She had just got back home with Kayleigh in tow but there was still no word from Brenda: she sounded rather worried. Gerry Heffernan, at his smoothest, said he'd be round later to give Sam a lift home and Wesley suspected that he'd be expected to provide the transport again.

After lunch, when Wesley announced that he was going

to visit the former owners of Chadleigh Hall, Heffernan pulled a face and said he could go alone. Wesley left him in the pub with a fresh pint of bitter on the table in front of him.

Neil had already provided him with the Iddacombes' address and he drove out of Tradmouth towards Bereton, aware of the vast expanse of sea to his left. He had once seen a map of the coast on which all the known shipwrecks were marked: hundreds of them, all lying beneath the waves, keeping their secrets. Just like the *Celestina*.

He spotted Bear Head lighthouse on the headland, the squat white tower that had once guided ships around the treacherous coast now sitting serenely beneath the cloudless blue sky. He drove on until he came to a gravel track and, keeping the tower in sight, arrived at his destination. The building at the base of the tower was low and whitewashed. From a distance it had looked pristine, but close up it was clear that it needed a fresh coat of paint. He parked beside an ageing grey saloon car and knocked on the glass front door.

The lady of the house answered. She was probably in her seventies with tight grey curls above a thin, suspicious face. She greeted him with a hostile 'Yes?' and looked poised to shut the door on him. Anxious to prove he wasn't a criminal, a Jehovah's Witness or a door-to-door salesman, Wesley produced his warrant card and asked whether he could have a word with Mr Iddacombe about Chadleigh Hall. The woman opened the door reluctantly to let him in.

'You have a very interesting house, Mrs Iddacombe,' Wesley commented, making conversation.

She said nothing as she led him into the living room, a surprisingly dark space with small square-paned windows. The room was a mess. Unwashed cups stood on the coffee table and the plain red carpet showed up every biscuit crumb.

'Please excuse the state of the place, Inspector. My cleaner was supposed to be coming this morning but she didn't turn up.' Mrs Iddacombe sounded annoyed. 'I'll call my husband. George!' she bellowed in no particular direction.

A few seconds later George Iddacombe appeared, a tall gentleman with a military bearing and a moustache to match.

'Brenda still not turned up?' he asked, hardly seeming to notice Wesley. 'Bloody unreliable.'

Wesley introduced himself and received an inquisitorial stare. 'I'm sorry, I couldn't help overhearing ... is your cleaner called Brenda Dilkes?'

'Yes. How do you ...'

'And you were expecting her today?'

'Yes. Why?'

'It's just that we'd like a word with her ourselves.'

The Iddacombe looked at each other as if his words confirmed all their worst fears about their errant cleaner.

'Perhaps if she turns up, you'll let me know.' Wesley handed Mr Iddacombe his card.

'Inspector, eh?' George Iddacombe stared at Wesley, curious. 'Come about Brenda, have you? What's she done? You said you thought she was light fingered, didn't you, dear?' His wife said nothing. 'Caught up with her at last, have you?'

Wesley wasn't sure whether the man was joking. He had an old-fashioned, clipped way of speaking. A relic of the British Empire; a man out of his time.

'Actually I'm here about another matter. I understand you received a visit from a friend of mine: an archaeologist. Dr Neil Watson.'

Iddacombe nodded, wary. His wife began to bite a fingernail.

'I believe you used to live at Chadleigh Hall, sir?'

'When I was a child.'

'But children can notice a lot. Do you remember anything odd happening? Or any old family stories of a girl disappearing?'

272

'You're talking about that skeleton, aren't you? Your friend mentioned it when he was here but ... I didn't say anything because it was a bit of a shock coming out of the blue like that.' The old man sat down and invited Wesley to do likewise.

Mrs Iddacombe opened her mouth to speak but thought better of it. She picked up some dirty cups from the coffee table and walked out, giving her husband a warning glance.

'When I was small I used to have a nanny who liked ghost stories. I remember she told me a tale once about someone being walled up in a secret room somewhere in the house. Frightened the life out of me, she did.'

'Where did she get the story from?'

'I suppose it was just a local legend. One of these things that gets about.' He hesitated. 'I asked my parents about it and they were furious and they told me never to mention it again. And then they sent the nanny away, which was a shame because I ...' He hesitated. 'I liked her. And I was sent away shortly after ... boarding school.' The stiff upper lip quivered slightly and Wesley suspected that the old man had just described a time of great sadness.

'When was this person supposed to have been walled up? Recently or ...'

'Oh, I shouldn't think so. It was just a story; you know how these old legends get about.'

Mrs Iddacombe had returned and stood behind her husband's chair protectively. 'It's all nonsense, you know ... ghosts and skeletons ...'

'A skeleton was found, Mrs Iddacombe. And I'm afraid we have to ask questions when a body's found,' Wesley stated, earning himself a suspicious look.

He stood up. 'Thank you, Mr Iddacombe. You've been very helpful. If Brenda turns up, please let me know.'

'I hope she does,' said Mrs Iddacombe. 'I've got the grandchildren coming over later.' She looked around her in despair.

But Wesley had other things on his mind than Mrs

Iddacombe's domestic problems. 'By the way, Mr Iddacombe, do you know what happened to your nanny?'

'I've really no idea,' the old man said sadly. 'She didn't keep in touch.'

Wesley drove away from the lighthouse, wondering why a nanny's indiscreet story had provoked such anger in the Iddacombe household all those years ago. Perhaps the parents were just concerned that she would give her young charge nightmares. Or had there been more to it than that?

He toyed with the idea of going straight back to the police station but instead he made his way to the hospital mortuary, where Colin Bowman greeted him like a long-lost friend and provided him with a large cup of freshly brewed coffee and a biscuit from a box marked 'Fortnum and Mason'.

'I wondered if you've discovered any more about the Chadleigh Hall skeleton,' Wesley said after he'd munched through his third biscuit.

'Funny you should mention that, Wesley. I was about to ring you. I sent away some samples for testing and I've just had the results back. Traces of arsenic were found in her hair.'

'She was poisoned?' This was something he hadn't expected.

'Not necessarily. Arsenic was commonly used in all sorts of things in the past, even wallpaper. Did you know there's a theory that Napoleon was poisoned by absorbing arsenic from his green wallpaper?'

Wesley smiled. 'I'll take your word for it. So this means she was either poisoned deliberately before being put in that room to die or that she lived at a time when arsenic was easily absorbed from her environment.'

'Either, I suppose. But somehow I just have this mental picture of a young girl being turned into a helpless invalid by being slowly poisoned. It happened, you know. There were many cases . . .'

'But you have no proof?'

'Sorry. No. But I still have the feeling that she was in that room a long time – perhaps a century or two. But that's good news for you, isn't it? It means that it's not your problem.'

But Wesley felt that it was his problem. As he walked back to the police station, he felt that he needed to find out who the girl was and who had brought about her horrible death. The murderer or murderers may well have died years ago but he still wanted to know. He felt that someone should tell her story and that she shouldn't be left as a forgotten pile of bones in a mortuary drawer.

Denise Fishwick kept Brenda Dilkes's key – in case of emergencies. She had only had to use it twice in the five years she'd had it. Once when she'd let the gas man in to mend the cooker and another when Brenda had locked herself out.

She had seen the police car call by earlier and leave when the officers received no reply. Denise had hidden herself behind the curtains – a great skill with so much of her to hide – and munched a packet of biscuits as she watched the morning's entertainment. But now somebody was ringing the door bell. Once. Twice. Three times. Urgently.

Denise ambled towards the front door, her large hips swaying, like a ship in full sail. She found it hard to move quickly and rarely even tried.

When she opened the door she found a tall, well-dressed woman standing on her doorstep. She had seen her in the driving seat of the smart four-wheel-drive that had dropped Brenda off once when her car was out of action. Brenda had told her about her: Carole Sanders, the rich and generous employer who obligingly looked after Kayleigh whenever she was asked. Denise could have done with one of those herself.

Denise smiled, showing a row of uneven, stained teeth, her smooth plump face folding into dimples.

It was Carole who spoke first. 'Sorry to bother you but I've been expecting Brenda to come for her daughter but she's not turned up. Do you know where she is, by any chance? I can see her car outside but . . .'

Denise shook her head.

'Have you got a key to her house? Only I'm a bit worried and . . .'

'You just hold on and I'll fetch it.'

It seemed an age before Denise returned, apparently unhurried. Carole asked her to come with her; to have a look around next door to see whether Brenda had left any clue as to her whereabouts. It had been a while since she had last heard from her and little Kayleigh was starting to ask where her mother was.

Hearing this last piece of information, Denise felt she had no choice but to do her bit.

She waddled in front of Carole Sanders – conscious of the taller woman's simple elegance; the plain, well-cut dress and skilfully tied scarf contrasting with the faded cotton frock that strained over her own ample bustline – and held the key out before her. She stepped aside to allow Carole to enter the house first and watched as the other woman stepped lightly over the cheap nylon carpet that had never looked clean since Brenda had bought it. Carole called Brenda's name but there was no reply.

Denise followed her into room after room, all empty but showing recent signs of occupation, and she was reminded of something she had seen on an 'unexplained mysteries' programme on the telly – that ship, the *Mary Celeste*. A half-drunk cup of tea; a half-eaten sandwich; a magazine flung on the settee open at a page on how to get your man – something that had never brought Brenda much luck: Kayleigh's father was a ship – or rather a sailor – who had passed in the night some nine years before.

It was the silence which Denise found disturbing. She waited at the bottom of the stairs while Carole went up to the bedrooms: she found stairs difficult and, besides, she

276

had an uneasy feeling that she might want to make a quick getaway.

When she heard Carole Sanders scream, she knew that her instincts had been right.

Chapter Twelve

I am sorry to say that many lives were lost on the night of the wreck – and not all, I suspect, owing to the cruelties of nature.

It was many months later that I came to Tradmouth and found the port as busy as ever: the river was a forest of masts and sailors roamed the quayside, some the worse for drink. I watched as cargoes were loaded onto the ships that waited to sail off to distant ports: some to the fishing grounds of Newfoundland; some to the West Indies and the Americas carrying supplies for settlers in the New World; others to Spain and France to return with cargoes of port and wine.

And then there was the darker side of Tradmouth shipping; the privateers sailing from the port looking for foreign ships to bring back as prizes, to make rich men of their masters and crew. As a clergyman, naturally I disapproved of this unwholesome enterprise, but I was well aware that many respectable shipowners were involved – Mercy Iddacombe included.

I was surprised to meet with Captain Smithers on the quayside outside the offices of Mistress Iddacombe's company. He greeted me with much courtesy and I enquired after his wife, Mary Anne's, health. It was then he informed me that she would be sailing with him on his next voyage, if she was well enough, and this news pleased me, as I had been concerned about the attention he had paid to Mistress Iddacombe when we had all dined together. He was to take command of a new ship called the Celestina *and she was to carry a cargo of great value. The Captain was clearly proud of his new command, more prestigious than the* Jane Marie *with her cargo of household goods bound for the settlers of Newfoundland.*

It is sometimes as well that we cannot know what the Almighty has in store for us.

From An Account of the Dreadful and Wicked Crimes of the Wreckers of Chadleigh *by the Reverend Octavius Mount, Vicar of Millicombe*

'So who found her?'

'Mrs Sanders,' Wesley replied.

Rachel Tracey nodded knowingly. 'The boss's latest lady friend?'

'I hardly think she merits that title yet,' Wesley corrected with the hint of a smile. 'The dead woman was her cleaner and she was doing her a favour by looking after her daughter, Kayleigh, while she was at work. Brenda was supposed to be picking the little girl up from Mrs Sanders' house but when she didn't arrive and wasn't answering her phone, Mrs Sanders came round here and found ... well, you know what she found. It gave her a terrible shock and she's worried about the effect it'll have on the little girl. Nice lady, Mrs Sanders.'

'So you've given this blossoming romance your blessing?'

'He's thinking of asking her out for a meal, not booking the church. I despair of the station gossip machine sometimes.'

Rachel walked over to the window and looked out. She could see Gerry Heffernan standing beside a large four-wheel-drive car with a middle-aged woman who was dabbing her eyes with a crumpled tissue. He looked as though he was longing to put a protective arm around her shoulder but hadn't quite summoned up the courage.

'The doc thinks it's suicide, I take it?'

'Looks that way.'

Wesley said nothing more. He climbed the stairs, making for the bedroom where the scenes of crime officers and Colin Bowman were going about their mournful tasks.

Colin greeted Wesley at the door in an inappropriately hearty manner. But Wesley's eyes were drawn beyond him to the figure on the bed. Brenda Dilkes lay there as if asleep, her eyes closed and her arms by her side. An apparently peaceful death. An empty pill bottle stood on the grubby white beside table beside a tall clear glass bottle that had once contained vodka.

'Definitely suicide?' Wesley asked.

'I think so but I'll be able to tell you for certain when I've done the post-mortem.'

'Did she leave a note?'

'I don't think anything's been found. Sorry, Wesley, I must go. Duty calls.'

Colin disappeared down the stairs with a cheery wave, leaving Wesley at the doorway watching the busy scene in the bedroom. It had the feeling of a film set where the star on the bed was pretending to be asleep surrounded by bustling technicians and make-up staff who would be unseen in the finished product. But Brenda Dilkes wouldn't sit up when the scene was ended. Her sleep was the real and permanent thing.

There was nothing Wesley could do, so he turned and walked down the stairs, back to Rachel and normality. But his mind was still on Brenda Dilkes. She had given her daughter Sally Gilbert's necklace to present to Pam as an end-of-term gift and she had helped to hide the stolen computers. Whatever was going on, Brenda had been involved. And now she was dead.

Was it remorse? Fear of being caught? Without a note,

he supposed they'd never know. Perhaps it had all become too much for her. Whatever the reason, she hadn't thought of Kayleigh.

He wandered outside. Carole Sanders had gone and Gerry Heffernan was talking to a couple of uniformed constables. His eyes lit up when he saw Wesley, hungry for information.

'Colin says it's probably suicide. What did Mrs Sanders say?'

'She said that Brenda had been a bit down lately, as if she'd had something on her mind. And she thought it was only a matter of time before her nasty habits caught up with her.'

'Nasty habits?'

'She found it hard to keep her hands off other people's property. She used to pinch things, even from Carole.'

'I suppose the necklace could have come from one of the people she cleans for . . . or a hotel guest.'

'It could have come from anywhere Brenda Dilkes had been. I'm really surprised she didn't have form. Who else did she clean for?'

'I've just been to see the Iddacombes. She cleaned for them and they hinted that she was light fingered. Where's Mrs Sanders now?'

'She's gone back home to Kayleigh. She says she's left her in the tender care of her nephew, Jason. She's going to have to break the news. I don't envy her. Poor kid.'

Wesley looked at his watch. There was nothing he could do here: as Colin Bowman had said, it was a probable case of suicide. But there were questions he'd wanted to ask the dead woman. Principally where she had obtained Sally Gilbert's necklace. He began to walk back to his car and Gerry Heffernan fell in behind him.

'I nearly forgot, Wes. Robin Carrington wants a word with you.'

'What about?'

'He didn't say.'

'When's he being taken back to London?'

'When we've finished with him. I hope that'll be sooner rather than later.'

'We've not really got much on him, have we? Only the Monks Island carpark ticket. There's nothing to suggest that he ever met Sally Gilbert.'

'That's why we're holding him. We're ...'

'Waiting for something to turn up?' Wesley smiled. 'Now where have I heard that line before?'

They drove back to the station in amicable silence. As soon as they arrived, Wesley announced that he was going straight to the cells to see what Robin Carrington had to say, promising to call Gerry Heffernan if it turned out to be something interesting ... like a confession to Sally Gilbert's murder.

When he reached the cells, the custody sergeant showed him to Robin Carrington's private apartment: tiled walls; a thin plastic-covered mattress; and the heady aroma of stale urine and disinfectant. When the sergeant peeped through the spyhole he saw Carrington sitting with his head in his hands. When the door was unlocked the prisoner stood up.

Wesley stepped into the cell. 'You wanted to see me?' he said quietly.

He still found it difficult to believe that Robin Carrington was a cold-blooded murderer. If he had met him at a social gathering he would have thought him a pleasant man, hardly the aggressive type: and Neil had obviously taken a liking to him.

Carrington had insisted that the murder had been his wife, Harriet's, idea and that she had administered the fatal injection of insulin to the unfortunate victim. But was he to be believed? And at the back of Wesley's mind was the thought of the other deaths, all falls from cliffs, all at the same time of year, all with the same smell about them. Robin Carrington came down to Devon at the same time each year and the carpark ticket had been found in his vehicle. He had been involved with the death of one stranger, so why not more? But as to a motive, Wesley hadn't any ideas as yet, and he still wasn't certain that the deaths were linked.

Carrington looked pathetically pleased to see him, like a man shipwrecked on a desert island coming face to face with another human being. He held out his hand. Wesley shook it. A man is innocent until proved guilty.

'Have you something you want to tell me?' Wesley began. 'Would you rather go to the interview room or . . .?'

'No. It's nothing . . . I mean it's nothing about the case. I believe you're a friend of Neil's – the archaeologist working on the shipwreck.'

'That's right.'

'In fact I met your wife the other day.'

'She told me.'

There was an awkward silence, as though Carrington had just realised that social pleasantries might be inappropriate.

He gave an apologetic smile. 'It's just that I promised to let Neil see a book I'd found in a second-hand shop. It's about the Chadleigh wreckers and it mentions the captain of the *Celestina*. Is my stuff still at the cottage?'

'Yes. Is the book called *An Account of the Dreadful and Wicked Crimes of the Wreckers of Chadleigh*?'

'You've seen it?'

'I spotted it when we were having a look round. I thought Neil might be interested and I meant to ask you about it.'

'I'd be grateful if you would give it to Neil. I would have done it myself but . . .' He gave a weary smile. 'I don't get out much these days. Am I allowed my papers and my laptop? I've almost completed the family tree I was doing for my clients in the States and . . .'

'I don't see why not. Next time I'm near the cottage I'll get them for you.'

Carrington looked him in the eye. 'You're very kind, Inspector. Thank you.'

Wesley turned and knocked on the door for the sergeant to let him out. Then he turned back. There was one last question he wanted to ask.

'What exactly were the dreadful and wicked crimes of the wreckers of Chadleigh?'

'Murder; robbery; rape. You name it, they did it.'

But before he could elaborate, the door swung open and Wesley was glad to step outside; out of the closed, narrow world Robin Carrington would be inhabiting for some time to come.

Steve Carstairs looked up as Wesley entered the office. Then he glanced across at Trish Walton. He'd let her do the talking.

Trish stood up. 'Sir, have you got a moment?'

Wesley strolled over to Trish's desk. 'What is it?'

'Steve and I have dug out all the files on Marion Bowler and I've been looking for more information on those other deaths you asked about; the next of kin and so on. I've got the files together and made a list of all the names and addresses for you.'

'That's brilliant, Trish. Thanks.' He turned to Steve. Better not leave him out. 'Thanks, Steve.'

Steve blushed and buried his head in his paperwork as Wesley strode into Gerry Heffernan's lair, holding the files that Trish had placed in his hands. Heffernan looked up.

'What did Carrington want? Confessed to all our unsolved crimes, has he?'

'He just wanted to tell me about a book he promised to let Neil have, that's all.'

'No mention of the Sally Gilbert case?'

'None at all. But don't worry, I'm still following up this other lead: those deaths in July each year.'

'So you reckon we've got a serial killer who goes around shoving people off cliffs, do you?'

When Heffernan put it like that, it seemed unlikely. 'I

think it's worth looking into. Have you rung Carole to see how she is?'

'I thought I'd leave it. I can't help thinking about that poor little kid – Kayleigh, isn't it? Wasn't she in Pam's class?'

Wesley nodded. 'What'll happen to her? Has she any grandparents she can stay with or ...'

'I suppose Social Services'll sort all that out.'

Wesley put Trish's files down on Heffernan's desk, keen to change the subject: the thought of little Kayleigh's situation depressed him. 'Trish and Steve have been digging out the details of the July deaths. I'd like to visit some of the relatives and ask a few questions. I might be barking up the wrong tree but ...'

'If you've got a hunch, Wes, go for it. Let me know how you get on.'

'So what's the latest? Has Sebastian Wilde been charged?'

'Charged and released on bail. I didn't mention it to Carole.'

'She's bound to know by now.'

'It's not been her day, has it? Her brother having his collar felt and her cleaner topping herself.'

A faraway look appeared in Heffernan's eyes, as though he imagined himself as the knight in shining armour slaying those unpleasant dragons for his lady.

Wesley looked at his watch. 'I'll have a look through these files and make some phone calls. Then I'll get home and see how Pam is.'

'You do that, Wes,' said the chief inspector, his mind on other things.

The next morning Wesley left Pam sleeping, confident that he had been forgiven for the incident of the necklace. They had made love the night before and had lain, warm in each other's arms, until Michael had decided that enough was enough and had started to cry. Pam had got up to see to him and Wesley had fallen asleep and had stayed that way until he woke refreshed at seven. He had decided not to mention Brenda Dilkes's death to Pam, knowing that the thought of little Kayleigh being alone, left to the mercies of official-dom and the care system, would upset her. He would break the news in his own time.

At half past eight he arrived at the office, prepared for a day that would be busy, even if it didn't turn out to be particularly productive.

At nine o'clock he set out for his first appointment.

According to the files Trish had found, Marcus Charles Gibbon had died on the twentieth of July the previous year, aged thirty-four, leaving a widow and three-year-old daughter.

He had left the house one day without saying where he was going and three hours later he had been found dead at Coreton Cove in the grounds of a National Trust property near Queenswear over the river, his broken body lying sprawled on some rocks at the foot of a path down to the cove. He had never shown any interest in Coreton House or its grounds and his presence there was inexplicable. He had been seen outside the nearby café half an hour earlier but there were no witnesses to what had happened on the path, which was known to be dangerous, a notice at the top instructing visitors to stay away from the edge. A verdict of accidental death had been recorded and the path down to the cove was now closed to the public, awaiting repairs and safety improvements. Marcus Gibbon's death had made the headlines of the local paper and had merited a few passing words in the national dailies. It seemed that dying was the most remarkable thing Marcus Gibbon had done in the course of his short life.

Wesley took Rachel with him to visit Marcus's widow, Linda, who lived in a small semi-detached house on the outskirts of Neston. When he had phoned, Linda had said she would be at home: it was her day off. She had sounded almost eager for a visit from the police – for a visit from anyone, for that matter.

The door was opened a few seconds after Rachel rang the door bell. Linda had clearly dressed up for the occasion and put on a layer of make-up. She showed them into the small, conventionally furnished living room. The place was unnaturally neat, and Wesley had the impression that she'd tidied it in preparation for their visit. She made them tea – in her best wedding-present china – and sat down to face them; the anxious hostess trying to anticipate her guests' every need. Wesley had the feeling that visitors were rare and she wanted to make the most of the company.

'Is that your daughter?' Rachel pointed to a photograph on the mantelpiece – a plain little girl in a fussy pink frock, smiling awkwardly at the unseen camera.

'Yes, that's our Jade. She's at my mum's. I thought . . .'

Wesley smiled. 'We're very sorry to bother you, Mrs Gibbon, but, as I said on the phone, we'd like to ask you a few questions about your husband's death.'

Linda Gibbon nodded eagerly. She relished the opportunity to talk about Marcus: so many people she knew avoided mentioning him at all.

'What did Marcus do for a living?' Wesley began.

'He worked as a salesman at a car showroom – Beckers, on the road into Neston – but he got made redundant a few months before he died. He was looking for work and he thought he had something lined up in Newton Abbot. When he went out without saying where he was going I thought it might be something to do with a job.'

'You didn't know he'd gone to Coreton House?'

Linda shook her head vehemently. 'I told the police at the time that I'd no idea what he was doing there. I mean, he wasn't interested in old houses and gardens and I don't think he'd ever been there before. I suppose he might have decided to go there on the spur of the moment. I don't know. It's all a bit of a mystery.'

Linda's initial eagerness for company had yielded to quiet sadness as the young widow remembered the last time she had seen her husband alive. He had seemed excited when he'd left the house that day, as though he was expecting something good to happen but didn't like to mention it to Linda in case his plans didn't come off. He had given her a cheerful kiss as he left – and he had never come back.

'Did you ask him where he was going?' Wesley was thinking of Sally Gilbert; how she had seemed excited as she said goodbye to Lisa Marriott before setting off for an unknown destination.

'He said he had a meeting and he'd tell me all about it when he got back. But he did say it was something that might solve all our worries.'

'What worries?' Wesley asked quickly.

Linda looked at him pityingly. 'What kind of worries do people usually have? Money, of course. I gave up work when Jade was born but we were all right. Then when Marcus was made redundant we found we couldn't manage. We had to start selling things and we even thought we'd have to lose the house. Of course, that was paid off when he died so . . .' Her voice trailed off.

'So what did you think he meant?'

'At first I thought it might be about a job: but I'm sure he would have told me if it was. Then I wondered if it was some get-rich-quick scheme, but I hoped it wasn't. All the get-rich-quick schemes I've ever heard of have ended up costing people money rather than making it.' Linda Gibbon was clearly a realist.

She hesitated, as though she had something on her mind. 'He got a letter a couple of days before he died – sort of important looking, marked strictly private and confidential – and I did wonder at the time whether it had anything to do with . . .'

Wesley sat forward, listening intently. 'You didn't mention it to the police?'

'Well, I didn't know if it was important.'

'So why mention it now?'

Linda thought for a few moments. 'I've thought about it

a lot since ... gone over and over it. I asked Marcus about it and he just said he couldn't tell me about it yet, which was odd because we never usually had secrets from each other, but ... But he seemed sort of ... pleased about it, excited. Perhaps I should have told the police about it at the time but I was in shock and ...'

'Do you think the letter could have been connected with where he went on the day he died?'

'It might have been, yes. He'd seemed a bit on edge since it arrived – as if he was sort of ... expecting something but didn't like to tell me or count his chickens before they hatched.'

'Did you ever find the letter?'

Linda shook her head. 'No. I looked for it, just out of curiosity really. But I never found it and it wasn't ...' She hesitated, close to tears. 'It wasn't in his pockets or in the car when they found him.'

Wesley and Rachel looked at each other. 'What did this letter look like?' Wesley asked.

'I never saw the letter itself but the envelope looked expensive: that thick cream paper with the address typed. There was a sort of blue line across the black. It looked as if it was from a firm – you know ...'

'Official?' Rachel suggested.

'Not from the tax man or anything like that but it looked as if it was from a solicitor or something. Important ... with "strictly private and confidential" typed on it.'

Wesley had the envelope Lisa Marriott had given him. He produced it, swathed in protective plastic, and handed it to Linda. He saw a spark of recognition in her eyes.

'Was the envelope like this one?'

'Yes,' said Linda, turning it over. 'It was exactly the same.'

After their visit to Linda Gibbon, he and Rachel called on the families of the three other victims on his list. All had died in late July by falling off cliffs, each in different years.

Two had been thought to be accidents, and the case of the third, Marion Bowler, had clearly been a murder, as yet unsolved.

Their next call was to the partner of the late Gilda Flemming, an artist who had taken up residence in the village of Stoke Beeching a year before her death. She had given up a career as a teacher and had sold all her assets to buy a small cottage in the village. As her partner was also an artist, and not a particularly successful one, money had been tight. The cottage was shabby and run down so things didn't seem to have improved since Gilda's death.

Gilda had gone for a walk one day and had never come back. Her body had been found at the foot of a cliff at Stoke Beeching. Verdict: accidental death. She had died uninsured and, the partner had told Wesley mournfully, money was now even tighter. He couldn't remember whether she had received a letter before she died: he tended not to notice that sort of thing. But, now he thought about it, she had seemed quite elated when she had gone out on the day of her death, as though she had some exciting secret. And she hadn't told him where she was going, which was unusual.

The next victim on their list was a John Millwright, a middle-aged man who lived on the outskirts of Morbay with his wife. He had fallen from cliffs near Bloxham on the twenty-second of July two years previously, and his wife had had no idea what he had been doing on an isolated cliff top when he was supposed to have been doing the weekly shop at the supermarket. There had been a suspicion at first that, as John Millwright was experiencing serious financial difficulties, he had taken his own life. But his widow, the last to see him alive, had assured the coroner of his cheerful state of mind when he had set out on his final journey, so it was concluded that his death had been a tragic accident.

When Rachel and Wesley called on Millwright's widow, Paula, there was nobody at home in the freshly painted white bungalow that stood in a suburban avenue on the edge of the sprawling seaside resort.

They were about to walk back down the crazy-paved front path towards the car when an elderly lady appeared round the side of the bungalow next door and eyed Wesley with undisguised suspicion.

'Can I help you?' she asked warily, keeping her distance.

Wesley produced his warrant card. 'We're looking for a Mrs Millwright. Does she still live here?'

The woman hesitated, not taking her eyes off Wesley. 'Yes. What do you want her for?'

It was Rachel who spoke. 'We just want a word with her. Nothing to worry about. Do you know when she'll be back?'

'Can't say I do.'

Wesley could tell the woman was lying. All the crime prevention publicity about bogus officials and suspicious callers had been etched into the psyche of Mrs Millwright's neighbour.

When he handed the woman his card, she took it and held it by the corner as though she suspected it was impregnated with some deadly poison. 'When you see Mrs Millwright again will you ask her to ring me or Sergeant Tracey as soon as possible. Tell her it's nothing to worry about. It's just a few questions we'd like to ask her.' He gave the woman what he considered to be a reassuring smile and left her studying his card.

'At least the neighbourhood watch around here seems efficient,' Rachel commented with a smile. 'I wouldn't like to be the burglar who tries to get past that one.'

The last visit was the one Wesley was dreading. Twenty-three-year-old Marion Bowler had left her parents' home on the afternoon of the twenty-fifth of July four years ago and had never returned. Her body had been discovered at the foot of the cliffs at Little Tradmouth, and there were clear signs of a struggle on the cliff top. According to everyone who knew her, Marion had been a nice girl. She worked in a local building society and was saving up for a round-the-world trip with her boyfriend. Inspector Stan Jenkins, now retired, had been in charge of the case, and Marion's boyfriend had been the chief suspect because they had quarrelled shortly before her death. But there was little solid evidence against him, certainly nothing that would stand up in court. Marion's killer had left no clues and Stan Jenkins had never managed to bring him to justice. Just another unsolved crime.

Wesley was glad that Rachel was with him. She always had the right words to say to grieving relatives – and Marion's parents were still grieving, even after four years. As they sat sipping tea in the Bowlers' drab front room in their small, neat bungalow, Wesley had an uneasy feeling that he was intruding. He would rather have left the couple, prematurely aged with grief, alone, but if his suspicions were correct, they might have vital information.

But they were unable to reveal anything they hadn't told the police a thousand times already. Marion had seemed excited before she went out that fateful day, elated even, but they knew of no official-looking letter. However, Marion had always been down first in the mornings and had collected the post from the mat, so if there had been a letter for her, she would have got to it first.

Wesley left the Bowlers' house with an increasing certainty that there was something in his theory: now all he needed was proof.

'What do you think?' Rachel asked as Wesley turned the car towards Tradmouth.

'I think there's a link but I can't for the life of me think what it could be. The victims don't seem to have anything in common. They're different ages, different occupations.'

'So how many have there been?'

'If our theory's right, Sally Gilbert would have been the fifth. But there might be some before Gilda Flemming that we don't know about yet.'

'There must be something connecting the victims. Something we're missing.'

Wesley glanced at her. 'Of course, they may have nothing in common at all. The deaths might be exactly what they seem: either accidents or unconnected murders.'

'Do you really believe that?'

Wesley smiled. 'As the boss would say, I've got a feeling in my water. I keep thinking about the victims being excited and being secretive about where they were going – and those letters Sally and Marcus Gibbon received. There's something odd going on and it's just a matter of finding out what it is.'

Rachel said nothing for the rest of the journey. Wesley parked the car at the police station and she climbed from the passenger seat, showing rather too much leg. Wesley averted his eyes.

He wanted to talk to Gerry Heffernan. He climbed the stairs to the CID office and made straight for the chief inspector's lair. Heffernan was examining his hair in a small mirror which he shoved back in the desk drawer hastily as soon as Wesley crossed the threshold. Wesley said nothing as he sat himself down, but he noticed that Heffernan looked embarrassed: vanity had never been one of his weaknesses in the past.

'Well, have you found out anything useful?'

'I've talked to the relatives of three people on our list and I think we might be on to something. They all confirmed that the victims went out without saying where they were going and that they seemed excited about something; as if they had a secret. The wife of one of them remembered that he got an official-looking letter a few days before his death and the envelope was identical to the one Sally Gilbert received. The relatives of the others weren't aware of any letters but that doesn't mean that the victims didn't receive one.'

'What was in those letters?'

'The victims never showed them to anyone and they were never found among their possessions.'

'And never found on the bodies?'

Wesley shook his head. 'The murderer must have ensured that he got them back somehow. Perhaps he told them to bring the letter to the meeting to confirm the person's identity and then asked them to hand it over?'

'But why?'

Wesley shrugged. He didn't have an answer.

'Were the victims linked in any way?'

'Not that I can see.'

Heffernan leaned back and closed his eyes. After a few seconds he opened them wide. 'I saw a film once – can't remember what it was called. These soldiers left one of their comrades to die in the desert. Anyway, he survived and later on he went round getting his revenge. He bumped them all off one by one.'

Wesley smiled. 'One of the victims was a young woman of twenty-three. I hardly think . . .'

'Then there was another thing I saw on the telly. Someone was hanged and this relative of theirs went round bumping off members of the jury who found him guilty. What do you think?'

Wesley had to hand it to his boss, this idea fitted better: twelve unconnected people being brought together at random to wreak society's revenge on wrongdoers. 'It's worth checking if any of them had been on jury service. If we find they were all on the same case . . .'

'And the case might have been heard in July . . .' Gerry Heffernan grinned. At last they were getting somewhere.

'Or it may all be coincidence and Trevor Gilbert may have bumped off his wife after all. But I'll have that jury-duty idea checked out. You never know. Do you still have the key to Robin Carrington's cottage?'

Heffernan looked up, surprised at the change of subject. 'Why?'

'Carrington's asked me to bring him his computer and some papers he was working on. And he has a book that he wants to give to Neil.'

'So you're running errands for our villains now, are you?

Is that what they call modern policing?'

'I have to go up there anyway. I've got to call in at Chadleigh Hall and give the builders the go-ahead to resume work on that room.'

Heffernan opened his drawer and threw Wesley a bunch of keys. 'There you are. Don't let Carrington take advantage of your good nature.'

Wesley put the keys in his pocket and turned to go. With any luck he'd find Neil at the cove. And the drive would give him a chance to think.

Wesley Peterson turned the key in the front-door lock of Old Coastguard Cottage and stepped into the hallway. He shut the door behind him and listened, frozen to the spot. There was something about the thick, hostile silence of the empty house that made him uncomfortable, as though the house itself resented his intrusion.

He walked towards the living-room door and had an uneasy sensation that he was being watched.

But he was unprepared for the thing that swooped down on him, aiming for his face, silent apart from a rush of air and a soft beating of wings. The shock brought him to his knees, his arms shielding his head.

Then there was silence. No further attack; no sound. After a few seconds he summoned the courage to uncover his face. He looked up and saw, in the corner, a small bird staring at him with shiny jet eyes. The swift had fallen down the chimney and was slumped on the ground, terrified and exhausted.

Wesley stood up and moved towards the creature, creeping softly. 'You gave me a shock,' he whispered as he picked it up gently, aware of the little body trembling in his hands as he carried it over to the front door. He opened the door, released it into the air and watched as it wheeled away, no worse for its ordeal. Then he turned his attention to the cottage, feeling foolish that the tiny harmless creature had made him so afraid.

If Robin Carrington had any link with Sally Gilbert, surely there would be some clue here. He decided to begin upstairs and work his way down. The place had already undergone a search and nothing had been found, so Wesley concentrated on the hidden places: the back of the huge, glowering Victorian wardrobes; the abundance of loose floorboards. But there was nothing there and nothing downstairs either. He gathered Robin Carrington's papers and put them into a carrier bag, then he zipped the laptop into its case.

He examined the book Robin had promised to lend to Neil, *An Account of the Dreadful and Wicked Crimes of the Wreckers of Chadleigh*. Wesley would have liked to have read it himself but he had enough dreadful and wicked crimes of the present day to think about. No doubt Neil would give him the edited highlights over a pint one day in the future.

Wesley left the house, careful to lock the door behind him: you couldn't be too careful, not even in an isolated spot – the modern thief was more mobile than his historical counterparts. He looked at his watch. It was one o'clock: lunch-time. He had spotted Neil's distinctive yellow Mini in the carpark of the Wreckers along the lane.

Sure enough he found Neil in the pub, perched on an ancient wooden pew near the unlit fire. Matt sat by him, swallowing his beer like a thirsty man. Wesley went to the bar and ordered something non-alcoholic: he was on duty.

'How's it going?' Wesley asked as he sat down.

'Okay. It'll be good to get back in a nice muddy trench, though.'

'You can say that again,' mumbled Matt.

Wesley delved in the carrier bag by his feet and brought out the book. 'I've got something that'll interest you. You remember Robin Carrington?'

'How could I forget him? It's not every day that you have lunch with a murderer. He said he'd lend me a book about the Chadleigh wreckers. Is that it?'

Wesley handed it over and Neil opened the book carefully. 'Great,' was his only comment as he flicked through the pages. It wasn't long before he gave in to temptation and began to read. Wesley strolled to the bar to give Matt a hand with the next round of drinks, fearing that it would be some time before he could get any sense out of Neil.

Neil barely looked up as Matt put the beer in front of him. He was away with the wreckers.

Matt looked at Wesley. 'Have you found out who murdered that woman yet? The one we fished out of the sea?'

'We're still working on it, I'm afraid. Following up leads,' Wesley replied apologetically. 'I presume Neil's told you all about the skeleton at Chadleigh Hall?'

Matt nodded.

'We're allowing the builders back to clear out the room and I wondered if you and Neil would like to come over.'

'The owners of the *Celestina* lived at Chadleigh Hall.'

'That's why I thought you'd be interested.'

Matt looked at Neil. 'Well, I wasn't intending to dive this afternoon so I'm up for it. What about you?'

Neil looked up from the book and nodded. 'Okay,' he muttered before returning to the narrative. Whatever was in the book, Wesley thought, it must be fascinating.

They ate lunch. The Wreckers didn't go in for anything fancy but they did a good plate of fish and chips. Wesley ate hungrily. The sea air had given him an appetite.

When they arrived at Chadleigh Hall, Wesley brought the car to a halt in front of the building alongside a large silver Mercedes, as shiny as a new bullet. Dominic Kilburn was there, which was good: Wesley wanted a word with him.

The three men made their way to the room that had once been Miss Snowman's study. The small chamber was still cordoned off with police tape – just in case the bones had been found to be those of Alexandra Stanes or the Iddacombes had revealed some sinister wartime incident that would necessitate a murder inquiry being set in motion.

But all the Iddacombes had given him were vague mentions of nebulous stories told by some young nanny many years ago: legends that had faded with time but which had had their origin in truth. No smoke without fire. Wesley removed the tape and stepped into the room, then he heard a voice behind him.

'I thought I saw you arrive.' Dominic Kilburn was standing in the doorway. He wore a smart grey suit and a look of irritation on his face, as though he was expecting trouble. He looked at Neil and Matt with something approaching distaste. 'What are these two doing here? Shouldn't they be down at the cove?'

'They've come to give me a hand. I've got some good news for you, Mr Kilburn: we're now fairly satisfied that the skeleton's old so there's no need for us to launch an investigation. You can carry on in here now. But I've asked Neil and Matt to be here when your men clear out the room; just to have a last look and make sure we haven't missed anything. I'm assuming you can spare somebody. It won't take long.'

Kilburn grunted. 'I suppose so. I'll get Ian and Marty to give you a hand: they're the ones who caused all the trouble in the first place.'

Wesley looked Kilburn in the eye. 'But they weren't the first people to find it, were they, Mr Kilburn? Your father and Peter Bracewell found it back in 1964 when you were doing some building work for the girls' school. They must have told you about it.'

Kilburn stood silently, studying his feet.

'Well, Mr Kilburn?'

'I remember my dad saying something about finding a skeleton but I didn't take much notice. He said he'd just blocked up the hole again and kept quiet about it 'cause he didn't want the job dragging on. Before I started all this work I asked him about it but he's not all there now – he wouldn't say anything and I thought he might have been having me on all those years ago.'

298

'Why didn't you ask Peter Bracewell about it when your father first told you?'

'By the time Dad had told me, Pete had buggered off. Rumour had it he'd run off with some girl and I never saw him again. Let's put it this way, I didn't know if my dad was joking when he told me about it ... trying to scare me with stupid ghost stories. But when a skeleton actually turned up I wasn't surprised.'

'Why didn't you tell us all this when it was discovered? It would have saved us a lot of trouble.'

'Because I didn't want Dad bothered. I thought he might get into trouble for not reporting it and ... well, I just thought it best to say nothing.'

Wesley understood. He might have done the same himself. 'How's your son?'

'I think he's learned his lesson. I've got him working in my office where I can keep an eye on him.' He looked at Neil. 'Sorry if that makes things awkward, Dr Watson. I know he was helping you out.'

'That's quite all right,' Neil said quickly. Oliver Kilburn and his crony Jason Wilde had never been the most reliable of volunteers and they weren't missed.

'I don't suppose you've found anything on the wreck yet?' The old confidence was creeping back into Kilburn's voice.

'No gold, if that's what you mean. We brought up another nice cannon yesterday and more pottery.'

This wasn't what Kilburn wanted to hear. He turned to go. 'I'll leave you to it, then. I'll go and tell Ian and Marty that they're needed.'

'There goes a disappointed man,' said Neil quietly when Kilburn had disappeared from sight. Matt nodded solemnly in agreement.

'What do you mean?' Wesley asked.

'He was hoping for rich pickings from the wreck. Gold and jewels.'

'The locals might have got them if they plundered the wreck.'

Neil shook his head. 'Nah. There was never anything like that on board. Just a load of old iron. Mind you, it was reputed to be carrying crates of gold coins and jewels at the time and the insurance claim mentioned a valuable cargo. I think someone was working a scam. Either the owner fiddling the insurance or some of the crew or the men who loaded the ship substituting iron bars for the gold. Whichever it is, at least we've got an interesting story.'

'And you're sure there's nothing down there?'

'Do you know, Wes, I've never come across anything you could describe as treasure in the whole course of my long and distinguished archaeological career,' said Neil with a grin. 'And the wreck of the *Celestina* is, sadly, no exception.'

Before Wesley could reply, Ian and Marty appeared at the door. Ian scratched his backside and Marty looked wary, as if they were about to be accused of something.

Wesley decided that it would be up to him to take charge. 'We've got the go-ahead to clear out the room where the skeleton was found.' He tried to sound cheerful about it. 'This is Neil and Matt. They're archaeologists and they just want to see if anything interesting turns up. Let's make a start, eh.'

Marty and Ian looked at each other and said nothing. Then they entered the jagged doorway to the small chamber and began work.

'What do you want doing with this chair?' Marty asked.

'That's up to Mr Kilburn.'

'Better take it outside to the skip,' Ian muttered. Wesley had the feeling that the two men would rather be elsewhere.

'No,' said Neil quickly. 'It's probably an antique. Just bring it out of the room and ask Mr Kilburn what he wants to do with it.'

They worked quietly, carrying the chair between them: it was a great solid oak thing, heavier that it looked. Wesley, Neil and Matt crammed into the small room. Neil had brought a torch and he swung it round, lighting up the thick layer of cobwebs and filth on the walls and floor.

Marty and Ian were hovering in the entrance, whispering together conspiratorially. Then the whispering stopped and Ian looked sheepish. 'Can I have a word?' he said.

Wesley stepped out of the tiny room to join them. 'What is it?' He sensed that a confession of some kind was about to be made.

Ian took something from the pocket of his jeans, something small and shiny. 'Er . . . when we found the skeleton I, er, went inside to have a look and . . .'

'And you found something?' Wesley guessed.

Ian nodded. 'It was on the floor by the chair. I just picked it up, like, and forgot about it.'

He handed Wesley a plain gold ring, made for a tiny finger. Wesley thanked him and took it over to one of the huge sash windows that allowed the sunlight to flood into the room.

He screwed up his eyes and held it up to the light. He could just make out letters inside.

'I didn't know what to do with it. The missus said it wouldn't be worth much and . . .'

Wesley turned to him. 'Do you mind if I hold on to it for a while?'

Before Marty and Ian could say anything, Neil and Matt emerged, chatting, from the skeleton room. Wesley called them over.

'Ian found this ring near the skeleton,' he said, careful not to sound as though he was blaming the blushing builder for withholding evidence. 'I think there's an inscription inside. It looks like IS and MAI. Any ideas?'

At first they shook their heads. But something was nagging at the back of Neil's mind. Something he'd seen recently. He walked over to the window and stared out.

Wesley waited, gazing out over the grounds: they were worth looking at with their leafy trees and untamed greenery. Such a pity Dominic Kilburn was planning to turn them into a golf course like a thousand other golf courses.

Neil swung round suddenly, making the two builders jump. 'The *Celestina*. Her captain was Isaiah Smithers and he married a Mary Anne Iddacombe. IS and MAI.'

'But what would Mary Anne's wedding ring be doing in that room? She's buried in the local churchyard with the rest of the people from the *Celestina*.'

Neil shrugged. It was a good question.

Chapter Thirteen

It distresses me to write that Captain Smithers' new command, the Celestina, *was lost with all hands on the night of the twenty-fourth of July 1772. The loss of a ship is an all too familiar tragedy on our treacherous Devon shores but I did not know the whole truth of the matter until Joseph Daniel, a villager of Chadleigh and thus one of the souls in my care, made full confession of his wrongdoings at the trial of Jud Kilburn.*

I learned at Kilburn's trial that on the night the Celestina *was lost, Jud Kilburn called upon the said Daniel to tell him that a wreck was expected that very night and that there would be rich pickings for the whole village. Daniel waited without a thought for the poor souls on the ship for, like George Marbis before him, he was so sunk in greed and wickedness.*

Later Daniel spotted Jud Kilburn near to the notorious inn known to all as the Wreckers with a man he recognised as a servant from Chadleigh Hall. He saw Kilburn hurry off with the man and he hoped the gentry hadn't discovered Kilburn's plans, for if they had they would have put an end to the villagers' main source of prosperity. And without the rich pickings from the wrecks, many might go hungry.

From An Account of the Dreadful and Wicked Crimes of the Wreckers of Chadleigh *by the Reverend Octavius Mount, Vicar of Millicombe*

Wesley took the plastic evidence bag containing the wedding ring out of his pocket and stared at it.

'What's that?' He looked up and saw Rachel standing by his desk. He hadn't even heard her approach. 'Is it Sally Gilbert's?'

'I've a strong suspicion it belongs to a lady called Mary Anne Iddacombe.'

'Who's she?'

'Possibly the Chadleigh Hall skeleton, but that's just a tentative theory at the moment.'

The office was alive with activity. Sally Gilbert's photograph smiled down from the notice-board at the far end of the room, flanked by more gruesome photographs: Sally dead, swollen and putrefying. Beside the pictures were lists of suspects and lines of enquiry to be followed in the chief inspector's untidy handwriting. The pictures of the Chadleigh Hall skeleton had been taken down as soon as it was realised that it wasn't their duty to investigate it, leaving a large vacant space on the board. Wesley wondered how long it would be before that space was filled with the photographs and details of those who had died in late July each year for the past five years. Or was it all just a grim coincidence: an unlucky time of the year for some?

Rachel spoke again. Wesley was so deep in thought that her voice made him jump. 'I've checked out whether any of those people had done jury service. Two had and the rest hadn't. And of the two who had, one, John Millwright, had done it a long time ago and the other, Marcus Gibbon, had done it the year before he died. There's no apparent connection between them. Sorry.'

'Not your fault. Thanks for trying.'

'How's your wife?'

Wesley noticed how Rachel could never bring herself to say Pam's name. Or maybe it was his imagination. 'She's fine. Much better now school's broken up and she can put her feet up a bit.'

'She taught the daughter of that woman who killed herself, didn't she?'

'Brenda Dilkes – yes.'

'Did she have much to do with Brenda?'

'Not really. But it was Brenda Dilkes's daughter who gave her Sally Gilbert's necklace. If only we knew where Brenda had got it from.'

'Could have been anywhere. According to that Mrs Sanders she wasn't averse to helping herself to anything that took her fancy. I'm surprised that Brenda gave a gold necklace away. I would have thought she'd have flogged it.'

'Me too. I wonder if she didn't realise its value. She might have thought it was just costume jewellery. Or perhaps when Kayleigh nagged her for a present for her teacher she just gave it to her to keep her quiet. Either that or she knew where it had come from and she wanted to get rid of it.'

'That's possible.' Rachel smiled. 'Have you heard how the great romance is going?'

Wesley shook his head. He had other things on his mind than Gerry Heffernan's love life.

As if on cue, Heffernan opened his office door and bellowed. 'Wes. Have you got a minute?'

Wesley made for the boss's office, conscious of Rachel's eyes watching him. He shut the door and sat down.

'I've had a couple of our lads out on Monks Island. Nobody at the pub remembers anyone answering Robin Carrington's description. It's my bet he's lying. I reckon he killed Sally Gilbert.'

'Why?'

'How should I know? Maybe he's a nutcase who likes pushing people off cliffs when there's not an R in the month. Your guess is as good as mine. But don't forget, he comes down here alone every year at the same time so, if your serial killer theory holds up, I'd say he has to be our prime suspect.'

'And the necklace that was in Brenda Dilkes's possession?'

A satisfied grin spread across Gerry Heffernan's face. 'While you've been out at Chadleigh Hall there's been a development. The phone number of Old Coastguard Cottage was found in the book by Brenda Dilkes's phone with the name "Robin" written by it. It seems that our Brenda used to frequent the Royal Oak in Tradmouth and she was in the habit of picking up men there. I've had a word with Carrington and he admits he picked her up there last year. He says he went back to her place for a bit of how's your father. He denies that he's seen her recently but we only have his word for that. Maybe she picked that necklace up from somewhere she cleans. Or maybe Carrington gave it to her. Let's face it, Wes, he's the best suspect we've got at the moment. Unless you've got any bright ideas.'

Wesley shook his head. He had ideas all right but they were still half formed, nebulous. And the boss was right: it looked as if Carrington was in it up to his neck ... whatever 'it' was.

Gerry Heffernan leaned forward on his desk, sending a pile of papers fluttering to the floor. He made no attempt to pick them up. 'Right, Wes, what have we got?'

'Robin Carrington has to be suspect, I suppose, but I can't think of a motive. There's Sebastian Wilde: he had means and opportunity to kill Sally and I suppose the motive could have had something to do with the Nestec robbery – or perhaps he and Sally were having an affair. There's Trevor Gilbert, of course: Sally's wronged husband. He has to be a prime suspect. Then there's Mike Battersley – he was having an affair with Sally but there's no proof that he was anywhere near Monks Island on the day in question.'

'And there's no proof he wasn't. Same goes for Trevor. What about this serial killer theory, Wes? I must say it still seems a bit far fetched to me.'

'I'm waiting to speak to the wife of one of the possible victims but ...' Wesley hesitated. 'I really think there could be something in it. I've talked to a few people now and all the deaths ... well, there's something about them: the same smell, if you know what I mean. Lisa Marriott mentioned that Sally had received a letter and one of the victim's wives said he had had a letter too before he died – a letter he didn't show her – and it was an identical envelope to Sally's. It might be nothing. I might be putting two and two together and making five.'

Heffernan looked him in the eye. 'Yes, Wes, but what does your gut instinct tell you?'

'I think there's something in it.'

Heffernan sat back. 'See what else you can dig up, then. But don't forget the Chief Super can be very sensitive about his overtime budget. By the way, did you find anything interesting at Chadleigh Hall?'

'We might have a name for our skeleton.'

'About time too.' The chief inspector looked at his watch. 'Get along home, Wes. It's about time your Pam saw something of you. And that little lad of yours.'

'Have you had a chance to ask Carole for that meal yet?'

Heffernan looked at Wesley mournfully. 'Not yet.'

Wesley shut the office door quietly behind him and picked up his jacket, all the time aware that Rachel was watching him.

For several days not much happened. Wesley Peterson felt that he was drifting along on a raft of paperwork, going nowhere in particular.

There was a quiet despondency in the office. All the enquiries the team had made had yielded nothing. No links had been found between the possible victims of Wesley's supposed serial killer. Nothing was found to suggest that any of their suspects had actually killed Sally Gilbert. All they had was suspicion. Solid evidence was harder to find. Even Gerry Heffernan seemed unusually subdued.

Wesley felt that he was leaving home each morning to go through the motions, but he tried not to let Pam see his frustration. He had broken the news of Brenda's death and she had asked what Kayleigh was going to do: he had discovered that she'd gone to her grandmother's in Plymouth, the best arrangement as far as Social Services were concerned. Pam seemed relieved that at least the child was being looked after by family. She'd been fond of Kayleigh Dilkes.

Pam was looking better and was settling into the holiday routine. She had a chance to be with Michael without watching the clock, and she had begun to see friends again. Della was a regular visitor while Wesley was at work: she was exploiting her invalid status and begging lifts to Tradmouth from neighbours and friends. With this new-found domestic tranquillity, Wesley found himself wondering why he felt so restless.

It was Friday morning when the call came. As soon as the phone on his desk rang Wesley picked it up and recited his name. Then there was a long silence at the other end of the line before a nervous 'hello'. A woman – by the sound of her voice not young – asked whether he was the officer who'd spoken to her neighbour the previous week. Wesley thought for a moment and then it came to him. Mrs Millwright. The widow of the man from Morbay who had fallen to his death from cliffs near Bloxham two years before. He had left his card with the formidable neighbour and the message had obviously got through.

But the call didn't raise his hopes; he expected Mrs Millwright to know as little about her husband's death as the other victims' families had. But at least a visit to that street of white bungalows in the Morbay suburbs would get him out of the office. He would take Rachel with him. Elderly ladies usually took to Rachel.

However, Paula Millwright wasn't quite as Wesley had imagined. She was a slim woman with a helmet of golden blonde hair – the type that comes out of a bottle. She wouldn't see fifty again but she was determinedly making the most of what assets she had left. As she led them into her pink sitting room she explained that she'd been away for a few days in the Cotswolds with a friend when they'd called. Wesley guessed from the sparkle in her eyes that the friend was male.

'We're here to ask you a few questions about your late husband's death,' Wesley began as he sank into a large pink armchair.

Paula Millwright suddenly looked worried. 'Why?'

'It's nothing to worry about, Mrs Millwright.' Rachel's voice was soothing, reassuring, like that of a nurse holding a patient's hand during a particularly nasty medical procedure. 'We'd just like you to tell us what happened on the day he died. We're afraid there's something the police might have missed at the time.'

'The police tried to make out it was suicide at first. But I never thought he'd killed himself. I told them . . .'

'Told them what?' Wesley asked.

'That it couldn't have been suicide. He was happy when he went out that day . . . sort of excited, as if he was expecting something nice to happen. I mean, we'd had problems with money and all that but he said things were looking up.' She looked Wesley in the eye. 'Those were the last words he ever said to me, you know. Don't worry, pet. Things are looking up.'

'And you said this at the inquest?'

''Course I did. At least the coroner listened to me. He said it was a tragic accident and that people didn't realise how dangerous the cliffs were around this part of the coast.'

'Do you think it was an accident?'

Paula Millwright shrugged her narrow shoulders. 'Well, I still can't think what he was doing on top of a cliff when he was supposed to be doing my shopping but I know it wasn't suicide. He seemed so . . .' She searched for the word. 'So optimistic when he went out.'

'Why was that, do you think? Had something happened? Is there anything you remember now that you didn't tell the police at the time?'

She thought for a few moments. Wesley and Rachel sat on the edge of their seats watching her, willing her to remember something, anything.

'Well, I suppose there was the letter.'

Wesley leaned forward, his heart thumping. 'What letter?'

'It looked official – not from the Inland Revenue or anything like that; more like one of those letters you get from solicitors: thick expensive paper and beautifully typed. You know the sort of thing. Marked strictly private and confidential.'

Wesley produced Lisa's envelope from his pocket and Paula gave a nod of recognition. 'Yes. It was exactly like that one. How did you know?'

'When did it arrive?'

'A couple of days before he . . .'

'Did you see what was in it, by any chance?' If only the woman was nosey; if only she had been in the habit of reading her husband's private correspondence.

'Well, not really. I mean, I only saw a couple of lines.' She blushed. 'He'd been very secretive about it so when I found it lying in his sock drawer . . .' She looked to Rachel for support. 'I mean, I didn't like John having secrets from me. It's not on, is it? We'd stuck together for richer, for poorer . . . usually poorer. We'd pulled together when he got made redundant and money was tight. It's an awful thing to say but since he died I've been so much better off. I mean, the house is mine now and I did very well out of the insurance. But before that times were very hard. We had to sell our car and I'd have been worth a fortune now if we hadn't had to sell off some of our insurance policies. But he'd never sell his life insurance. I want you to be comfortable if I go, he used to say.'

'So what was in the letter?' Rachel steered the woman

back to the matter in hand.

'Well, I found it and I started to read it but I didn't get very far. I heard John outside the bedroom door so I put it back in the envelope and shoved it back in the drawer. He was unemployed and at home all day so I didn't get another chance until he went out to the supermarket to do the shopping ... at least, that's where he told me he was going. When he'd gone I went and looked for it again but it wasn't there. He must have taken it with him.'

'Or thrown it away?' Rachel suggested.

'No. I looked through all the bins for it. It wasn't there.'

Rachel couldn't help smiling. Mrs Millwright had been thorough in her nosiness. Rachel would have done the same herself in the circumstances.

'Was the letter found on his body?'

Paula Millwright shook her head. The hair was so stiffly lacquered it hardly moved. 'I was in such a state that for one reason or another I didn't mention it to the police until after the inquest. Of course, they weren't interested. They said the case was closed. I expect they thought I was just a grieving widow trying to grasp at anything that would prove John hadn't killed himself.' She looked down at her hands. 'Perhaps they were right. It's always been at the back of my mind that the coroner was wrong. When I think about the debts he had and ...'

'What was in the first few lines of the letter?'

She frowned, trying to remember. 'It was something about him being a beneficiary, I think it was. Then it said something about being confidential and it mentioned money ... a considerable sum. There was a lot more but that was all I managed to see,' she said, disappointed. 'When I told the police about it they just said it probably wasn't important.'

Wesley and Rachel looked at each other. Was this how the victims were lured to their deaths? By a promise of wealth? By greed – or just a desperate need for money when times were hard? Wesley imagined that the letter instructed the victim to keep its contents secret and to bring it with them to a meeting place so that the evidence could be destroyed. Clever. But why?

'Was there any sort of company name on the letter?'

'Oh yes. It was a Tradmouth address. I tried to look them up in the phone book and the Yellow Pages later on but they didn't seem to be in. I thought about getting in touch with them after John died to find out what it was all about.'

'Can you remember the address?'

'I wrote it down.' She thought for a moment. 'I thought it might be one of those confidence tricks and I was going to check it out if John showed signs of getting involved in anything.' She stood up and walked over to a light-wood sideboard, unfussy and modern – probably acquired during her years of relatively affluent widowhood.

She opened a drawer and took out a small black book. 'Here it is. Iddacombe Finance. Seventy Ship Street, Tradmouth.

Wesley wrote the address carefully in his notebook.

Neil Watson had read the book Robin Carrington had lent him with great interest. At last he knew exactly what had happened to the *Celestina*, the object of all their attention for the past weeks. And there was more to discover – matters the Reverend Octavius Mount had glossed over, for reasons best known to himself.

Neil was determined to piece together the whole story. That was why he was sitting in the reference library in Exeter with a book open in front of him, its yellowing pages stiff with age. He read the words again, more slowly this time, taking them in, accustoming his eyes to the old-fashioned print; the S's that took the form of F's and the archaic language.

But the story was clear enough. Jud Kilburn had been a notorious wrecker – a ruthless murderer who hadn't hesitated to end of the lives of countless men, women and even

312

children for his own gain. He had eventually been brought to justice. Neil was reading a contemporary account of his trial.

But he was unprepared for Kilburn's outburst from the dock, his every word carefully reported. Words that would have shocked judge and jury alike.

When he had finished reading, Neil sat back and smiled to himself. It all fitted. He knew the truth at last.

There was no 70 Ship Street. The numbers on that narrow but handsome Georgian thoroughfare only reached the low forties. Most of Ship Street contained buildings that had once been the elegant town houses of wealthy shipowners, now converted into offices of the discreetly professional kind: solicitors, architects, accountants, dentists – all with their names engraved on polished brass plates, reliable and respectable. Whoever had chosen it as the address of Iddacombe Finance had done their homework.

Wesley was back in the office, sitting at his desk with a cup of tea in his hand, when Steve Carstairs sauntered in. He hesitated, as if making a decision, then came over, avoiding Wesley's eyes.

'Er, you had a call earlier. Neil Watson. Said could you get in touch. Claims he's found out something important.'

Steve turned to go. He never spent any longer talking to Wesley than was absolutely necessary. And he had been worse, more surly and resentful, since Harry Marchbank had shown his ugly face in the office again. Wesley thanked him with scrupulous politeness: hopefully Steve would settle down again now Harry was off the scene and back in London giving the Met a bad name.

Wesley looked at the telephone, tempted to ring Neil right away. But there were more pressing matters. He found Gerry Heffernan in his office, looking through a file marked 'Budget' with an expression of blank boredom on his face.

'How do they expect us to catch villains when we've got

to deal with crap like this?' He flung the file to the floor and the contents spilled out. 'Pardon my French, Wes, but if I'd wanted to be a flaming accountant I wouldn't have joined the force. What's new?'

Wesley told him. He gave him chapter and verse on Paula Millwright and her late husband's letter.

'So he gets a letter from a company that doesn't exist then the letter disappears when he conveniently falls off a cliff. Why him? Who'd want him dead?'

'I haven't the faintest idea.' Wesley thought for a moment. 'But I'd like another word with Trevor Gilbert. There's something nagging at the back of my mind and . . .' He hesitated.

'Anything you're ready to share with Uncle Gerry?'

Wesley grinned and shook his head.

'I said I'd pick Sam up from Carole's again after work.'

'You mean I'll pick him up. Have you never considered learning to drive, Gerry?'

'Can't teach an old dog new tricks,' Heffernan growled.

'I've been thinking.'

'What about?' Heffernan bent down wearily and began to pick the budget papers up off the floor.

'Iddacombe Finance. Brenda Dilkes cleaned for the Iddacombes in that lighthouse. And the owners of Chadleigh Hall were called Iddacombe. It's not a common name.'

'All roads lead to Chadleigh Hall, eh? Think there's some connection with your skeleton?'

'How could there be? But it does indicate some link with the present-day Iddacombes. Or somebody who knows the history of the hall.'

'Robin Carrington and his family trees. He knows all about the Iddacombes. And he comes down here every July.'

Wesley looked at the boss expectantly. This was surely more than a wild guess. The coincidences were just too great.

'Carrington's victim – or rather his wife's – was murdered in an insurance scam. Could Carrington have been insuring the lives of all these unconnected people and then bumping them off one by one?'

Wesley shook his head. 'Sorry, Gerry, it's a good idea but under English law you're not allowed to insure the lives of complete strangers for no good reason. They stopped that in the eighteenth century. The Gambling Act of 1774.'

Heffernan looked at him, astonished. Wesley smiled. 'I had that idea myself when I'd seen Mrs Millwright so I called up an insurance company and that's what they told me. It's something called "insurable interest".' He shrugged. 'It was a good idea while it lasted.'

'So if it was Carrington, why did he do it?'

'If it is him, he's not telling. He admits to having known Brenda Dilkes – mainly in the biblical sense – but he denies all knowledge of Sally Gilbert and the other possible victims. And he denies giving Brenda the necklace.'

'And the Met want him back. They're sending someone to pick him up later today. Apparently the French police are still looking for Harriet.'

'Harry Marchbank's daughter?'

'So he says. I've never felt sorry for Marchbank before but . . .'

'They say adversity makes you a better person.' Wesley mumbled the platitude hopefully, although he had his doubts in Harry Marchbank's case.

Gerry Heffernan scratched his head and said nothing.

'I'm going to have another word with Trevor Gilbert. I want to see if there's anything we've missed – any common denominator. The only thing I've come up with so far is that most of the victims seemed to be going through hard times financially.'

Heffernan pushed his paperwork to one side. 'Hang on, Wes, I'll come with you.'

Wesley had wanted to see Trevor Gilbert alone – he sensed the man might be more open in a one-to-one situation. But Gerry Heffernan looked so keen to get out of the office he knew there was no way he could put him off.

As he drove out to Trevor Gilbert's house on the edge of Tradmouth, Wesley's mind was on the common denominator. But he couldn't for the life of him think of one.

They found Trevor Gilbert at home. He hadn't felt like going into work that day. The atmosphere at Nestec wasn't good, he told them as he shuffled out to make them a cup of tea. Now that Sebastian Wilde was facing charges and the workforce knew the reality of the company's financial situation, the formerly happy ship had turned into a storm-tossed hulk. Things looked bad. Redundancies were expected.

But financial disaster was nothing new to Trevor, he explained to the two officers sadly. The one thing Sally had excelled at was spending money, he said, and her credit and store cards had had more exercise than a top Olympic athlete. But at least the mortgage had been paid off on her death, so whatever happened Trevor would keep a roof over his head.

At that point there was a noise upstairs. Something falling over, perhaps. Or a footstep on a bedroom floor. Trevor made no comment and Wesley didn't ask.

Wesley didn't know whether he was imagining it, but he thought Trevor looked a lot happier, more relaxed. Perhaps it hadn't been Sally's death which had kept him awake at night: perhaps it had been covering up for Sebastian Wilde's misdemeanours. Perhaps the truth had been that he wasn't as upset by his wife's death as he'd first appeared: perhaps she had pushed him that little bit too far when she had gone off to 'find herself' in the arms of Mike Battersley.

Trevor looked at Wesley expectantly. 'Have you got anyone for Sally's murder yet?'

'Not yet. Sorry. But we're following up a few new leads.' Wesley sipped tea from the cracked mug Trevor had

316

given him before continuing. 'Did Sally ever borrow money from anybody?'

'She borrowed all over the place. Running up dirty great bills on her credit cards, getting loans.'

'Did she ever receive demands for repayment . . . or any threats?'

'Nothing out of the ordinary.'

'I know I've asked you this before, but did she seem worried about anything?'

Trevor shook his head.

'Have you ever heard of or dealt with a company called Iddacombe Finance? Did Sally borrow money from them?'

Another shake of the head. 'I've looked through all her papers but I don't remember that name. Sorry.'

'Was Sally's life insured?'

Trevor grinned. 'Why do you think I'm looking so cheerful these days? Now if she hadn't gone and sold her endowment policy, I'd be prancing about on the deck of my own yacht by now.'

Wesley had been examining the mug, ensuring that his mouth didn't come into contact with the more unhealthy-looking cracks. He glanced up. 'Endowment policy? What do you mean?'

'She had one of those insurance policies – endowment policies, they're called. You pay in so much every month then the insurance company adds profits and you pick up a big lump sum at the end of twenty years or so. People use them as a way of saving. They work as life insurance as well, so they pay out a big sum if you die before the policy matures.'

Wesley nodded. He had bought one of these policies as a long-term investment when he and Pam had first married, but he had been too busy at the time to take much notice of the ins and outs, and until Trevor had mentioned it he had forgotten all about it. 'Go on.'

'Well, the policies keep increasing in value, so if you've had them for long enough you can sell them to raise cash –

317

there's quite a market in them: people buy second-hand policies through agents as investments. Sally had had hers for years and she sold it through an advert in the paper.'

Gerry Heffernan gave Wesley a nudge, causing him to spill his tea. 'So would whoever bought her policy be able to claim any money now she's dead?'

Trevor looked puzzled. 'Do you know, I've never thought of that. I've no idea.'

'You don't happen to know who bought it, do you?'

'Sorry. She was just after the cash to pay off her credit card bill. She wasn't interested in who bought it.'

'You haven't got the advert she answered, have you?'

Trevor got up. 'I'll have a look through the bureau. She kept all that sort of thing in there. Hang on.'

Ten minutes later Trevor Gilbert handed them a piece of paper with a name and address. Wesley thanked him and put it in his pocket, feeling that they might be on to something at last.

Trevor was showing them out, acting the perfect host, when Wesley heard another noise from upstairs. But this time it was clear that it was footsteps. And they were getting nearer, treading softly on the landing. Wesley looked up. Sebastian Wilde's secretary was standing at the top of the stairs, slightly dishevelled, minus her glasses and wearing what looked like Trevor's dressing gown. Wesley looked away tactfully, but he noticed that Gerry Heffernan was staring upwards with undisguised curiosity. Wesley nudged his arm. It was time to leave.

'Did I really see what I just saw, Wes?' Heffernan asked as they got into the car.

'Yes. I think she was comforting the distraught widower.'

'Is that what they call it nowadays? Where to now?'

'Back to the station. I think we've got some phone calls to make.'

Wesley walked into Heffernan's office and sat down.

'I've just called a local insurance broker who gave me the low-down on these endowment policies. He said that they're extremely popular in this country but rare in the United States apparently.' He smiled at this bit of useless information and hesitated, gathering his thoughts. 'Anyway, the broker told me that when people sell their endowment policies before they mature to raise cash, the life insurance element still applies to the policy's original owner, not the new one – even when a complete stranger buys that policy. If the person who originally took out the policy dies, the new owner picks up the loot. The life insurance is never transferred.'

'So the rule about not having a financial interest in bumping off a stranger doesn't apply?'

'Precisely. Anyone who invests in buying a second-hand endowment policy collects the insurance money if the original owner dies.'

'So if the original owner dies shortly after you buy the policy . . .'

'You've hit the jackpot. No paying out the premiums every month to keep the policy going and no waiting for years before you get your hands on the big pay-out.'

Heffernan sat there for a few seconds taking it in while Wesley made for the door.

All it took was four phone calls. One to Paula Millwright, one to Linda Gibbon, one to Gilda Flemming's partner and one to the parents of Marion Bowler. Wesley could feel his hands shaking with excitement as he finished the last call. Some time before they died all the victims had sold endowment policies through an advert in the local paper. He had found it. The missing link.

He almost felt like celebrating, inviting the whole team to the pub for a well-earned drink. But he told himself that it was early days. He had possibly found out why the killer had struck. But he still had no idea who that killer was.

All they had to do now was to track down the advert and find out who had placed it. Surely it wouldn't be long now.

An hour later Paul Johnson and Trish Walton returned from the offices of the *Tradmouth Echo* with the disappointing news that the advert had been placed by telephone and no individual's name had been given. However, the payment had been made by a firm called Chadleigh Holdings.

The CID office was beginning to resemble a call centre. Sixteen police officers sat at their desks in front of computers, telephone receivers apparently glued to their ears. Chadleigh Holdings had to be traced. If it was a registered company, there would be a list of directors. If it had a bank account somewhere locally, one of the banks would know. Whoever had placed the advert had used an accommodation address; a seedy corner newsagent's in one of Morbay's less desirable areas. The proprietor couldn't remember who had picked up the correspondence – or didn't want to remember. Presumably the endowment policies themselves would have been bought with some kind of cheque. Someone somewhere must know who was behind Chadleigh Holdings.

But it was a Friday afternoon and it was getting late. Commerce has an irritating habit of not working police hours, and many banks had already closed and their staff gone home.

And a call from Colin Bowman only made matters worse. He announced to Gerry Heffernan in jovial tones that the toxicology report on Brenda Dilkes's body had just come through from the lab. His initial diagnosis of an overdose of sleeping pills and alcohol had been understandable in the circumstances as a quantity of pills and an empty bottle had been found beside Brenda's bed. Given this fact, Colin had been rather surprised to find that a completely different drug had been discovered in the body. Someone had replaced the relatively mild sleeping pills that Brenda had been prescribed with something much stronger and more deadly when taken with alcohol.

Of course, Brenda might have done this herself but it did look suspicious.

And there was always the possibility, Colin added cheerfully, that Brenda Dilkes had been murdered by person or persons unknown.

Chapter Fourteen

On the night of the twenty-fourth of July the Celestina *ran aground near the rocks at Chadleigh Cove shortly before midnight. Joseph Daniel testified to the court that he was roused by his neighbours and, as they climbed down the steep path to the beach, he could hear screams and desperate cries in the still night air. There was a light on the cliff top; a lantern tied to a horse to lure the ship to its doom.*

He saw the broken ship not far from the shore, alive with clambering bodies, ropes tied around their waists for safety: villagers seeing what pickings they could plunder. Daniel saw a young woman half conscious at the waterline, and he stated that he saw Jud Kilburn have his pleasure of her before pushing her head beneath the water. But later Daniel himself was attacked. As he helped himself to a barrel from the wreck, he felt rough hands hauling him round and was stunned by a fist in his face. Through streaming blood, he recognised his assailant as Isaiah Smithers, the Captain of the ship, who had married the daughter of Mistress Mercy Iddacombe of Chadleigh Hall. Daniel put up his hands to defend himself, but when no further attack came he opened his eyes and saw that Smithers had been brought down by Jud Kilburn, who was now directing operations on the shore. The Captain fought back but Kilburn was the stronger and Smithers staggered away, collapsing into the water. Kilburn dragged him out, as though trying to save his life, but the Captain was dead.

A short time later the soldiers arrived from Plymouth and Daniel fled, fearing arrest. It was the next day when he heard that Kilburn had been taken.

I am pleased to say that Jud Kilburn, that most wicked of men, who had, like his father before him, led the villagers of Chadleigh away from the paths of charity and right, paid the price for his crimes on the gallows. But even arrest and imprisonment did not cure him of his wickedness and focus his thoughts on his fate in the world to come. He perjured himself at his trial, making wild and wicked accusations against his betters, even under oath. These lies and his lack of remorse ensured that the law granted him no mercy and a huge crowd cheered as his body jerked at the end of the hangman's rope.

And so I finish this account of the dreadful and wicked crimes of the wreckers of Chadleigh and trust that the innocent will receive their reward and the guilty their punishment.

From An Account of the Dreadful and Wicked Crimes of the Wreckers of Chadleigh *by the Reverend Octavius Mount, Vicar of Millicombe*

Gerry Heffernan asked Wesley to drive him to Gallows House: Sam was expecting a lift home. Wesley agreed. It would give him space, a chance to think before he returned home to domestic chaos.

When they arrived Sam was waiting for them, sweaty and dishevelled after a day of manual labour. As soon as he climbed into the back seat of Wesley's car, his father got out. 'Just want a word with Carole. Won't be long.'

'Are you going to mention Brenda?' Wesley asked. But the chief inspector was already making for the front door.

Wesley looked at Sam. 'So what do you think?'

'What about?'

'Your dad and . . .?'

'If he's happy, I'm happy.' He hesitated. 'Although Rosie has different ideas. She reckons it's insulting to Mum's memory but . . . I don't know. It's a funny situation.' He shrugged his shoulders. 'Still, life must go on, know what I mean?'

Wesley nodded. He knew what Sam meant all right.

Carole Sanders answered the door and led Gerry Heffernan into the drawing room. 'Would you like a cup of tea?' she asked, sounding almost coy.

'No thanks, love. I can't stay long. I've got Wes and Sam outside waiting for me.'

The piano lid was open. He walked over and played a small snatch of Chopin. When he turned round he saw surprise on Carole's face.

'Sorry, love. Couldn't resist it. Lovely piano.'

She didn't answer.

'Look, I'm sorry about your brother. I hope . . .'

'If Sebastian gets himself into trouble that's his own fault. I know you were just doing your job.' Her sad smile reassured him a little. At least that was one problem out of the way.

'Er . . . I was wondering . . .' He looked at her. She was standing, head tilted to one side expectantly. Then he suddenly lost his nerve. 'Er . . . I just thought I'd better tell you we're treating Brenda's death as suspicious. We think someone might have killed her.'

Carole's hand went to her mouth. 'But who'd want to . . .? Are you sure?'

'Pretty sure. Sorry if it's come as a shock, like, but . . .'

Carole didn't seem to be listening. 'Poor Brenda. Do you have any idea who . . .?'

'We've got our suspicions, love. Don't you worry. We'll get him.'

Carole gave a weak smile. 'I can't help thinking of little Kayleigh. She's gone to stay with her grandmother but ... Poor Brenda,' she repeated 'Why? I know she was a bit ... well, her lifestyle was a bit free and easy. But who'd want to harm her?'

Heffernan looked at his watch. 'I'd better be off. I just thought I'd keep you up to date and ... er, I wondered ... would you like to come out for a drink one evening ... er ...?'

Carole smiled. 'That'd be nice. But aren't you busy with ... ?'

His eyes met hers. He felt suddenly flustered and he heard himself saying, 'Yeah. When things are quieter, eh?' There was a moment of awkward silence as he searched for something else to say. 'Er ... Sam says your garden's coming on a treat.'

'Yes.'

He shifted from foot to foot, feeling he'd made a mess of things and not knowing quite what to do next. 'I'll see you soon, then.'

When Carole had seen him out he almost ran over to the waiting car.

'Well?' asked Wesley as he climbed into the passenger seat.

'Don't ask, Wes. I didn't realise I was so out of practice.'

He sat back and caught a glimpse in the side mirror of Sam sprawled in the back seat, grinning.

Wesley was surprised to find a crutch in his hallway when he arrived home that evening, hanging from the banisters as though its owner had abandoned it after some miraculous cure. Della was around. He took a deep breath before opening the living-room door.

'Wesley. Don't worry, the cavalry's arrived. I'm giving you two an evening out.' Della held out her arms, beaming widely, playing the fairy godmother.

Wesley bent to kiss her. 'How's the leg?'

'Improving. A friend offered to give me a lift here and I thought I'd surprise you and baby-sit ... give you a night of freedom. But be back by eleven thirty– that's when he's picking me up.'

Wesley had somehow known that Della's chauffeur would be a 'he'. There was a noise behind him and he turned round to see Pam standing in the doorway. She wore trousers and a simple white silk top. She looked good, radiant. Wesley never ceased to be amazed at the difference between the term-time Pam and the school-holiday Pam.

She put her arms around him and kissed him. He put his hand gently on her swelling abdomen; their growing child. 'How are you feeling?'

'Fine. I thought we could go to that pizza place on the quayside then on to the Tradmouth Arms. Neil's rung three times asking if you were home yet. He wants to talk to you. I told him we'd meet him at the pub.'

Wesley had no chance to say anything before Della started shooing them out of the house, as though trying to get rid of them. 'Go on, you two. I can manage here. Off you go.'

They knew better than to argue. Wesley suspected that Della might use the opportunity for some impromptu entertainment of gentlemen callers to relieve her boredom – like a teenage baby-sitter inviting her boyfriend round. But Michael was far too young to have his morals corrupted, so he might as well leave her to it.

Then he remembered something he wanted to tell her. 'Do you remember that girl who disappeared from your old school – Alexandra Stanes?'

'Was it her you found walled up in that room?' Della asked eagerly.

'No, far from it. She's living on the Tradmouth council estate. She ran off with one of the builders who were doing alterations at the school.'

Della laughed. 'At least she had the courage to escape, which is more than I ever did. So did you ever find out who it was in that room?'

'No. But it seems that the skeleton's old so we're not involved officially any more.' He remembered the other question he had been longing to ask Della. 'Do you remember a girl called Carole Wilde? She was Alexandra Stanes's friend.'

Della screwed up her face in concentration. 'Carole Wilde – the name rings a bell.'

Wesley looked at Pam. 'It's just that she's living near by. She's widowed and my boss, Gerry, seems to be taking rather an interest. His son's been doing her garden for her.'

'It's about time Gerry got himself fixed up. I've even thought of taking him on myself,' Della added mischievously.

'She'd eat him alive,' Pam whispered as they made for the front door.

Pam and Wesley passed a pleasant and uneventful hour and a half consuming Pizza Margheritas and garlic bread at the small Italian restaurant overlooking the river before making for the Tradmouth Arms. Their route took them past St Margaret's church, and as they passed the faint sound of the organ and choir seeped through the ancient walls. Wesley thought he could just make out the tune of 'For Those in Peril on the Sea'. Gerry Heffernan would be in there practising for next Sunday's service.

This reminder of his boss set Wesley thinking about Carole Sanders. She seemed a nice woman, from the little he'd seen of her, and, according to Gerry, her brother's arrest for the Nestec robbery hadn't affected her attitude towards the police in general and Gerry in particular. Sam was still working on her garden and all could be right with Gerry's world – if he could get his act together and find the courage to ask the lady out.

He glanced at Pam. She was wearing a plain silver chain

around her neck; he recognised it as one she'd had for years, since their student days. Kayleigh Dilkes's gift would have looked better. But it had belonged to Sally Gilbert and hadn't been Kayleigh's to give. Once again he found himself wondering how Brenda had got hold of it. Had she stolen it from the hotel? Had she been given it as she had claimed? By Jason Wilde or the Iddacombes? Or by Robin Carrington?

But then, if the theory about the cliff-top killings held water, taking Sally's necklace was a stupid mistake for the killer to have made. Careless when the killer had gone to such lengths to be careful. Brenda could have answered his question. But Brenda was dead – possibly murdered. Which was significant in itself.

As they entered the Tradmouth Arms, Wesley forced himself to forget about work, telling himself that there was more to life. He spotted Neil waiting for them in the corner of the dimly lit bar. He had his feet up on a stool as he sipped his pint – the picture of relaxation. For a moment Wesley envied him.

Pam sat down beside him and Neil looked at her appreciatively. 'You look nice. Mine's a pint, Wes.'

When Wesley returned with the drinks Neil and Pam were deep in conversation, their heads bent together over something, whispering. Wesley almost felt as though he was intruding until Neil looked up and grinned.

'We're looking at that book Robin Carrington lent me.'

'I don't know how you're going to get it back to him. They took him back to London today.'

'Poor sod.'

'He murdered a woman for the insurance money then he burned down a house.' This sort of automatic liberal sympathy for the criminal always irritated Wesley: there might be a few wrongdoers who deserved it but Robin Carrington wasn't one of them – even though, against his better judgement, he had found himself liking the man.

'I thought it was his wife who did the dirty deed,' said

Neil, amused at his friend's prickly response.

Wesley didn't reply.

'Want to know what I've found out about the Chadleigh wreckers?' Neil asked.

'And what have you found out?'

'There was a man called Jud Kilburn who organised the villagers of Chadleigh to plunder ships that were wrecked on the coast. And he made sure of a steady supply of wrecks by luring ships onto the rocks.'

'Everyone knows that things like that went on in the West Country. I read about a family of wreckers up in North Devon near Clovelly who were supposed to have pickled and eaten their victims.'

Pam pulled a face.

'Well, I don't think Jud Kilburn went that far. But he stood trial for murder, robbery and rape amongst other things.'

'Was he found guilty?' Pam asked.

'Oh yes. He was hanged at Exeter in 1772. It was said that he plundered over a hundred ships, although that might have been an exaggeration. But it says in this book that he made accusations against other people, implying that someone influential was behind it all. He said he was only obeying orders.'

'Well, he would say that, wouldn't he,' Pam said dismissively, before draining her glass of mineral water. She was longing for something alcoholic but her condition forbade it.

'Was this Jud Kilburn any relation to our dear friend Dominic Kilburn?' Wesley asked.

'I shouldn't be surprised. They seem to have a lot in common. Anyway, I went to Exeter to look up the court records of the time to see exactly what he said at his trial.' He paused.

'Go on,' said Pam, eager to hear more.

'When I first read it, I assumed that he was just desperate to put the blame on someone else – you know, just throwing accusations around. But then I thought about

329

the skeleton in Chadleigh Hall ...'

'You think the skeleton has something to do with the wreckers?'

Neil leaned forward. 'Now you've got to imagine you're back in 1772. You live in the village of Chadleigh. There's the usual set-up: the parson and the squire – only the parson lives in Millicombe and nobody takes too much notice of him and the squire lives up in the big house and in a different world. No, the main man in the village is the blacksmith, Jud Kilburn. He's the one who leads everyone down to the shore when there's a wreck – he even makes sure there's a steady supply of wrecks to keep the village in comfort. You've seen him rape women who are washed ashore alive; you've seen him rob; you've seen him slit sailors' throats and cut people's fingers off to get at rings. You don't argue with Jud Kilburn: you know what he's capable of.'

'So?'

'Eventually Kilburn's caught by a detachment of soldiers from Plymouth who have been sent to sort out the situation. He's brought to justice and people who have been his accomplices give evidence against him to get themselves off the hook. To read the trial report you'd think that Jud Kilburn did it all single handed, whereas in reality virtually the whole village was in on it, and those that weren't turned a blind eye to what was really going on. But when Kilburn stood trial something unexpected happened.'

'What?' Wesley was impatient to know the rest of the story. He looked at Pam and saw that she was listening intently.

Neil paused to take a drink, looking from one to the other, enjoying the suspense he had created. 'As I said, Jud Kilburn began to throw accusations around at his trial. He said that someone else was the brains behind the whole operation. He even claimed that the *Celestina* had been wrecked on this person's orders and that the captain's wife hadn't been on board. He said that she'd found out what

330

was planned and had threatened to tell the soldiers so that her husband would have a chance of survival. But then she was murdered to prevent her from talking. Of course, nobody believed Kilburn. Everyone knew that the captain's wife, Mary Anne, had been aboard the ship: she had been buried in the churchyard with all the other victims. But what if she hadn't been? What if someone else was buried in her place? There must have been a lot of confusion with bodies being pulled from the sea.'

'Go on,' said Wesley impatiently.

'Jud Kilburn said that Mary Anne Smithers was walled up in a small dressing room off one of the bedchambers to prevent her warning anyone. Hence the wedding ring with her initials – Mary Anne Iddacombe. He said that she'd been drugged and tied up in there. And he said he'd sealed up the room himself.'

'Why didn't anyone go and look in Chadleigh Hall to see if he was telling the truth?'

'Because the whole story was dismissed as Jud Kilburn's attempt to dodge the gallows. He was found guilty and the judge said all his accusations were to be treated as rubbish. Nobody bothered investigating because nobody believed him. And of course there was the small fact that the judge was a friend of the person he was accusing. I had to go back to the original trial transcripts: even the author of that book about the wreckers says he told wicked lies at his trial, but he doesn't say what they were. And because everyone assumed he was lying, nobody bothered to check. He also said that there was no treasure aboard the *Celestina*, only iron: it was all an insurance fraud. Nobody believed that either. But I know from our excavations that he was right. Jud Kilburn was telling the truth.'

'So who did he say was behind it all?' Pam asked.

Neil said the name and Wesley nearly choked on his beer.

*

Saturday passed quietly in the CID office. A statement had been taken from the owner of the Morbay newsagent's, who was still very vague about who had picked up the Chadleigh Holdings letters. Quite a few people used the shop as an accommodation address: it may have been an elderly lady or a middle-aged man or a fair-haired young woman, possibly Brenda Dilkes – on the other hand it could have been a young man who vaguely fitted Robin Carrington's description. If it had been a regular customer, the newsagent said, he would have known. Presumably, Wesley thought, whoever was behind Chadleigh Holdings had made sure they didn't run the risk of becoming a familiar face.

Wesley told Gerry Heffernan what Neil had discovered about the Chadleigh Hall skeleton and the chief inspector greeted the news with relief. If it dated back to the eighteenth century, then it definitely wasn't his problem. One less thing to worry about.

Wesley knew he was right. But somehow he couldn't get the image of those small, sad bones out of his mind. Mary Anne Smithers, née Iddacombe – if it was her – still haunted him. Maybe she was trying to tell him something.

Monday morning saw all hands on deck in the CID office with Gerry Heffernan strutting between the desks like a ship's captain on the bridge waiting for the first sight of land. Everyone was telephoning banks and other financial institutions, trying to trace an account in the name of Chadleigh Holdings.

At ten o'clock exactly, Trish Walton struck lucky. Chadleigh Holdings had an account at a bank in Morbay. They were on to something at last.

Wesley and Heffernan rushed out as Trish was warning the bank manager of their imminent arrival. They'd waited long enough, and they were anxious to get the case cleared up once and for all. If their suspicions were correct, whoever was behind Chadleigh Holdings was clever ... and dangerous.

*

Much to Gerry Heffernan's surprise, the bank manager turned out to be a woman. Mrs Simmons was in her thirties with short brown hair and a businesslike suit. She greeted them with a brisk handshake. Wesley had the impression of an actress playing the part of a successful businesswoman – or the popular conception of the successful businesswoman: there was a softness and uncertainty in Mrs Simmons' eyes which belied her apparent coldness.

'You do appreciate this information is confidential, Chief Inspector?'

'Of course.' Heffernan slouched in his seat and scratched his stomach. 'You can rely on our discretion, love. But this is a murder inquiry.'

Mrs Simmons stared like a frightened rabbit when the word 'murder' was mentioned and pushed a file towards him as if she wanted nothing more to do with it. It was Wesley who opened the file and began to read.

When he reached the names of the two authorised signatories of the Chadleigh Holdings account – Brenda Dilkes and Sandra Bracewell – he looked at Gerry Heffernan and took a deep breath. Somehow this wasn't what he had expected.

They returned to the office, and as Wesley pored over the print-out of Chadleigh Holdings' bank account, he noticed something odd; something that shouldn't have been there.

Every year for the past five years a few thousand pounds had been withdrawn, presumably to purchase the endowment policies from their hapless owners. Then a substantial five-figure sum had been deposited some time later, presumably the policies paying up on their former owners' deaths. These large sums were swiftly taken out of the account, leaving just enough in for next year's purchase. Neat. A regular income for someone who didn't baulk at committing murder to make a living.

But there was something out of place. Five and a half thousand pounds had left the account a few months earlier, presumably to buy Sally Gilbert's policy. But then a similar sum had been withdrawn a couple of weeks later. Wesley scratched his head. Had there been another death? Had they been too preoccupied to notice that it fitted the pattern? After sticking to one murder a year so as not to arouse the suspicions of the various insurance companies who had been obliged to pay up, was the killer getting greedy?

He took the print-out over to Trish Walton's desk and asked her to make a phone call. Half an hour later she walked up to his desk with a triumphant grin on her face.

'You were right, sir. There was a second advert placed in the *Echo* a couple of weeks after the one Sally answered.' She looked him in the eye. 'Does this mean there'll be another murder?'

Wesley shook his head. He wasn't sure what it meant. He phoned the bank. There was nothing else he could do for now.

And then a call came from the Met.

Robin Carrington had escaped from the magistrates' court in London by climbing out of a lavatory window. And Harry Marchbank's guvnor would be eternally grateful if the Devon force would keep a look out for him just in case he headed back. As the French police hadn't caught up with Harriet yet, it was assumed that he'd try to reach her somehow, and if the phone number of Old Coastguard Cottage was the only way she had to contact him ...

But although Wesley made cooperative noises down the phone and assured his London colleagues that they would be on constant lookout in case Carrington showed his face on their patch again, his mind was on other things.

There was a killer about – and if that killer wasn't

caught soon, there was a chance that he or she would kill again.

Two officers were dispatched to bring Sandra Bracewell in for questioning. They had orders to keep things low key. Just a chat down at the station.

As it was coming up to lunch-time and they couldn't do anything more until Sandra had been brought in, Gerry Heffernan suggested that he and Wesley get out of the office to have something to eat. They could buy a pasty and eat it back at his place, washed down with a decent cup of tea. Wesley agreed. He too felt he needed a change of scene.

They walked through the busy streets to Baynard's Quay, stopping to buy their lunch on the way. It was good to be out of the office. And perhaps it would help them to think.

'You keeping your eyes peeled for Robin Carrington?' Heffernan asked, not sounding too concerned. 'That lot in the Met couldn't organise a piss-up in a brewery – I mean, how did they let Carrington give them the slip? He's hardly in the same league as the Krays.'

'Somehow I can't see him coming back here. He'll make for Dover or Folkestone.'

'You reckon?'

Wesley didn't answer. Recent developments had caused him to lose interest in Robin Carrington.

'So Sandra Bracewell's behind these murders?'

'That's what it looks like. Her and Brenda both worked at the Tradfield Manor – that's how they must have got to know each other.' Wesley didn't sound too certain. 'And if Sandra's planning another one, getting greedy, that's when they start making mistakes. The bank is tracing who the latest payment was made to but Mrs Simmons said it could take some time. I told her it was urgent.'

'You should have laid it on thick, Wes. You should have

said it was a matter of life and death. It might be if whoever sold Sandra that policy is walking into her trap at this very moment.'

'I'd never have had Sandra Bracewell down as a murderer,' Wesley said as Gerry Heffernan unlocked his front door. 'In fact Miss Snowman said she wasn't too bright.'

'She pulled off that successful disappearing act all those years ago and arranged for those letters to be sent. You can never tell. Or maybe it was Brenda who did the actual murders.'

'But she was murdered herself, so Sandra must be the brains behind it. And we had her down as the Chadleigh Hall skeleton.'

As they entered Gerry Heffernan's living room from the narrow hall, he spotted an envelope on the mantelpiece and picked it up. On it was scrawled a note in the untidy handwriting Rosie Heffernan had inherited from her father.

'Gone to work. Ship Shape's sending me to that lighthouse again. Be back later. R.' Gerry Heffernan smiled to himself before screwing up the note and throwing it in the fireplace.

But Wesley bent down and picked it up. Then he took it over to the table and flattened it out.

'Isn't that taking recycling a bit far, Wes?'

Wesley didn't answer. He was examining the expensive-looking cream envelope with the thin blue line running along its gummed edge. There was another note on the back in faint pencil. Wesley screwed up his eyes to try to make out what it said.

He handed the envelope to Heffernan. 'Does this look familiar to you?'

Heffernan took it and turned it over. 'Yes, but . . . There must be loads of 'em about.'

Wesley's mobile phone rang and, after a brief conversation, he turned to Heffernan.

'That was Trish. The bank's got an address for us.'

Heffernan looked at the paper bag in his hand which contained his pasty. He supposed he could eat it on the way.

Chapter Fifteen

The accused stated that on the night before the Celestina *was lost he visited Chadleigh Hall, the dwelling of Mistress Mercy Iddacombe, a widow, her son James and two daughters, one married to the* Celestina*'s master, Captain Isaiah Smithers. He was asked by the said Mistress Iddacombe to look out for the* Celestina *and put a lamp on the cliff top to guide her into the cove. The* Celestina *and her cargo were heavily insured, although the accused claimed that the cargo was worthless and that there was a sailor on board who had been paid by the said Mistress Iddacombe to hole the ship's hull and cause the vessel to founder at that point so that he could come ashore and make himself known to the accused.*

The accused stated also that this conversation was overheard by the wife of the Captain of the said ship who had been forced by illness not to accompany her husband on the voyage. This lady, Mistress Mary Anne Smithers, became sorely distressed at the prospect of her husband's ship being wrecked and threatened to tell the authorities of her mother's plans. The accused then stated that Mistress Iddacombe gave her daughter a strong dose of opium and ordered the accused to place her in a room which was then bricked up and all trace of it removed. The accused stated that Mistress Iddacombe was deeply jealous of her daughter as she and the said Captain

338

Smithers had been lovers and the Captain had abandoned the mother to marry the daughter. He also said that Mistress Iddacombe had been giving poison to the said Mary Anne Smithers and that she had issued orders that Captain Smithers was to be saved from the wreck and brought to her. However, the Captain died after a fight on the shore.

The judge directed the jury to disregard these wild accusations as Mistress Mary Anne Smithers had been identified as one of those who died in the wreck of the Celestina *and Mistress Iddacombe was a respected shipowner who had lost not only her daughter and son-in-law, but also a great treasure of gold and jewels aboard the* Celestina. *Such lies against an innocent lady, he said, were further proof of the criminal character of the accused.*

From an account of the trial of Judah Kilburn, 14 September 1772 at Exeter

The last thing they wanted to do was to alarm Ms Theresa Palsow of 14 Nelson Crescent, Neston. Wesley and Heffernan sat in the car for a few moments staring at the house, a new box on an estate a bus ride from the town centre.

'Better get it over with,' said Heffernan.

They got out of the car, watched by a group of curious children circling on bicycles, and walked up to the white UPVC front door. As Wesley rang the bell he could hear a baby crying inside and hurried footsteps in the hallway before the door opened to reveal a thin young man with a goatee beard. He wore a faded T-shirt decorated with milky vomit around the left shoulder and had the harassed look of a house husband.

'Mr Palsow?' Wesley asked, holding up his warrant card.

'No. Carter. Palsow's my partner's name.'

'Is that Theresa Palsow?'

'Yeah. Why? Is she okay? Has something happened?'

'Nothing to worry about, Mr Carter. Just routine.' Wesley said, trying his best to sound reassuring. 'Is Ms Palsow in?'

'No. You've just missed her. She's gone out.'

Wesley came straight to the point. 'Do you know if she's sold an insurance policy recently? An endowment policy?'

Carter frowned. 'Yeah, a few weeks back. Why? What's all this about?'

'May we come in?'

Carter led them into a living room, half decorated and strewn with brightly coloured plastic toys. A young baby sat gurgling in a bouncing chair near the fireplace.

'How did she sell the policy? Through a broker or ...?'

'No. She answered an advert in the paper. We needed some ready cash. Why? What is this?'

Wesley produced Sally Gilbert's envelope. 'Do you know if Theresa's received a letter like this recently?'

Carter took the envelope from him and studied it, frowning. 'She got one exactly like it the other day.'

Wesley and Heffernan looked at each other. 'Did she show you what was inside?'

Carter shook his head.

'Do you know where the letter is? Can we see it?'

Carter told them to hang on and left the room. As soon as he was out of sight, Gerry Heffernan bent down to make a fuss of the baby, pulling faces and entertaining the infant with a cloth rabbit which he found lying on the floor near by. Wesley had always known that the boss was a big softie on the quiet. But when Carter returned he straightened himself up and looked serious.

'I can't find it. I've looked in all the usual places and ...'

'Did she tell you what was in it?'

Carter was beginning to look worried. 'No. I asked her

but she said she couldn't tell me yet – said it was going to be a surprise for me. I thought it was something to do with my birthday – it's tomorrow. Why? What's all this about?'

Wesley glanced at the cheap carriage clock on the mantelpiece. 'Do you know where she's gone?'

'No. She took the day off work today. Said she had something to do. Said she was meeting someone.'

'Who?'

'I don't know.'

'Please, Mr Carter. Is there anything else you can tell us? Anything at all? What were her exact words?'

He thought for a moment. 'She just said she was meeting someone. And she said she might have a surprise for me when she got back. She was in a good mood when she left . . . excited, like a kid at Christmas.'

'And you didn't ask her where she was going or who she was meeting?'

'Of course I did but she wouldn't say. Look, what is all this? I've got a right to know.' The baby, sensing tension, started to cry. Carter bent down to pick it up.

'Can you give us her car registration number? And have you got a recent photograph?'

'I'm not saying any more until you start telling me what the hell this is all about!' Carter yelled, holding the baby so tight that it started to cry again.

Wesley faced him, knowing that if he hadn't had the baby in his arms he would probably have thrown a punch by now. He understood how he felt but he couldn't reassure him. And he had never been much good at telling blatant lies so he tried the truth. 'Look, there's a possibility that Theresa might be in danger. That's why we have to find her.'

Carter stared at him, dumbstruck, before reciting the details of Theresa's car. Then he placed the baby on the grubby sofa and began to pace up and down.

Wesley stepped out into the narrow hallway and put through a call to the station. All patrols were to look out for

Theresa Palsow's rusty white Ford Fiesta. It was urgent. Possibly a matter of life and death.

He returned to the lounge, where he found Gerry Heffernan with the baby on his knee. Under other circumstances the big man's display of softness would have made him smile. But his attention was on Carter, still pacing up and down in a world of his own.

All of a sudden the pacing stopped. Carter swung round to face them. 'Last night she asked me the best way to get to Tradmouth Castle. She's not local, see. Comes from Somerset.'

'She just asked this last night, out of the blue?'

Carter nodded.

Wesley saw that Heffernan was passing the baby to its father: at least it would give him something to take his mind off Theresa.

'We'll ask a WPC to come round and give you a hand; just while we make sure your, er ... Theresa's safe,' said Wesley, aware that his words were hardly a comfort.

They left the house quickly, hoping they were wrong.

Pam Peterson had just lifted Michael into the child seat of the supermarket trolley when she heard a familiar voice.

'Hello, Pam. How are you keeping?'

She turned round and saw Jackie Brice grinning at her over a trolley piled with groceries. 'Hi, Jackie. I'm fine, thanks. Enjoying the holiday?'

But Jackie had spotted Michael. 'Hasn't he grown since I last saw him.'

Michael grinned happily. Like most babies, he had taken to Jackie immediately.

'I read about Kayleigh's mum in the paper,' Jackie said, turning her attention back to Michael's mother. 'Isn't it awful? Poor little Kayleigh. Such a selfish thing to do when you've got a little one depending on you.'

'She must have been desperate. Poor woman.'

The two women observed a few seconds' silence as they

contemplated Brenda Dilkes's death.

'Have you heard how Kayleigh is?' This had been worrying Pam ever since she'd heard the news.

'She's gone to Brenda's mum – she only lives this side of Plymouth. It's terrible for the poor little maid. She's such a nice child. I met her on the way to the shops just before Brenda passed away and she was chattering to me like she does.' Jackie raised a finger, as though she had just remembered something. 'You know you were worried about that present she gave you? That Brenda had spent too much on it?'

Pam nodded.

'I asked Kayleigh where her mum had got it.' She laughed. 'Well, you know how nosey I am.'

'And did she tell you?'

'Oh yes.'

'So where did she get it?'

Jackie Brice told her.

Gerry Heffernan chewed his nails as Wesley drove.

'Can't you go any faster?'

Wesley put his foot down.

Heffernan's mobile began to sing its cheerful rendition of 'The Ride of the Valkyries' in his jacket pocket. He answered it, and after a series of grunts he turned to Wesley. 'Sandra Bracewell's not at home: she told her husband she was going to visit her old school friend, Carole. Put your foot down, eh?'

When Wesley spotted the sign to Tradmouth Castle, he swung the car off the main road.

Theresa Palsow parked her car by the small café to the side of Tradmouth Castle, relieved that the ancient vehicle hadn't decided to break down on the way. But soon that wouldn't be a problem. Soon she'd be able to afford a new one.

She looked around. There weren't many people about,

only a young dark-haired man coming out of the gift shop and an elderly couple sitting on a bench beneath the ruined walls of the old part of the castle, gazing out to sea. Perhaps it was them. But it seemed unlikely. Surely Iddacombe Finance's executives would look more business-like. These two seemed more like pensioners who had all the time in the world to sit on benches in beauty spots and watch the world go by.

She took the letter from her bag and read it again. She had read it so many times since its arrival that she knew it off by heart.

'Dear Ms Palsow, I am writing to inform you that the will of one of our clients has named you as a beneficiary. I was informed by our client before his death that he wishes the matter to remain strictly confidential and it is a con-dition of his will that you should tell nobody about your receipt of this letter, not even your spouse or closest rela-tives. If it is found that this condition has been broken you will, of course, forfeit the considerable sum of money that is owing to you. This condition may seem unusual but it is due to delicate personal considerations that can only be revealed to you at a face-to-face meeting under conditions of the strictest confidentiality. As our Tradmouth offices are undergoing extensive refurbishment at the moment, I feel it might be best for us to meet informally at a neutral location. I suggest that the café at Tradmouth Castle would be a most suitable venue where we can discuss the matter over tea. I look forward to meeting you outside the café on Monday, 6 August at 3.30. Please bring this letter with you as proof of your identity. Yours sincerely, B. Dilkes.'

Theresa smiled. This was the sort of thing she had dreamed of; the sort of thing that happened to other people. There would be no more debts; no more loans; no more threats and demands for payment. The sale of the endow-ment policy had paid off most of her debts but now, for the first time in her life, she'd be able to afford a few little luxuries. She felt a warm glow of happiness as she contemplated a life without the constant worry of bills shooting through the letter box like guided missiles.

As she put the letter in her pocket, she saw that the elderly couple had stood up and were looking in her direction. Theresa locked the car door and stood quite still, watching as they made their way slowly down the steps. The man was holding the woman's hand, helping her down.

They were coming towards her. She took the letter from her pocket and held it out ostentatiously. With any luck, her troubles would soon be over.

'I've been trying Carole's number but there's nobody in. Wherever Sandra's gone, it isn't there.'

'Is Sam working at Carole's today? Has he got a mobile with him?'

'He doesn't tell me what he's up to and he usually forgets his mobile anyway. How much farther to the castle?'

'Not far now.'

But as they rounded the next bend, Wesley saw a slow-moving tractor ahead.

'Theresa Palsow?'

Theresa swung round. She hadn't heard the footsteps behind her.

'Yes,' she answered, holding the letter with trembling hands. She didn't know why she felt nervous: perhaps it was the thought that this might change her life. But, she told herself, she had nothing to lose.

'May I have the letter? Just to verify that you are who you say you are.' When Theresa handed over the letter, it was opened and read.

'Good,' said the stranger after a few seconds, smiling encouragingly. 'Do you mind if we go for a short walk before we have our tea? Some of what I have to tell you is highly confidential and I don't want to risk being overhead. Let's take the footpath over there and have a little chat, shall we?' The stranger smiled again. 'Work up an appetite. I believe the café's cream teas are excellent.'

Theresa was unused to walking and she didn't know whether the cheap sandals she was wearing were up to it. But she followed the stranger obediently. If there was a fortune at stake, she would willingly sacrifice a pair of plastic snakeskin mules.

'This way,' said her companion pleasantly.

'That's her car.' Wesley jumped out of the driver's seat and looked around. A tall couple had just emerged from a people carrier and were busy coaxing two children away from electronic games with dire threats and promises of ice cream.

'Let's try the café.' Wesley made for the entrance and Heffernan followed. Most of the tables inside were occupied but there was only one person Wesley recognised.

'Mrs Iddacombe,' Wesley said as he marched up to her table. 'Is your husband here with you?'

Mrs Iddacombe shifted in her seat and looked slightly nervous. She was obviously surprised to see them there. 'He'll be back in a minute. We're here to meet my daughter and the grandchildren.' She hesitated. 'Is something wrong, Inspector? Is it about our cleaner, Brenda? I can't help thinking of her poor little girl, you know.'

'It's not about Brenda this time, Mrs Iddacombe.' Wesley pulled a smiling snap of Theresa Palsow from his pocket. 'Have you seen this woman here today?'

Mrs Iddacombe put on a pair of glasses and stared at the picture, obviously uneasy. She looked up. 'Here's my husband,' she announced with what sounded like relief.

George Iddacombe had just entered the café. The woman and the two sulky children from the people carrier were with him. The children were staring at Wesley with undisguised curiosity.

'George.' Mrs Iddacombe called her husband over. 'Isn't that the woman we saw in the carpark earlier? The one you said looked a bit . . .' She didn't finish the sentence.

'A bit tarty. That's right, dear.' He took the photograph from Wesley. 'Oh yes, that's her. I saw her going off up the cliff path. Ridiculous in those shoes.'

'Was she with anyone?' Heffernan asked.

'Yes, I believe she was.'

'Man or woman?'

'Can't say I noticed. Wearing trousers and a hat . . . too far away to see. Sorry.'

Wesley and Heffernan had no time for social niceties. With a quick goodbye they left the Iddacombe tribe to it. They were in a hurry.

Even though the sun wasn't shining it was warm and Wesley felt the sweat dripping from his forehead as he followed the 'Public Footpath' signs. Gerry Heffernan lagged behind, talking on his mobile, asking for back-up.

If their hunch was right Theresa Palsow was up here somewhere with the killer. And Wesley only hoped they weren't too late.

As he hurried along the path he could see the sea to his left. It was a dirty grey today, reflecting the cloudy sky, but there were plenty of boats bobbing and skimming along its calm surface. Ahead of him were two distant figures. He couldn't see clearly but one appeared to be a young woman and the other was taller and shrouded in a thin blue cagoule that billowed out in the breeze.

He turned to see how Heffernan was doing but his boss was still some distance away, puffing and panting. He shouted a few well-chosen words of encouragement, but when he turned back he saw that the figure in blue was alone.

It was hard to tell at that distance whether it was a man or a woman. It could have been Sandra; it could even have been Robin Carrington. The figure disappeared into the bushes that lined the path but there was no time to follow.

Wesley had to know what had become of Theresa

Palsow, but he dreaded the sight of her broken body lying on the rocks below the cliff.

He ran towards the edge, but it seemed an age before he reached the spot where he had last seen her. His legs felt as if they were weighted with lead as he tried to hurry, but he told himself to move, to summon every ounce of energy. There was a chance, just a slim one, that he could do something.

He peered down the cliff, feeling a little dizzy as he gazed at the greedy, foaming water lapping around the jagged black rocks below. He couldn't see her. Either he had been mistaken in his assumptions and Theresa Palsow had walked away ahead of her companion into the safety of the bushes or the sea had already carried her body away. He stood, breathless, close to weeping tears of frustration. Had they been just too late?

Then he heard a small sound over the background roar of the waves below. A squeak – a bird, perhaps. Then the sound came again and Wesley recognised it as a muffled voice crying for help. He started to jog along the cliff edge, peering down, and suddenly he spotted a splash of colour against the grey of the rock. A summer dress. Theresa was down there, sobbing and clinging to the rock face, her feet on a wide grassy ledge. She was safe. She was alive. She had been lucky.

He called down to her to hold on and assessed the chances of getting her up to the top of the cliff by himself. If he climbed down to her, it would mean that there would be two to rescue instead of one: sometimes heroism only made things worse. He stood, heart pounding, staring down at her as he took his mobile phone from his pocket. It was probably a job for the rescue helicopter.

He heard Gerry Heffernan's breathless voice behind him, asking what was going on.

'She's okay, Gerry. She's managed to reach a ledge. But there's no way anyone can get down to her safely so I've called the coastguard. You stay with her, eh? Keep her talking. I'll get after . . .' He didn't finish the sentence. He supposed the figure in blue had been Sandra Bracewell, but until he knew for certain, he hardly liked to say the name. And the fact that Robin Carrington was free nagged at the back of his mind. He had known Brenda; what if he had known Sandra too? What if he was behind the whole scheme? What if it had been Robin who had disappeared into the bushes?

'Go on, then,' Heffernan said, staring down at Theresa, who stood stiffly on her ledge, hardly daring to move.

Wesley guessed that the killer had gone up the higher path and doubled back to the castle. He began to jog back along the path. He didn't want to let the murderer get away . . . not when they'd come this far.

All three generations of the Iddacombe family had just emerged from the café, as though they had sensed that something exciting was about to happen. The children had lost their bored expressions: a real-life police chase was better than any computer game, but somehow they had expected it to be noiser, more like the telly.

George Iddacombe spotted Wesley and waved him over imperiously. 'I say. Are you still looking for that young woman?'

'We're looking for the person she met. Have you . . .?'

Iddacombe pointed down the road to his right. 'Someone went down there a minute ago in a terrible hurry. I think it was the same person who was with the young woman . . . blue cagoule and one of those floppy sunhats. Nearly got run over by a car . . . some people just don't look where they're going.'

Wesley rushed off, leaving George Iddacombe in full flow. He ran down the road, hoping that the killer hadn't already driven off.

He ran on, mocked by circling seagulls overhead. As he rounded a bend he saw someone running ahead of him, the figure in the blue cagoule he had seen with Theresa Palsow

349

... the murderer. But all he could see now was the back of the floppy canvas sunhat he or she wore, he couldn't see the face.

He shouted, and as the figure swung round to face him the shock made his heart lurch. He took a deep breath before he spoke.

'Mrs Sanders, can I have a word?'

Carole Sanders began to move quickly towards a large four-wheel-drive car parked by the roadside, her knuckles so tightly clenched that they showed as white bones beneath the flesh. She reached the car and fumbled in the pocket of the cagoule.

She turned to Wesley. 'I'm so glad I've seen you, Inspector. I'm just going to ring the emergency services. Something awful's happened. Sandra asked me to meet a woman she knew and as we were walking she slipped and fell. My mobile's in the car.' She looked at him innocently. 'Unless you want to ring ...'

'It's all in hand. She's okay.'

'Thank goodness for that.' Carole put her hand to her heart in a gesture of relief.

'We know all about the endowment policies.'

'The what?'

She looked at him, puzzled, innocent, and Wesley hesitated, fearing that he'd got the whole thing wrong. But after a moment of doubt he decided to continue. There was nothing to lose.

'It was a while before we latched on to how and why you did it,' he began, walking towards her slowly. 'The letters were a clever idea, and so was putting the account in the names of your cleaning woman and your old school friend. I suppose you paid them something for opening the account and signing the cheques: I bet they were grateful for a bit of easy money. Did they know what they were involved in? Or did they find out? Is that why you killed Brenda Dilkes?'

'I've no idea what you're talking about,' Carole Sanders

350

answered. She sounded confused, so convincing that he was beginning to believe her.

'We'd like you to answer some questions about an attack on the woman on the cliff top.' He tried to sound confident but he didn't feel it.

'Attack? I told you ... she slipped. It was her idea to go as far as the cliffs – I was nervous because I'm not keen on heights. I told her not to go too near the edge but ...'

'Where's Sandra Bracewell?' he asked. 'Her husband said she was on her way to see you.'

He noticed that her hands were clenched tight again, her only sign of unease. 'She called in on her way into Tradmouth. She said she had an urgent appointment: that's why she asked me to meet this woman. She asked me to get a letter off her. She said it was important.'

'So where is she now?'

'How should I know?' She looked him in the eye, open and innocent. 'Whenever Sandra's done it's got nothing to do with me. All I did was meet this person for her.' Her eyes began to brim with tears and she fumbled in the pocket of the cagoule for a tissue.

Wesley stared at her. He didn't know what to believe any more.

When they returned to the station Gerry Heffernan shut himself in his office, not to be disturbed. He was only too glad to leave things to Wesley for the moment.

Wesley was pleased that he had asked him to stay with Theresa until the helicopter arrived. He wouldn't have wanted him to witness Carole being pushed into a patrol car. But he couldn't shield his boss from reality for long.

Carole Sanders was still sticking to her story that Sandra had asked her to keep the rendezvous for her. And she still insisted that Theresa's fall was an accident and challenged them to prove otherwise. In any court of law it would be her word against Theresa's – and as he had just discovered that Theresa Palsow had a past conviction for obtaining money by deception perhaps things might not be as straight-forward as he'd hoped if Carole got herself a good defence lawyer. There was no sign of the letter Theresa claimed she had received from Iddacombe Finance: but then Carole could easily have disposed of it by throwing it into the sea, even though she had said that Theresa fell before she could hand it over.

But Wesley was still uneasy about Sandra Bracewell. She appeared to be missing and the search he had ordered of Gallows House and its outbuildings had proved fruitless.

He sat at his desk, turning his pen in his fingers, aware that Sandra's husband, Peter, was downstairs, pacing the station foyer. He felt for the man. His and Sandra's relationship may have started on shaky foundations – the posh schoolgirl from 'Virgins' Retreat' and the builder's labourer – but it had stood the test of time.

He picked his jacket up from the back of his chair and walked over to Rachel's desk. 'If anyone asks I'm going over to Carole Sanders' place to see if the uniforms have found anything yet.' He glanced across at the chief inspector's office. He could see Heffernan through the window, head down, pretending to be absorbed in witness statements. There was no need to tell him where he was going.

He drove the short distance to Gallows House and swung the car into the drive. Ahead of him he saw two police cars parked next to a pick-up truck. Three men were unloading stone flags from the back of the truck. One of them, the youngest, stopped what he was doing.

'What's going on?' There was a look of concern on Sam Heffernan's face. 'The police won't tell us anything. Has there been a break-in? Is Mrs Sanders all right?'

Wesley saw that Sam's two colleagues were watching him with expectant curiosity but he didn't feel inclined to give too much away. 'We're investigating a serious crime but Mrs Sanders is unharmed,' he said, aware that he was sounding as if he were reading a formal statement to the press.

352

Sam shrugged. 'Okay. I'll have to ask Dad about it tonight, then.'

'I wouldn't, Sam.'

'Why not?'

'Leave it a couple of days, eh?'

Sam looked at Wesley, puzzled.

'So can we unload this stuff or not?' asked one of Sam's colleagues hopefully, searching for some excuse to slope off.

Wesley looked at the York stone slabs waiting to be taken round to the back of the house, and he couldn't help wondering whether Carole Sanders would be in a position to appreciate her newly landscaped garden for the foreseeable future. 'Well, I suppose you might as well get on with it, as you're here.'

Slowly, reluctantly, Sam's fellow workers began to unload the slabs and take them round the side of the house. Wesley, following behind, heard a barrage of colourful oaths and when he reached the back garden he found the three men standing there, staring at the spot where the patio would soon be laid.

'Something wrong?' he asked.

'Some bugger's been digging this up. We left it all even last night ready to work on it tomorrow. Look at it.' The young man stared at Wesley accusingly. 'Was it one of your lot? Bloody police,' he added under his breath as an afterthought.

Wesley looked down. A rectangular hole about three feet deep had been dug in the smooth sandy soil. The uniformed officers who'd searched the place had assumed it was the gardeners' work.

'Was Mrs Sanders expecting you today?' he asked the puzzled gardeners.

It was Sam who spoke. 'No. We told her we wouldn't be coming. We were supposed to be working on a job in Stokeworthy, but then the York stone was delivered to the yard so we thought we'd drop it off on the way.' He looked at Wesley innocently, unaware of the implications of what he had said.

Wesley looked down at the hole and knew it for what it was: an empty grave waiting for an occupant. A grave that would be filled in before the gardeners showed up again to cover it with slabs of stone. Something told him that Sandra Bracewell might not be far away, either dead or waiting for Carole Sanders to come back so she could dispose of her.

He ran to the front of the house, where half a dozen uniformed officers in shirtsleeves were preparing to leave. They looked mildly annoyed when Wesley gave the order to search the whole place including the outbuildings again, and half an hour later they reported that their efforts had been fruitless. There was still no sign of Sandra Bracewell. She wasn't anywhere on the premises, dead or alive.

For a few moments he suspected that Carole Sanders might have been telling the truth; that something had gone wrong with Sandra's plans and she had sent her innocent friend, Carole, to retrieve incriminating evidence for her.

But someone had dug the hole in the patio: and that someone hadn't been the gardeners or the police. It may have been Sandra, preparing to dispose of Carole on her return. But why?

As the officers climbed into their cars, Wesley sat down on the front doorstep and put his head in his hands.

'So what's going on?'

Wesley glanced up and saw Sam Heffernan looking down on him. 'They're looking for a woman,' he said.

'Who? Carole?'

'No, a friend of Carole's. Her name's Sandra Bracewell.'

'And you think she's here? Is she supposed to be hiding out or what?'

Wesley didn't answer.

'Tried the loft?'

'Yes.'

'The cellar?'

'There isn't one.'

'Yes there is. There's a wine cellar under the pantry. There's a trapdoor.'

Wesley stood up so quickly that he felt dizzy. 'Show me.'

Sam led the way into the kitchen. He opened the pantry door, squatted down and pulled the ring set in the floor. When the trapdoor was open, Wesley knelt down and felt inside, looking for a light switch. His searching fingers found it and soon the tiny cellar was flooded with light.

Sam was talking, asking questions, but Wesley wasn't listening. His eyes were on the small, lifeless figure, slumped like a rag doll on the cold stones beneath.

Peter Bracewell wept. Wesley and Rachel waited patiently and dispensed tea and sympathy in the interview room – you couldn't rush these things. It was over half an hour before he felt up to answering questions.

'What can you tell me about Chadleigh Holdings?' Wesley began quietly.

Peter dried his eyes and blew his nose on a white handkerchief wet with his tears. 'There's nothing much to tell.' He hesitated. 'A few years ago Carole set up a bank account in the name of a company and she asked Sandra and another woman, her cleaner I think it was, to sign the cheques. She said it was all to do with stocks and shares and she didn't want anything in her name because of tax. I don't understand these things but it sounded ... well, it's the sort of thing people do when they're in the know, isn't it.'

Rachel nodded. 'Go on.'

'All Sandra had to do was sign a cheque about once a year and Carole gave her a hundred pounds each time – I suppose she paid the other woman the same. I thought it was generous but ...'

'And you had no suspicions?'

Peter shook his head.

Wesley looked down, studying his hands. He didn't like what he had to say next but it had to be said. 'Mrs Sanders denies everything, you know. She claims that Sandra was behind the whole thing.'

'Sandra wouldn't hurt a fly,' Peter said indignantly.

'One of the victims' handbags was found at your home.' Wesley hated himself for playing devil's advocate, but someone had to. 'And when we called at your house the other day I noticed that you had a brand-new car in your drive. Where did you get the money for that?' He knew the question was impertinent but Peter Bracewell would face some tough questions from Carole Sanders' defence lawyer at any trial – and Carole would pick the best available. She could afford to.

Peter sat up straight and looked mildly offended. 'If you must know, my father died last year and left us some money. You can check if you like.'

Wesley left the interview room, satisfied that Peter was telling the truth. He could only think that Carole had considered Sandra, like Brenda, a liability. Like Brenda, Sandra had been drugged. The same method for both.

He guessed that Carole was about to wind up Chadleigh Holdings. Perhaps she was planning to open a new account with different signatories, keeping one step ahead of the game. Carole Sanders was a clever woman and a convincing one – until he had found Sandra, he had almost believed in her innocence. He just hoped that she wouldn't wriggle out of their clutches for lack of evidence that would stand up in court. If Sandra wasn't in a position to testify against her, Carole's lawyers would try to twist the facts to her advantage.

When he entered the CID office Steve Carstairs looked up. 'Your wife phoned.'

'Thanks, Steve,' Wesley said, making a mental note to ring her when he had a free moment.

'She said it was urgent. Said it was about Kayleigh.'

Wesley picked up the receiver and dialled his home number. After a long conversation, he caught the attention of DC Paul Johnson, who was returning from the photocopier. 'Paul, will you get round to this address and take a statement from a lady called Jackie Brice. Come back as soon as you've got it: it's urgent. Okay?' Paul took the sheet of paper Wesley held out to him.

As Paul hurried out, Wesley smiled. Carole Sanders was a clever woman all right but she had made a serious mistake.

An hour and a half later, as he and Rachel made their way down to the interview room, he felt in his pocket and his fingers touched the evidence.

'What are you smiling at?' Rachel asked.

'I didn't realise I was.'

'You look pleased about something,' she said, her head tilted to one side coquettishly. 'Are you going to tell me what it is?'

'You'll find out.'

He opened the door. Carole Sanders was sitting there beside a plump solicitor who wore a suit that was beyond a policeman's pocket.

'My client denies all the charges.'

'So she's sticking to the story that Sandra Bracewell was behind it all?'

'Indeed. We've been over it time and time again. My client had been very worried about Mrs Bracewell's mental state and erratic behaviour for some time. This whole thing has been most distressing for her, and the fact that Mrs Bracewell chose to kill herself at Gallows House . . .'

Wesley sat down and leaned across the table. The solicitor fell silent.

'My wife is a teacher. One of the pupils in her class last year was called Kayleigh Dilkes, daughter of the late Brenda Dilkes.' He noticed that Carole Sanders' mask of injured innocence had slipped and she was starting to look uncomfortable. 'Kayleigh gave my wife a rather expensive necklace as a present. My wife felt awkward about this and asked where the necklace had come from.' He looked at the solicitor. 'Indeed, whether it was Kayleigh's to give. Kayleigh assured her that her mother had been given the necklace. Her mother used to be your cleaner, didn't she, Mrs Sanders?'

'She cleaned for lots of people,' Carole said defensively. 'She cleaned at one of Dominic Kilburn's hotels and for a family called Iddacombe and . . .'

'Is that where you got the name Iddacombe Finance from? The letters the victims received were all from a firm called Iddacombe Finance promising them a lot of money.'

'I don't know what you're talking about.'

'Theresa Palsow, the woman who fell from the cliff today, said she received a letter from Iddacombe Finance. She said you asked for it as proof of her identity. She says you took it.'

'I've never heard of Iddacombe Finance. Sandra had asked me to get a letter off her but she said she hadn't brought it with her.' She spoke the words with such confidence that Wesley could almost have believed they were true.

He leaned forward again, confidentially. 'The necklace Kayleigh Dilkes gave my wife was identified as the one Sally Gilbert was wearing on the day she died. And I think we can assume that her murderer took it. So how did it get from Sally Gilbert's neck into the possession of Kayleigh Dilkes?'

'I really have no idea,' Carole said innocently. 'Perhaps Sandra gave it to Brenda at work. They both work at the Tradfield Manor, you know.'

'Where is this leading?' the solicitor enquired in a bored voice.

Wesley picked up Jackie's statement and began to read. 'I met Kayleigh Dilkes and, aware that Kayleigh's class teacher, Mrs Pamela Peterson, was worried about the origins of a necklace Kayleigh had given her as a present, I asked her where her mother had obtained it.'

'Is this relevant?' the solicitor said uneasily.

'Kayleigh said that she got it off an Auntie Carole, who's very nice and gives her mummy things. I asked her if she was sure about this and she said she was.'

The solicitor shifted uncomfortably. 'I hardly think the hearsay evidence of a child . . .'

Wesley looked at Carole, who was sitting stony faced, then produced a plastic bag from his pocket containing an envelope. 'And there's another thing. This envelope came from your house. You had written a note on it for your landscape gardeners. One of them, our chief inspector's son, put it in his pocket and forgot about it until his sister needed some scrap paper to leave her father a note.' He looked at the solicitor, who was glowering at him suspiciously, and pulled another plastic bag from his pocket with another envelope inside, feeling rather like a conjuror producing rabbits.

'And this envelope was received by Sally Gilbert. Her murderer sent it, arranging to meet her on Monks Island. It's identical to the one Sam Heffernan took from your house, and Theresa Palsow says it's identical to the one she received – the one you took off her. And it's an unusual make. Very expensive: only available at one outlet in Tradmouth. You like expensive things, don't you, Mrs Sanders? You have a part time job, I believe?'

'Yes.'

'Where?'

'In Tradmouth.'

'What kind of work do you do, Mrs Sanders?'

'I work in an insurance office.'

'Is that how you hit on the idea of getting a regular income through murder?'

'I advise you not to answer,' the solicitor said, loudly, for the benefit of the tape.

She pressed her lips together and said nothing.

'And there's something else,' Wesley said casually. 'We've found your thumbprint inside the flap of the envelope you sent to Sally Gilbert. I'm sorry, Mrs Sanders, but it looks as though we have enough evidence now to prove your guilt.'

Wesley smiled and waited. Rachel stared at the woman, watching for any sign. The solicitor fidgeted.

There was a knock on the door and Trish Walton tiptoed in and put a note in Wesley's hand. When he had read it he looked Carole Sanders in the eye.

'I forgot to tell you that Sandra Bracewell was still alive when they found her.'

Carole's eyes widened. 'I thought you said she was dead.'

'I didn't say she was; you assumed it. She was rushed to intensive care and the doctors thought it was touch and go. They said if she'd been found half an hour later she might not have made it. But you'll be pleased to know she's just come round, so we hope that soon she'll be able to give her side of the story.'

Carole sat back as though she'd been slapped in the face.

The solicitor leaned across to her. 'You still don't have to say anything.'

Carole turned to him and opened her mouth to speak, but she bit back the words.

'It's over, Carole,' said Wesley softly. 'We've got Theresa's evidence, Kayleigh's evidence, the fingerprint evidence ... and Sandra. And the letters had to be written on a computer. I can send someone to the office where you work to have a look at the one you use: even if the letters have been deleted they can still be found by our people from Forensics. And of course there might be some forensic evidence from Brenda Dilkes's place.'

He sat there expectantly for a few seconds before addressing the solicitor. 'I suppose you'll be wanting a word with your client?'

But before the man had had a chance to answer, Carole began to speak quietly. 'Do you know what it's like to be used to having everything then suddenly it's all gone ...

taken away?' She played with her wedding ring. 'My late husband was a gambler: he lost all his money then he went through mine ... all the money my parents had left me. I'd put the house in my name so a least we kept a roof over our heads, but everything else went to feed his nasty little habits. We had debt collectors knocking on the door and we lived hand to mouth for years.'

She paused. Wesley noted the hard determination on her face. She looked quite unlike the pleasant, motherly Carole Sanders he had first met. Was she just good at acting a part? he wondered. Or perhaps it was her crimes which had enabled her to become the comfortably off lady bountiful they had first seen. Perhaps she had just been willing to go farther than most to achieve the station in life she yearned for.

She continued. 'When he died I sold up and moved back to Tradmouth. Gallows House needed a lot of renovation and, although I could afford to buy it, I couldn't afford the redecoration or lifestyle to go with it. I took a job with an insurance company doing the typing to make ends meet and when I found that money was still tight I thought I was going to lose the house and I began to get desperate. I was brought up with certain expectations, you see. I expected a nice house, a cleaner and expensive things around me and ...' She paused. 'Then one day somebody in the office made a joke. They said a good way to make easy money is to buy up a stranger's endowment policy, bump them off and collect on the insurance. You can't insure a stranger's life but endowment policies are different. People sell the policies to raise cash – traded policies, they're called – but what they often don't realise is that the life insurance which applies to the original owner isn't sold on with the policy – if the person who originally took the policy out dies, the new owner gets the money.'

'Go on,' Wesley prompted gently.

She stared at her hands. 'It took months of planning and more months before I plucked up the courage to do it. I knew I had to be careful so I set up Chadleigh Holdings to buy the policies and I put the bank account in Brenda's and Sandra's names. Then I opened an account in the name of Smith at a large bank in Exeter for the proceeds.' She hesitated. 'I bought a policy from a woman in Stoke Beeching and . . . we met outside a café and I suggested that we go for a walk.' She twisted her wedding ring round and round. 'I didn't think I could go through with it. Her name was Gilda and she was an artist. She kept talking – telling me about herself and . . . she was a nice woman. I . . .'

'You killed her.'

'I thought I wouldn't be able to do it at first but then she went near the edge and I just reached out and pushed her. Just one shove and it was all over.' She looked up at Wesley, her eyes wide. 'I collected nearly thirty thousand pounds. It was so easy.'

'And what about the others?'

'I was only going to do it once but after I began renovating the house the money soon ran out and . . . well, the next time wasn't so bad. And it just got easier every time.'

'Even though Marion Bowler and Sally Gilbert put up a fight?'

'When you've done it once . . . once you've crossed that line, murder is easy, Inspector,' she said, almost in a whisper. 'I didn't enjoy it, you know. I just regarded it as something that had to be done. I remember when I was a child and we had a holiday on a farm. The farmer's wife asked me if I wanted chicken for dinner and when I said yes she took one of the chickens in the yard and wrung its neck. She said that if we wanted to eat chicken . . . well, it had to be done, didn't it. A few days later I asked if I could kill one.' She stared down at her hands.

'And did you?'

She nodded. 'She told me how to do it. She said it's best just to get on with it and not to think about what you're doing. She was right.'

'So you never thought of your victims?'

A shadow crossed her face. 'Sentimentality was one luxury I didn't allow myself.'

Wesley glanced at Rachel, who was sitting stiffly upright, a look of disapproval on her face.

'Surely the policies had to be transferred to you legally. How did you manage that?'

'I used my old family solicitor. I told him I was using the policies as an investment, buying one a year, paying the premiums and waiting for the big lump sum at the end – people do that, you know: it's quite common. I told him I was using the name Chadleigh Holdings for reasons of my own. He's nearing retirement and he didn't ask too many questions. And of course he could never know that the policies were paying out rather sooner than expected.' She smiled. 'He even said he was glad I was using what little money I had wisely. I suppose you could say I'd hit on the perfect crime, really – killing complete strangers – and I thought that if I kept to one a year it wouldn't arouse any suspicions. Most of the policies were from different insurance companies and . . .'

'But how did you persuade the people to go to the edge of the cliffs?'

'Oh, that was easy. I just put them at their ease, got them talking. They all trusted me, you see.'

She leaned forward and Wesley looked at her: a pleasant-faced, motherly, middle-aged woman. He had no doubt that her last statement was true. If he hadn't known better he would have trusted her himself.

'I really don't advise you to say any more,' the solicitor muttered half-heartedly. But Carole ignored him.

'They were only too glad to go wherever I suggested. They thought they were coming into money and money's one thing people will do anything for, Inspector. Especially those who don't have any.'

'You planned two murders this month,' Rachel snapped. 'Why was that? Were you getting greedy?'

'It wasn't greed – I was going to do the second one to help

out my brother. Sebastian's firm's in difficulties, you see.'

'How did Brenda and Sandra get involved?' Wesley asked.

'I didn't want to put any of the accounts in my own name and they were only too happy to sign the cheques. I only had to tell them it was for tax reasons and they accepted it. People do all sorts of little fiddles to reduce their tax bills, don't they?'

'What about Sally Gilbert's necklace? Did you give it to Brenda or did she steal it?'

She thought for a moment. 'The latter, I'm afraid. Brenda was light fingered ... not that I was going to make a fuss. In fact that necklace was my first mistake. The woman struggled and it came off somehow. I don't know why but I put it in my pocket and when I found it there later I didn't get rid of it ... I know I should have done, but I didn't.'

'Why did you plan to kill Brenda and Sandra?'

She shook her head, an expression of sorrow on her face. 'I didn't want to but they were becoming liabilities. Little Kayleigh was a real chatterbox: she told me her mother had given her a gold locket to give to her teacher – she described it and I suspected it was the one from Monks Island. I checked and found it wasn't where I'd put it so I guessed what had happened: Brenda's light fingers again. Anyway, Kayleigh said her teacher's name was Mrs Peterson.' She looked up at Wesley. 'And I remembered you'd said that your wife was a teacher at Kayleigh's school. I couldn't take the risk that you would be able to identify it so I had to ensure that Brenda wasn't in a position to tell you where she got it.'

Wesley stared at her, shocked. Horrified that his casual remark about Pam's job – a bit of idle, friendly conversation – had led to Brenda Dilkes's death.

'Don't worry, dear, it wasn't your fault,' she said, as though she had read his mind. Suddenly, with those words, she became the motherly, sensible woman again; the type of woman who would be at home at the Women's Institute or helping with meals on wheels.

'What about Sandra?' he asked. He had to keep reminding himself that this woman was a killer.

Carole shook her head sadly. 'I feel bad about Sandra . . . after all, we'd been at school together. But she kept questioning me about Chadleigh Holdings. She kept asking if there was any chance of her and her husband buying and selling shares if there was a profit in it. She'd told Peter all about it, you see, and she kept on and on about it every time I saw her. Sandra was always short of money but then she had this windfall when Peter's father died and she was looking for somewhere to invest it. The silly girl should never have run off with Peter. She'd had everything and she threw it away.' She hesitated. 'Just like I did once.'

'So you decided to kill her?' asked Rachel.

Carole Sanders sighed. 'I was afraid that she was getting suspicious. She was even hinting that I should pay her to keep quiet – not in so many words, of course: Sandra was more devious than that. She always was, even at school. The way she fooled everyone when she ran away with Peter showed that. I made sure she and Brenda didn't suffer.'

'But they hardly deserved to die. None of them did.'

Carole sat expressionless and didn't answer. Wesley turned off the tape and she suddenly looked up. 'Tell Gerry I'm sorry. He's a nice man.'

Wesley nodded curtly and marched from the room with Rachel following behind.

They walked down the corridor in silence. Then Rachel spoke. 'How could she have killed all those people in cold blood like that?'

'I suppose that after she'd psyched herself up to do the first, she made herself think of her victims as a means to an end. She didn't allow herself to think of them as people. If she had, surely she couldn't have done it.'

'I've never met such a cold bitch.'

'I heard of another one the other day.' Wesley smiled.

'There was a lady called Mercy Iddacombe who killed her own daughter just to stop her warning anyone that a ship was going to be wrecked and dozens of people murdered.'

'How could anyone do something like that?'

'They do say that after you've done it once, murder is easy ... that was Carole Sanders' excuse, anyway.'

When they reached the office they heard laughter coming from Heffernan's lair. Bob Naseby was in there and they were sharing a joke.

'Are you going to tell him what she said?' Rachel asked quietly.

Wesley thought for a moment. 'Best leave well alone, eh?'

He reached his desk and opened the drawer. Rachel, standing behind him, spotted a small jewellery box inside. 'Been spending your hard-earned cash?' she asked.

He picked up the box. 'It's for Pam,' he said as he opened it. 'Do you think she'll like it? It's to replace the one Kayleigh gave her. What do you think?'

'Lovely.' She looked down unsmilingly at the small gold heart lying against the red velvet.

As she walked away, Steve Carstairs looked up from his computer screen and winked.

Epilogue

News came through on a quiet Monday afternoon three weeks later that Robin Carrington's body had been found. He hadn't made it back to Devon: he had been found dead with multiple injuries, lying near his parked hire car in a country lane not far from Dover, apparently the victim of a hit-and-run driver.

Perhaps he had been on his way to France: as far as anyone knew his wife, Harriet, was still over there, as yet undiscovered by the French authorities. Harry Marchbank's inspector at the Met told Wesley that Harry was taking some leave, and that he had mentioned going on a short trip over to France. Wesley couldn't help wondering whether Harry's trip across the Channel and Robin's death were connected in any way. But perhaps he was letting his imagination run away with him.

Neil Watson's only comment when Wesley had told him of Robin's death was that he hoped he had had time to send the Smithers of Connecticut their family tree. And he said no more on the subject until the day he and Wesley met at Chadleigh Hall's small and neglected chapel overlooking the sea to tie up loose ends and put Chadleigh Hall's past to rest once and for all.

Neil arrived at the chapel first and found the door wide open. Curious to see inside, he entered without waiting for Wesley. Dim light crept in through the arched windows, filtered by the tall yew trees growing outside: rampant nature had taken over in the churchyard many years ago. As Neil's eyes adjusted to the gloom, he could see a dark figure standing by the tombs that lined the far wall.

'Dr Watson. Glad you could make it. How many more are coming? Do you know?'

Dominic Kilburn walked slowly towards him but Neil ignored his outstretched hand. 'A few. My mate from the police and . . .'

'Good. I did wonder whether I should contact the press.'

Neil scowled. 'And did you?'

'I've been so busy planning the hotel opening it slipped my mind.'

'Good.'

Kilburn shot him a look of disapproval.

'Tell me, Mr Kilburn, are your family local?'

'Yes. Devon born and bred,' he answered smugly.

'Do you know if you're descended from a Jud Kilburn? He was hanged for wrecking and murder back in 1772.'

Kilburn's face reddened. 'I shouldn't think so for one moment,' he snapped. Neil guessed that he'd hit a raw nerve.

'So have you any plans for this chapel?' Neil asked, looking around.

'I'm turning it into a gym.'

'A what?' Neil frowned with disapproval. He wasn't known for his piety, quite the reverse, but even he would draw the line at filling an elegant eighteenth-century chapel – even a disused one – with weights and rowing machines. 'Won't the tombs get in the way? Or will you have people vaulting over them?'

Kilburn looked unsure whether to take him seriously. 'I own this estate so I can do what I like,' he said peevishly.

Before Neil could think of a cutting reply, he was interrupted by a familiar voice. 'Has the vicar arrived from Millicombe yet?' Wesley Peterson walked into the chapel, looking around, noting the building's pleasing proportions.

'Not yet. But Mr Kilburn's here . . . representing Kilburn Leisure,' Neil added pointedly.

Wesley shook Kilburn's hand. 'Good of you to come, Mr Kilburn.'

'The least I could do, seeing as she was found in my hotel.'

'I hear you're intending to market the room where the skeleton was found as "the haunted room".'

'Yes. That part of the building was to have been offices but now it's a luxury suite. The marketing opportunity was too good to miss.'

'And the chair the skeleton was found on?'

'A special feature of the room, of course. It's polished up nicely, as a matter of fact.' Kilburn said this matter-of-factly, the profit motive overcoming any question of bad taste.

He reached in his pocket and produced a handful of glossy vouchers. 'We open on the second of September. I hope you'll join us for our introductory special offer – two main courses for the price of one in the restaurant. We've got ourselves a top French chef. And there's details of our special offer on health club membership too.' He passed a leaflet to Neil, who looked as though he would have discarded it at once had there been a bin handy.

'I'm sorry you won't be working on our wreck any more, Dr Watson.' Kilburn didn't sound particularly sorry.

'It was a great experience but I'm afraid I've got other projects I need to be getting on with. But I've compiled a report to be sent to the body that deals with historic wrecks and . . .'

'Still no sign of the treasure?'

'There never was any treasure.'

Dominic Kilburn looked at Neil as though he suspected him of lying, and there was a moment of tension between them, which was broken only by the sound of a booming voice.

'Vicar not here yet?' They looked up and saw a large

369

figure blotting out the sunlight in the doorway.

'Come in, Gerry, we're just waiting for her.'

'Her?'

Wesley and Neil exchanged a covert grin. Gerry Heffernan appeared to have recovered from his recent disappointment. Carole Sanders' name hadn't been mentioned since her arrest. Perhaps the boss realised that he'd had a lucky escape.

'And the Iddacombes from the lighthouse said they'd come, seeing as she's family.'

'Robin Carrington would have liked to have seen this,' said Neil wistfully.

Wesley looked at him, wondering whether the fact that Carrington had committed murder had quite sunk in. For Neil it had seemed incidental, less important than Carrington's interest in the *Celestina*.

Gerry Heffernan pointed to the wooden box that lay at Neil's feet. 'Is that her, then?'

'Yes. That's Mary Anne. The vicar said we could put her near her husband.'

'Yeah.' Heffernan looked around the little church, dusty and unused; long since deconsecrated and in the middle of nowhere. No faithful congregation except the occupants of the fine tombs lining the walls. It was a dead place: as dead as the old Iddacombes who rested there.

Wesley began to walk around, examining the names carved on the tombs. He came to the grandest and stopped. 'Here she is,' he said quietly.

Gerry Heffernan walked over to join him. 'Who?'

Wesley stood back and let the chief inspector read the name for himself.

'Mercy Iddacombe. She lived to a ripe old age.'

Wesley said nothing. As he looked at the tomb, he thought of Carole Sanders. But she had been caught – Mercy hadn't. Even when her guilt had been revealed, nobody had believed it.

The Iddacombes turned up, suitably solemn in funeral

black, and when the vicar arrived the little party followed her outside to the small grave dug near the oak tree. Mary Anne's bones, which had sat for so long in that small dark room, would rest in earth at last.

Historical Note

In the late eighteenth century villagers in the Scilly Isles prayed, 'We pray thee, o Lord, not that wrecks should happen, but that if any wreck should happen Thou wilt guide them into the Scilly Isles for the benefit of the inhabitants.' Further afield, the girls of Tristan da Cunha were somewhat bolder. They prayed, 'Please, God, send me a wreck that I may marry.' A wreck was considered a blessing in many isolated coastal communities, such a blessing that the villagers of the West Country sometimes gave the Almighty a helping hand by luring ships inshore: a lantern tied to a horse or to a cow's horns on a cliff top often worked a treat.

Shipwrecks provided rich pickings for the people who lived on the wild coast of Devon and Cornwall. In 1750 a Dutch galleon carrying wine and brandy was wrecked on Thurlstone Sands, and it was said that as many as ten thousand came from all parts of Devon to plunder the cargo. They were kept at bay only by the arrival of soldiers from Plymouth, and the drunken leader of the mob was killed by falling on a solider's bayonet.

In maritime law a vessel that is driven ashore is not said to be a wreck if any man or domestic animal is still alive aboard her: and if she isn't a wreck then her cargo must be restored to her owner. Misunderstanding of this law in days gone by meant that survivors of shipwrecks were some-

372

imes murdered by their potential rescuers. Seafarers feared
⸱⸱s, and when the steamer *Delaware* went aground in 1871
near the Scillies, two survivors who were about to be
rescued by locals had stones in their hands, fearing that
they'd have to fight for their lives. In 1772 the rich cargo of
the *Chantiloupe* was plundered when she went ashore in
Bigbury Bay in South Devon. One of the survivors, a lady
related to the famous Edmund Burke, was stripped and
robbed of her jewels by wreckers from nearby villages.
They cut off her fingers to steal her rings and murdered
her, burying her body on the foreshore. In 1900 children
digging in the sand discovered another of the wreckers'
victims; a man buried in a shallow grave, probably one of
the *Chantiloupe*'s crew.

However, the most gruesome tale of Devon wrecking
comes from Clovelly in the north of the county. A family
called Gregg were reputed to have lured ships ashore then
robbed, killed, pickled and eaten more than a thousand
hapless victims.

But those who sailed the seas in the eighteenth and nineteenth centuries didn't have to contend only with land-based
wreckers. Shipowners sometimes risked their vessels,
because if a ship sank they could claim the vessel's value
plus the cost of its cargo from their insurers. Sometimes
worthless cargo would be substituted for the valuable one
insured and an owner would hire a 'wrecker', a man who
signed on as a member of the crew and sabotaged the ship
in a seaway where he was likely to be rescued.

It wasn't unknown for women, like Mercy Iddacombe in
this book, to be involved in the shipping business. A
shipowner from Bideford called Widow Davie was such an
astute businesswoman that she acquired a reputation for
being a witch: the sailors on her ships believed that she
knew everything they did, even when they were in port
thousands of miles away in Virginia or Newfoundland.

There are several tales of sealed rooms in Devon – a few
complete with skeleton. But I feel I must mention the story

of Chambercombe Manor near Ilfracombe where a secret room containing a skeleton was discovered. The remains were reputed to be those of a young woman murdered by local wreckers, possibly the daughter of their leader, who left her in the room to starve.

It was dangerous to go to sea, but it seems that for some life was just as risky on dry land.